Praise for Gliding Flight

'A book you'll feel homesick for as soon as you've closed it'
PETER BUWALDA, author of *Bonita Avenue*

'A well-balanced, complete novel that stands out because of its many themes and quirky, eccentric characters, whose tragicomic character traits are movingly identifiable'
JURY, DIORAPHTE PRIZE

'The Dutch Annie Proulx'
OPZIJ LITERATURE PRIZE

'A captivating story about a heartwarming adolescent'
Algemeen Dagblad

'A book you do not want to leave, and finish with a sigh of pleasure'
De Telegraaf

'A lively, exciting and funny novel, which is told with great energy and momentum. A completely convincing picture of the bizarre fantasy world of a lonely adolescent'
DUTCH FOUNDATION FOR LITERATURE

'Goemans shows, once again, how agile a narrator she is'
Trouw

'Anne-Gine Goemans has written a very special and beautiful book'
De Volkskrant

ANNE-GINE GOEMANS (1971) is a Dutch journalist and novelist. Goemans debuted in 2008 with the acclaimed novel *Unfolding Grounds*. It won the Anton Wachter Prize for best Dutch debut and was longlisted for the prestigious Libris Literature Prize. For her second novel, *Gliding Flight*, Goemans won the Dioraphte Literature Prize and the German M-Pioneer Award for literary newcomers. *Gliding Flight* has been translated into five languages and film rights have also been sold.

NANCY FOREST-FLIER is a New Jersey-born translator who moved to Europe in 1982 and has worked in the Netherlands since 1988. Her literary translations include *The King* by Kader Abdolah, *Dissident for Life* by Koenraad de Wolf, *We and Me* by Saskia de Coster, *Mr. Miller* by Charles den Tex, *Departure Time* by Truus Matti, *Hex* by Thomas Olde Heuvelt, and most recently *The Story of Shit* by Midas Dekkers. Nancy also translates children's literature and has translated for numerous Dutch museums and institutes, including The Anne Frank House and the Kröller-Müller Museum (home to the world's second largest Van Gogh collection).

Gliding Flight

Anne-Gine Goemans

Gliding Flight

Translated from the Dutch
by Nancy Forest-Flier

WORLD EDITIONS
New York, London, Amsterdam

Published in the USA in 2019 by World Editions LLC, New York
Published in the UK in 2015 by World Editions Ltd., London

World Editions
New York/London/Amsterdam

Copyright © Anne-Gine Goemans, 2011
English translation copyright © Nancy Forest-Flier, 2015
Cover image © Mischa Keijser
Author's portrait © Merlijn Doomernik

Printed by Sheridan, Chelsea, MI, USA

Library of Congress Cataloging in Publication Data is available.

ISBN 978-1-64286-008-5

First published as *Glijvlucht* in the Netherlands in 2011 by De Geus.

This book was published with the support of
the Dutch Foundation for Literature

N ederlands
letterenfonds
dutch foundation
for literature

Twitter: @WorldEdBooks
Facebook: WorldEditionsInternationalPublishing
www.worldeditions.org

Book Club Discussion Guides are available on our website.

For Lucy, Wester and Flint

With a dream in your heart you're never alone.
—BURT BACHARACH & HAL DAVID

It is easy to keep from walking;
the hard thing is to walk without touching the ground.
It is easy to cheat when you work for men,
but hard to cheat when you work for Heaven.
You have heard of flying with wings,
but you have never heard of flying without wings.
You have heard of the knowledge that knows,
but you have never heard of the knowledge that does
    not know.
Look into that closed room,
the empty chamber where brightness is born!
Fortune and blessing gather where there is stillness.
—*The Complete Works of Chuang Tzu*

Translated by Burton Watson

I

Hello, Christian!

My name is Gieles. I saw you flying with your geese on an
air show. I thought it was a magical spectacle. You were
very high in the sky with your flying two-seater motorbike. My father says you were flying with geese barnacles,
but I have certainty they were geese lesser white-fronted.
I apologise for my French. I have big problems with your
language. I try to do good.
I am for years impassioned by the geese. I have fourteen
years old. I have two brown geese, American Tufted Buff.
They wear a tuft, very beautiful and very elegant.
Like you I am a goose explorer and I am training my geese
for a project. My geese listen moderately average. They are
not shy. Indeed, sometimes they are insolent. They resemble the children of Dolly, my neighbour lady. My neighbour lady is above average good-looking.
I do the training with a stick. The stick is not for violence
but for obediencing. I always use different stick. When
geese know my stick longer, the obediencing disappears.
This is not desirable.
Your migrating varieties excel in listening. My compliments, also on behalf of your wife. Your geese regard you
and your wife as an adoptive father. My geese regard me, I
cry, as a cousin or brother to obtain tricks on. Just like the
children of my neighbour lady on whom I babysit.
I live in the Netherlands, next to an airplane path. Geese

next to an airplane path gives difficulties, you will observe! I am in great agreement. Fortunately my geese do not fly through the path. That comes, I cry, from my training (I have a small pride in this). Rest assured, my geese do not live in captivity. Captive birds are a scandal that should be terminated. My geese live in liberty on our campground. It is a campground for people who adore airplanes. They collect airplanes as if it was postage stamps.

You ask of course, why does the boy write? I do not write in order to fly in the two-seater motorbike with you, although for me that would really be spectacle. Being the same high height as the geese in the sky, together with the migrating varieties past the cumulus clouds! Unfortunately, your professional tourism is too expensive for me. I am writing you for a very different motive, for the content of our mutual training of the geese.

Gieles hesitated. How could he make contact with this man—this world famous goose specialist, meteorologist, pilot, filmmaker, ornithologist, photographer, writer, vegan and activist—and ask him the most important questions without revealing too much about his incredible scheme? It had to be kept secret. Gieles stood up from his desk and walked to the open attic skylight. Leaning out with his arms on the roof tiles, he gazed over at the runway. Less than sixty metres away was a straight black strip with lights embedded in it, as well as pastures and fields. In two minutes' time Gieles could be out on that runway, causing chaos. He wouldn't have to do a thing. Just standing there would be enough to get himself on every TV station in the country. But then his father could kiss his job as an airport bird controller goodbye.

Gieles looked over at the lights of a descending plane. The sky was calm. The only vibration of air that could be seen was around the wings. The roaring of the engines swelled steadily. He walked back to his laptop and filed the letter to the Frenchman Christian Moullec in a special folder. He had come up with just the right name for the folder: *Expert Rescue Operation 3032*.

In thirteen weeks and four days his mother would be coming home on flight 3032. Ellen had never been away so long before. Last week she had flown to Africa in the wake of a flock of wild geese. Geese migrated to survive. He understood that. But he didn't understand why his mother had to migrate. She went to places where there was nothing to eat or drink. His mother was migrating backwards, going against the flow. The birds would have thought she was out of her mind.

He went downstairs to the kitchen where Uncle Fred was sitting at the table peeling apples. 'Hey, Gieles,' he said cheerfully. Uncle Fred was always in a good mood. 'I've got peels for the geese.'

Gieles poured himself a glass of milk, swallowed it down in one gulp and wiped the moustache from his upper lip. The smoothness there irritated him. Not even a sign of peach fuzz.

His father and Uncle Fred were fraternal twins, but they didn't look at all alike. Willem Bos hardly had any hair left, while Uncle Fred had way too much with his mass of salt-and-pepper curls. His father held himself as erect as a statue of a powerful statesman. Uncle Fred, on the other hand, had a slight build and a shuffling gait, the result of childhood polio. He rode around on a mobility scooter and walked with a crutch. He refused to use a cane. There was something about the crutch that suggested a temporary condition (not that his leg was ever going to heal).

The brothers' personalities and hobbies were also different. His father was fond of birds and comic books. Uncle Fred liked cooking and literature. The only things they had in common were their height—almost two metres—and taking care of Gieles.

'Don't forget the goose poop,' Uncle Fred said, handing him the peels wrapped in newspaper. 'We have guests. A married couple.' He sounded pleased.

Gieles got a shovel and bucket from the barn. The deal he had made with his father was simple and straightforward: he could keep two geese as long as they didn't fly. The minute they took to the sky, they'd have to go. He was also responsible for caring for the geese, which mainly meant shovelling shit. The geese crapped about once a minute.

Next to the old farm was a pasture, where Uncle Fred ran a campground. He had recently gotten the campground listed in a farm-camping guide, although it didn't meet any of the criteria. No peace and quiet here. The planes took off and landed at about the same punishing tempo as the geese's bowel habits. The guide said it was a niche campground, which was absolutely true. It wasn't popular with families. The plane spotters who camped here were solitary figures by and large. The fact that the campground was not a success didn't bother Uncle Fred in the least. Nothing bothered him. He looked at the grey film of jet fuel covering the wooden sign that said WELCOME TO THE HOT SPOT and shrugged his shoulders.

The geese came toward him, greeting him with outstretched, swaying necks. Gieles patted the tufts on their heads and set the bucket of peels in the grass. They stuck their heads into the bucket with little enthusiasm, then began pecking at his thighs. The geese preferred the speculaas cookies that they were more or less addicted to. But Gieles only fed them speculaas during their training sessions, knowing that otherwise they wouldn't listen to him at all.

Parked on the edge of the pasture was a trailer that looked like a spaceship. A woman was standing in front of it. She waved at him and motioned to him to come over. He planted his shovel in the ground like a flag pole and walked up to her with the geese at his heels, begging for food. The woman's face was full of creases and cracks, like an antique painting, but her eyes were as clear as a girl's. As if they had been restored somehow.

'Hello, ma'am,' he said politely. 'Everything all right here?'

Gieles enjoyed being excessively polite to old people. There was something sad about them, he thought, because they were going to die soon.

'Excellent,' she said kindly. 'What I wanted to ask you is that my husband and I want to barbecue tonight. Is that all right?'

'No problem, ma'am. Just as long as you don't build a campfire. That might confuse the pilots. And don't fly any kites,' he joked.

She smiled. 'Silly boy.'

The door of the spaceship swung open and her husband came out. He was wearing a pair of aviator glasses and a body warmer with pockets stitched onto it. A pair of binoculars dangled from his neck. And the knobby knees and fossilised calves that stuck out from beneath his shorts looked like they were wasting away.

The man began rubbing the rounded curves of the spaceship with a handkerchief. Dispensing with all formalities he got right down to business. He didn't even give Gieles a chance to say hello. 'Look at that. Mirror finish, huh?'

Mirror was right. Gieles could see his reflection in the door, and he noticed that his hair was standing straight up. He ran his hand over his head.

'The origin of the Airstream,' said the man proudly, tucking his aviator glasses into one of the pockets, 'lies in the American aerospace industry. The wings are missing, but otherwise ...'

A descending Cityhopper drowned him out. They waited patiently until the sound died away.

'Where was I?' The man tugged at his white eyebrows. 'What's your favourite?'

'My favourite what, sir?'

'Plane,' he said, sitting down in a lawn chair. Gieles didn't have a favourite. The aviation industry left Gieles completely cold.

'The Antonov 225, sir,' he lied. The biggest plane in the world, number one for many spotters.

The man screwed up his face. 'That Russian hulk? Let me tell you something. I once waited hours for an Antonov, and all for nothing. The Russians can have their Antonov.'

'And the Boeing 747 400,' said Gieles to oblige him. 'They're awesome too, sir.' All plane spotters loved the 747 400.

He clapped his wrinkled hands. 'That's what I like to hear! One phenomenal looking plane, especially when it's frozen. Wingspan?'

Gieles gave him a puzzled look.

'What's the wingspan?' It was obvious from the way the old man asked the question that he already knew the answer. 'Sixty-four-point-four metres,' he said, looking at a plane through his binoculars. 'An Airbus A321. My wife goes for the take-offs, I love the landings. You?'

Gieles couldn't care less. A landing plane wasn't even

in the same league as a flock of descending geese. Suddenly appearing with all that cackle and flapping of wings. Then sweeping over the land like a wave that finally, slowly, disintegrates.

'I love geese when they land,' said Gieles, and he cast a glance at his geese, who were pulling up clumps of grass. 'The racket they make when they come down. The last metres before they hit the ground. They're really funny then. As if they can't remember what they're supposed to do.'

Gieles spread his arms and pretended to be losing his balance. 'Once they've landed, they strut around like anything. That's from pride. Sometimes they cover three thousand kilometres! They come all the way from the northernmost tip of Norway, and they all start shrieking together. "We're back! We're back!"'

The man and his wife looked at him in amazement.

'Geese talk to each other all day long,' Gieles went on. 'Just like a bunch of women, my father says. And they're never alone. They always fly together. The whole family.'

'Goodness,' said the woman with wide eyes. 'I didn't know that. But how do they know which way to go? The sky is so—how shall I put it?—so vast. It's easy to take a wrong turn.'

Gieles crossed his arms self-confidently. Geese were his speciality.

'The most important things are the sun and the stars.' He spoke the words with an air of importance. 'They're migration signposts. And the little ones learn from their parents. Chicks straight from the egg don't know anything at all. When they overwinter for the first time, they fly with their parents to learn the way. Sometimes it's thousands of kilometres.'

The woman listened attentively to Gieles while her

husband spotted the next plane.

'And the chicks that have no parents? Who do they learn from?'

'There's always an aunt to take care of them,' said Gieles. 'Or a nice uncle.'

'Oh, of course,' she sighed, sitting down in the other lawn chair. 'How many geese do you have?'

'Two, ma'am. Just these two.'

'But they shit for ten,' said the old man disdainfully. 'Better to have a dog. They don't shit nearly as much.'

They watched silently as another plane descended. One of the geese was foraging along the bank of the canal. In the four years he had had them, not once had the geese ever gone into that filthy water. They never even considered it.

'Very dangerous, geese near a runway.' The man squeezed the binoculars so hard that his knuckles turned white. 'I'm sure you've heard of that emergency landing? On the river in New York?'

Heard of it? Gieles's eyes lit up like fireflies on a dark night. The emergency landing on the water—a 'ditch'—had made a huge impression on him.

'The Miracle of the Hudson, sir,' Gieles exclaimed. The words rolled off his tongue in such an orderly fashion that it made him sound like a news presenter. 'On January 15th, 2009, Captain Chesley Burnett Sullenberger of US Airways landed on the Hudson after a flock of Canada geese flew into his engines. He felt as if he had been hit by a gigantic bolt of lightning.'

Gieles mimicked being struck by the lightning, his body jolting, and then continued. 'Captain Sully—everybody calls him Sully, and that's what's printed on the T-shirts and mugs and underpants—Captain Sully saved all hundred fifty-five passengers of flight 1549.'

'He checked the plane twice for stragglers,' the man added excitedly—this was a boy he could talk to—'before evacuating, the last man to leave the sinking ship. Which actually happened, because the landing had torn open the whole bottom of the aircraft.'

'And then these little boats came sailing out from everywhere to pick up the passengers,' continued Gieles happily. 'But I'm sure you know that, sir.'

'Hey,' the man roared over the noise of a descending plane. 'Cut it out with that "sir" stuff! Makes me nervous!'

He waited for the sound to die down. 'Johan and Judith.' He pointed to his wife, who stood there staring at Gieles in silent amazement with her restored eyes. 'Goodness, you sure do know a lot! This boy sure does know a lot, doesn't he?'

She placed a hand on her husband's liver-spotted arm. 'Johan knows everything about airplanes and crashes. He's been collecting plane crashes in scrapbooks since 1972. With all the details. And if he can find photos he pastes them in, too. Other spotters call him a crash freak. Isn't that right, Johan?'

'Hmm.' A Boeing was hanging heavily in the air a few kilometres away.

'They're very lovely scrapbooks,' she declared. 'It's not the death and sensationalism that Johan is interested in, but the chain of events.'

'I was sure I could do it,' said Gieles in English.

'Excuse me?' said the woman.

'That's what Captain Sully said. After his act of heroism.' Gieles tried to imitate his voice by relaxing his vocal cords. 'I was sure I could do it.'

The man followed the plane until the tail disappeared behind a row of birches. Then he said, rather severely, 'So you know damn well how dangerous geese are for aviation.'

'My geese can't fly,' Gieles lied. 'They've lost the knack.'

'Look,' said the woman, delighted. 'Kenya Airways. What cheerful colours. It looks just like the tail of a tropical parrot. I adore parrots. They make me think of fireworks.'

'Next time we come here,' said Johan, 'I'll bring my scrapbooks along. Then I'll show you that even a couple of geese in the engine can do a lot of damage. A whole lot of damage.'

'What a wonderful place to live,' his wife interrupted, inhaling deeply. 'Right near the airplanes, yet out in the country.'

'Tremendously beautiful spot,' nodded Johan in approval. 'That's all I can say.'

She turned halfway around in her chair and pointed to a little wooded area further up on the other side of the road.

'I wonder who planted those trees there. Such young trees right out in the polder ... It's like a fairy tale.'

'Environmentalists,' said Gieles.

'What a terribly nice gesture.'

'Why?' asked Johan suspiciously, putting his aviator glasses back on.

'They didn't want a runway to be built here. So they bought a piece of land from our neighbour and planted trees on it. But the court said the trees had to go, so they moved the trees over there.' He pointed to the woods. 'My mother calls it "the woods in exile."'

For Gieles, the summer with the environmentalists was the best he'd ever had. Suddenly there they were. They came chugging along in a smelly diesel bus, and Gieles couldn't see how the bus could hold so many people and so much stuff. He watched as they unloaded their tents, generators, duffle bags, sleeping bags, kerosene lamps and pans. In one afternoon, Gieles's boring view of the polder turned into a non-stop circus performance. Dozens of dome tents were pitched around a trailer that was painted in rainbow colours. The environmentalists tied hammocks to wooden poles and their children hung paper streamers in the branches. It looked gorgeous, thought Gieles, who didn't dare go out to size up the situation until the end of the afternoon. His friend Tony went first.

The activists were very nice. They gave them lemonade and cookies and asked them all kinds of questions: how often Tony and Gieles played in the woods, what they thought of the airport, whether they were often sick or found themselves coughing a lot. Gieles chuckled when the environmentalists talked about the importance of 'their woods,' when what they meant was the scrawny little clump of trees in the middle of a wasteland. Everywhere there were piles of grey sand with bulldozers and dump trucks driving through them. It was one big sandbox, where men in orange overalls walked around with notebooks. The construction of the new runway was in full swing. Now it was a matter of waiting for the court ruling.

Every day, new people came to visit the encampment. According to Uncle Fred they were celebrities, which must have been true because there were photographers and journalists there as well. The celebrities shouted that they were opposed to the runway. But once the runway was built, you never heard them say another word about it. They never came back. Now the celebrities were flying over the roofs of the houses of Gieles and his neighbours.

Gieles's house was on television countless times that summer. Reporters kept asking Uncle Fred what he thought of the idea of airplanes landing in his backyard.

'You can't stop it,' he declared. And actually it wasn't even his backyard. Uncle Fred had been bought out. His own house was located right *on* the future runway; it had to go. That's why he moved in with the family of his twin brother. It had been a practical decision, too. When Ellen was flying, Fred could take care of Gieles and do the housework.

Gieles knew that Uncle Fred never answered the journalists' questions. Uncle Fred was never for or against anything. He never identified with any particular side, as if the matter didn't concern him. He took everything in stride. Be a river, not a mountain: that was his motto. The river was friendly to the activists. He brought them homemade fennel soup and sausage rolls, and let them take showers at the farm. When the guy ropes of the sprawling encampment got all tangled up, he offered them the pasture as an additional place to pitch their tents. That's what inspired him to start a spotters' campground.

The river was friendly to the activists' enemies, too. When the military police appeared in the farmyard to go over some questions of public safety, he gave them a bag of cherries. And when the airport people came over to talk about sound insulation, he served them coffee and apple pie.

Gieles fervently hoped that the environmentalists would never go away. And he wasn't the only one. All the neighbourhood children spent more time in the woods that summer than they did at home. They played hide-and-seek and danced wildly to the music from Rinky Dink, an environmentally-friendly sound installation driven by bicycle power. A man with a braided red beard taught Gieles how to make a tent with bamboo sticks. He painted wooden leaves that were suspended from the branches of a metal tree. Sometimes Gieles ate with them from big pans of beans that had been cooked to death. They ate at long tables, and often the discussions became so heated that Gieles thought they were going to start fighting. He heard words he hadn't heard before, such as 'free state,' 'mafia,' 'court order,' 'occupation.' And he learned how to curse for the first time. 'Prick' and 'asshole' were already familiar to him, but 'twat,' 'cunt,' 'motherfucker' and 'cocksucker' were new. His friend Tony couldn't get enough of the curse words.

When his mother came back from abroad she would go take a look at the camp, sometimes still in her uniform. The environmentalists were nice to Ellen. No one paid any attention to her stewardess outfit. Gieles even suspected that the men of the camp were flirting with her.

In the evening, Gieles would stare at the encampment through his attic window as long as he could keep his eyes open. Some of the activists sat around the campfire, others lay entwined in hammocks. Someone played the guitar. Flashlights blinked on and off in the dome tents and made the woods look magical. One man hauled a bucket of dishwashing water out of the canal he'd just pissed into. Once Gieles saw a bare bottom sticking out of a hammock. Whether there was one person or two in the hammock was impossible for him to tell.

On the day the woods were cleared by court order, the environmentalists got ready to resist to the bitter end. They promised a raging battle, a guerrilla war. Gieles was on the environmentalists' side, of course. He and Tony made a slingshot out of wood and a rubber band.

But the battle never materialised. When two police-men closed off the road so the camp could no longer receive supplies, the tents were taken down in silence. The only reminder of the environmentalists was the metal tree with its wooden leaves, but even that disappeared within a couple of days. The airport had won.

Since the runway's completion, the short distance between it and the farm had been drawing Gieles like a magnet. The first time he and Tony had tried to bridge the few forbidden metres was with a blowpipe and paper. They shot spitballs at the runway from his attic window until the ink from the paper made them nauseous. This led to a game with a slingshot and a whole series of variations that became increasingly less innocent.

The shootings ended for good when a homemade paint bomb exploded against the flank of a Cityhopper. The idea for a paint bomb had come from a squatter who lived next-door to Tony and his family. The house had stood empty since the opening of the runway. No one wanted to live there any more, except the squatter. He was the one who taught Tony and Gieles how to make the bombs, a procedure that involved dipping balloons in candle wax at least forty times. That, said the squatter, would produce a bomb that could smash a double-glazed window. Gieles and Tony didn't want to smash any double-glazed windows, so they only dipped the balloons twenty times. The very first shot was a direct hit. For a moment the pilot was under the impression that a big bird had crashed against the cockpit, but there was something suspicious about the blue colour. From the attic window Tony and Gieles could see the flashing lights of the military police. Terrified, Gieles grabbed one of the balloons and squeezed it so hard that the paint squirted all over his bedroom. There was no point in denying that they were the culprits.

Gieles emptied his glass of cola, and when the woman offered him another syrup waffle he accepted it. Her husband had fallen asleep. His chin was hanging loosely over his body warmer. The binoculars rested on his lanky legs. Gieles thanked her and went back to cleaning up the goose shit.

His father had called the environmentalists a bunch of boneheads. Leaving without resistance: that, according to him, made you a bonehead. But for Gieles the environmentalists were heroes, and since that summer he had felt a deep longing to be a hero himself. He had done the occasional heroic thing, but that didn't make him a hero. Two years before he had rescued a German shepherd from the canal. The dog hadn't been able to scramble up onto the bank himself. Gieles pulled him out by his collar and the dog ran away. No one had seen his act of heroism, so it didn't count.

The Frenchman Christian Moullec was a hero. In his flying two-seater motorbike he saved lesser white-fronted geese by showing them the way to their winter quarters.

His mother was a hero. At the risk of her own life she travelled from one dried out place to another (for reasons that were incomprehensible to him) to teach poor Africans to cook on solar-powered stoves.

Captain Sully was the biggest hero of them all. Without a doubt. *I was sure I could do it.* Americans adored him. They drank coffee from I ♥ SULLY mugs. They wore T-shirts with THANK YOU CAPTAIN SULLY, SULLY IS MY HOMEBOY, OLD PILOTS NEVER DIE on them. His name was on pillows, mouse pads, bumper stickers, calendars and dog shirts. Women wore panties bearing the words TRUE HERO FLT 1549. He was sexier than Johnny Depp, greater than Jesus. Jesus could walk on water, but

Captain Chesley Sullenberger could land on water and bring a hundred fifty-five people to safety.

Another hero of immense proportions: Jan-Ove Waldner. The best table tennis player ever. Also called the Mozart of table tennis. Gieles had no idea why, but it sounded good.

His father was a kind of hero. He drove birds from the runways to keep the passengers safe. Gieles suspected him of driving the birds away to save them from the airplane engines. Obstinate birds were shot, but not by Willem Bos. He never shot. Except at pigeons. His father despised pigeons.

Gieles went to the barn, shovel and bucket in hand. In just a few more months he'd be a hero himself. He would personally see to it that his mother never wanted to go back to Africa again. Everyone would be hugely impressed.

In the barn he picked up the bamboo stick and the tin of speculaas. When he shook the tin the geese came running. He gave them a couple of cookies and put the tin in his backpack. Then he prodded their feathery backsides with the stick.

Strutting with pride, their tufts held jauntily in the air, the geese crossed the road. When they got to the environmentalists' woods they began to graze in the grass. Gieles looked up at the camera that was mounted to a lamppost.

The airport tolerated the geese because his father had told them they were flightless farm chickens that had never flown a metre in their lives. His father had authority.

If only they knew.

Idiots.

They passed a derelict house whose garden was overrun by wild blackberry bushes that were creeping up the outer walls. Gieles noticed that part of one bush was growing in through a broken window, as if the house were being devoured. Behind the uninhabited ruin was a grassy path leading to the shed. He pushed open the corrugated metal door. The shed was empty, except for a couple of aluminium boats and a disassembled tractor. The geese waddled in, their tails wagging. They were eager to get started.

'Stay,' he said to the geese, articulating distinctly. He held up his hands as if he were pronouncing a blessing.

'Stay.'

Slowly Gieles started walking backward, repeating the command. The geese stayed where they were but became restless. They wiggled up and down and began cheeping. At a distance of less than twenty metres Gieles again called out 'stay!', but this time they took a running start and flapped up to him awkwardly, flopping down at his feet and cackling with wild abandon.

'Damn!' said Gieles in frustration. 'You guys are supposed to wait till I give the sign! With my stick!' They pecked at his pants' leg. Gieles pushed the geese away. 'First listen. Then cookies.'

He began walking backward once more. 'Sit! Stay!'

2

At the end of the afternoon they watched scenes of an earthquake on television. A woman stood wailing in front of a mountain of rubble that until very recently had been a house.

'Good thing Ellen isn't there,' said Uncle Fred, opening the newspaper. They were sitting side by side on the threadbare couch with the English tea-rose pattern.

Gieles tried to imagine what it was like for the earth to shake. A shaking roof was normal for him. When the heavy cargo jets took off at night, the roof pounded like an old washing machine.

Gieles zapped from the earthquake to Animal Planet. A grooming bonobo and her baby were sitting under a tree. Gieles's friend Tony had a lot in common with monkeys. He was muscular in a stocky sort of way and there was something threatening about his body language. He had a habit of scratching the zits on his chin and putting the pus in his mouth. It was revolting. Even so, Gieles still hung out with him. After the runway had been built almost everyone in the neighbourhood had moved away.

One of the males grabbed the female from behind.

'Bonobos spend almost the entire day delighting in each other's company,' said a voice.

Uncle Fred glanced up from his newspaper. Gieles quickly zapped to another station. Recently it was impossible for Tony to carry on a conversation without talking about screwing, as if he had already done it a gazillion times and Gieles was doomed to be a virgin for the rest of his life. It's true that he was too much of a chicken to talk to girls, which was why he spent so much of his time on the internet. He had met someone on a website. She called herself Gravitation. He had logged in as Captain Sully. The e-mail correspondence between them had been fairly vague.

His father's airport service car came into the yard. It was a bright yellow jeep with transmitters and sound equipment on the roof. The equipment was meant to keep birds off the runways. He had recordings of dying birds that sent ice cold shivers down your spine. The screeching of a terrified seagull was especially effective at keeping other seagulls away.

His father got out of the jeep with his phone to his ear. He looked grave. Gieles zapped to soccer. A little while later his father came into the living room with a beer in his hand.

'Hey, guys,' he said, dropping onto a dark grey sofa that had once matched the rest of the interior. When Uncle Fred had moved his own furniture into the living room—the English tea rose couch, a mahogany sideboard and a glass tea table—unity of design went out the window.

'How'd it go?' Uncle Fred asked his twin brother.

'A close shave,' said Willem Bos, never a man of many words. Whenever he did speak, he got it over with as quickly as possible. Occupational disability, he called it. He had adjusted the rhythm of his sentences to the take-off and landing of the airplanes.

'Thousands of migrating starlings flew over the runway and down into the fields. Close shave.'

He said it at the end of every workday. Close shave.

Uncle Fred and Gieles didn't even hear it any more, nor did Willem Bos expect a response. Swallows, seagulls, geese, bats, owls, starlings, lapwings, oystercatchers, buzzards, swans: hundreds of thousands of birds made a stopover at the airport. The sky was a tangle of migratory routes, invisible to most people but not to his father. When Willem shut his eyes he could see all the bird highways take shape before him. His job was to keep the birds at a safe distance, an overwhelming task when you considered what was involved.

Willem Bos took a sip of beer and settled down to watch the game.

Uncle Fred hoisted himself up with his crutch. 'Supper's almost ready.' He click-clacked into the kitchen.

Gieles set the table and sat down to eat. They only sat in the same seats when his mother was away. He had a view of their narrow backyard, the canal and the runway. The black water glistened in the evening sun. The nose of a plane appeared in the kitchen window and came to a halt. The crew and passengers couldn't see them. His mother had once had to wait in a plane that was idling in front of their house. All she could see when she looked in the windows was the reflection of the plane itself.

'Thursday evening we're experimenting with a robot bird,' said Willem. He ate his macaroni in big bites. Everything about his father was big: his mouth, his ears, his nose, his hands. His movements. Women found him handsome in an exciting sort of way. They stole glances at him but didn't dare strike up a conversation. Sometimes women from Uncle Fred's book clubs came over, and they would suddenly get all theatrical if his father happened to walk into the room.

Willem Bos looked at his son. 'Maybe you'd like to

come along? To see the robot bird, I mean.'

'I think I have time,' said Gieles.

His father pushed the empty plate away and let his hands rest on the table.

Gieles wanted to take hold of that powerful hand, but he was afraid it would seem childish. He looked at his own hands. They were baby hands compared to his dad's. They hadn't done anything yet. He'd never even laid a finger on a girl's body, let alone *in* a girl's body. In kindergarten he'd rooted around in a girl's backside with his finger, but it might just as well have been her nose. There had been a practical reason for it. They had been playing that the felt-tip pen was a thermometer, and the top got stuck inside her. Gieles wanted to get the top out. The teacher got mad if they didn't put the tops back on the felt-tips. She was afraid they would dry out. (She was also afraid of lice, sour milk, mud in the construction corner, scraped knees and lots of other things.)

After supper Gieles went to his room. He had half an hour before he had to leave. He turned on the fan and the laptop and wiped his forehead. It was early May but it was stifling in his room. The airport had had the roof insulated with thick mattresses that were supposed to muffle the noise of the planes, but they turned his room into a pressure cooker. The worst thing was that the sound insulation made his hair stand on end. He was always walking around with a permanent static charge.

Gieles wanted to do some more work on the letter to Christian Moullec, but he noticed there was an e-mail from his mother. It was the second message she'd sent since she left. Gravitation was also online. He quickly read the last sentences of his mother's mail.

'And I can't take off the burka either, even though it's

forty degrees. I miss you and think about you, and I hope you spend just a teensy bit of time thinking about all those people living in such terrible poverty here. Love, Ellen.'

Gieles didn't want to think about all those people, so he closed the mail. Africans made him feel so incredibly depressed. He'd rather think about the virtual girl. Gravitation. He wondered why she called herself that. It was as if she wanted to imply that she was fat, but she didn't look fat in the little photos. She had pitch black dreadlocks and a pale, oval face. It said in her profile that she had fourteen piercings. Gieles wondered where they were. He could only see one, in her eyebrow. He couldn't get a clear picture of Gravitation because of the dreadlocks and the black make-up. Her green eyes were beautiful, he thought. They were the same colour as the scum on the fish bowl when it hadn't been cleaned for weeks.

He could start with her eyes, but that was corny. Keep it simple.

Captain Sully: 'Hi, what are you up to?'

Gravitation: 'Nothing. Playing with my rabbit and listening to music.'

Captain Sully: 'What you listening to?'

Gravitation: 'Fever Ray. You probably don't know her. Fever Ray is this Swedish woman. She changes every day. Just like me. This morning I dyed my hair.'

Captain Sully: 'What colour?'

Gravitation: 'Violet.'

Weirdo. Violet dreadlocks.

Captain Sully: 'Did you dye your rabbit, too?'

Gravitation: 'Fuck off.'

Captain Sully: 'I have rabbits, too. Hundreds.'

Gravitation: 'You live at a petting zoo?'

Captain Sully: 'Ha ha. No, I live on a dead-end street next to an airport runway. There are lots of rabbits near the runway. And hares.'

Gravitation: 'Cool.'

Captain Sully: 'There are lots of birds and foxes and stuff near the runway, too. My father calls it a wildlife area. I have two geese.'

Gravitation: 'Geese are great!'

She's pulling my chain. Nobody thinks geese are great.

Gravitation: 'What are their names?'

The geese had no names, but that might sound like he didn't care enough about them. He scanned his room in search of suitable names. On his bookshelf he spotted the rows of comic books that had belonged to his father.

Captain Sully: 'Asterix and Obelix. And your rabbit?'

Gravitation: 'Just plain rabbit.'

Captain Sully: 'How old is he?'

Gravitation: 'Five. And you?'

Captain Sully: 'About four.'

Gravitation: 'No. *You!*'

She has to be older than fourteen.

Captain Sully: 'Sixteen. And you?'

Gravitation: 'Almost seventeen.'

She's almost three years older than me! That means I pretty much don't even exist for her!

Gravitation: 'I'm moving out as soon as I can. I hate my parents.'

Shit, I have to be at Dolly's in ten minutes.

Captain Sully: 'I've got to go to work.'

Gravitation: 'Where?'

Babysitting wasn't cool, Gieles decided, so he thought of the part-time job Tony had in his father's shop. His father was a butcher.

Captain Sully: 'In a butcher shop.'
Gravitation: 'I'm a vegetarian.'

3

Dolly lived with her three little sons at the bend in the runway. The house was wedged in between two abandoned houses that looked just as dilapidated as hers. Empty houses were cancerous growths, Dolly said, that should be cut out immediately. But that didn't happen. There she was, stuck in the most nauseating place in the universe. On rainy days, when the polder was dull and grey and the only thing that shone was the asphalt, she repeated her theory over and over again like a mantra.

Gieles didn't know whether she was right or wrong. But over a year ago her husband had died of a heart attack. One morning she found him dead in their bed. It was a mystery, said the doctor, but not according to Dolly. She was convinced that it had to do with the airport and the empty houses. The noise of the airplanes ate away at him the way fungus hollows out a tree. She could feel the cancer demons beaming their rays right through the walls. Since then, Dolly cursed the house, the neighbourhood and her life, but she never managed to get away. A FOR SALE sign had been hanging in the front yard since her husband's death. Not a single person had come to look.

Dolly opened the door. She already had her jacket on and her face was carefully made up. She smiled. 'Hello,' he said, and put his backpack with the laptop under the hat rack. Gieles was eager to get back online.

Gieles thought Dolly was sexy, but sometimes she was

scary, too. She could light into her children like a crazy lady. His father and mother never yelled or hit. Gieles had gotten a smack on the head, but just once. That was after the incident with the paint bomb and the Cityhopper. His father pulled him out from under the bed, where he had been hiding. He was covered with blue paint. That was the one time his father had hit him.

Dolly could get a certain expression on her face that made you want to look the other way. She never did it with him, but she did with his mother sometimes. If his mother was at a birthday party, for example, and she started talking about African children with chopped off limbs and smashed skulls, Dolly's eyes would narrow. He realised that her expression had something to do with disapproval.

He walked into the living room and was met by Skiq and Onno, Dolly's two oldest children, who jumped all over him, whooping loudly. Dolly went to the dining room table, where there was a suitcase containing bottles of vitamins. Two evenings a week she sold the vitamins at living room gatherings. During the day she worked in her own beauty parlour. Gieles wondered if she took the pills herself. She always looked so tired.

'Jonas is already asleep,' Dolly told him as she shut the lid and pulled the suitcase off the table.

'I'll carry it,' said Gieles. He shook Skiq off his back and dragged himself up to her. (Onno had wrapped his arms around Gieles's leg and was trailing along behind him.)

'Cut it out, Onno,' she snarled. Then she went outside, high heels clicking. Gieles put the suitcase on the back seat of the worn-out old Nissan. The inside of the car smelled of her perfume.

'You're an angel,' she told him.

She had called him that before. 'I don't understand

why your mother leaves such an angel alone,' she had said.

Dolly stroked his static hair and laughed. 'Try a wooden comb. That helps. There's one in the bathroom—or in my bedroom. On the window sill, I think.'

She gave a quick wave to the boys, who were standing at the window. A plant fell from the window sill and both of them saw it. It was the ficus.

'Goddamn it,' cursed Dolly.

'I'll clean it up,' he said.

She got in her car and opened the window. 'Don't forget their medicine!'

Inside the boys were fighting over the ficus. The pot lay on the floor in three pieces. The soil was all dried up, and everywhere there were brown leaves covered with a layer of dust. Dolly hardly did any cleaning since the death of her husband. Not very smart, Gieles thought. She'd never find a buyer that way. On the other hand, he didn't like the idea of Dolly and the children leaving.

Gieles put the plant in the dish pan and turned on the water, which was soaked up by the ball of soil around the roots. On the counter was a ten euro note for babysitting.

'I need glue,' said Gieles. 'If you guys stop screaming, you can help.'

They both ran to the hall closet and came back with their hands filled with tubes of glue.

'I only need one.' He placed the shards on the table. The boys spread glue on the broken pottery.

'Put your hands on the cracks and push.'

He thought of his mother. She had scars on her arms from a car accident in Zambia. Or was it Malawi? He didn't remember. When Gieles asked what the long, thin stripes were on her arms, she answered, 'Glue joints. I fell apart, and they glued me back together.'

After a couple of minutes Gieles said they could pull their hands away.

'Nice,' said Onno. 'Now Mom won't be mad.'

Skiq lined the tubes up in front of him and began to count. 'There are eighteen,' he said.

'Why do you have so much glue here?' asked Gieles.

The boy shrugged his shoulders. 'I think because lots of things break.'

Gieles picked up his laptop. 'Go watch TV.'

The brothers stretched out on the couch, zapping, while Gieles installed himself at the table. Fuck. No Gravitation. He read the mail from his mother.

'Sunshine,' she wrote. His mother had been calling him that for as long as he could remember. 'I'm writing you in the classroom of a little school in Budunbuto. It's a poor village without running water but with eight brand-new computers donated by a Dutch company. A heart-warming initiative. Unfortunately, seven of the computers broke down because of all the airborne sand. Tomorrow I'm giving the women of the village a cooking demonstration. They're used to cooking on wood, but there's not a tree to be found in the whole area. Compared with Budunbuto our polder is an overgrown jungle. Fortunately I can spend today resting from the journey. It took almost a week to get here. I'm used to inaccessible places and bandits, but my guide really beat them all. He chewed khat non-stop. Munched down entire bushes of the stuff like a goat, so that he totally lost touch with reality. He actually thought I was a female hyena and he was the male counterpart. I'll spare you the details. I'm glad I'm here, although sometimes the dust drives me nuts. It gets on and into everything.

There's nothing I'd rather have than a cold shower, but the water is being rationed. And I can't take off the burka either, even though it's forty degrees.'

He had already read the bit about the burka.

'There's nothing good on TV,' said Skiq, grabbing his black Michael Jackson hat.

'Can I show you the moonwalk?' The hat was hanging low over his eyes.

Gieles slammed the computer screen shut and walked over to the cabinet where the CD player was stored. All the CDs were scrambled up together, none of them in boxes.

'Number four!' shouted Skiq. '"Billie Jean", it's already in it.'

Skiq stood in the middle of the living room with his hat tilted at an angle over his face. He held the brim with one hand. The music started and Skiq began shaking his narrow hips. Then he made punching movements. His little brother imitated him from the couch. While snapping up the heel of one foot he pushed the other foot back.

'You do it better than Michael Jackson,' said Gieles.

Onno jumped down from the couch, right on top of his brother. They began fighting.

'Time for bed,' said Gieles, pulling the boys apart. They continued their quarrel in the bathroom, first fighting over toothbrushes, then over their medicine. All three children had asthma. Dolly blamed their illness on the airport, too.

'If you guys put your inhalers in your mouth now, I'll let you ride in Uncle Fred's scooter the next time.'

They both inhaled their medicine and went out to the hallway.

'You can't come in my room,' Skiq told Gieles.

He stood in the doorway, blocking the entrance.

'Skiq still wets the bed. He has a piss alarm,' teased Onno.

'I DON'T WET THE BED, YOU STUPID PRICK!' screamed Skiq, punching his brother in the stomach. Onno fell against the wall and began to cry.

The youngest boy woke up and started bawling, too.

'We're not gonna start beating each other up,' said Gieles, pulling them apart once more. It took half an hour to calm the boys down. Gieles went into Skiq's bedroom last. Skiq was lying with his back to the door. Next to his head was a little black box attached to a cord. The cord disappeared under the duvet.

'Is that the alarm?' asked Gieles.

The boy said nothing. His angular shoulders protruded from the duvet. Skiq was a boy of delicate build. When Gieles horsed around with him he could feel the bones right through his skin. He made Gieles think of a grasshopper. Dolly had named Skiq after an English hardcore band. Gieles was afraid that Skiq would never become hardcore.

'I wet the bed sometimes, too,' Gieles lied, but he immediately regretted saying it. Later Skiq would tell Dolly.

Totally unconvinced, the boy turned around. 'Really?'

'Joke. But Tony does,' said Gieles. 'And Tony is sixteen already and you just turned nine.'

Skiq looked relieved.

'And Tony drives a motorbike.'

'Don't tell anybody. Promise?'

'Promise.'

'Gieles?' the boy asked.

'Yes?'

'Are we ever gonna play table tennis again?'

'Sure.'

He walked past Dolly's bedroom. The door was open. It was a mess, clothes lying and hanging everywhere. The ironing board was about to collapse under a mountain of laundry. Gieles went in. He looked on the window sill behind the closed room-darkening curtains, but there was no wooden comb to be seen among all the pots of desiccated cactuses. He sat down on the unmade double bed. The room was suddenly ablaze with lights from a descending plane. Gieles squeezed his eyes shut. It felt like stadium lights were penetrating the curtains and shining right on him. The plane landed and taxied past the house. For a moment it was dark, but just a few minutes later the room was bathed in light again. Gieles stretched out on the bed. On the nightstand was a framed photo. He saw Dolly in a white wedding dress. Her dead husband had his arms wrapped around her waist. Gieles thought they looked happy. The light flared up again, blinking, and then ebbed away.

Gieles's parents were not married. His mother thought marriage was nonsense. Whenever she got all agitated about the state of the world, his father would joke, 'Will you marry me?' That made her laugh. But for the past year his father had stopped making those jokes.

Gieles turned over on his stomach and smelled the same sweet fragrance he had smelled in the car. Yawning, he threw his arms around the pillow. His hands encountered a strip of pills and a small piece of velvet. In the airplane light he saw that it was some kind of Zorro mask.

He thought about Gravitation and her green eyes. She liked Swedish music and animals. The next time he'd tell her everything about the behaviour of his geese.

He thought about table tennis. He'd spent trillions of hours playing table tennis with Tony, but ever since

Tony had started getting zits and acting irritating they didn't play any more. He daydreamed about Dolly. Did she sleep naked? That was a thought that made the lower part of his body come to life.

A high, shrill noise brought him back to reality. It sounded like a fire alarm. Stumbling over the clothes, he ran out into the hall. He expected to see metre-high flames shooting up the stairwell, but he saw and smelled nothing. The sound came from Skiq's room, from the little black box. The boy didn't even wake up.

4

I am like you training my geese for a project. I cannot run
into the details. It is secret and surprise for my mother.
Like your rescue flying, my project is also an action of
rescue. As I already wrote, my geese do not excel in
listening. They behave sometimes completely stupid.
When I give them an ordering, I want them to stay in the
same place, even when I am no longer visual. But when I
am not visual for the geese, they start looking for me.
They panic and search for me and they are consummately
happy to see me. I must punish, but I have trouble. They
are not making a serious mistake. They are following the
nature. I try to be goose. I cry, Christian Moullec. How to
stay in 1 place?
I look in book for dog. The dog is also like geese the best
friend of the person. I try with a low voice. Sit and stay.
But they do not listen. I do not scream. In the book dog it
says: screaming orderings is useless. The book is right.
My neighbour woman Dolly screams orderings at her
children on whom I babysit. The children also scream,
but they do not understand each other.
Book for dog says for training use an open stream of
water. But for leaking they have fear. As I already wrote to
you, my geese see me as a cousin or brother. They do not
see me as head of the platoon.

Tony's mother stood at the window with one hand on her
hip. The telephone was clamped between her shoulder

and her ear. From the back, Liedje looked like a high school girl. Her jeans were stretched tightly across her bottom. Her hair was long and golden blond. Gieles sat on the couch gazing at Liedje.

'My God, honey,' she said, 'you never told me. I had no idea.' Then she turned around. With her tan face full of wrinkles and her creased lips, she was Tony's mother again. She was wearing a low-cut gold-coloured sweater. Her tanned cleavage was so full of crevices that it looked as if a tic-tac-toe board had been gouged into it. Tony called his mother 'lame-o,' 'ass wipe' or 'weasel,' depending on his mood. He had an inexhaustible collection of metaphors on hand to describe her.

Liedje lit a cigarette and went back to the window. She nodded her head vigorously and kept repeating 'uh-huh, uh-huh, uh-huh' and 'oh my God' as she plucked at the mint green lace curtains. Liedje was a mint green fiend. Everything in the house was mint green: the couch, the toilet seat, the kitchen cabinets, the door mat, the dog basket.

Tony put two glasses of cola on the coffee table and flopped onto the couch. On TV there was a black girl dancing with four black men. They hardly had anything on. Gieles looked over at Tony, who was slumped down with half his back on the seat of the couch. He was muscular, but he wasn't much to look at. His eyes were small and too close together and his nose was the colour of a veal cutlet (and just as shapeless). Maybe it came from eating all that stuff from his father's butcher shop.

Working with a thumb and forefinger, Tony squeezed a pimple on his chin. He wiped the pus off on his pants, next to a dark grease stain.

Liedje rubbed a sleeve of her gold sweater over the display cabinet. Liedje was very neat; she followed Tony and his little sister around all day with a damp cloth and the dustbuster. Inside the display cabinet were miniature motorcycles. The whole family collected them. Liedje's were mint green.

Liedje was silent for a while, said 'oh my God' and 'uh-huh' for the umpteenth time and hung up.

'That Polman woman got cancer, too,' she said absently.

'Which Polman woman?' said Tony, followed by a burp.

'Renee,' said Liedje.

'Renee from the gay café.'

'Cut the crap,' she said with irritation. 'The woman's name is Renee Polman.'

'Sick Renee with her vayjayjay.'

'God, you're disgusting. I don't know where you get it from.'

'Big hairy deal.'

'The woman is only sixty-five! That's a very big deal! And lay a towel down before you sit on the chairs with your filthy pants. How many times do I have to tell you?'

His mother made noises that sounded like she was chasing away a cat.

Big hairy deal. Tony said that all day long. Big hairy deal, and he said it with a look on his face as if he were telling the whole world to go fuck themselves.

'Thanks for the cola,' said Gieles, and rushed out behind Tony.

There were white angel figurines in the front yard whose wings had been spray-painted mint green. Airplane spotters who were driving by often stopped in front of the house to take a look. It wasn't a big house but it certainly was striking with all that green. Tony lived with his parents and little sister on the same road as Dolly. It used to be a lively neighbourhood before the runway came. Each spring the residents organised a street party, and in the winter they put braziers and pans of pea soup out on the sidewalk. Now only four of the houses were occupied. Even the squatter who knew how to make paint bombs had moved away. It was spooky, he thought. The airport had built the runway right through the heart of the community. Residents who lived in the danger zone were bought out, and those who refused to leave were dispossessed.

Tony and Gieles walked to the backyard shed. Two motorcycles and a motorbike were lined up side by side. Liedje's Kawasaki looked as good as new. Not a spot of dirt on it anywhere.

Tony put on his father's helmet and tossed his own helmet to Gieles. Gieles smelled it first. The inside smelled like scalp. The idea that Tony, with his wet chin, had had this helmet on his head, was truly disgusting.

'Hurry up,' said Tony impatiently. He had already ridden his souped-up motorbike out of the shed. Pebbles flew in every direction.

'What exactly are we gonna do?' asked Gieles. He shut his eyes and put on the helmet.

'Nothing. You know. Grab a bite by the chink.'

They rode slowly past the security camera. True to form, Tony gave it the finger. The whole area was full of security cameras. The airport was perpetually on guard. Gieles had charted the position of every single camera. He knew exactly where the gaps in the system were. That would be essential for *Expert Rescue Operation 3032*.

Once they crossed the intersection, Tony stepped on the gas. Gieles tried to relax. Tony started screaming a story. 'I'm now in an alliance guild!' Tony shouted. 'For eighteen years old and older!'

He was probably talking about World of Warcraft. Tony gamed himself silly in a virtual world that consisted of elves, trolls and dragons.

'I'm member 250!' Every time he turned halfway around, the motorbike swerved. 'I have priority with everything because I play more than twenty hours a week!'

They were going eighty.

They took the main road to the shopping centre. Tony parked his motorbike in front of the snack bar and walked in. Standing behind the glass case were a small man and a woman. They were Chinese. Tony ordered something unintelligible that the woman immediately understood. He came here every day. She scooped some French fries into the deep fat fryer and slid in a frikandel. Tony sat down on a bar stool with his helmet on his lap. He lit a cigarette and threw some money into the slot machine. Smoking in the snack bar was prohibited.

'I have to buy something,' said Gieles, who was standing behind him. 'Be back in a minute.'

Outside he took a deep breath of fresh air. He walked down the shopping street and passed a small group of girls he knew from the higher grades at school. Reflexively he smoothed down his high voltage hair.

Once inside the department store he went to the sunglasses department. Gravitation had asked for photos. First she talked about Scandinavian music and metal bands, then she said she was a fan of Jake Gyllenhaal 'drip drip drip.' He didn't understand what she meant by Jake Gyllenhaal and 'drip drip drip,' and wrote back that he thought he was awesome, too. Then he made the mistake of declaring that, like her, he was a fan of the metal bands Lostprophets, Cradle of Filth and The Vandals.

'Real original,' she wrote back, promptly asking for photos.

Naturally she'd see that he was younger. That's why he needed the sunglasses. He stared into the display mirror and tried to look impressive by squinting and rubbing his hand over his chin. Satisfied, he noticed that his hair was lying down flat. It probably came from the greasy helmet. He exchanged a nonchalant glance with himself.

Then he pulled up the left corner of his mouth. He had seen Elvis do that on one of Tony's mother's DVDs. Sometimes she watched Elvis for days on end, especially his performance in the black leather suit. Gieles had to admit that it did look cool when he did that thing with his mouth.

He saw that one of the sales clerks was watching him. She was smiling at him in a motherly sort of way, leaning against a pillar. Gieles felt like an idiot. Embarrassed, he grabbed a pair of sunglasses from the display. They were dark grey with mirror lenses. He didn't dare put them on, afraid the woman was still laughing at him. At the checkout he discovered that the sunglasses far exceeded his budget. So he paid with his bank card and left the department store.

Halfway down the street he saw Tony coming with a boy he didn't like. The boy's father ran a waste processing plant, which you could tell somehow just by looking at him.

With his head lowered he turned into a side street and went into a CD shop. He wandered through the shop for a few minutes and looked outside. On the other side of the glass was a red mobility scooter. His jaw dropped. The body in the scooter was far and away the fattest body he had ever seen in his life. The double chin looked like a swimming tube with a head bobbing around inside it. The rest looked like an explosion that was just barely being contained by a grey sweatsuit. Gieles was convinced that the shop window was creating a funhouse mirror effect. So much fat—it just wasn't possible. He went to the doorway to make sure his eyes weren't playing tricks on him.

Gieles stared at the enormous mass, mesmerised. It took a few minutes for him to realise that all that flesh was home to a single human being. The flesh belonged to a man, and the man was clearly in trouble. The back tyre of his scooter was flat. The man tried to pull himself up, but at the halfway point he gave up and dropped back onto the seat. Minutes passed. Tony and his little waste-processing friend were nowhere to be seen. Gieles just stood there and the man just sat there, immobile and abandoned. He didn't ask anyone for help. Passersby looked at him as if he were stuck fast in his own shit.

Gieles made up his mind to slip out of the shop and take the bus home. He hurried outside.

Don't look!

But he couldn't help himself, and at that very moment their eyes met. The man gazed at him with fierce intensity, as if he were the last remaining dog in the animal shelter and Gieles was his final hope. It would be rotten to pretend he hadn't seen him.

Reluctantly he walked up to the man. 'Sir … you have … a flat tyre.'

'I know,' came a voice from under the layers of fat. 'The problem is that I can't go any further. It would ruin the rims.'

He pronounced the last words with such defeat that Gieles felt even more sorry for him.

'Can you walk?' asked Gieles.

'If I hold onto something I ought to be able to manage

it.' He had a thin man's voice, smooth and fluid. 'I live right back there.'

'I can drive the scooter,' Gieles heard himself say, much to his alarm. 'My uncle has one, and I drive it every now and then.'

'I gladly accept your offer,' the man said with relief, and he held out his hand.

Gieles looked at the lump of blubber with dismay. Then he shook it, trying to hide his disgust, and his entire hand disappeared inside it, as if he were putting on a baseball glove.

'Super Waling. Pleased to meet you.'

'Gieles,' he said. 'Gieles Bos.'

With immense effort, Super Waling hoisted his mountainous body out of the mobility scooter. Gieles didn't want to look, so he turned his face upward, to the sky. A plane flew overhead, its white belly appearing very vulnerable.

'Can you provide me with a little counterweight?' the man gasped. 'Yes, yes, there ... in the back ... yes ... yes, right ... very good ...'

Gieles sat down in the scooter. The seat was still warm. He choked down his saliva with difficulty. The man held onto the back of the seat with his right hand while Gieles drove at a snail's pace. After a hundred metres the man came to a stop, swaying slightly. 'I appreciate this enormously,' he said with a long-winded wheeze. 'Really ... enormously ...'

Running away was out of the question. The colossus heaved himself forward in slow-motion.

They passed shops and a restaurant. UNLIMITED SPARE RIBS it said on the sign. Gieles wondered whether that applied to everyone.

After an eternity they stopped at the orange front

door of a small house in a new subdivision. The man unlocked the door with trembling hands.

'Come in,' he gasped, out of breath.

'I really have to go,' said Gieles to the gigantic expanse of back as the man slowly shuffled his way into the living room. He didn't answer.

He's gonna drop dead. I'll wait until he's sitting down and then make a run for it.

The man sank into a big armchair. Gieles stood at the doorway.

'Have a seat.' His face was covered with strange purple splotches.

'On second thought, pour yourself something to drink ... you've earned it ... there in the kitchen ... at the end of the hallway.'

I'll walk to the front door and run away.

Gieles didn't run away. He walked obediently to the kitchen, which looked as if it had never been used. The refrigerator was surprisingly small. Its contents surprised him, too. He had expected buckets of mayonnaise, chunks of cheese, mountains of sausages, kilos of cooking fat. But all he could see were a couple of packs of dairy products. The crisper was full of cans of grape soda. Gieles took one out and studied the wall, which was papered with folders from probably all the home delivery services in the area. Gieles never ate take-out. Uncle Fred didn't like it.

A soft humming sound was coming from the living room.

Gieles snuck to the door. The armchair in which the lump of fat was sitting had turned into a vibrating recliner. His stomach heaved like a waterbed under his sweatshirt. The sweatshirt was made of the same soft fabric as children's pyjamas. Dolly's youngest son slept in pyjamas like that.

Gieles coughed. The back of the chair rose immediately.

The man pressed a button that made his lower body vibrate twice as fast. Then he lowered the leg support.

'This chair can give three-dimensional massages,' he said.

'Can I get you something to drink, too, sir?' asked Gieles bluntly.

His name had escaped him. Super? And then? Something with a W.

Super Waffle?

'I'm fine,' he said, and pointed to an end table next to the massage chair. There were bottles of water on it and a stack of books. 'And no "sir". Let's not stand on formality. Have a seat. Yes, that's good. Make yourself comfortable.'

Gieles sat down on the edge of the leather couch and clamped the can of grape soda between his knees. The wall opposite him was one big mountain landscape. It was the first time he had ever seen wallpaper like that. The tops of the mountains were covered with snow. The lake in the valley reflected the mountain range. The wallpaper looked so real that it made Gieles feel cold. Hanging on another wall were bizarre paintings of buildings that looked like castles. It wasn't the image that struck him as strange so much as the colours it was painted in. Fluorescent purple and orange, bright green, canary yellow. The colours hurt his eyes.

'The big three. The Lynden, the Cruquius and the Leeghwater,' said the man, who had followed his gaze. 'It's because of them that we're sitting here right now. God made the world, but the Dutch made their own country. Those three pumping stations sucked the whole Haarlemmermeer dry.'

Gieles took a closer look, and through the hysterical colours he made out a group of steam pumps.

'I have to do a report at school on the history of the steam pumps,' said Gieles.

Super Windhole?

The man perked up with delight. 'Well, you've come to the right place. I know everything about the pumps. I give … well, I used to give tours there.'

His lower body was still vibrating. His socks were spotlessly white. Gieles wondered where his shoes were.

'Personally, I find the Cruquius the most impressive. Some people called her a vomiting monster. But I think she's beautiful, with that round Victorian exterior. At one time she was the most powerful steam pump in the world. No one could pump as much water as she did. Did you know that the Cruquius has the world's biggest cylinder?'

He turned the massage chair off, and soon the sloshing mass of flesh began to calm down.

'It isn't always fun being the biggest of something, but in her case I think it's a real plus.'

Neither of them spoke. Gieles was just about to get up and leave when the man suddenly asked him, 'Do you have any hobbies? I like the Swiss Alps and steam pumping stations.'

Gieles stared at him in amazement.

'Oh, yes,' he added with a smile. 'I also like Country Western music. And you?'

The man looked sincerely interested.

'I like table tennis,' stammered Gieles. 'And geese.'

'You like table tennis and geese,' he repeated, pushing himself up in the chair.

'Well, not exactly "like." I think they're funny. I have two at home. They're American geese. Tufted Buff geese, with that tuft, you know. They look like they have a lump on their heads.'

'Are they pets?' he asked. 'I mean, do these geese live in the house?'

Gieles chuckled and squeezed the can of soda. 'No. If they did, we'd be knee-deep in shit. They walk around outside, but they act like house pets. They're as alert as watch dogs. If a stranger comes by they bark, and when they see me they start wagging their tails. They're two females,' Gieles added. 'They can also open the kitchen door with their beaks. Uncle Fred, my father's twin brother, isn't too thrilled about that. Because then they shit all over everything and eat whatever they find. Uncle Fred calls them feathered vacuum cleaners.'

The fat man laughed a contagious laugh.

'But they're also real smart,' Gieles rattled on. 'I'm training them for a special project. I can't say anything about that though. It's a secret.'

He tried to infuse the last words with as much significance as possible.

'What fantastic geese you have,' the man said. 'Were they born at your place?'

Gieles was now sitting so far forward that he almost slipped off the leather seat. 'No, thank God! One of our neighbours had an incubator. When the chicks hatched, they gave him a good long look. With one eye. When a goose wants to look at something very closely, he does it with one eye.'

To demonstrate, Gieles squeezed his right eye closed. 'That's what my geese do. If I have a new stick, for instance. I use a stick to teach them to listen to me. I train them with it. I don't hit them, of course. But then they fix me with that black eye of theirs. My neighbour's chicks thought he was the mother goose. They followed him around all day long. It drove him crazy. They even slept with him in bed. Otherwise they'd just keep on peeping.'

No one had ever laughed so heartily at his goose stories. 'A goose can live to be thirty years old,' Gieles went on, warming to his subject.

'Thirty?' He laughed again and wiped his forehead with a handkerchief. 'Poor man. Thirty years with geese in your bed. How's your neighbour doing now?'

'No idea. We live near the airport runway and he let the airport buy him out. And then I got two geese from him. My father won't let me have any more. They were different than the ones I have now, but since then I've gotten pretty good with geese.'

'And you haven't been bought out?' the man asked gravely.

Gieles shrugged his shoulders and took another gulp of grape soda. 'No, my father wanted to stay. He figures we were there first. My mother doesn't really care. She's never home anyway.'

The man was silent and bit his lower lip. 'That's very noble of your father,' he said meditatively. 'Not letting yourselves be bought out, regardless of the price.' His voice had a kind of militant tone.

Gieles wondered how old he might be. The man had no wrinkles. Every groove was filled in with butter. But his hair was in pretty good shape. He had auburn hair that shone like the fur of a stuffed lion in a shooting gallery at the fair.

'Your geese,' he asked. 'What are their names?'

No one had ever asked about their names before, and now it had happened twice in close succession.

'I never named them,' said Gieles. He didn't have to lie. This was someone he didn't have to impress.

'Deliberately?'

'No, I just never got around to it. But a name can be pretty handy.'

'It certainly can,' said the man guardedly. 'What kind of geese did you say they were? Tuffs buffs?'

'Tufted Buff,' Gieles corrected him.

'If they had names they might be more responsive. You said you were training the geese?'

Gieles nodded. Maybe that was the problem. They didn't listen well because they didn't have names. He'd ask Christian Moullec about it, although he realised it might be a complicated job for a French ornithologist with hundreds of geese of his own.

'But it's up to you, of course. I don't want to stick my nose into your affairs.'

Super Waling! That was his name!

Gieles looked at him with one eye, the way his geese did. He couldn't imagine an adult taking an interest in his life. Uncle Fred was caring, his dad never asked him anything and his mother conveniently assumed that he was doing fine. That's because the rest of the world was doing so badly. They had AIDS, they were hungry or they butchered each other. But this ten-tonner actually listened to him.

'Can I offer you a tour in the Cruquius?' Super Waling asked him. 'For your report?' he hastened to add.

The question sounded so sincere that Gieles immediately said yes, much to his alarm. He had completely lost track of space and time.

'Fantastic!' the man said happily. 'Just tell me when you can go. In the meantime, I have some material for you to read, if you like.'

'Material?' repeated Gieles stupidly, watching as the man attempted to get out of his massage chair. Relocating his weight was a regular mass migration.

'I have a story,' he puffed, putting his feet on the floor, 'about … the … land reclamation. It's the first part.'

PART I

Ide & Sophia

He was expected to take up his father's trade, but Ide Warrens preferred to follow his own dreams. So he brought Sophia along with him without letting their parents know. She was barely fifteen years old, but she suited his dream perfectly. Sophia was not particularly beautiful. Her front teeth were broken off like bits of chalk and her face was asymmetrical, but he didn't care. Sophia was the most big-hearted creature Ide Warrens had ever met. Her caresses, her laugh, her humour, her fury: she was extravagant in everything she did, a rare trait in their part of the country.

They left Zeeland and arrived two weeks later on the other side of the world. The girl never complained during the entire journey, even though her plump thighs had turned black-and-blue from the bumping of the covered wagons they rode in. Her feet, too, were battered by the long trek.

Sophia sat down on the sidewalk in front of a cafe, looking with curiosity at the unfamiliar village square before her. Hillegom. She had never heard of it. Farther on she saw a linden tree with a pear-shaped opening in the trunk. She smiled. She was crazy about hollow trees. Limping forward, she went up to the tree and squeezed herself inside, along with her suitcase. She stroked the bark. Then she carefully took off her shoes and saw that her woollen socks were stuck to the blisters. With a jerk she tore off one sock and examined the bloody, blistery expanse. It looked awful. Her right foot was even worse.

'Sophia!' she heard Ide calling. 'Sophia!'

Peering through the cleft in the tree she could see him walking nervously back and forth. He had been searching for a place to spend the night. Once more he called her name, but she waited to respond. She stared out at him, forgetting her feet, and a glorious feeling ran through her. Ide was finally hers alone. She pressed her hand against the brocade shawl she had stolen from her mother, along with the two gold rings. At the end of this adventure she swore she would give the things back.

She began to whistle as Ide walked away from the tree. He looked around, scanning the square and following the sound of her whistle. First his boots appeared in front of the tree opening, and when he crouched down she could see his face. 'That looks bad,' he said, glancing at her feet. She pulled her skirt up over her knees. The red hairs on her legs were a shade darker than the curls on her head, and a few shades lighter than her pubic hair. Ide had examined and kissed every millimetre of her body.

'I need jenever.' With her chin she pointed in the direction of the cafe. Without asking any questions, Ide stood up and returned with a bottle of jenever. He looked on with surprise as Sophia poured the liquor over her feet.

'I learned this from my father,' she explained. Her father was a modern-minded physician. He abhorred the practice of bloodletting and the opium drinks his colleagues prescribed.

Ide's mother had been keeping house for the doctor and his wife for twenty years. According to his mother, the doctor had more brains than the mayor, the minister and the schoolmaster put together. The way she said this bespoke total veneration. Ide's father despised the doctor. In fits of drunkenness he would beat his wife, which for the moment made him think he was striking the physician as well. This gave him a pleasant feeling. But as soon as the man was sober again he regretted what he had done.

Ide hated his father's short temper and his mother's black eyes. His greatest fear was that she would have to stop working for the doctor. Her job was Ide's only means of access to Sophia.

Sophia tore a strip of cloth from her petticoat and wrapped it around her heel. Then she poured a splash of jenever over it and took a swig from the bottle. 'Pretty good,' she said, sucking on her tongue. She firmly pulled Ide's battered hands into the hollow tree and rinsed them clean with the liquor.

'That stings.'

'Stinging is good.' Sophia licked his fingers off. Laughing mischievously, she opened her suitcase. She set aside the doll she slept with every night and pulled out a pair of socks from the jumble of clothes. 'Come here.' Obediently he squeezed his head and limbs inside. His torso remained outside the tree, as if he were stuck in the birth canal. Her father had dealt with that problem many times: babies who wouldn't come out and midwives who called on him for help.

'Shut your eyes. Come on, nothing's going to happen.'

She grabbed his right hand tightly and emptied the sock. Ide heard her giggle as she pushed something cold onto his finger. He opened his eyes.

'I'm not a woman!' he shouted, looking at the ring with disapproval.

'And now you have to put this one on me.'

Sophia held up her mother's ring.

'Too big,' Ide concluded.

'Put it on my thumb. It fits—look. From now on I'm Mrs Warrens.' Speaking in a falsetto voice to imitate the tone of his mother, she said, 'Mrs Warrens. Pleased to make your acquaintance.'

She laughed with her mouth wide open, so that Ide got a good look at her crumbling teeth.

Then she stopped abruptly. 'But you must never hit me? Is that clear?' As she said this, she gave Ide a slap on his cheek. Not hard, but hard enough to leave a red mark.

'I don't wear jewellery.'

Ide tossed the ring in her lap and stood up. 'Come on, let's go. It'll be dark soon.'

The landlord raised his eyebrows doubtfully when the couple entered the inn. They were still youngsters, and such an amusing sight that it made him chuckle. The blond, blue-eyed giant was at least three heads taller than the girl. They didn't even bargain over the high price.

He gave them coffee, and bacon with potatoes, which they attacked with relish. They were starving. Sophia abandoned her good table manners and imitated Ide, who shovelled the food in with his spoon.

'Delicious potatoes,' said Ide, smacking his lips.

'Dune spuds,' replied the landlord. 'We pamper our potatoes as if they were eggs. That's why they taste so good.'

Standing behind the counter he sized up the young guests and felt embarrassed about the high rate he had charged them.

'You come here to work on the polder?' the landlord asked as he served them a stack of syrup waffles and a pot of coffee.

Ide and Sophia nodded, chewing busily.

'Then I don't envy you.'

'I'm strong,' said Ide, and he made a muscle.

'He's as strong as a draft horse.' Sophia pinched his upper arm and kissed it unashamedly. She realised how fine it was not to have to hide her love for Ide and kissed the muscle once again.

It was the first time they had ever slept in a box bed together. At home they had explored each other furtively in the dark corners of the doctor's house. Although the box bed was stuffy and cramped, to them the space seemed endless. Sophia climbed on top of Ide and brushed her breasts over his face until his cheeks glowed. She plunged her tongue into Ide's mouth and ran it around till both of them were breathless. Ide could taste the jenever, and he felt intoxicated without having had a drop to drink. The straw on the dilapidated plank bed poked him in the back, but he couldn't feel it. She pulled on his lip with her teeth and thrust her tongue into his ears and nostrils.

With a face wet from sweat and saliva, Sophia got down on her hands and knees and offered Ide her backside. Ide pulled himself up and bumped his head against the wooden ceiling. He gazed at her sloping back with admiration, while a feeling of perfect happiness came over him. He had no hunger, thirst or pain. All he had was Sophia. He needed nothing else.

Ide languidly stroked her bottom, sticky with sand. Sophia responded to his caresses by impatiently pressing against his erection. 'Hey, what are you waiting for?' she said hoarsely, looking over her shoulder. 'Let's go for a ride!'

The next day, 20 May 1840, Ide Warrens reported to the foreman behind the Treslong farmstead. They weren't the only ones. The yard was swarming with hundreds of men, women and children, and all of them looked impoverished. Sophia gazed with astonishment at the sallow mothers and their even sallower children. She was on an adventure. For her none of this was real. She could always go back to another life, a luxurious existence filled with clean fingernails, tea services and pastries, poetry evenings, her mother's smell of lavender and school books. But these people had absolutely nothing to do with her world. Everything on two legs here was filthy and penniless. Generations of poverty had preceded them. You could see it in their crooked backs, dull hair, drab skin, hobbling legs, sickly eyes, toothless maws.

Sophia knew she was no beauty, but her imperfections paled in comparison with so much physical infirmity.

She found a tree and sat down beneath it to give her feet a rest. Some of the men were busy building shanties from reeds and straw. Others just hung around, bored. Drinking, chewing tobacco, shouting, drifting.

Sophia tried to understand what they were saying, but it was all a cacophony of dialects. Leaning against one of the shanties was a little girl. She couldn't have been more than four years old and she was crying long strings of snot. Sophia thought for a moment that she was wearing black pants, but her legs were dark from the filth. The only thing the little girl had on was a torn shirt.

'Is that sack of shit yours?' someone yelled. 'I hope not!' came the bellowing response. With her eyes narrowed to slits, Sophia peered at a bunch of young male specimens. Suddenly one of them turned and ran up to the crying child. He was a wiry guy with a birthmark on his face. The mark was shaped like a star. The man picked up the crying girl by the back of her shirt so her head hung down. He ran a finger between her buttocks as if he were about to take a lick from a pot of syrup, then smelled his finger.

'Nope, this rag ain't mine!' he shouted, letting the child drop where he found her.

Sophia glared at the men with rage. She jumped up and ran to the little girl, who was lying on the ground, crying. Carefully she picked up the child, surprised at how light she was. She weighed practically nothing. Then Sophia strode back to the men and spat at them. But they were only interested in their drink. The people here paid no attention to each other.

It wasn't until she returned to the tree that she realised how much the little girl stank: it was the smell of decay. She took a nightgown from her suitcase and on it she placed the child who promptly fell asleep, lying on her side, her little knees drawn up to her chin. Sophia studied the stinking child with a mixture of tenderness and disgust. Lice and nits were tumbling all through her mass of tangled hair. Her shirt and legs were caked with crusts of dried shit. Sophia swallowed hard. She had gone with her father sometimes when he made house calls and had seen a thing or two: women on the edge of death after childbirth and men who had turned blue from cholera. But this little girl was by far the foulest creature she had ever seen in her life.

Ide stood in line to present himself to the foreman. He turned his head away when the child was dumped on the ground like a sack of garbage. It wasn't that it left him cold, but he wanted to stay focused on the good things, not the bad. He looked around intently for something to cheer him up. The people near him all looked so miserable. Sophia was sitting behind the trunk of a tree, and all he could see of her was a bit of her back. So Ide turned his gaze to the horizon. He didn't believe in God. His parents had raised him to be so God-fearing that he had lost his faith altogether. But he did trust in nature. There was little about nature that frightened him.

The land he was standing in was gentle and green. There were canals and pastures alternating with poplars that were arranged around the farms in perfectly straight rows. When he looked north he could see the edges of a forest. The sweeping expanse of the landscape eased his mind. Ide understood how life was lived here without having any knowledge of the area. Orderly and consistent. They didn't like extravagance here, you could see that.

Ide stared into the distance and saw the sails of a passing ship against a clear blue sky. In only a couple of years the lake would be filled in.

'Name?' a voice barked.

Ide looked up and saw a head of frizzy flaxen hair sitting behind a table. It looked like the sea foam that washed up on the beach, the kind he used to kick at when he was a boy. Unlike all the others, this man did not wear a hat.

'Name!' he repeated impatiently.

Ide blurted out his name. His thick Zeeland accent sounded impenetrable.

'*What?*'

Ide said his name again.

'Hidde Warren,' wrote the man without a hat. Silently he turned the notebook around so Ide could read it. 'Correct,' Ide guessed. He couldn't even read his own name. Without knowing it he had become untraceable on paper.

'Work starts at three-thirty. You get seventy cents a day and you sleep in that shanty.' He waved a brown finger off to the side.

'You mean that shack without a roof?' Ide asked the yellow top of the man's head. This was a man who only cared about his papers.

'Sophia, my ... my wife, is with me, too.'

'Suit yourself.'

'But there's no ... uh ... it's a shack without any ...'

'Something wrong with your legs?' the man shouted, pounding his fist on the table. 'Next!'

Ide walked over to Sophia. Her eyes were still dark with anger. She told him about the brutal way the little girl had been treated and pointed to her dirty sleeping body. Ide didn't want to look at her. He wanted to build a roof on the shanty so he could protect his beloved from the elements.

'We're taking her with us,' said Sophia maternally.

'Out of the question.' He gave the child a quick glance. 'Her pa and ma are around here somewhere. You can't just pick someone up and carry them away.'

'She has no one!' cried Sophia. 'What kind of mother lets her child walk around like that! The lice have made her sick. They've sucked all the blood out of her!'

'Sophia, all the children here are skinny and sick. Just look!'

She crossed her arms angrily. She knew he was right, but she refused to look at the other children.

The next day Sophia was awakened by screaming. She would have to get used to it, although she did not find it unpleasant. Her parents seldom raised their voices let alone scream, even when Sophia drove them to their wits' end with her tempestuous disposition.

She beat the straw out of her clammy clothes and hair. Standing up was barely possible, the shanty being no more than a metre and a half high. Yawning, she went outside. The air was still hazy with morning dew. She wondered where Ide was now. He had left that night after having made a thatched roof. A neighbour man had helped him in exchange for the half-filled bottle of jenever.

She looked around and saw only women and children walking between the shanties. They were all hard at work, but Sophia had no idea what they were doing. She kicked absently at a stone and ground her heel into the dirt. She tried to find the filthy child she had dressed in her nightgown. The nightgown had been much too long.

'Hey! Carrot Top!' shouted two little boys who were running around in bare feet.

'Fuck off!' Sophia shouted back, cupping her hands around her mouth like a trumpet. 'I'll get you yet!'

'Lay off with that shouting,' snarled a passing woman.

'Then I won't do it again!' Sophia screamed in a kind of snort.

The woman looked at her with surprise and pulled the corners of her mouth into an awkward grimace. Her face was friendly but dog-tired, framed by two braids.

'Where's your mother?'

'My mother? I'm here with Ide, my husband. We're from Zeeland.'

Sophia spoke the words as genteelly as she could, without an accent.

The woman looked suspicious. 'Then you must have married very young. How old are you anyway?'

'Old enough.' She held up her thumb with the ring on it. 'Say, do you know where the men are working?'

'Just follow the canal straight out in the direction of the lake.'

Sophia skipped past the shanties. Once she reached the pasture and began walking through it she forgot the steaming, stinking shantytown. She filled her lungs with the May air and walked along the canal. When the shanties were far enough behind her she had a drink of water. No people meant clean running water, her father always said. She washed her hands and feet and splashed some water between her legs. She wiped her bottom with plantain leaves and used a twig to scrape the dirt from under her fingernails. Hungry, she peered at the farm that lay beyond a row of trees. She wouldn't ask for food; that was beneath her station. She would borrow something from the land, and one day she would return it.

She crept through the grass until she reached the field. Quickly sizing up the white-flowered plants that were growing there, she pulled one from the ground. A stalk broke off. Looking to one side she saw two women lying on their bellies further on. They were digging up the plants with their hands. Sophia followed their example and took as many plants as she could carry. Back at the canal she removed the leaves from the potatoes and rinsed them off. They weren't full grown but they tasted all right. Whatever she couldn't eat she wrapped up in her shawl to save for Ide.

On her way to the lake she passed the two women. Her greeting was met with looks of suspicion. Back home in Zeeland everyone said hello to her. Sophia turned around and stuck her tongue out at their backs. 'Stupid cows,' she said, and laughed heartily at her own behaviour, which her parents would absolutely not have tolerated.

She heard them before they came into view. It was a mixture of raw voices and scraping shovels. The sound they produced was lively, as if it held some secret promise. Then she saw them, the polder boys. They were lined up in long rows, digging a trench. The earth they shovelled up formed a small dike between them and the lake. For the first time she was standing face to face with the most notorious lake in the whole country: the Water Wolf, which kept devouring more and more land and therefore had to be tamed. Thousands of polder boys would overpower it and bury it in its own watery bed.

Sophia was shocked by the size of the lake. This was no modest puddle, no damp pit. She realised for the first time that it would be years before the men were finished digging a canal around the lake. And then they would have to pump all that water away. How much time would this venture take?

She would fall terribly behind in school, the costly private lessons that her mother insisted were so good for her development.

'You live up to your name,' her teacher had said.

'Sophia' meant 'wisdom.'

But what good was a name like that if she wasn't allowed to study at the university? What was the point of learning Latin if she could never become a doctor? And what was development, anyway? Marrying a rich merchant from Tholen? Bearing children?

Sophia had always felt like an observer. She saw how her father made a name for himself as a doctor, and how he proudly called himself the first hygienist in Zeeland. In the evenings he would share his knowledge with her, but she knew that her thirst for learning would never be rewarded. Sophia would have to gaze out the window as life passed her by. Year in and year out. Until her face had attained the same dull colour as the needlework on her lap.

Ide Warrens was Sophia's ticket to freedom, but her parents would never allow her to marry him. They liked him well enough, but marrying Ide was not advancement. It wasn't even stagnation. It was a decline, to be measured in light years.

Suddenly she saw Ide, rising head and shoulders above the crew of polder boys. His cap and his face were black with mud. He was clever, but he couldn't read. That would be her project. She would educate him single-handedly.

Full of high spirits, Sophia ran up to him. When she got to the edge of the boggy trench she stopped and called his name. He walked up to her, shovel in hand. She kissed his dirty mouth and gave him the potatoes wrapped in the shawl. His neck was gleaming with sweat.

The pit boss was standing behind him. 'Tell her she has to leave. The last thing we need around here are dames.'

'She's already going,' Ide said, and gave the shawl back to her.

'What am I supposed to do there?' asked Sophia angrily.

'Well, housework. That kind of thing.' Ide glanced back at the boss nervously. He couldn't let himself be fired. His father would break his legs.

'But we don't have a house! We have a stinking hovel without windows or furniture.'

'Please, just go home.' Ide gently pushed her away from the trench. 'I'll be back this afternoon and I'll be good and ready for those spuds.'

Sullenly, Sophia walked back to the shantytown.

At one of the first shanties she saw the woman with

the braids and the dog-tired face. Sophia followed her through the narrow doorway.

'Hi,' she said when they got inside.

'You again,' the woman noted. She knelt down on the hard dirt floor and tried to start a fire in a pit. Lying along the edges of the shanty were piles of straw and blankets.

'How many people sleep here?' asked Sophia with surprise when her eyes got used to the dim light.

'Ten men and me.'

'That's a lot! Ide and I have the whole shanty to ourselves.'

'That's what you think.' The woman looked at her with contempt. 'One of these days you'll end up with ten others in that shack, just like us. And if you're not careful, you'll be sharing every hole in your body with them, too.'

Sophia's eyes widened. She was too overcome to say another word. She'd never heard anything so lewd before.

The woman lit a branch and laughed. Her mouth was a dark cavern.

'Don't worry. You're married, aren't you?'

Sophia nodded and coughed. The room was already blue with smoke. There was no chimney; the only way for the smoke to get out was through the hole that served as a doorway.

'Are you married, too?' asked Sophia hopefully.

'Over the broomstick, with Hayo. It's not official.' She rose with difficulty. 'But it's just enough to keep the other fellows away from me. And this helps, too.' She tapped her bulging dress. Only now could Sophia see that she was pregnant.

Sophia wished she could shake off the grim feeling

that had taken possession of her. 'You're having a baby!' she cried through her coughing, and stuck her head outside to get some fresh air.

The woman shrugged her shoulders laconically. She picked up a frying pan and put it on the smouldering fire. Then she poured some batter from a bowl into the pan. The stuffy shanty was filled with the smell of pancakes. It made Sophia's mouth water. She tried to hold them back, but the tears suddenly began streaming down her cheeks.

'Jesus, girl,' said the woman with irritation. 'What have you got to cry about?'

'Nothing,' bawled Sophia.

'Listen,' said the woman, 'when you've reached the end of your tether, there's always jenever. Jenever washes everything away.' She picked up an earthenware jug, took a long swig and wiped her mouth off with the back of her hand.

'It's not that,' wailed Sophia. 'The problem is that I can't cook. I can't do anything.'

Sophia learned quickly. She struck up a peculiar sort of friendship with the pregnant Akkie from Friesland, from whom she learned all the unwritten codes. The norms and values in the shantytown could be counted on two fingers. Rape and murder were frowned upon. Otherwise it was every man for himself, Akkie instructed, except when your own people were being attacked from the outside. Then you had no choice but to form a community. No one was to be trusted, especially the contractors, the police and the Belgian polder workers. The Belgians, Akkie informed her, snapped up all the work and earned more than their husbands did. She believed it was perfectly permissible to kick a Belgian to death or set him on fire.

In addition to these survival lessons, Akkie showed Sophia how to cook. It was simple. The food was so monotonous that it allowed for little experimentation. Pancakes with bacon, bread with bacon and potatoes with bacon were the daily fare. And when there wasn't any bacon for the bread, they spread potatoes on it.

In Sophia's parents' home there was always butter, fish, meat, cheese and pastries on the table. The food was prepared by their cook, a tall woman with hips like hams big enough to feed the entire village. Sophia often watched the cook as she stood over a pan and slowly stirred while her body swayed along. Never in a hurry. Always cheerful.

'Take it easy,' she would say to Ide's mother, who plodded and sighed her way through the housecleaning in the doctor's home.

Then the cook would conduct Ide's fragile mother to a chair and make her eat a bowl of cinnamon pudding.

In the meantime the cook would scrub the mussels clean, humming as she went. Sophia's father believed that shellfish cleansed the kidneys and activated the bladder. The kitchen smelled like a harbour as the screeching mussels opened in the pan.

'White, tender and plump. And right to the brim. That's what men like.' The cook winked. Ide's mother blushed and bowed her head and quickly took another bite, while Sophia's eyes flashed with pleasure. Sophia loved the cook's risqué talk.

They could have stolen her food at home for all she cared. She never had an appetite. She was certainly never hungry. She lived her life indoors for the most part, staggering from one meal to the next until she could no longer taste the difference between lamb stew and pork roast.

There was nothing indoors that interested her. Sophia loved being outside, in the street. She loved the smells, the sounds, the bright colours in the market, the hollering vendors trying to sell their wares. Sometimes she was allowed to go to the market with the cook, a visit that took hours because the cook moved so slowly. Every step was a supreme effort. If Sophia listened closely she could hear the cook's flesh quiver.

Sophia soaked up the market in every detail. Wrangling women. Chickens in cages. Flies on a fish head. The smell of roasted coffee and wine. The cook holding up a skinned rabbit with disapproval and shouting 'this isn't fresh!'

And then the offended market vendor: 'Not fresh? That rabbit is so fresh that the grass is still green in its mouth! It doesn't get any fresher than that.'

'*An men urehul!*' she'd exclaim in her thick Zeeland dialect. 'If that beast is fresh then I'm as skinny as a scallion!'

The cook's haggling, always with a coquettish undertone, was a ritual Sophia enjoyed immensely. Sometimes the cook let her give it a try.

'Tell him they're as old as shrivelled up dog balls,' the cook would whisper.

And Sophia would giggle and say, 'The potatoes are old, sir.'

'Tell him we feel so sorry for the poor dog balls that we'll take three kilos for two cents.'

The cook's lessons in bargaining served Sophia well. At the market stalls in Hillegom she did her utmost to spend as little money as possible on food. Except this was no longer an amusing game. Now bargaining was a matter of necessity. Sophia's mouth began to water. She smelled sausages and eels. She smelled freshly baked bread, artichokes and spices. She smelled the sweet flesh of partridges and oxen. She sniffed the gentle fragrance of sugar and butter. She let her hands glide over the skins of apples. But she couldn't buy any of those delicacies. She looked at them, stored the fragrances in her memory and went back to the shanty to make pancakes for Ide and the shanty's eight new inhabitants.

The men they were forced to share the shanty with came from every corner of the country. They slept on straw with rags as blankets, far enough from Sophia to keep from touching her yet close enough to make every inhale and exhale audible. At night she counted all the different sounds she heard until she fell asleep. Crying babies. Coughing children. Snoring, farting men, scratching and rubbing themselves in their sleep, anesthetised by alcohol to keep the cold away. Quarrelling couples. Scurrying rats and mice. Screaming, babbling, moaning, groaning, panting, hawking, scolding, wailing, puking, bawling. And Ide's heavy breathing on her forehead.

In the shantytown it was never silent. It amazed her that people were capable of producing so many noises. At home, in the doctor's brick residence with its spout gable, all she could hear was the refined tick of the Frisian grandfather clock.

Three a.m. brought an end to the nightly clamour. The men got up to go to work. Ide released himself from her arms. He lay on his back and she stretched half her body across his to keep from feeling the damp earth. He carefully slid out from under her and left. It was quieter without the men. The oxygen returned. During the few hours that followed Sophia got her deepest sleep.

The division of labour was unequivocal. Sophia took care of the housekeeping, the men brought in a bit of money. Sophia didn't see much of Ide. He easily worked sixteen hours a day. The men worked as long as there was daylight. Sophia didn't complain, although the adventure was sometimes unpleasant and harsh. The wedding ring was stolen from her suitcase, as were a pair of socks and a pair of underpants. She was also bothered by the filth that the polder people wallowed in. Their skin was even dirtier than the rags they wore. They had no idea what they were doing. They shat where they ate, put out smouldering fires with urine and drank the ditchwater they shat in. The authorities had brought in a filter to purify the drinking water but no one knew how to use it.

Sophia tried to instil in Akkie an awareness of hygiene, but to no avail.

'You must wash your hands,' Sophia admonished. Akkie peeled potatoes with blackened fingers. She left black smudges on the white vegetables. 'You'll never get rid of the runs that way.'

'These,' said Akkie, holding her hands in front of her, 'are working hands. They're supposed to look like this. You don't have working hands.'

Unperturbed, she kept on peeling.

They sat outside on stools in the shadow of the shanty. It was a hot day.

Sophia had no idea how old the woman was. She looked as if most of her life was behind her, even though a child was growing in her belly. One corner of Akkie's mouth was torn. Unbalanced diet, would have been her father's diagnosis. Sophia resolved to 'borrow' some apples from the local farmers, and perhaps a chicken.

'What are you doing here, anyway?' Akkie asked, looking at Sophia pointedly.

'What do you mean?'

'You know, just what I said. You're not like us. Look at your hair, your hands, your face. Nothing on you is broken. Your face is crooked, but that's all.'

'I don't have a crooked face,' said Sophia defensively.

'Yes, you do,' said Akkie, and she rolled up her sleeve. 'Look, that's a burn.' She pointed to a wrinkled spot on the inside of her forearm. 'And this dent was once a whopper of a festering sore. It's deep enough to drink out of now.' Akkie pushed back some hair on the side of her head. 'Smacked with a rake.'

'How horrible,' whispered Sophia. 'Who would do such a thing?'

'My brother,' she said off-handedly. 'He did such a thing.'

As if that weren't enough, she kicked off her old shoe and turned her foot toward Sophia. Two toes were missing.

'When I was eight, my toes froze. My pa twisted the dead stumps off my feet with a pair of pliers.'

Sophia said nothing, while Akkie kept on peeling and put her foot back in her shoe.

'I wanted to be with Ide,' said Sophia after a while. 'That's why I went with him. His mother was our housekeeper.'

'Housekeeper?' cried Akkie. 'What was your pa then? Mayor? Minister? King? Ha! Get out of here!'

The Frisian woman's voice was hard. 'Honey, find somebody else's leg to pull. If you had a housekeeper, you wouldn't be sitting here now with your ass in the mud.'

Akkie stood up, shaking her head. She walked into the shanty and came back with a bottle of jenever.

'I gotta do me some dancing,' she said, taking a long

pull from the bottle. 'At home I danced my legs off. But here there's not a damn thing to do.'

'You and Hayo,' asked Sophia, hoping that Akkie's cynicism would disappear. 'Was it love at first sight?'

'Love?' she said contemptuously. 'Of course not. We were just drunk. And that's where this came from.' She thrust her belly forward and put the bottle to her mouth. 'Here, take a swig. It kills the vexation.'

Sophia became skilled in stealing food. Her greatest asset was her normal appearance. In no time at all, the grubby people of the polder began to develop a bad name. They stank, pilfered, drank, fought, screamed and begged. The local population avoided them like an outbreak of typhus.

But not Sophia. She could go anywhere in the market without being shunned. She knew the art of keeping up a conversation while stashing a piece of bacon under her brocade shawl, a shawl that had offered shelter to eggs, beans, peas, pig's trotters, buckwheat and parsnips.

One day, as she was slipping in a piece of cheese, she looked out of the corner of her eye and saw the little girl whom the men had dumped on the ground like a gob of spit. Sophia recognised her own nightgown. Half of it had been torn away and the rest was encrusted with dirt. The child was rummaging around the stalls in bare feet and begging for food, her filthy little hand held aloft. Everyone looked at her with contempt and disgust. The little girl was the very image of misfortune that the populace hoped to keep outside their door. Poverty and disease were lurking everywhere and ready to pounce. Cholera, holy fire, scabies, syphilis, smallpox: the people were scared to death of them.

Sophia followed the little girl through the market.

When the child got to the fish stalls she was chased away with hisses. The pork seller tried to kick her, but his wooden shoe missed her head.

Rage welled up in Sophia. It started in her belly, bubbled upwards and ended on her tongue. She planted herself in front of the pork seller, legs wide apart and hands on hips.

'Your pigs have more decency than you'll ever have. They should put *you* in that sty.' Her voice was remarkably calm. Before the pork seller was able to utter a word in response, Sophia had turned her backside to him. She walked away with her nose in the air, close on the child's heels. When they reached the linden tree she stopped her. Squatting down, she smiled at the little girl, who stared at her with vacant eyes.

'Are you hungry?'

Her eyes showed no sign of life. The only colour in her face was the yellow ooze in the whites of her eyes.

'Is your mother here, too?'

She smelled the pungent odour of excrement.

'Can you talk?'

There was a crust of snot and blood on her upper lip.

'Come on, I have food for you.'

The girl silently followed Sophia into the hollow tree. Sophia settled herself once again at eye level and motioned to the girl to come in through the opening in the bark. The girl obediently followed her instructions. She could easily stand up inside the tree. After looking all around her (prudence was in order), Sophie reached under her shawl, broke off a piece of cheese and put it in the little upraised hand.

The child didn't eat, she devoured the food like a famished beast—slobbering, gulping and smacking her lips. Insatiable, she kept holding out her little black claw while uttering bestial cries. She bolted down the entire chunk of cheese and one piece of sausage. When everything was gone, she followed Sophia around like a bitch in heat. Any more stealing that day was out of the question; Sophia was far too conspicuous with the stinking child in her wake. Together they returned to the shantytown. On the way back, the little girl stopped on the sandy path and vomited her guts out.

5

Gieles read the story three times. Who were Ide and Sophia? Had this Super Waling written the story? Impossible. He was way too fat to write about certain things, about sex.

On her hands and knees. Her bottom, sticky with sand. Impatiently pressing against his erection. Her tongue in his ears and nostrils.

The tongue part was disgusting, Gieles thought, but it excited him.

He put the story in his desk drawer. There amid all the junk he saw a crumpled up ticket. It was admission to the air show of Christian Moullec and his wife Paola that he had gone to the year before with his father and Uncle Fred. His mother had been spending two weeks in some bone-dry Sahel country at the time.

Gieles picked up the ticket and looked at the photo of Moullec in his magical flying two-seater motorbike surrounded by the lesser white-fronted geese. Moullec had grey hair, just like Captain Sully. Gieles had been looking up with thousands of other spectators, but he felt as if he were the only one—as if Christian Moullec were putting on the show just for him. Music by Ennio Morricone swept across the grounds and a guy at a microphone was blaring a story about Moullec that Gieles already knew, but it didn't bother him. He was enjoying the spectacle.

When the guy bellowed through the loudspeakers

that geese always return to the place where they had learned to fly, his father had said, 'Let's hope Ellen does the same.' Uncle Fred said soothingly that quarrels were a fact of life.

It was at that moment that Gieles first realised that things were not going well between his parents. He put the admission ticket on top of the story about Ide and Sophia Warrens and closed the drawer.

He decided to skip the appointment he'd made with Super Waling (Gieles really didn't want to be seen with a walrus like that) and turned his attention to the game board that was lying on the desk. Using white masking tape he had made a runway across the full width of the board, and had pasted a yellow and a blue goose on the runway. Then he had stuck pins in the cardboard that were topped with little coloured balls. The pins were the security cameras. Naturally he'd have to make sure that the cameras didn't film him leading his geese onto the runway for *Expert Rescue Operation 3032*. That was a crime. But they *would* have to show him later on as he, Gieles Bos, chased his birds away from the runway. That was an act of heroism.

Gieles had once seen a platinum blond TV reporter ask Captain Sully, 'But how did you do it?' How do you safely land an Airbus in which both engines have been disabled by a couple of geese?

The woman looked at Sully as if he were a sex machine who had also invented the electric light. WWSD was emblazoned on T-shirts and caps. 'What Would Sully Do?' Americans asked themselves when faced with a problem. Sully had become a compass for making life choices.

Gieles stood in front of the mirror above the sink in his room and combed his hair, which was always standing on end. Then he put on the new sunglasses with mirror lenses. 'Gieles,' he said, with the same rapturous tone as the platinum blond reporter. 'How did you do it? How did you manage to get those geese out of the way at the very last second?'

'Well, let me tell you,' said Gieles nonchalantly, thrusting his chin forward. 'I was standing near the runway waiting for my mother. She had never been away so long before and I wanted to wait for her at home—so we'd be able to wave to each other. But suddenly I saw two geese out on the runway.'

The reporter would gape at him with fear and adoration. Of course he wouldn't tell her that he had ordered the geese to go there himself.

Gieles crossed his arms. 'By now everyone knows how dangerous geese can be for airplanes. Do you know Captain Chesley Burnett Sullenberger? The pilot who parked his plane on the Hudson on January 15th, 2009?'

The reporter would nod enthusiastically and exclaim, 'But of course I know him! Who doesn't? Now we finally have our own Dutch Sully!'

'Gieles!' he heard his father call. 'We've got to go!'

Gieles took off his glasses and hid the game board behind a partition where his old toys were stored.

His father was already outside, in the barn. He was standing at a workbench that had a row of fox tails hanging above it. The fox tails were russet with white tips. Killing birds was painful for Willem, but he had no problem hunting foxes and rabbits. After he shot a fox he would cut off the tail and dip the raw flesh in denatured alcohol to keep it from rotting. Then he would tie off the tail with a piece of string to allow the flesh to dry and have fur hats made from the pelt. Everyone got a hat, even his fellow bird controllers. But no one ever wore them.

His father held one of the tails under his nose and turned it around as if it were a glass of wine. Then he hung the amputated body part up again and walked out of the barn.

They got in the car and headed for the demonstration of the robot bird, listening in silence to the monotone radio conversations between the cockpit and air traffic control. Every plane was directed through the air space affably and efficiently by an unknown voice. 'Eight-zero-nine, you can land.'

Gieles had downloaded the conversation between Captain Sully and air traffic control. Spectacular! 'We can't do it. We're going to be in the Hudson.'

Not a hint of emotion. As if Captain Sully had said, 'Hey, I'm stuck in traffic. I'll be getting home a little late,' while he and a hundred and fifty-five passengers were flying straight to their deaths. And then the air traffic controller had said drily, 'I'm sorry.' ('Doesn't matter. I'll put your dinner in the microwave.')

A couple of hundred metres further on they passed Dolly's house. Gieles remembered the smell of her messy bed and thought of Super Waling's story. It got him agitated. *Her tongue in his ears and nostrils.*

Imagine Gravitation or Dolly pushing her tongue into his ears. How would that feel?

He had sent her a photo of himself posing in front of his father's service car. In another one he was standing with his geese. He had plastered his hair down with gel. The sunglasses did the rest.

Gravitation had reciprocated with a photo of herself pressing her rabbit against her pale white upper body. He regarded this provocative pose as a sign of approval. Something like: You look pretty good.

His father was leaning against the car window in his

leather jacket, peering into the sky. Then he looked down at the road. He did that all the time, even when he wasn't on patrol. His eyes went up and down, from the sky to the road, from the road to the sky. He possessed the rare talent of being able to see things from a bird's perspective. Why does a bird do what it does? That one question formed the basis of his thinking and defined his behaviour. According to his mother, his father had been a bird in a previous life.

They passed the fence that was under camera surveillance and for which Willem Bos had a special pass. In the distance they saw a couple of seagulls flying against a pale sky hung with grey clouds that looked like ice floes.

Willem Bos held the walkie-talkie to his mouth. 'Gulls in midfield. I repeat: gulls in midfield.'

'Runway free,' came the reply after a pause. 'Situation under control.'

The car's dashboard was a bag of tricks. Press the button and a panic-stricken starling shrieked across the farmland. That farmland, according to Willem Bos, was a very big problem, apart from the infinite number of invisible intersections in the sky. When the runway was built, the experts had condescendingly shrugged their shoulders over the fact that agrarian areas tend to attract birds.

Standing in the midfield between the two runways were his father's fellow bird controllers and the robot man. Unlike his father, the bird controllers were dressed in green. They looked like forest rangers. The robot man was wearing a faded turtleneck and jeans and was standing a couple of metres away from the group.

Willem Bos parked next to the other yellow cars and walked up to his colleagues, sauntering like a cowboy.

They greeted him and gave Gieles a few brotherly slaps on the back.

Then Willem Bos walked up to the robot man and introduced himself, and Gieles shook the man's hand in turn. He forgot his name immediately. Lisping and inhaling deeply through his nostrils, the robot man launched into a description of the invention he had worked on for three hundred and fifty hours.

'Just show us the bird,' Willem Bos interrupted. He had crossed his arms. The robot man was disconcerted by the interruption but quickly recovered and went to work. He opened a chest in the trunk of the airport service car and took out his invention. They all shrank back. The robot was a gigantic bird of prey with cold eyes and a hooked beak. Its dark brown wings spanned at least a metre and a half.

The robot man held the monster over his head, making his own body look even punier. One of the bird controllers whistled through his teeth. 'Whoa,' he said, deeply impressed. 'You can hardly tell it from the real thing. A perfect white-tailed eagle.'

'A golden eagle,' corrected the robot man. 'Notith the tail.' He turned the bird halfway around, still holding it over his head. 'It hath a black terminal band,' he lisped.

'We don't get any golden eagles around here,' said Willem Bos. 'Plenty of buzzards, goshawks, kestrels and falcons. But no golden eagles.'

The robot man began sweating under the weight of his invention.

'I saw a white-tailed eagle once,' said one of his father's colleagues, rubbing his moustache. 'Above the dunes. But that was a long time ago. We're talking about the end of the seventies. And from that distance it could have been a great spotted eagle. You can never be sure.'

The other bird controllers nodded in agreement. 'I once mistook an escaped turkey vulture for a buzzard. But you don't expect to see big ones like that out here. Buzzards can be very aggressive.'

The bird controller now turned to Gieles. His colleagues knew the anecdote by heart. 'I know this farmer. He was out haying once on his land and suddenly this buzzard attacked him. The buzzard planted its claws into his hair and scalped him right then and there. Pieces of scalp this big.' He created an implausibly large shape with his hands. 'Really. Pieces that big.'

'Okay,' said Willem Bos, looking up into the dark sky. 'Get going with that thing.'

'It'th called Golden Eagle,' the robot man said, slowly dropping to his knees. Gieles wanted to help, but the robot man absolutely refused.

'Thith ith no toy,' he said. Very carefully he placed the golden eagle on the ground and pulled the wings out further. Gieles saw that the feathers had been painted with the utmost precision. There must have been a thousand of them. The robot man stroked the wings, then took the remote control out of the trunk.

'Golden Eagle ith ready,' said the robot man, lifting the bird up over his head again with one hand.

'Make sure you stay away from the runways,' warned Willem Bos as the robot man ran onto the field. Gieles watched a plane taxi by. Maybe he was seeing things, but he could have sworn that the passengers were craning to look out of the little windows. Willem Bos and the other bird controllers chuckled at the scene before them. There stood his father—big, secure and completely relaxed. Gieles wanted so much to be able to stand like that someday.

'You know who he reminds me of?' said the man with

the moustache. Now the robot man was running back in their direction. 'That environmental bunch that came here and cut holes in the fences. They were just as lanky and nervous.'

'Maybe he's an activist, too,' Willem Bos suggested.

'Or a terrorist,' said his colleague. 'With a bird as a thuithide bomber.' He burst out laughing.

They made a few more jokes about the lisping robot man, and just when they thought his technology had let him down, the invention took to the skies.

The majestic wings whooshed like windmill blades. The yellow-tinted body gained altitude with ease. Once it was high enough, the bird began gliding through the atmosphere. Anyone who didn't know better would have sworn that the golden eagle was scanning the earth for cadavers.

The robot man had his bird fly toward a pole mounted with runway lights. A kestrel had settled on one of the lamps. A kestrel was one bird you didn't want in an airplane engine. Recently a Boeing 747 had crashed in Belgium because of a kestrel. No fatalities, but the plane had snapped like a dry twig. The kestrel looked up at the unfamiliar assailant, gauged its chances and fled.

The golden eagle drove off a couple of seagulls, six partridges, a group of magpies and dozens of starlings. The bird controllers began to reassess their opinion of the robot man.

'Can I give it a try?' asked Willem Bos after an hour. A few drops of rain had fallen and no one felt like getting drenched.

'Thertainly not,' said the robot man. His nostrils had become one big imploding nerve. His eyes shot back and forth from the golden eagle to the bird controller. 'I'm the only one who can handle the controlth.'

'What a load of crap,' said Willem Bos. 'Even a kid can make this trinket work.'

The rain put an end to their discussion. 'The bird's getting wet,' warned one of the bird controllers.

'Rain ith no problem!' cried the robot man.

It began to rain harder. The controllers ran to their cars for shelter. Gieles stood beside his father, who remained outside.

The robot man made his bird fly even higher. Gieles threw back his head and peered into the sky as the rain streamed down his face. The golden eagle must have been at least sixty metres off the ground. Its wings glided on the wind.

'Too high!' shouted Willem Bos. 'You're going too high! You're losing control!'

The robot man set off at a run and went after his bird, which was no longer flying in a straight line but lurching dangerously in the direction of the runway. Airplane headlights could be seen approaching in the wet airspace. Willem Bos took off in pursuit.

'GOLDEN EAGLE: LAND IMMEDIATELY' came the announcement from the speakers in the service car. 'FINAL WARNING. GOLDEN EAGLE: LAND IMMEDIATELY.'

The robot man did not respond. Leaping like a gazelle, he tried to catch up with his invention. But it was impossible. One of the bird controllers stepped out of his service car with a flare gun. He stood with his legs astraddle and aimed at the golden eagle, which was buzzing the edge of the runway threateningly. Gieles screwed up his eyes against the brightness of the approaching airplane lights. He followed the flare as it raced toward its target. But the golden eagle banked to the left, away from the bang and the smoking powder. The bird floated on outstretched wings as if it were borne up by an immense updraft. Suddenly it plunged forward and began losing altitude. Its mechanical body came spinning downward. The robot man jerked at the remote in an effort to regain control.

Panting and leaning over with his hands on his thighs, Willem Bos watched the gyrating bird. Just as the tyres of the airplane hit the asphalt, the golden eagle crashed into the grass. The robot man ran up and hurled himself onto the bird. There was little left of it. Its styrofoam body had broken in two, spewing out its metallic entrails of screws and wires. There were nasty tears in the wings. The yellow beak and head were shattered beyond recognition.

Moving with great strides, Willem Bos approached the robot man. Gieles had never seen him like this before. His father did not anger easily.

'You imbecile!' he roared, planting a hiking boot on one of the wings. 'You'll have everybody after you now, asshole! The entire airport!'

Then he turned around and walked away.

The soaking wet robot man stared at his bird, his nose frozen in a painfully inhaled grimace. Gieles sat down next to him and picked up the shattered head. He placed all the parts in one of the battered wings. Then using a detached piece of string he tied the eagle up into a manageable package.

Gieles fervently hoped it wouldn't rain on the day of his rescue operation.

Rain was disastrous.

6

That night Gieles dreamed about the crashed golden eagle. But instead of a bird's head, the creature had long black hair and a head that looked like his mother's. He woke up in a daze. It was only six o'clock.

Gieles began to worry that *Expert Rescue Operation 3032* might not be safe. He calculated his chance of success at ninety percent, provided the geese listened to him. And that was the problem. They followed after him when they were supposed to stay put, and stayed put when they were supposed to take off.

On the other hand, Captain Sully's chance of success couldn't have been more than one percent. But he was well prepared. He had things under control. The captain followed the landing instructions, even when the runway had turned to water. He stuck to his schedule. Gieles had to have a schedule, too.

He paced back and forth in his insulated room until the solution presented itself. Then he grabbed the partition from the junk corner and turned it over.

Perfect. With a black felt-tip he wrote out the schedule on the back of the wooden partition.

'May: train for stay command
June: train for up/down command
July: train for all commands—stay/up/down
August 7, 11:40 a.m.: Mom comes back'

Gieles looked at the outline with satisfaction. This afternoon, after school, he'd work on training the geese and finish the letter to Moullec.

He got dressed and went to the kitchen. Uncle Fred was reading the newspaper.

'What a brouhaha with that robot yesterday,' he said, taking a sip from a mug with a picture of DC-2 on it. There was a jagged crack running through the plane. Why the coffee didn't leak out was a mystery.

'I can understand why your father blew his stack, but it really was tough luck for the inventor, too. I heard he had worked a long time on that bird.'

'Three hundred and fifty hours,' said Gieles as he spread peanut butter on a piece of bread.

Uncle Fred pushed the newspaper towards Gieles. It was the free regional paper that came every week through the mail slot.

'Speaking of tough luck, take a look at this.' He tapped his finger on the front page photo, obviously amused.

Gieles recognised him right away. Super Waling.

He was sitting on his mobility scooter, which was sunken deep in the mud, and smiling meekly as the firemen pulled him out with a rope. Gieles read the caption.

RUNAWAY SCOOTER

While on assignment for this newspaper, correspondent Waling Cittersen van Boven found himself in a potato field along the Hoofdweg. His mobility scooter had bolted and refused to turn left on the bicycle path, causing Cittersen van Boven to end up in the mud. The fire department managed to free him from his perilous predicament. Fortunately our correspondent came out unscathed, and after his wild ride he continued on to the line-dancing finale at the Fokker Dancing School. Read his lively report on page 3.

Gieles wanted to say he knew him, but he swallowed his words along with the peanut butter. This wasn't the kind of guy you bragged about knowing. He was even embarrassed about having helped him in a crowded shopping centre. But why hadn't Super Waling told him anything about his work for the newspaper?

Gieles took another look at the photo. He could hear the echo of the man's contagious laugh and felt himself brighten up, just as he did at Super Waling's house.

'This guy must really be ashamed of himself,' said Uncle Fred. 'Being so fat that the fire department has to haul you out and then ending up in the newspaper.'

'He's not *that* fat,' said Gieles with irritation. Calling him up and cancelling was what he really ought to do. That was more decent than not showing up at all.

'Seems to me I've seen him before at a lecture,' said Uncle Fred, putting on his reading glasses. 'Except he was thinner then. You often see that with overweight people. They always get fatter, seldom thinner.'

Uncle Fred studied the newspaper photo again more closely and repeated his last name a few times. 'Cittersen van Boven. That name sounds familiar. You wouldn't know by looking at him, but it seems to me it's a noble name. It wouldn't surprise me if he was from a rich family.'

For the rest of the morning Gieles couldn't get Super Waling out of his mind. He had become a mystery. By twelve o'clock the tub of lard had attained the status of table tennis celebrity Jan-Ove Weldner. Gieles told his teacher he had stomach flu and raced home on his bike. Uncle Fred and his father weren't there. He stormed up the stairs to the attic and googled 10,340 hits for Waling Cittersen van Boven. A huge number of the articles he wrote for the regional newspaper came to the surface.

Gieles read the headlines. LECTURE ON SWISS ALPS AT PUMPING STATION. VAN MARELS CELEBRATE 50 YEARS TOGETHER. NOW: SPEED DATING AT THE PUMPING STATION. FARMER FINDS 150-YEAR-OLD SAILOR'S BOOT. GET MARRIED AT A PUMPING STATION. GOLDEN ANNIVERSARY FOR A GOLDEN COUPLE. MOUNTAINEERING MEGASTORE OPENED. PUMPING STATION RESTORED. PLATINUM ANNIVERSARY IN DEPARTURE HALL. PLAYBOY TAKES PICTURES IN PUMPING STATION. COUNTRY WESTERN SHOW AT WEDDING FAIR.

The overview went further, with many more stories about pumping stations and old married people. Gieles searched and searched, but he couldn't find anything about Super Waling himself—whether he was from a noble family, as Uncle Fred had claimed, or whether he was swimming in money. The last didn't seem likely. Super Waling lived in a tiny house.

Gieles heard the geese. He walked to the little window in the hallway and saw Tony in the yard. The geese were honking at him from a safe distance, their necks twisting angrily. They didn't carry on with anyone else that way. Tony kicked some pebbles at them and lumbered to the back door with his hands in his pockets. Gieles clicked away from the stories by Super Waling and the photo of Gravitation with her almost naked torso, holding her rabbit. He also reversed the partition with the training schedule on it.

Tony stomped up the stairs and entered the room.

'I heard you went home sick.' He plopped down on the bed and stretched out full length. Reaching behind his back he pulled out a book.

Tony was in his second year of vocational training at the local high school after having been left back twice. Gieles had just started at the college prep level.

'You really missed something this afternoon,' said Tony, leafing through the Dutch-French dictionary.

Gieles spun around in his desk chair and crossed his arms, balling his fists under his armpits. Conversations with Tony usually started by him saying, 'You really missed something.' Usually it wasn't anything spectacular, but Tony always managed to make him feel excluded with that remark.

'You know Becky? Becky Boobs?'

Of course Gieles knew her. Everybody knew Becky with the big tits.

'This afternoon they caught her in a closet with a janitor. That Moroccan. They were fucking.' Tony made bumping movements with his hips and looked at him triumphantly with his slanted eyes.

Gieles certainly had missed something.

'Who caught them?' he asked with as much indifference as he could muster.

Tony noticed the agitation in Gieles's voice and calmly continued leafing through the dictionary. '*Boobs* isn't in here ... *Cunt* is. *Chatte, con.* I leek your leetle chatte. French is for fags. *Gimmie bossie*,' said Tony.

Gieles raised his eyebrows quizzically.

'"*Gimmie bossie.*" That's what that Flippertong guy says to all the babes. He's from the Antilles.'

'Who caught them?' Gieles repeated impatiently.

'That stiff from biology.'

He tossed the dictionary onto the floor and lit up a cigarette, blowing smoke rings with pursed lips.

'You can't smoke in here,' said Gieles, leaning toward him with an empty cola can.

Tony kept smoking anyway, burping as he exhaled. The smell of onions enveloped Gieles's face.

'By the way,' Tony began, 'I think we've outgrown the

first-name stuff. Real guys call each other by their last names. So, Bos, from now on I'm Keijzer.'

'Fuck off, Tony. Give me a break.'

'Fuck off, Tony,' Tony said, imitating him with a whiny voice and sitting up.

'You coming with me to the mall?' He asked as if nothing had happened.

'No. I have homework.'

Tony left the room, trailing smoke. Thirty seconds later he slammed the back door loudly, causing the geese to start honking all over again. Tony picked up a handful of stones. He was about to throw them when he noticed someone from the campground looking at him. It was Johan, the old man with the fossilised legs.

Gieles tried to redirect his thoughts, turning his attention yet again to the picture of Gravitation holding her rabbit up in front of her breasts. She was being provocative. Maybe she'd strip on the webcam for money.

Gieles stood up. He had to concentrate and stick to his new training schedule.

He shook off his thoughts of Gravitation and went downstairs and out to the barn, where he picked up the bamboo stick and cookie tin. The geese came up to him as soon as they heard the sound. He drove them energetically along the edge of the woods and down the grassy path to the shed. There was a pasture next to the shed where a couple of cows were grazing. In a few weeks he would move his training programme to the pasture. After all, his rescue operation was going to take place outside anyway.

He pushed open the corrugated metal door and assumed his position. The geese circled him, pestering him for food. 'One for Tufted and one for Bufted,' said Gieles, giving each one a piece of speculaas. He had given them names.

'Tufted and Bufted,' he repeated, and he thought of Super Waling, who would be disappointed if he didn't show up for the tour.

'Stay,' Gieles ordered. Both geese looked at him with one eye. 'Stay.' Slowly he walked backwards to other side of the shed.

7

My letter to you goes pitiful slow. There are always orderings from people. Remove goose poop. Sit the babies.
But I will not harass you further on. You have formidable
problems! Your website says in Lapland almost all geese
lesser white-fronted murdered by hunters. Another scandal that must be terminated. The sky is high. Fortunately
human beings cannot be everywhere.
I want to write you that in my country this year many ten
thousands geese were murdered, and in America 500,000
geese were murdered !!!!! With gas!!!! For the traffic of
air!!!! Perhaps you are familiar with Captain Sullenberger.
The formidable chauffeur of flight 1549 that emergency
landed on the Hudson with geese in the machinery. Then
the Americans said, O the geese must die. There are too
many of them in the air. There are too few Sullys. O, then
we will lead them to the chamber of gas.
I say to you, I am not per se against the chamber of gas. My
father was earlier owner of a gas tank. The gas tank was in
our barn. See in your mind a rolling garbage pail with a
gas tube. The gas tank was the final destination of
pigeons. Pigeons are the cause of enormous overburden-
ing. One day in my youth I hid myself from Tony in the
gas tank. It was for the joke, but my father died of fright.
The gas tank disappeared.
For you I have at the moment two questions. The easy one
is whether you donate a name to your geese as an instru-
ment of listening? Birdie, Tarzan, Chippie? Book for dog

says: choose two-syllable name. For the master, two sylla-
bles are suitable for the calling away in the woods. What
do you say? What do you think of: Tuf-ted! Buf-ted!
A new question on which I crack my head. It is about how
to school the ordering 'fly'. I want to make the geese fly up
with silent accessory. That is, not with a screaming voice. I
want to correspond the ordering 'fly' so they listen at
great distance. Stick does not work. Do you know a silent
accessory?

Uncle Fred was calling him. He sounded excited. He was
standing at the table, bending down over a cardboard
box.

'Take a look at this,' he said, but his salt-and-pepper
curls blocked the view. Gieles heard a peeping sound.
Uncle Fred straightened himself, and then he saw them.
Two goose chicks. More down than feathers and two
weeks old at the most. They were as big as drinking cups.

'I have no idea how they got here.'

He peered at the little creatures through his reading
glasses. 'All at once there they were, in the yard.'

Gieles picked up the smallest chick, who peeped anxiously. He could feel its heart muscle beating wildly
against the palm of his hand.

'Someone who knows we have geese probably threw
them over the fence. But who?' Uncle Fred wondered.

Gieles stroked the yellow breast with one finger. He
knew that geese don't like to be stroked on the back. The
chick stopped peeping.

Uncle Fred picked up the other chick, who began hiss-
ing angrily.

'So small and already so fierce,' he said, and carefully
examined the creature. 'Hey, tough guy, take it easy.'

'They're hungry,' said Gieles. 'We should get that special bird feed for them.'

He was thinking about Gravitation. A picture of him with the goose chicks would drive her wild.

'Oh, no. Not that. These birds have got to go. Your father will never approve.' He resolutely put the chick back in the box.

'But where are they supposed to go?' asked Gieles indignantly.

Uncle Fred put his reading glasses on top of his curly head. 'We've got to get rid of them. Two more geese, right next to the runway? Impossible.'

Gieles could feel the little goose pooping in his hand. It was a small watery dollop.

'It could cost your father his job.'

'But he doesn't have to know about it,' said Gieles, fully aware that Uncle Fred couldn't say no.

Throwing one arm into the air in a theatrical gesture, Uncle Fred hobbled over to the kitchen counter. He leaned his crutch against the counter top, filled the dishpan with water, and began washing the dishes restlessly. 'I don't know, Gieles. They get so dependent on you. How do you see this working out?'

Gieles shrugged. 'I'll just keep them in my room until they get stronger, and in a couple of weeks we'll take them away. Just like we did with that jay.'

Uncle Fred turned around and wiped his hands on his pants. He gave Gieles a look of despair. 'Then I'm out of the loop,' he said. 'I haven't seen any chicks.'

'You haven't seen any chicks,' Gieles repeated, picking up the box.

He took the goslings up to the attic and spent the whole afternoon outfitting his bedroom up for them. The dish from an old rabbit hutch would serve as their toilet. The fox tail fur hat became their new sleeping quarters. Gieles put the hat next to his bed. He slid the goose toilet under his desk along with a saucer of water, fresh grass and some pieces of apple. Then he put the chicks in the dish.

'This is where you guys poop and pee. And that's your food.' He pointed to the saucer. 'And this,' he bent down and held up the hat, 'this is where you sleep.'

He wondered whether the smell of the fox fur would frighten them. The chicks looked at each other uncomfortably. The bigger of the two started pattering through the dish. Sniffing curiously, the chick began to follow the electrical wires that ran along the wall. Gieles pulled all the plugs out of their sockets. Then he closed the attic window.

That evening he was kept awake by peeping. The big chick slept in the dish from the rabbit hutch, but the little one was restless. It wandered forlornly through the room as if it were looking for its mother. Gieles was reminded of the neighbour who had taken his geese to bed with him for so many years. His father claimed that no woman would have him because the man always smelled of goose poop.

One night couldn't hurt. Just one night, to get a little peace and quiet. Gieles put the chick in the fur hat, which he placed next to his pillow. He laid his hand in the hat and felt the chick seek out his warmth and nestle up to his fingers. The peeping died away.

Gieles closed his eyes. Gravitation had been on line this afternoon, and he had solemnly promised to mail her photos of the chicks. He fantasised about the provocative images he hoped she would send him as a reward.

8

At one-thirty Gieles left for his get-together with Super Waling. When he reached the woods in exile he bumped into the old lady with the restored eyes. She had been picking mint and she began to talk to him, so that he was forced to get off his bike.

'How nice to see you again,' she said. She was wearing a comical straw hat decorated with fake flowers. 'We're going home later. To do the laundry and pick up medicine for Johan, things like that. But we'll be back soon. We love it around here.'

Gieles had never heard anyone say they loved it here. He smiled at her and the woman laughed sweetly, and they both said goodbye. He biked down a straight road in the shadow of a row of poplars. Last night, as the chick slept contentedly in the palm of his hand, his curiosity had won out over his embarrassment. He would keep his date with Super Waling. There was something else that led him to make this decision, but Gieles couldn't quite put his finger on it.

He could see Super Waling in the distance, a colourful dot against the background of a black polder landscape. Gieles could still make a u-turn. The chances that Super Waling could see him were small. He slowed down. The dot gradually grew bigger until he saw the colour. Red.

He couldn't bike any slower or he'd fall over. He wanted to turn around. The idea of being spotted with the fattest man around was suddenly unbearable. He put on his brakes and got off. But the dot became a life buoy that waved at him. Biking away would be cruel. The buoy rolled up to him and came to a stop right next to his front wheel.

It seemed as if Super Waling had become even fatter since their meeting two weeks before. His body was squeezed into a sweatsuit. 'Hey, Gieles! I'm so glad you came!' said Super Waling with surprise.

Gieles said hello in an unintelligible mutter and looked around nervously.

Whale.

'Shall I go first? If we ride side by side no one will be able to get past us.'

Super Waling turned his scooter around and led the way. They rode on the bicycle path through the open countryside. The glances from the oncoming traffic did not escape Gieles. Some drivers even slowed down to get a better look at the big man.

A densely packed row of trees to hide behind would be a welcome sight. Or a field of sunflowers to divert the attention of the gawking motorists. Palm trees and an azure blue sea would make Super Waling less conspicuous. But in the polder there was nothing to hide behind. Everyone could see you. Everyone looked at you, because there was nothing else to look at. Everything was open and exposed. For the first time he hated the landscape. Gieles cycled more slowly in order to break the connection between them. But Super Waling looked over his shoulder and let Gieles catch up.

He forced himself to think of something horrible, things that were much worse. He thought about his mother's e-mails, which were becoming increasingly sombre in tone. In the first years she described the unusual flowers she saw. She shared her surprise about strange dishes and made jokes about them ('Sunshine, you're not going to believe this, but yesterday I ate stir-fried mealworms!'). But now it seemed as if she had lost her astonishment and sense of humour somewhere along a sandy path.

She wrote about African women who got raped when they went to the desert to search for bits of firewood. Or about the two-year-old girl who was eaten by a dog. Ellen had seen it happen, and once she got home she just kept carrying on about it. No detail was left out. His father didn't want her to tell such gruesome stories when Gieles was around. But his mother said these weren't stories, they were reality. And, she insisted, it was never too early to get used to reality.

He thought about Dolly with her tired eyes. When he had gone there to babysit the week before she had been storming around, ranting and raving. Dolly had been given an offer for her house that she said was insultingly low. Even a construction shack would bring in more than that.

Just as the next gloomy thought came bubbling to the surface, Super Waling stopped.

'Here we are!' he shouted happily with his ageless face. They were standing side by side on the dike, looking up at the gigantic pumping station.

With all that brooding, Gieles had forgotten about the pumping station. The building looked like a failed attempt at a castle with arms growing out of it. The iron arms stuck straight out through the dungeon windows and groped for the sky.

'Look how gorgeous she is,' sighed Super Waling. 'So gracious and powerful and completely untouched by time. She's every bit a lady. More than a hundred and sixty years old.'

Super Waling cast Gieles a beaming smile.

'Use your imagination. Forget the cars, the street signs, the traffic lights. Forget the butt ugly apartment buildings that lack every sense of decorum. Focus on *her*. Look at her robust cast iron arms. Those arms pumped out three hundred and twenty thousand litres of water—a minute! Now that's what I call impressive,' he said, riding down from the dike to the pumping station parking lot. No one else was there, much to Gieles's relief.

'These days we think it's a real achievement when somebody on TV belches the national anthem. I apologise for the crude example, but people do crazy things to get attention.' His voice broke. 'I think it's impressive that human beings were capable of pumping out an entire lake with only three pumping stations. An enormous lake! Where we're standing right now! Eight hundred million cubic metres of water, Gieles! The invisible suddenly became visible. Just imagine what a sensation the bottom of that lake produced.'

Gieles tried to imagine, but the pumping station and the bottom of the lake failed to come to life. His questions kept distracting him.

Can he see his own cock?

Super Waling pulled out a bottle of water and a can of grape soda from the linen bag that was in his basket. He gave the can to Gieles.

'I brought Part Two for you,' said Super Waling. 'About Ide and Sophia Warrens. I don't know whether you've read the first story at all or even whether you liked it. Maybe you didn't think much of it.'

'Oh, no,' Gieles replied quickly. 'I thought it was great. I want to read the rest, too.' Gieles felt his cheeks reddening because he had asked for Part Two with such enthusiasm. He didn't want Super Waling to think that all he cared about were the dirty parts, so he tried to come up with a proper question.

'The lake,' Gieles began, racking his brains. 'Was that really so … so dangerous?'

Super Waling smiled and took a few sips of water.

'Close your eyes. Go ahead. No one is watching you. Close them. That's right. And keep them closed. Imagine we're in a sailing ship. You know, one of those ships from long ago with a big bulging wooden hull that looked as if it had eaten too much. Brown sails are hanging from the mast, but there's not a flutter of wind. So we're bobbing with the current, on our way to Amsterdam to deliver hundreds of kilos of peat. We warm ourselves in the watery November sun and tell each other tall tales about the Water Wolf, which was the lake's nickname. Usually the Water Wolf keeps a low profile, but when he's angry—watch out! His fierce waves are as high as the foothills of the Bavarian Alps, and they devour one fishing boat after another. Dikes burst, and the poor wretch with the horse and wagon who's trying to make a run for it doesn't stand a chance. The Water Wolf catches up with him and eats him in one gulp. Just like that! Gone! Like a snake that prefers to dine on living prey. That's what we tell each other, but we aren't afraid because the water is calm and we haven't noticed that the seagulls and cormorants are flying restlessly over the surface of the lake. We're deaf to the dogs making a racket on the distant farms. We're blind to the eels shooting away lickety-split. The eels are as deaf as posts, but they can feel the vibrations. And make no mistake,' he whispered—Gieles noticed that now Super Waling himself had closed his eyes—'there are plenty of vibrations. At first the water is as smooth as a baby's bottom, but now a wave emerges out of nowhere. A single wave, but what a wave! A tidal wave!'

Super Waling opened his eyes and gave Gieles a penetrating look. 'The Water Wolf turns out to be an unstoppable monster who gets bigger and bigger the closer he comes. We stare with open mouths. We don't even have enough time to get frightened or to escape, for suddenly the monster lifts us up to his full height—fifteen, twenty metres! We see our wooden houses and church towers looming up. And when the monster reaches his highest point we can even see the English coastline. For one second we seem to be standing still, but then the monster takes a nosedive. Raahhhh! With enormous force he spits us out on land, where we're smashed to smithereens. Nothing is left intact, neither us nor our ship. We break body parts we didn't even know were breakable. The monster slinks hundreds of metres inland and gobbles up everything in his path. When his hunger is finally appeased, he withdraws and takes us with him. Into the depths.'

Super Waling took a sip of water.

'All that's left of us is my copper tobacco box and your boot. That's the way it happened. Our own tsunami on November 1st, 1755. Right here. On this very spot.'

'How can that be?' Gieles asked, unconvinced.

'An earthquake in Lisbon set off a deadly tremor in the lake.'

'Really?'

'Yes, sir.'

'Well,' said Gieles, and he meant every word, 'that makes a terrific story for my school report.'

Super Waling started up the scooter and rode into the pumping station, cart and all. Gieles parked his bike in the bicycle rack next to the entrance.

Upon entering they were greeted by a lady sitting behind the ticket counter, who immediately stood up and walked over to them. 'Hello, Waling,' she said. She spoke the words very courteously, as if he were someone important.

Nobility!

The slender elderly woman with red, protruding eyes made Gieles think of something reptilian. A kind of gecko. The woman took Super Waling's hand as if she were weighing it. 'How are you and how is your health?' she asked.

'Excellent,' said Super Waling, placing his slab of a hand over hers. 'Couldn't be better.'

'I saw you in the newspaper,' she cried with alarm. 'Good heavens! Stuck in the potato field.' Her gecko eyes protruded even further as she spoke.

'Saved by the firemen,' smiled Super Waling. 'Life is full of surprises. May I introduce Gieles Bos? An extremely kind young man who rescued me on another occasion when my buggy broke down.'

Gieles smiled shyly.

'Some people are never rescued,' she said, patting his hand. 'You're lucky, Waling.'

'How right you are,' he said, turning his attention to Gieles. 'He's doing a report for school on the pumping station. A few folders would come in handy.'

'Of course.' The woman walked to the counter.

The sound of muted applause could be heard from somewhere in the building.

'A wedding,' she explained, handing Gieles a stack of folders. 'In the Water Board Room.'

Super Waling nodded and rode over to the stairs where a wheelchair elevator had been installed. In a practised motion he rolled onto the platform and began the ascent. His thighs bulged out over the seat.

'I saw that piece in the paper, too.' Gieles slowly climbed the stairs beside him. 'I didn't know that was your name. Waling Cittersen van Boven.'

The elevator came to a halt with a slight jolt.

'Sometimes you change so much that your name no longer fits you,' said Super Waling. 'I chose my nickname myself. Which, by the way, is more the exception than the rule. Usually other people give you a nickname. In grade school the kids called me mama's boy. And they were completely right. But this time I beat them to it.'

He smiled a mournful smile.

Super Waling rode his cart off the platform and clapped his hands as if he were trying to drive something away, thereby bringing the topic to a close.

The steam engine was in the tower. It was soaring and gigantic, as if the engine were crashing out of the building. 'She still works,' he said proudly. 'Which is a good thing. Who knows, we may have to use her again if we ever get flooded.'

'You really think so?' asked Gieles. He gazed into the pumping steam engine. The upward pressure made his hair stand on end.

'Well, water is supposed to flow. People used to understand that much better than they do today. They lived *with* the water back then. When floods threatened their homes, they packed up their stuff and set off for higher ground.'

Super Waling got ready to climb out of his scooter. With one hand firmly grasping a pillar he pulled himself upward as he talked. His sweatshirt began creeping up, exposing the skin of his stomach.

'We don't accept the fact that water seeks its own level ... We want to bend everything to our will ... yessss,' groaned Super Waling as he hung from the pillar, '... we defy all the laws of nature ... but ... pfffffff ... at the same time we demand ... a risk-free ... society ...'

Then he straightened himself up, jovial and proud as an overheated nuclear reactor.

'Carry my bag for me, would you?' he asked. 'There's something in it I want to show you when we get to the top. The most beautiful thing about the steam pump isn't inside the tower but on top of it.' He pointed to a narrow spiral staircase.

Gieles took the linen bag and put his own backpack in the basket of the mobility scooter. He raised his eyebrows.

'Don't worry. I've been up there a hundred times. What am I saying—a million times. I can climb those stairs with my eyes closed.'

He waddled over to the stairs. Gieles was reminded of the chicks. He hoped they wouldn't shit all over his room. And he hoped the little one wouldn't panic. She didn't like to be alone.

Super Waling made an awkward bow. 'After you, sir.'

Gieles looked up at the cramped turns in the staircase. 'Are you sure?'

'Absolutely. Go ahead. The thing isn't going to collapse. It's indestructible,' said Super Waling, slapping the cast iron handrail.

Gieles began climbing the steps, which were decorated with four-leaf clovers.

'How's it going with your geese?' he heard him ask. He was halfway up, while Super Waling was only on the third step. His cheeks had turned the same colour as his sweatsuit. Gieles was afraid his head would explode.

'Good. I got two new geese chicks a couple of days ago. Uncle Fred found them.'

'Do they have … grmmmm … names?'

'No. I don't know if I'm allowed to keep them or not. My father doesn't know.'

Super Waling was panting. His swimming-tube neck was soaking wet.

'You can … ,' he wheezed with a look of determination. '… You can name them after the people you're … humgrrr … fond of.'

Gieles was just about to tell him that he had named his two other geese when Super Waling tumbled forward. He expected him to bounce all the way down the stairs, but his right arm got caught between two bars. Gieles was at his side in a couple of jumps, crouching over his head. Super Waling was lying with his right cheek pressed against one of the steps and he looked anything but comfortable. His lips hung heavily down as if the rubber band in his mouth had snapped.

'You okay?' Gieles had no idea what he was supposed to do.

'Not bad,' Super Waling replied weakly. 'Although something tells me I'm not going anywhere.'

His body was blocking the stairs. Gieles had no intention of climbing over him. Super Waling's sweatshirt had slid up and his pants had dropped a bit, exposing kilos of backside.

'Are you religious?' Super Waling asked.

'No. I don't think so.' Gieles sat down on a step with Super Waling's bag on his lap.

'Me neither. Not any more. Used to be … before all the trouble started … Oh, I'm just blabbering … But suddenly a psalm came into my head. Be pleased, O God, to deliver me! O Lord, make haste to help me! … That's pretty funny. I don't really remember the rest.'

Gieles looked around in a panic. 'You're not gonna die, are you?'

'Of course not. This is no big deal. My arm hurts a little, that's all.'

Gieles looked at his arm, which was hanging through the bars at a strange angle. His hand was all splotchy.

'Before I forget,' said Super Waling, trying to look cheerful. 'The second part of Ide and Sophia is in my bag.'

Gieles opened the bag. The story was inside a red folder between the cans of grape soda. He also saw two pairs of binoculars.

'Something to read to kill time,' he joked, wincing in pain.

In the adjacent room they could hear a door being opened followed by the buzzing of voices. 'The wedding guests,' Super Waling observed hopefully.

'Let's call them.'

'Hello,' Super Waling said weakly. 'Can you hear me?'

Gieles began to call them, too. Louder and louder. After the fourth time he roared, 'HELP! HELP! HELP US, DAMN IT!' He never cursed when he was around adults, but this was an emergency.

That worked. A few of the wedding guests came to the pumping station tower, but they didn't look as if they were interested in freeing Super Waling from his predicament.

'What's going on here?' Gieles heard someone ask.

'Is that your father?' asked a woman in a cobalt blue dress. She looked stunning.

'No,' said Gieles, blushing scarlet. 'Just a ... someone who ... uh, who ...'

Gieles could no longer concentrate. His ears were ringing. His legs were wobbly. His voice shook. The wedding party got bigger and bigger but he couldn't make out what anyone was saying. He felt as if he were in a merry-go-round and could only pick up snatches of conversation.

'I'm not getting involved in this ... the buffet is ... hee hee hee! ... at my daughter's wedding ... own fault ... hoo hoo! ... full moon! ... damn! ... ha ha ha! ... does this guy have an air valve? ... fat chance! ... woo hoo hoo! ... where's his valve? ... hey, the buffet is ... eating and drinking ... opened! ... ha ha ha!'

'Get the receptionist. Please.'

Super Waling's voice sounded dignified and calm. 'Get Mrs Geerts.'

The merry-go-round didn't stop turning until the guests had left and Mrs Geerts came to do what she could for Super Waling.

'Poor, poor Waling.' Her voice was heavy with sorrow. Her gecko eyes were moist. 'And now this. On top of everything else you've had to go through.'

She walked around the staircase and lovingly inspected his hand. 'I'll call an ambulance,' she said, and went up the stairs to straighten out his disarranged pants and sweatshirt. 'Poor Waling.'

PART II

Ide & Sophia

'My father says everyone is born with a gift,' said Sophia. She was lying with Ide in the grass under an oak, right near the lake. It was Sunday, the only day of the week that the men didn't work. The sun shone through the canopy of leaves.

Ide lay on his back with his hands folded behind his head. Sophia was sitting astride him. In less than two months' time his fine facial features had turned into furrows. Sand, sun and wind had eroded his skin. Sophia followed the lines with her finger and wondered how deep they'd get. She stroked his pale blond hair and kissed the veins in his neck. Ide's body had taken on impressive proportions with all the excavation work. He looked like a fully trained fighting dog in the prime of life. She pounded on his chest with her fist. It was as hard as ice.

'Only people of a certain standing are born with a gift.' Ide spoke without irony.

'Not true,' Sophia smiled. 'It has nothing to do with what cradle you end up in. Everyone can do something special. You, for example, are the best lover in the whole world.'

She dropped forward, giggling and pressing her pelvis against his bare belly. She had yet to put her underpants on. Ide and Sophia had been making noisy, exuberant love. Their moments alone were few and far between. In the shanty they were constantly surrounded by men. 'And not only that,' she said, giving him another powerful push, 'but you can also draw beautifully.'

Ide didn't drink—it wasn't a question of principles; he just didn't like it—but he did draw. While the polder boys got tanked up at the countless nearby pubs, Ide retreated with a piece of paper and a pencil. He drew landscapes. Not as they really were, but as they someday could be. Utopian landscapes of the drained lake. He fantasised about the exposed lake floor, strewn with mysterious treasures and shipwrecks. And rising from that virginal floor he depicted picturesque villages, fertile orchards, spacious country houses, flowing streams and lush pastures filled with horses and cows.

'That's where we'll live,' he would say emphatically, pointing to the most beautiful farm with the biggest barn beside it. 'And this is where I'll plant fruit trees. Your fruit trees.'

He could fantasise endlessly about the new land, their new existence. He daydreamed about all the gold pieces he'd find once the lake was drained.

'Tell me about us again,' Sophia whispered. She lay on top of him, motionless, her lips near his ear. 'What does our life look like? What do we look like?'

'We live in the best farmstead around, with ten hectares of land and ten farmhands.' Ide's voice sounded sleepy and hoarse. 'We have sixty cows, five horses and pantries full of food and clothes. On Sundays your pa and ma come to visit, and they take our children out for a walk.'

Sophia felt a stab of guilt. She had promised herself that she would write a letter to her parents in Zeeland, telling them about her adventures and the life she was leading. Her real life.

Feeling restless, she raised herself up and sat down

next to Ide. She looked at the water. The polder boys were besieging the lake from its banks, but it just kept rippling unperturbed on. Or maybe not. Maybe something was brewing in the heart of the lake and it was getting ready for a counterattack.

Ide sat up as well. He shook the grass from his hair and pulled his shirt down. 'You're not pregnant, are you?' he asked suddenly.

'Pfff, fortunately not,' said Sophia. 'I'm not even bleeding yet. You first have to bleed down there before you can have children.'

'And when does this bleeding start?' he asked uncertainly.

'How should I know? Not for a long time, I hope. I don't even want to think about having a baby in that filthy shack. Even a farmer wouldn't keep his cattle there.'

Sophia thought about the children in the shantytown with their hungry, torn mouths. She had fed them bits of bread on a few occasions but had given up on that practice. Her charity only led to aggression. The children fought each other for every crumb.

The only one she fed was the little girl, because she was lonelier, sicker, dirtier and more wretched than all the others. The child never spoke, but she couldn't be deaf. When Sophia asked her to stick out her tongue, she had responded immediately. Her tongue was covered with a grey coating. The mother of the child, who had seven other bags of bones running around, was completely indifferent.

Once Sophia tried to wash the girl in the canal. First she rubbed the most stubbornly encrusted places with grease, hoping to loosen the dirt. Then she immersed her in the water. She washed the girl's hair with bleach to delouse her. Although the washing must have been painful, the child didn't flinch. Sophia never did get her clean. It was as if the dirt had been burned into her skin.

'No,' said Sophia, her voice firm. 'This is no place for children. I want our children to go to school. A good private school. At the poor schools they beat the children.'

'Don't worry,' said Ide, pulling her onto the grass.

'I'm not worried,' said Sophia. She bit the forearm that was wrapped around her neck. 'At the poor schools they fill birds with dried peas and throw them at the children. And when a child brings the bird back, he gets a smack. Or they rip off a piece of ear.'

She licked the impression that her teeth made on Ide's skin.

'Salt,' she said. 'I can taste the sea.'

'I threw a bowlful of salt into the sea once,' said Ide.

'What for?'

'I don't know. I was little and I wanted to know if I could make the sea saltier.'

Towards evening they walked back to the shantytown, where the usual carousing was in full swing. The atmosphere was explosive. Ide joined his crew and Sophia went looking for Akkie, the Frisian woman. Akkie was sitting with a few other women, leaning against the shanty. 'Little Sophie!' she shouted with an unsteady voice, slapping the wooden bench with her hand. 'Come shit down.'

Sophia obeyed and took a sip of the jenever she was offered. 'What's going on?'

'Problems, trouble,' said Akkie scornfully. She brought her face up close. Her red eyes were crossed from the drink.

'The fucking Belgians beat up a couple of our men.'

Sophia tried to steer clear of her rotten breath.

'And now our men are gonna go take care of the fucking Belgians.'

Sophia looked at them. She could hardly imagine them fighting in their condition. Even their caps hung limp from the alcohol. A little further on, one fellow tried to piss against a tree but never got any further than the tips of his boots. The only sober one was Ide Warrens. No one said anything about it. Ide was too big to pick a fight with.

'Those fucking Belgians are shinging dirty shongs about ush,' slurred Akkie. Saliva was running down her chin. 'About our little twats. They shay we're whores ... and they think they're better 'cause they get more money, and those fucking Belgians ...'

'You shouldn't drink so much,' interrupted Sophia with irritation.

'Don't drink sho muuuuuch!' repeated Akkie, snorting and spluttering.

Sophia wiped the spatters from her face. 'Yes. It's bad for the baby.'

'Little Sophie!' shouted Akkie. 'You got a lot to learn. Ha ha. Bad for the baby! Did you hear that? I'd rather have 'm dead than alive. If that brat gets a life like mine, I'd sooner wring his little neck ... fucking Belgians!' screamed Akkie. 'Bastards!'

The other women laughed and drank until the first raindrops fell and everyone fled into their own shanty.

No one could work the next day on account of the rain. It was early in the morning and the men had gathered in front of the shacks. They stood there tightly packed, like the peels of an onion. 'Let's go kick out the Belgians!' came the call from the innermost peel. The outer peels cheered in agreement. Ide kept his mouth shut. He understood that he couldn't stay behind, but he wasn't planning on joining them, either. He'd go along and look the other way. Not because he was a coward, but simply because he had a different set of goals.

Their minds made up, the men took off in their muddy coats and boots. There were sticks and shovels to be seen. And liquor, of course. Always liquor. Two hundred strong, they began walking in the direction of Lisse, where the Belgians were supposed to be living.

They passed farms, villas and the hovels where the farmhands lived. The folk in the farmyard looked on anxiously as the polder boys passed. The farmers had no idea what was going to happen. The men looked impressive in their poverty. The biggest blockhead could see that they had nothing to lose.

Ide was almost taking up the rear. He towered over all the others. He saw the men in the front line: they weren't walking, they were marching. He saw the church tower looming up and the big market gardens. Some of the men vandalised the crops as they went and filled their mouths and pockets with anything edible. Ide was ashamed for them and stared at the horizon.

Sophia hadn't heard Ide leave. She drank with the women until the rain came and drifted into a comatose sleep. She was awakened by a cold, wet feeling. Standing up, she realised that the straw was drenched. Water was leaking into the shanty. She cursed wholeheartedly.

Her head felt as if it were being pressed under a rock. She stumbled outside and raised her face to the sky. Eyes closed, she caught the rain in her open mouth.

She stayed there for several minutes. The only sound was that of the rain. All the other sounds were drowned out.

When her clothes were soaked through she went back inside. Then she opened her suitcase and took out a damp skirt; there was no way she could keep anything dry in the sieve they lived in. She checked to see that the false bottom of the suitcase was still intact. Under the cardboard she kept the money she had earned with her stolen wares. She sold the food to the shantytown dwellers for a mere trifle.

She got dressed, dried her face, placed buckets and pans outside to catch the rain, tried to stop up the chinks in the shanty with reeds and twigs, started a fire, washed her hands, mixed batter, ground coffee, put on water, hummed and sweated. It was peaceful in the shanty—until the Frisian woman showed up. Standing before her with black bags under her eyes she looked like a leper. She sat down on a stool, her legs wide apart. The baby hung heavily between her legs.

'I'm out of coffee,' said Akkie.

Sophia made coffee without saying a word while eyeing Akkie critically.

'Don't look at me like that.'

'Like how?' asked Sophia defiantly.

'Angry. But I can't imagine why.'

Sophia poked at the fire viciously. 'Because of what you said last night. About your baby.'

Akkie looked at her with amazement. 'About my baby? What did I say? I can't remember anything.'

'That you'd rather have him dead than alive.'

'Oh, listen, honey,' said the Frisian woman kindheartedly. 'I didn't really mean it. I mean, my mother had sixteen kids and a bum for a husband. So even if you lose a few you've got plenty to spare. Understand? How many children did your ma have? Ten? Fifteen?'

Sophia stopped poking and stared into the fire. 'She

only had me. My father and mother only have me and they were overjoyed when they got me.'

There it was again, that gnawing sense of guilt. She had left like a thief in the night and still hadn't been in touch with them. Her father would surely be looking for her.

'If your pa and ma only have you it's a different story,' said Akkie not very convincingly.

They were both silent for a time. The rain lessened. The first women and children went outside.

'Hey, I don't mean it like that.'

Sophia handed her a bowl and Akkie blew into the coffee absently. The warm liquid brought colour back into her cheeks.

'The men,' said Akkie, relieved that she had found another topic to discuss. 'Did you know about the men?'

Sophia shrugged her shoulders.

'They've gone to teach the Belgians a lesson.'

The men walked on further to the next village. Ide didn't know how it happened—he hadn't heard about anything being planned—but suddenly he saw another group of workers come looming up. This group was at least as large as his. 'De Kaag, De Kaag,' they sang, 'the men from De Kaag.'

The two groups approached each other and greeted each other with cheers. They combined forces seamlessly, perfectly matched in their shabby appearance.

Now Ide Warrens was no longer taking up the rear but walking somewhere in the middle. He could see their power reflected in the faces of the villagers. They were scared to death. He still towered over the rest of the crowd. His height made him an obvious target, Ide reasoned, and he bowed his head.

The rain had almost stopped. He wanted to go back to work, although he knew he could forget about today's wages.

There was shouting and cursing at the front of the line. The contractors and foremen could all drop dead. They paid too little. They fined the men for things that weren't their fault. They let the workers eat filth while they stuffed themselves with goose liver.

Ide took a deep breath and called to mind his mother's freshly baked whole wheat bread. He could taste the warm bread on his tongue, the wheat, the salt. The soft butter with her homemade rose hip jam. His mouth began to water. He fantasised about the stove that would later grace their farmhouse with a chicken roasting inside. Ide swallowed his saliva to drive away the hunger. He hadn't eaten breakfast that morning.

To divert his attention he concentrated on the surrounding landscape. The cultivated fields, succulent and green. Bits of blue sky peeking out from the grey. Bright red poppies and white apple blossoms. The only thing that struck a false note were the polder boys. He felt filthy.

They came into Lisse. Women and their children fled into their houses. The streets were empty except for one man. The man looked distinguished in his hat and suit. He reminded Ide of Sophia's father. Unlike his own pa, the doctor had never lost his self-control. Ide regarded dignity and composure as the highest qualities a person could achieve. 'Stay calm,' Ide murmured as he walked.

The man in the street was standing with one foot in a shop, his other leg still outside. His curiosity seemed to be winning out over his fear. Ide hoped they'd leave him in peace.

Suddenly the group expanded to about five hundred

men. They must have come from shanties surrounding the lake.

Ide had heard about strikes but he had never taken part in one. And now here he was, right in the middle of a strike. There was nothing exciting about it. It left him cold.

In the distance they could see the shanties of the Belgians—twenty, twenty-five hovels that looked just as ramshackle as those in their own shantytown. The Belgians couldn't be earning more. They came closer. Once again, the residents scurried away like cockroaches.

Ide slowed down until he found himself at the tail end of the group. It was quieter there. The men at the back weren't so much walking as lumbering, which caused the mud to suck at the soles of their boots.

By the time Ide reached the shanties of the Belgians, the few things that could be plundered had been plundered. Broken chairs, torn shirts, crushed wicker baskets, household goods scattered everywhere. All was silence except for the suppressed weeping of the women and children, who hid themselves away in their shanties. Ide could feel their fear and hatred right through the reed walls. He was ashamed.

A wooden stool was lying on its side in the mud, its legs still intact. He wanted to set it aright but realised how idiotic that would be. He left the stool alone and kept telling himself that all trouble eventually comes to an end. His own childhood had taught him that. That his mother's black-and-blue spots went away by themselves, as did his father's bursts of aggression.

Ide decided to stop looking, but a dog crossed his field of vision. The dog was staggering, blood streaming from its mouth. Before he could formulate an idea of what he was seeing, two men gave the dog a final blow. The blade of the shovel that landed on the dog's fur made a dull sound.

They kept on lumbering, out to the lake. They found the Belgians within fifteen minutes. Ide slowed his pace and leaned against a tree, listening to the hundreds of footsteps squelching in the mud. The Belgians were still at work. There was no difference between them and the Dutch workers, Ide realised. They were digging the same canal and building the same dike. Like himself, they were just extensions of their shovels. No more and no less. They had no heart, no soul, no past and no future. Whoever dropped dead was out of luck. Or maybe in luck, depending on how you looked at it.

A boy came to stand next to him. Ide guessed him to be close to his own age. His scrawny face looked bruised. His cheeks hung over his cheekbones like wet laundry.

'Hopefully we can go back to work tomorrow,' said the boy. He raised his head with great effort and looked up at the sky. Then he put his hands on his forehead, put them back in his pockets and repeated the ritual. Each movement produced a tallow-like smell.

They heard screaming. The Belgians had stopped digging and were gathered together in a tight group. They were clearly in the minority. In the meantime, four of their bosses were speaking with the snorting head of the rebellion.

'My mother says that God will take revenge for draining the lake,' the boy continued nervously. 'She says that God creates land, not man. So He's going to punish us.'

'What crap,' laughed Ide, sitting down in the wet grass. He rested his forearms on his knees. The boy followed Ide's example and began to gnaw on his black fingernails. Ide thought of the sharp twigs Sophia used to keep her nails clean.

'I don't believe my mother either,' murmured the boy. He spit out a bit of fingernail. 'It wasn't our idea anyway. We're just doing the work. He won't punish us for that, will He?'

'Of course not.' Ide looked at a mosquito on his arm and squashed it, leaving a small bloody smear. 'Our biggest punishment is the mosquitoes.'

The boy nodded and showed off his bites as if they were war injuries. He was covered with them. 'Mosquitoes are terrible. And they're good for nothing. You get honey from bees. You can milk a cow. But mosquitoes—they're not good for anything as far as I can tell.'

The boy rattled on for a while about mosquitoes and God. It seemed like hours before they were finally ready to leave. Most of the men just stood together milling around. Ide closed his eyes, and he woke up when the troops started moving again. The boy next to him lay sleeping with his head between his drawn-up legs. He looked as if he had been about to turn a somersault and had changed his mind at the last minute. Ide shook him awake. The catastrophe seemed to have been averted.

'The Belgians are leaving!' passing voices chanted. 'We won!'

Ide waited till the end of the procession was in sight, and he gazed at all the jubilant faces. Suddenly their happiness caught on and Ide was cheered by their euphoria. The worthless had proven to be powerful. Their sheer scale commanded respect. Today they had risen above their humiliating existence. They were somebody. With great satisfaction they scattered themselves among the pubs.

Ide breathed a sigh of relief. Except for one dead dog and some smashed up household goods, the revolt had not gotten out of hand. He stood in front of a bar listening to the drunken songs, and glancing over at the other side of the road he saw dozens of immaculate uniforms and tall black boots.

'The army,' said a fellow who had walked outside in search of a tree.

The soldiers were equipped with weapons. Some of the uniforms had decorations on them, but Ide was clueless when it came to ranks and positions.

'Doesn't mean a damn thing!' shouted the man over his shoulder. He stood beside the tree with his legs planted far apart. Ide looked at the puddle of urine the man was standing in. 'If there are forty of 'em it'll be a lot. We'll make mincemeat out of 'em!'

Grinning, the man shook his penis back and forth and pushed it back into his pants. 'Get a load of him, that little guy, the one with the trumpet. Worthless lout. Just wait for him to blink his eyes I'll have that trumpet shoved up his ass. Bah-bah-bah!'

He cupped his hands around his mouth and made provocative noises. 'Toot-toot-toot!'

The Zeelander was glad when the man went back to the bar. He wasn't in the mood for trouble.

Suddenly he felt a hard push against his lower back. 'Ide Warrens! Where were you?'

Her voice was anxious, angry and happy at the same time. She pummelled Ide's chest a couple of times and pulled on his neck to kiss him. He bent his head down. Sophia was warm and sweaty and her breath smelled of jenever. She thrust her tongue deep into his mouth. The sound of cheering rose from the bar.

Ide pushed Sophia away. He threw his arm around her and began to walk. 'We're going back,' he said.

'Back? I just got here. I didn't walk that whole stinking way just to ...' She groped for the right words. She didn't want to call the shanty 'home,' and apparently Ide didn't either. 'Just to go right back from where I started.'

She pulled on his arm angrily, forcing him to slacken his pace.

'They set the army on us. There's going to be trouble.'

Intrigued, Sophia observed the uniforms on the other side of the square. She had never stood eye-to-eye with soldiers before. Suddenly she found herself at the heart of life and she had no intention of leaving. Pulling herself loose from Ide's grasp, Sophia came to a halt. 'The other women are here, too. Everyone is drinking to the good outcome.'

'Everyone has already had enough to drink.'

'Come on, there was no trouble, was there? No one was wounded?'

'They beat a dog to death. With a shovel.'

'A dog? Why would they do a thing like that?'

He knew he had her on his side. Before long she'd forget about her desire to stay, and rage would fill her heart.

'No reason. They did it for no reason. They were just bored.'

'How horrible! Was it the Belgians?'

'No, it was our boys who killed it. I believe it was just a young dog, a puppy. They hit him on the head.'

'The bastards,' she thundered. Her emotions swung up and down. He could see it in her eyes, which were drained of all colour. She began walking with him and cursing. 'Filthy shit heads. Dirty sons of bitches.'

They left the village. Little puddles of water had gathered in the sunken cobblestones. Ide diverted her attention with animal stories. There was one about a horse who rescued a girl from a burning haystack. Another about young kittens who were raised by a goat. On the way they caught up with a group of polder boys who had been slowed down by too much drink and too little sleep. No one was in a hurry. The day's euphoria had ebbed away, and soon they'd be nobodies again.

A few hundred metres further on they saw a group of men in the middle of the road. The men were standing in a circle facing inward. One by one they disappeared behind the row of backs. Ide slowed down while Sophia sped up. 'Come on,' she said. 'I want to see what's going on.'

When they got close to the backs, Sophia squatted down on her haunches to get a better look. Ide didn't have to stand on his toes. He had a perfect view—and what he saw made his stomach turn. On the ground lay a fellow with his legs drawn up and his face smeared with blood. His jaw was hanging at a strange angle, as if one side had become detached. His eyes were shut. Sophia probably saw him, too, for she covered her mouth with her hand and stifled a scream.

The men paid no attention to them. They were in a trance. Without saying a word they each took turns. One fellow stepped into the circle. He took his time as if he were lining himself up in front of a ball, then kicked the victim's rib cage with the inside of his boot. Blood gushed from the man's mouth.

Sophia screamed again. Ide grabbed her upper arm and tried to pull her away from the violence. One of the men looked around with a smirk on his face and then turned back to the centre of the circle.

For a second time the same fellow wound up and bored his heel into the dislocated face. The only thing Sophia could see was blood. The body seemed to be emptying out like a bottle. Snarling and snorting she tore herself loose. She dove right through the row of backs and stormed up to the man, who was returning to his place. Sophia sank her fingernails into his temples and scratched his skin away in a rapid downward motion. The man looked at her with surprise, wondering where on earth this little redhead had come from. Then Sophia sank her teeth into his arm. He grabbed a tuft of her hair with his left hand and pulled, but her teeth refused to budge. Ide grabbed Sophia around the waist, but the other men threw themselves on him. Sophia began striking out wildly in every direction, the arm still in her mouth. A piece of her scalp had been pulled out with her hair, but she didn't feel it. The man grabbed another tuft and pulled Sophia's head back so far that she had to let the arm go. Then he balled up his fist and planted it full in her face.

9

Gieles put Part II in his drawer. He spun around once in his desk chair and wondered what Sophia looked like after having had her face punched in. Maybe there was nothing left of her teeth at all. He took out Part I of Ide & Sophia and read it all over again. *Her front teeth were broken off like bits of chalk and her face was asymmetrical.* Maybe now her face was completely cockeyed. Or maybe they kicked her to death.

Gieles thought about Super Waling. It had been a week since he had left him with the gecko woman on the spiral staircase in the tower. Gieles had fled after they called the ambulance, and he hadn't had the courage to visit him. To ask him about his arm, which had been so weirdly twisted. To pick up his backpack, which he had left in the basket of the scooter.

To ask what the gecko woman had meant by 'on top of everything else you've had to go through.'

Was Super Waling suffering from some terrible disease that made him so fat? Was that it? Maybe he was dying.

Gieles googled the words 'fat' and 'disease.' A long list of possible illnesses unfurled itself on the screen. He mumbled the various disorders out loud. 'Underactive thyroid, disorders of the hypo ... hypotha ... lamus ... , family history of obesity, fluid retention caused by poor cardiac function, diabetes, syndrome X ...'

Syndrome X?

That sounded mysterious. He lay down on his bed. The chicks were rummaging around through the room. Although they were exactly the same age, one goose was growing more slowly. But the other may also have been growing too fast. They were two females, just like his two Tufted Buffs. Uncle Fred was very good at determining the sex of chicks. He held the chick in an upside-down stranglehold and pushed between the legs with his thumb and forefinger until something popped out. If nothing popped out, it was a female. Uncle Fred could also tell that the two newcomers had come from the same clutch. They were sisters.

The smaller gosling liked to sit on Gieles's lap and could only sleep when he put her in the fur hat next to his head. In the short time since she had arrived he had grown more attached to this little goose than to the geese who had been with him for four years. Like most birds, they kept a suitable distance. But this one was different. This gosling was as affectionate as a little kitten. Sometimes she seemed to purr when he ran his finger over her head. Her big sister, on the other hand, wasn't the least bit interested in intimacy. Her passion was food. She was a kind of Super Waling in bird form. All that eating made her shit constantly—and not, like the little gosling, in the rabbit dish.

Gieles looked at his schedule on the wooden partition. His mother would be coming back in ten weeks. Her absence was a nagging pain, like a fingernail cut too close to the quick.

He ran through the schedule and knew he was running behind. The 'stay' command was still a disaster, as was the 'fly' command. They just couldn't get the hang of it. He still didn't have a good method for getting the geese to take off. And then there was the problem of the canal. The geese would have to fly over the canal on command. But how?

Gieles stared at the slanted ceiling where the outlines of animals were still faintly visible. His mother had once painted the slanted part blue, with birds in the sky. Gieles had asked if she would make a lion, too. A lion with wings. When he got too old for the drawing, his father painted the ceiling white again. Sometimes the old outlines seemed to move. It was just like his mother, when he hadn't seen her in a long time. There wasn't much left of her except for a moving outline.

Gieles watched as the big goose chick used her greedy bill to pull an album out of the closet, *How to Identify Birds*. The albums had belonged to his grandpa. His grandpa used to buy Rizla rolling papers for his cigarettes, and in every pack there were bird cards that he pasted in an album. His grandpa must have had to smoke a hell of lot to fill all the albums with cards. After he died, he left the bird inheritance to his son, and Willem in turn passed it on to Gieles. Gieles had spent hours poring over the fascinating bird cards.

The goose tugged at the album like a wild animal tearing its prey to bits.

'Cut it out,' said Gieles.

Spitefully, the goose pecked a piece out of the cover.

'Hey! Cut it out!' Gieles sat up. He picked up a table tennis ball that was lying on his nightstand and threw it at the big goose. The ball struck her on the back and bounced across the room. As she went on impassively shredding paper, the little goose waddled after the ball.

When the ball came to a stop she paused to inspect it, walking all around it, bobbing her neck up and down and producing noises of approval. After a while she tapped the ball with her bill, then pranced up to it again and gave it another tap. Gieles and the big goose followed her movements. This time the ball rolled through the room more rapidly, making her quack with excitement.

Gieles picked up the ball. The little goose looked up at him with sharp eyes, her head cocked. Slowly he traced circles in the air with it, which she followed. The big goose responded by lying down. Suddenly Gieles whammed the ball against the floor with an outstretched right hand.

Service without effect.

The ball bounced, bounced, bounced, and at that point the little goose rushed in. She caught the ball with her bill, let it fall and scooped it up again. Gieles looked on, speechless. He stood up and ran downstairs.

It took forever for Uncle Fred to climb the stairs with his crutch. He stood at the doorway, panting.

'Good heavens, what a stench,' he said, making a face.

Gieles ignored the remark and picked up the ball, which was lying next to the little goose. She sat there waiting obediently. Then Gieles wound his whole body up and served the plastic ball with a thwack. Like something demented she pounced on her prey and even managed to balance the ball on her bill for a couple of seconds.

'Unbelievable,' whispered Uncle Fred, rubbing his polio leg. 'Unbelievable.'

After demonstrating her trick three more times, she produced a weary quack and walked over to the fox fur hat, which was under the desk. She scrambled over the brim of the hat and immediately fell asleep.

'That's no ordinary gosling,' said Uncle Fred, scanning the rest of the room. The big goose was sitting in the corner, gnawing on a loose piece of floor covering.

'And this, Gieles, is no ordinary room. What a mess.'

There was goose down and torn-up paper everywhere.

Hanging from a hole in the wall, which had been made by Tony during one of his bad moods when he decided to play darts with his pocket knife, were tufts of insulation. Gieles noticed he hadn't turned the partition around with the training schedule on it.

But Uncle Fred took no notice. He hobbled through the room, sniffing. 'There's more shit in here than oxygen.'

'I keep cleaning it up,' Gieles said apologetically, 'but the big one just shits non-stop.'

'Then you really missed something,' said Uncle Fred, pointing at the bed with his crutch.

Gieles knelt down next to the bed—right beside a big plop of goose poop.

'We can't have this. Those birds have got to go,' said Uncle Fred, opening the attic window wide. 'They stink and they're dangerous.'

'I don't want them to go,' said Gieles. 'They're domestic geese. They won't fly away. And if they do, we'll pinion them.'

Uncle Fred sighed. 'I'll talk to your father, but I can't promise anything. I'm afraid he's not going to agree this time.'

10

Sunshine,

You remember that minibus we used to have that we took on vacation? It was red and white, as if half a white bus had been soldered onto half a red one. Yesterday I took a taxi through Mogadishu and suddenly I saw that very minibus right in front of us. I forgot the stench and the dust and all I saw was us. You with your long brown hair. They thought you were a girl. So uninhibited. You used to yell 'I love you' at everybody, but no one in the Czech Republic understood you. Dad had made a big bed in the minibus that the three of us slept in. You were in the middle. You crept up and slept with one hand in my hair and one hand in Dad's, as if you were a neuron trying to connect us. I had strung clotheslines inside the bus from one side to the other, and that's where I hung your clothes and stuffed animals. You called them sleep streamers. All I wanted to do yesterday was open up the hatch of the bus and crawl back in time. Back to us. We kept following the minibus and I just wanted to cry, but I couldn't. There was an iron plate between my heart and my stomach. The minibus stopped near the market. The driver opened the hatch, and out rolled a big tangle of men and women with baskets and animals. As if a dirty, soggy sponge were being squeezed dry. Suddenly I got so angry. That swarm of Somalis with their mangy goats had contaminated the minibus. They contaminated my lovely memories of us.

I miss you.

Love, Ellen
(Oh, yes, please tell Dad that I didn't cut him off because he was angry but the line suddenly went dead.)

As if it were the most ordinary thing in the world, Super Waling rode into the farmyard. The pebbles crunched under the tyres of his mobility scooter. He was holding the black backpack up in the air like a trophy he had just won.

Gieles was busy setting up the table tennis table in front of the barn. The legs were rusted and the net was frayed. He wiped his hands on his pants, and as he walked towards Super Waling he scanned him for physical injury. No abnormalities, but it was too soon to tell.

'Forgive me for being so nosey, but I looked up your address in your assignment book,' he said excitedly, and handed him the backpack. Gieles looked into his eyes, trying to detect anything else there. He had written a detailed description of *Expert Rescue Operation 3032* in his assignment book, and he wondered whether Super Waling had read any further. But his eyes revealed nothing. They were gentle and friendly. There was no other story lurking behind them.

'I'll put my backpack inside,' said Gieles.

When he returned, Super Waling was looking at the geese, who were poking around his scooter with great curiosity. He wanted to bend over but his belly was in the way. Only now did Gieles see the bandage around his wrist.

'Are you all right? Your arm, I mean?' Gieles blurted out.

'Fantastico,' said Super Waling, pulling the sleeve of

his sweatshirt over the bandage. 'The ambulance personnel were most skilful at dislodging me from the banister and wrapping up my arm.'

He made a careless gesture. 'I'm chalking it up to experience. First the fire department, then the ambulance. I wonder which emergency service will come to get me the next time.' He laughed.

Gieles failed to see the humour. 'Sorry that I ...'

He groped for the right words, gazing at his sneakers and making a little hollow in the gravel. He thought of the wedding guests who had made fun of Super Waling, shrieking with laughter. 'That I left ...'

'Listen, Gieles,' interrupted Super Waling abruptly. 'It's all right. I had a terrific afternoon. I had wanted to show you the view from the tower. It's really breathtaking. But, well, things turned out differently. Too bad about the fall. For you. For me. For Mrs Geerts. For everybody. Done. Finished. Ended. And now tell me this,' he said, stroking the geese over their tufted heads. 'Are these your American geese?'

'This is Tufted and this is Bufted. Her tuft is longer.'

'You've given them names,' said Super Waling, beaming.

Gieles nodded. It surprised him that the geese allowed a stranger to pet them. They didn't even hiss.

'They look very cool with those tufts. And that gosling must be your new acquisition.' He was looking at the grass where the chick was sleeping. 'What a sweet little thing.'

'Yeah, and that's her sister.'

Gieles pointed to the pasture where the other gosling was tearing grass out of the ground.

'She looks famished.'

'No way,' said Gieles. 'She's just a little pig ... I mean ...'

Once again he felt awkward.

'Make sure the lady doesn't end up as corpulent as I am,' Super Waling laughed.

They spent a few minutes watching the voracious goose. Tufted and Bufted walked towards her but kept a safe distance. They were intimidated by the newcomer.

Gieles's father had been aware of their existence for a few days now. Gieles didn't know how Uncle Fred had managed it, but they were allowed to stay until they started beating their wings. Then they'd have to go. The second rule was that the geese were not to enter the house under any circumstances. Those were Willem Bos's own words.

Super Waling started getting ready to leave, but Gieles wanted him to stay. No one was home anyway.

'I read Part Two of Ide and Sophia,' Gieles said as he straightened out the frayed table tennis net. 'Did you write all that?'

'Yes,' said Super Waling, nodding tentatively. 'Did you like it?'

'Definitely. I thought it was great. Really, really great.'

'What a nice compliment. You're the first one to read it.'

Gieles didn't know anyone who could beam like that. He was like a gigantic firefly.

'I'm sorry that Sophia got beat up. Is her face all crooked now? Did that really happen?'

'Oh, yes,' said Super Waling. 'Ide and Sophia Warrens are my distant ancestors.'

Gieles considered his last words. Distant ancestors?

'My great-great-great-grandparents, to be exact. After the draining of the lake, Sophia kept a diary in which she wrote down her life story. All those writings have been carefully preserved.'

'So they weren't from the nobility?' asked Gieles with disappointment.

Super Waling burst out laughing. 'No, unfortunately. There's not a drop of blue blood in my family tree. If you really want to know what became of her, I'd be more than happy to give you Part Three. Or I'll send it by e-mail. Whatever you want. Maybe you'll find it useful. Is your report going well?'

'Pretty well,' said Gieles. He hadn't even started.

Super Waling took a sip of water from a bottle and surveyed the landscape as if it were a masterpiece.

'So your father refused to let the airport buy him out,' he said gravely. 'Now that's what I call noble. Very noble.'

'For us it was just convenient,' said Gieles. 'My father works for the airport.'

'Being bought out can have disastrous consequences,' muttered Super Waling as he stroked the head of one of the geese. The other goose nibbled on his monumental sweatpants. 'But don't let me hold you up any longer. I see you're about to play a game of ping-pong.'

'Table tennis.'

'Excuse me, sir. Table tennis. Who is your opponent?'

Gieles knew that Super Waling wouldn't laugh at him.

'My goose. The little one.'

He raised his eyebrows in amusement and opened his mouth to speak, but his words evaporated into thin air. They waited until the plane had passed the house.

'In that case,' repeated Super Waling, 'I would consider it an honour if I could be your spectator.'

Gieles grinned. 'It's her first lesson, you know.'

'Doesn't matter. Doesn't matter. It will be my first lesson, too. I don't know anything about this sport.'

'Then I'll teach you at the same time,' said Gieles, but he regretted it immediately because it put him in such an awkward position. Super Waling worked himself out of the mobility scooter, shouting 'that sounds like lots of fun!' with great enthusiasm.

'Okay,' said Gieles, averting his eyes. 'Okay. Then I'll go get the paddles. And the balls.'

By the time he got back from the barn, Super Waling was standing upright at the table. 'Lift up your heads,' he murmured. Those were the words written over the barn doors. 'You know that song?'

Gieles shook his head and kicked one of the legs to straighten the table.

Super Waling placed his hand over his heart. '"Lift up your heads, ye mighty gates, Behold the King of glory waits; The King of kings is drawing near; The Saviour of the world is here" … and I forget the rest,' he said. 'We used to sing that for Ascension Day at home. Now, what do you think? Am I in the right position?'

He said this with so much self-mockery that Gieles dared to laugh.

'You should be about a metre from the table.'

Super Waling took two steps back.

'The way you hold the paddle determines your technique,' he continued. 'Personally, I prefer the "shakehand" grip.'

'The shakehand,' repeated Super Waling.

'Yeah. You grab the paddle as if you were shaking hands with someone, but you stick your forefinger out. Look. Like this.'

He watched Gieles attentively.

'But you can also use the penhold grip, which is the favourite of the Chinese.' Gieles gave him a paddle. 'Left or right?'

'Right-handed. But left-handed today,' he said. 'You know, minor injury.'

'Left-handed is fine, too.' Gieles wondered whether he had broken his wrist.

'The most important thing is that you add something personal to your technique. Like an aggressive forehand drive or a sidespin loop.'

Super Waling looked at him with a face full of doubt.

'But when you're just starting out that's too difficult, of course. Right now the whole idea is to go back to the ready position every time you hit the ball. Like this.'

Gieles assumed the ready position with great deliberation. Super Waling tried to copy him, but without success.

'No, no. Not like that. Your feet should be closer together.'

He walked around the table and stood next to him. Only now did he realise how small Super Waling's feet were in their light blue Crocs. It amazed him that they were able to carry so much weight. His thighs were at least two times thicker than the length of his feet.

'They're really comfortable,' Super Waling said in his own defence. 'You can't even call them shoes. But who cares, I can't see them anyway.'

Gieles stood beside him in the ready position.

'Your feet have to be closer together,' he repeated.

'I'm afraid that's not going to work. My stomach ...'

Gieles did his best not to visualise the paunch between Super Waling's legs.

'Try to bend your arms. Ninety degrees. No, not so close to your body.'

Gieles guided his upper arms to the desired height without actually touching him. Super Waling looked as if he were flapping his wings. He followed a few more of Gieles's instructions and ended up in a totally contorted position.

Gieles walked back to his side of the table. He hit an easy high ball over the net. The ball bounced against Super Waling's stomach and onto the gravel.

'I'll get it. Just stay where you are.'

Super Waling managed to hit the fourth ball, but somehow he knocked it backward instead of forward. A following ball hit him in the forehead and bounced in a straight line right back to Gieles's side.

'Nice header,' he giggled.

'You'll never get past me!' Super Waling shouted.

He stood there motionless, only his left arm flailing up and down and the corners of his mouth curling higher and higher. His sweatshirt had crept up, giving Gieles a view of his belly (although it might just as well have been his butt). There was a deep vertical slit right in the middle of the mass of flesh.

He has two asses.

In the meantime the little goose had awoken. She waddled up to Gieles, but his attention was focused elsewhere.

'Think about your footwork!' shouted Gieles, who was jumping up and down fanatically. 'Get them going, make them move! Make use of the space!'

Super Waling began to bellow. He leaned on the table with his left hand and his body jolted up and down like an inflatable jumping castle.

'Oh, God! Move! Footwork!' He roared with laughter.

Finally Gieles let himself laugh, too. First timidly, but as soon as he got a look at Super Waling's Crocs he began laughing so hard that the tears rolled down his cheeks. It felt like a liberation. They both laughed, each for his own reasons.

Gieles didn't stop until he heard the sound of Tony's motorbike. Tony rode past slowly and then came back the other way, without greeting him. He hadn't done anything, and yet it seemed to Gieles as if his friend had opened fire.

11

Christian Moullec, my letter to you is still not ending. Very many things are happening to me. And people keep coming to me with orderings. Many things are happening to you, too. Your website writes that you almost had a collision in your flying two-seater motorbike with a plane of the army in Germany! It is a miracle that you and your geese did not have any nerve!

I bring you the nice news. I am now the connoisseur of four geese. I have two new puppies. Two sisters. They were foundling. One is very small, one is very big. Goose small excels in listening. I have great pride here. She plays the game of table ping pong with her bill. I tell you it is spectacle! If you and your wife happen to be in the neighbourhood of my house, I give you a welcome.

Now I present you with a new question. The goose very big eats extraterrestrial. Even in the sleep she keeps eating. The bill never does not rest. Uncle Fred says, she will burst into bits. Is extraterrestrial eating dangerous? For geese? And for people? Is extraterrestrial eating for people dangerous? Can they burst apart? Are you familiar with syndrome X?

I have worry about the food and the being fat and about my mother also. She is not fat. Rather on the contrary. She is as thin as the antenna on a walking-talking. My mother works in Africa. Africa is dangerous (I have knowledge with an internet girl and she wishes her parents in Africa). My mother does just like you the work of rescue.

She teaches people to cook on the sun. In Africa the trees and the roads are absent. She often loses the way. My mother is more there than here. I desire her here. With my project I am going to rescue my mother. She will shout: O, you are the hero! Then she will stay here for eternity. Humanity likes to hang around the hero.

Now I come once more to the point: what is your secret? What commands do you use for the excellent listening behaviour of your geese?

Before leaving for his babysitting job, Gieles looked at the new photos Gravitation had sent him. They were disappointing. He had hoped she'd send naked pictures of herself. Gieles had sent her photos of his new gosling—on his bed, in the fox fur hat, on his lap and on his shoulder.

'How adorable!!' she wrote with at least thirty hearts, and it felt as if she was talking about him.

But Gravitation didn't show any part of her body except her dreadlocks, which were always a different colour. She was like a jawbreaker. Her violet dreadlocks started out red and now they were pitch black again, just like her eyes and lips. She had drawn her eyebrows in the shape of barbed wire. He thought she was scary, like somebody going to a Halloween party, but he was careful not to say so.

Gieles hurried to Dolly's. She hated it whenever he was late. The unpainted front door was wide open. The two oldest boys were sitting at the table next to a pile of laundry. They were drawing. Jonas, the toddler, was in his diaper dragging around a plastic squirrel. Gieles sat down with the boys and pushed the laundry aside. The towels and sheets were the same drab colour as the chairs in the garden. White with grey spots. The boys didn't say much. They were completely absorbed in their drawing. Skiq had made a tractor with a strange snowman sitting on it.

Dolly came into the room and said hello, running her hand over his static hair. She was wearing red lipstick. Suddenly a mental image of Sophia's breasts popped into his head, brushing across his face. It wasn't the first time he had stood in for Ide Warrens. A few fantasies back, when he was in the shower, Sophia had spread her naked thighs for him on the shore of the lake.

'The boys are obsessed by this fat guy who rode past our house,' said Dolly. 'He was driving a little cart, just like Fred's.'

'A mobility scooter,' said Gieles, and his face tightened. Jonas was standing next to him, holding up his thin little arms. The kid hardly ever said a word. Gieles pulled him up onto his lap. Satisfied, he started chewing on the squirrel's tail.

'He was fatter than the moon,' said Onno.

'Liar!' shouted Skiq. 'But he did have a belly like ...' He looked around the living room and pointed. '... like that bean-bag chair. He was a big old bean-bag man.'

Dolly and the boys laughed.

'Is he staying with you at the campground?' She was standing so close that Gieles could smell her hair. The fragrance of her body flustered him.

'His name is Waling Cittersen van Boven.' He pronounced his name with great dignity.

She gave him a look of surprise and rattled off the name as if she were memorising a list of irregular verbs. Then she slammed her hand down on the table. The boys jumped and their felt-tips went flying.

'Waling Cittersen van Boven? He was my high school history teacher! He couldn't have been more than eight years older than me, but that man was thin and incredibly good-looking, I swear to God. All the girls had a crush on him. I did, too.'

She got a naughty gleam in her eye. 'Waling was so good at telling stories. Like when he taught us about the lake. It was weird ... as if we were right there. As if we had drained the water with our own hands.'

'That's the same man!' cried Gieles enthusiastically. 'Super Waling knows everything about pumping stations. I went with him to ...'

'Super Waling? What kind of idiotic name is that,' she interrupted with contempt. 'That fat guy can't possibly be *my* Waling.'

'I'm almost sure it's him.' Gieles never contradicted her but somehow he felt offended.

Dolly looked at her watch and ran upstairs.

Jonas was still chewing on the plastic toy and breathing with a raspy sound. His brothers were colouring in the snowman.

It irritated Gieles. 'Go make something else,' he said, taking the drawings away. They looked at him in bewilderment. 'It's not nice to draw people like that.'

'But he really *was* that fat!' cried Skiq.

'Go make some paper airplanes.'

'We're not allowed,' said Onno. 'Mom hates planes.'

Angry, Skiq left the table and began kicking the couch rhythmically.

Jonas slid off Gieles's lap and hit the chair with the squirrel.

Dolly came downstairs, her cheeks flushed. She handed Gieles a class picture that had been taken on a school playground. Gieles spotted him immediately, standing among all the girls with their earrings and square-shouldered jackets. He was wearing a black leather jacket and a white shirt. His face was tanned, his body thin. In no way did the Waling in the photo resemble the Super Waling of today, but his eyes betrayed him.

'There, you see? I was right,' she said, bending over Gieles.

Once again that intoxicating smell.

She ran her forefinger over the photo. 'What he taught were life-lessons, really. Waling had a gift for making us feel unique. Making us feel that we mattered. He actually *saw* you. He could listen to you as if you were the only person on earth who mattered.'

She stood up with a grim look on her face. 'That tub of lard could never be my teacher, not in a thousand years.'

She kissed her children on the tops of their heads. 'Be good and clean your plates.'

Then Dolly put on her jacket and turned to Gieles. 'There's a pan of pasta ready to eat. All you have to do is warm it up. I'll be back by nine o'clock.'

The boys were remarkably peaceful. They obediently ate their pasta with tomato sauce, did a little moonwalking through the living room and went to bed without screaming.

Gieles tried to do his homework but he wasn't able to concentrate. The photo of Super Waling as a handsome history teacher was lying on the table.

He put the photo in his assignment book and looked at Skiq's drawing. He had drawn two circles on top of each other with tiny little legs and hands sticking out. He had also drawn a tiny little weenie on the lower circle.

BEEN BAG MAN it said underneath. Gieles crumpled up the drawing and threw it away. Then he trudged up the stairs and laid down on Dolly's unmade bed, trying to focus on the airplane engines in an effort to keep his head from churning.

He looked at the wedding picture and suddenly remembered that Dolly's husband had died right where he was lying now. With a knot in his stomach he stood up, went downstairs and turned on the TV.

Dolly was home by nine-thirty. She always came home later than she said she would. Gieles had fallen asleep on the couch. She smiled. 'You look like a hippie with that crazy hair,' she said. 'You need a haircut. Come here.' She gently pushed him onto a chair. He sat there in a daze while Dolly rummaged around in the kitchen. She came back with a cape that she tied around his neck, and she dampened his hair with a plant sprayer. It smelled like cleanser. Then she ran a comb over his head. She did it quickly, as if she were afraid that one of the boys would wake up.

She started cutting. One wet lock landed on his cheek. She brushed it away and he closed his eyes. The cleanser smell had disappeared. Now what he smelled was Dolly. He wondered how Gravitation smelled. Smell was important, very important. Smell and eyes. If someone had ugly eyes their whole face was worthless, no matter how beautiful it was. Once she had written to him that she wasn't supposed to wash the dreadlocks with shampoo. Maybe a bit of soap at the most.

'Dreadlocks,' Gieles began, but he didn't know exactly what he wanted to ask. 'Have you ever ...'

Dolly stopped cutting, as if the word had frightened her. She made a disapproving face. 'Oh, no. No way. It's hair abuse.'

'Oh.'

'No. Making dreadlocks is the last thing I'd do. You end up with one big dry snarl.'

'Ow!' It felt as if she had cut through his ear.

'Sorry.' She inspected the damage. 'Still in one piece,'

she said, ruffling his hair a bit with her fingers. 'For little black kids, dreadlocks are fine. They have the right kind of hair. The structure of kinky hair is coarse. But you,' she said with a laugh, 'you have thin hair. Crazy, wiry, thin hair. But it's way better than those impossible heads of hair the boys have. Evert's hair was like that.'

She stopped talking and kept on cutting. The scissors made angry little clips.

Clip clip clip.

Gieles could hardly remember Dolly's late husband, although he hadn't been dead more than a year. He was always doing something. And at the street barbecue he usually spent all his time silently grilling meat.

'Evert's hair was always horrible.'

Clip clip clip.

'The only time I ever got his hair to look good was when he was dead.'

Clip clip.

'Ridiculous. It was a closed coffin. Not a single person saw it.'

Clip.

Gieles didn't know what he was supposed to say. As soon as adults starting talking about things like that his head got all foggy. He concentrated on the airplanes taking off. First he heard a high peep, accompanied by a low drone. As soon as the plane passed Dolly's house at full speed and started ascending, the sound switched to a wave that smashed against the asphalt with a roar.

'The day before Evert died, he told me I had to buy glue and toilet paper. For one whole month I bought a tube of glue and a package of toilet paper every single day.'

Clip clip.

'I just couldn't get it out of my head. At a certain point I made up a shopping list of things that I *shouldn't* buy. *No* glue. *No* toilet paper.'

She laughed. She laughed in a way that Gieles didn't recognise. Usually her laugh was abrupt, but this sounded kind.

'Even when I cut it, those spikes of yours keep sticking up.'

'Sorry,' said Gieles.

'Crazy kid. If my little monsters are just like you in a couple of years, I'll know I've been a successful parent.'

She stood in front of him and bent over, checking the length of his hair at the ears. Her red lipstick was faded. Blue eye shadow had gathered in the folds of her eyelids. Gravitation wore black lipstick. It looked like a hole had been shot in her face. He wondered whether he dared to kiss the hole. He didn't know much about her. He had no idea where she lived. Her parents grew strawberries. She hated her parents, school and strawberries, but he didn't know much more than that.

Clip clip.

'Were the boys good about going to bed?'

'Yeah. No problem.'

'They're always good about going to bed when you're here. When it's me, it's one big battle.'

Dolly took a small razor out of a leather case that was lying on the table.

'Head down.' The razor made scraping movements on his neck. 'The days go pretty well. And just when I think we've made it through the day in one piece, something goes wrong.'

Gieles swallowed. The scraping made a creepy sound.

'Then one of them lets a glass slip out of his paw, or they hurt each other ... At a certain point I just explode ... and then I see they're scared of me ... and the whole day, which was going pretty well, ends up hopeless again ... I mean ... I always go to bed feeling rotten.'

He squeezed his eyes shut and hoped that Dolly would keep paying attention to what she was doing.

'Then I get so goddamned angry at Evert. He can't ruin anything any more. He'll always be their hero. Their big dead hero.'

She unbuttoned the cape and blew away the little hairs from his neck.

'Do this.' She shook her head. Her black hair whipped up and down. Gieles did the same.

'Looking good again,' she said absently, staring pensively at the floor. Gieles also looked at the floor, which was strewn with an alarmingly large amount of hair. Worried, he ran his hand over his head. Not so bad.

'Gieles?' She rubbed her dark pants with her hands and leaned against the cabinet so heavily that Gieles thought she wanted to push in the door. 'Are you ever afraid of me?'

'Afraid?' repeated Gieles. He brought his hands down slowly and once again felt the anxiety he had felt when he came here to babysit for the first time a few months ago. The front door had been open and he had walked in. He could hear Dolly ranting in the bathroom. 'Fucking little brat! Look what you've done!' And then he heard a hard smack. Gieles had slinked out and rung the doorbell. One hour later you could still see the impression of Dolly's hand on Skiq's cheek.

'No, not at all,' he answered. 'Never.' And he saw that Dolly knew he wasn't telling the truth.

12

Gieles had invested heavily in speculaas. He had laid in twenty packs (there were no more on the shelves), but this would keep him going for the time being. Chuckling to himself, he put two packs in his backpack and stashed the rest under his bed.

That evening he sat in the kitchen and ate a sandwich for supper while the little goose drank water from the tap. She held her bill half open. A couple of time she stuck her head blissfully under the running water. Gieles had the place all to himself. Uncle Fred had gone to the Dutch poetry book club meeting. His father had his hands full with a flock of starlings. He had driven them away less than a week ago but they had returned in full force. Now the flock had grown to fifty thousand starlings and had taken up residence south of the airport. They flew around like an amoeba, moving back and forth as if they were all forming one gigantic bird. Gieles knew his father secretly enjoyed watching their air ballet.

He walked outside and set the little goose down in the grass near her ever-expanding sister. His father's fireworks could be heard in the distance. He counted five explosions, six. He didn't see any starlings though. Except for the airplanes the sky was empty.

Then from across the field came the old man: Johan, the crash freak. They had landed their spaceship back in the campground that morning. Gieles had no interest in chatting, but he didn't want to seem impolite. He wondered why the man didn't walk with a cane; he was in much worse shape than Uncle Fred.

'Good evening, sir. How you doing?'

'Johan,' he said, placing a withered hand on his body-warmer. 'My name is Johan. Could be better. I fell out of the Airstream this afternoon. Down the steps. My leg is stiff.'

Gieles looked at his legs. He noticed that the man was wearing his pyjama pants. They were wide and sporty. They might have been skate pants.

'What a drag,' said Gieles, wondering where Tufted and Bufted were keeping themselves. He wanted to do some training. Last night he had received an e-mail from his mother. It was the most depressing mail she'd ever written him. Gieles was convinced that if his mother spent much more time with the solar ovens there wouldn't be anything left of her.

He heard new explosions from not too far away.

'I have some buddies,' said Johan, peering up into the sky, 'who get thrown completely off kilter when they hear fireworks. Even a fireworks show reminds them of the war. Personally it doesn't bother me.'

Gieles saw the old man's wife gesturing behind him. She was wearing an apron and standing at the edge of the field, and she was shouting something that sounded like 'supper.'

'I have good memories of the war for the most part. I used to bike past the Germans as a young fellow and ...'

'Your wife,' Gieles interrupted, pointing over his shoulder. 'She's calling you for supper.'

He turned around slowly. 'Aha. The call of the little woman.'

He was about to set off on the return journey, his stiff legs in the flapping pyjama pants, when he turned to

Gieles. 'Before I forget, Gerard,' he said confidentially, almost pushing his nose into Gieles's. 'I brought my scrapbook. Of the plane crashes. You have to come see them.'

'I will.'

'Tonight?'

'Can't make it tonight.'

'Tomorrow? Come tomorrow,' he said urgently.

'I think that'll work,' said Gieles to get Johan out of his hair, and he took off.

He found the geese near the barn. Armed with the bamboo stick, a broom and a vuvuzela, he started off. This time he was going to try a few new things. He used the bamboo stick to direct the geese to the road.

A new series of firework explosions followed. His father was really letting loose. He had also recently let loose on the phone with Gieles's mother. He had hurled the word 'irresponsible' through his mobile phone at least five times during his call to Somalia. Gieles didn't want to listen and had run outside. He didn't want to think about it any more either, so he concentrated on the tall grass and the wagging goose tails.

Gieles dealt with his sombre thoughts about their fight by picturing them as a flock of starlings being shot to bits by his father. It worked. By the time he got to the shed his head was as empty as the pack of speculaas whose contents he had scattered across the concrete floor. The geese attacked immediately.

'Stay,' commanded Gieles while walking backwards. 'Stay.'

The geese stayed, even when he reached the end of the shed about seventy metres further on. They only had eyes for the goodies.

'Stay!' His voice resounded beautifully throughout

the interior. He had solved the problem of making them stay in one place in a way that was surprisingly simple: with a mountain of cookies.

The next phase in the schedule was to get the geese to fly to him on command. Gieles tried this by wildly waving the broom around.

No reaction.

He blew on the vuvuzela like a madman, but this, too, failed to excite them. Then he spread his arms and ran up to them, trying to imitate the sound of an airplane. 'Roahhh!'

The geese didn't even look up.

Maybe it was asking too much to get them to master two commands in one session. Maybe he would just have to be happy with what he had accomplished and try the vuvuzela again tomorrow.

On the way back the geese showed no interest in eating grass. They were stuffed full. Their stomachs were sticky brown blobs. He couldn't let them get too fat, of course, or they'd end up struggling with the mysterious Syndrome X. If that happened he'd never get them into the air. He'd have to be judicious in handing out the cookies. Discipline. Regularity. Things Captain Sully felt very strongly about.

It was just eight-thirty. Gieles could try Gravitation. A couple of days earlier she had been in the depths of despair. Her rabbit had died of myxomatosis. Gieles knew how terrible myxomatosis rabbits looked. His father had once picked up such an animal from the runway. Its head and backside were swollen like overripe plums.

His stomach tingled. She was online.

Gravitation wrote: 'I'm in deep mourning. If I could choose between my rabbit or my parents, I'd take my rabbit.'

Captain Sully: 'If you want, you can have one of my geese. You know, the one that eats like a vacuum cleaner. Everything gets sucked in. You can also use her as a paper shredder.'

Gravitation: 'Fuck off. My parents are nagging me to pick strawberries. They say I don't do shit. Do you know how awful strawberries are? With the fucking sun and the fucking hornets. I only want to do useful things. In an orphanage. Or work with sick elephants. What your mother does in Africa with those ovens sounds cool. Can I help her? I've been suspended and I really can't go back to school. NFW! My parents can go fuck themselves.'

Captain Sully: 'Picking strawberries may not be so bad. I really don't think helping my mother in Africa is a good idea!'

Gravitation: 'That's for me to decide. I'm going to Africa.'

After hesitating for a moment, Gieles decided to send his mother's last gruesome mail to Gravitation. If it were up to him, nobody he knew would ever go to help the Africans.

Sunshine,

I've totally lost my way here in Somalia. What a dramatic country. They're barbarians, cruel barbarians with mobile phones. One guide showed me a recording on his mobile phone of something his cousin from Kismayo had seen. Kismayo is a dangerous seaport in the southern part of the country.

I saw a young girl buried up to her neck. It was as if they had put her head on the centre spot for a soccer game. I couldn't see her face very clearly, any more than I could hear her. There was too much noise. On the bleachers there were hundreds of men screaming themselves into a frenzy. Near the girl was a pile of stones, easily enough to build a house. Next to that was a small group of men. There were also soldiers there, fully armed (as if the child could still get away). After a while the barbarians began to throw. Some of the stones were bigger than her head. When the girl's face was completely obliterated by blood, she was pulled up out of the hole by the hair. One guy, who was supposed to pass for a doctor, announced that she was still alive. They put her back in the hole and picked up more stones.

The guide said that the girl was thirteen years old. She was guilty of adultery: she had been raped by three men. Justice had been done, said the guide. I wanted to tear him apart, but I swallowed my anger. So I imploded, and it felt as if something inside me had been damaged. I just don't know what.

I'm forcing myself to drive away those horrible images by remembering you on your seventh birthday. We had buried you in the sand on the beach. You were lying with your head on a pillow of sand and you were laughing yourself silly. When Daddy made breasts on you with shells for nipples, you got mad and came bursting out of the sand. Sunshine, how I wish I had had that day stored in my phone.

To make matters worse, last night a shipment of stoves was stolen from the jeep. But what am I talking about?

Love, Ellen

Captain Sully: 'Are you still there?'

He waited another five minutes and repeated his question, but Gravitation had stopped responding. Gieles immediately regretted forwarding the mail. He was in such agony that he wasn't even aware of Tony suddenly appearing into his room. Gieles was badly startled but tried not to let on. He assumed Tony wanted to know who the fat guy was he saw him with out in the yard, standing at the table tennis table. But Tony didn't say a thing about Super Waling. He looked very excited.

'You got to come with me!' he shouted. His cheeks were crimson, but that could have been the acne. 'This you've got to see!'

It was almost nine-thirty in the evening and still light out. It never got dark around the runway. Gieles shrugged his shoulders. 'I've got homework,' he said, turning in his desk chair. 'A report.'

'Jesus, man, it sure is ripe in here!' said Tony, wrinkling up his ugly nose.

The smell of goose shit was still lingering in his room.

'You'll be sorry for the rest of your life if you don't come with me. This is a trillion times better than Becky Boobs.'

'Oh, all right.' No one was home yet anyway.

Tony led the way. He was in a hurry. On the back of his shirt was the company logo of his father's butcher shop: a happy cow. He was sure Tony was going to humiliate him with Super Waling.

'Come on!' said Tony, quickening his pace. Further on in the woods a black Fiat was parked. Nothing strange about that.

'Now duck down.' Together they crawled through the bushes. Gieles thought of the activists he'd played hide-and-seek with. They approached the side of the car. Suddenly the car began to shake. Tony lay flat on the ground and crept the rest of the way up to the car door. He motioned for Gieles to come closer and Gieles followed his example, with difficulty. They were lying side by side in the sand. Coming from the car was the sound of groaning.

'They're screwing.' Tony rocked his hips rhythmically against the ground.

'I know that,' Gieles whispered back. 'What's happening now?' he asked, trying to sound as bored as possible. He had broken out in a sweat.

'She's naked.' Tony looked blissful and sat hunkered down on all fours. Very carefully he held his cell phone up to the car window and took a picture.

Gieles gave him a jab. 'Cut it out,' he whispered.

Tony put the phone back in his back pants pocket and rose slowly till he could get a look inside.

'They'll see you!' Gieles tugged frantically on Tony's pants. He had never seen a naked woman before in the flesh, except for his mother. Naked on the internet didn't count.

Tony grabbed Gieles by the arm and pulled him up. First he saw the steering wheel, then two buttocks being firmly held by a pair of man's hands. The hands kneaded the buttocks and pushed them in every direction.

Gieles cautiously looked to the right and saw a pair of wobbling breasts.

They were the most beautiful breasts in the universe. He couldn't tell whose they were; the back of the seat was in the way. The hand grabbed one breast and squeezed it. Gieles's head was pounding.

'Shit!' panted Tony. 'I'm gonna come.' He made a wild grab for the stiff fabric of his jeans, leaning against the car door with his other hand. Suddenly the woman appeared at the window. She was flushed, her short hair sticking out in every direction. She looked as if she had been taken by surprise.

Gieles and Tony shot up and starting running. They hid behind the bushes. After a couple of minutes the Fiat lurched out of the woods. Waving his cell phone over his head, Tony began bellowing, 'Filthy letches! We took your picture!'

Tony looked at the display with satisfaction and shoved the thing under Gieles's nose. All he could see was a piece of buttock and three fingers, and the passenger's seat with clothes hanging on it.

'I can't see a fucking thing.'

'No, but it's enough for me to jack off to,' said Tony with a sneer. 'My dick is killing me,' he said, sticking his hand down his pants. 'I was just about to come.'

Gieles turned around. He didn't want to see Tony standing there showing off with his cock in his hand.

'Ahhh,' he groaned. 'My dick is on fire.'

'As long as you leave it alone,' said Gieles, walking away.

'I'll do it behind a tree.'

'Have fun!' shouted Gieles.

'Jesus, you're the life of the party! I give you a chance to see tits for the first time in your life and you take off!'

Gieles kicked at a branch, stopped for a moment and sat down reluctantly on a log.

'You know what I don't get?' asked Tony, sitting down beside him and pulling a crumpled joint out of a pack of cigarettes. 'That somebody would get it on with a babe like that in a rinky-dink Fiat. Man, I'd show up with a Porsche Panamera at the very least.'

'Or a Maserati,' said Gieles.

'Nah. Then you got your ass glued to the window. There's no room to fuck.' He offered him a drag. Gieles shook his head.

'I know. A Hummer Superstretch Limousine,' murmured Tony. 'That thing is at least twelve metres long. My uncle rented one when he got married. Unbelievably awesome. The night sky painted on the ceiling so you can have your own laser show. Thousand watt audio. LCD screens everywhere. Seats a kilometre wide. If I ever had the chance to screw somebody, my friend, it would be in a Superstretch. Easy and Superstretch.'

'And you always said you've done it before.' Gieles gave him a thump on his upper arm. He'd rather do it in a box bed than in a limousine. In a box bed with Sophia Warrens, spreading her breasts in his face like butter. And after that with Gravitation. Or both of them together.

Tony laughed a little sheepishly and took a toke. 'That guy was at it for a while. I must have been watching for ten minutes before I went to get you. And then all that time in the same position … I can fuck for at least half an hour before I come.'

Gieles burst out laughing and pulled the joint from Tony's hand. He inhaled and coughed. 'You don't even know where to stick it in.'

'If her cunt's wet enough I can go for hours. But I have to be on top. Fags lie on the bottom.'

'I once saw a couple of those activists fucking in a hammock,' said Gieles. 'But I didn't know it at the time. I thought they were pumping something up.'

'Oh, those guys,' sighed Tony, stretching out on the tree trunk. 'They had some really hot babes. Did you know that if a girl bites her lower lip it means she wants to give you a blow job? Really. And if she has dilated pupils it means she wants to fuck.'

'No, man, it just means she's stoned out of her mind,' Gieles giggled, inhaling deeply.

'*Gimmie offoo.*'

'Huh?'

'That's Antillean. Learned it from Flippertong. Gimme a drag.'

Gieles coughed and laughed at the same time and fell over backward. Only his lower legs were hanging over trunk of the felled oak tree.

'Flippertong! That's not a name! That's what you call a dolphin.'

'You know who's a mega juicy babe? Raven Alexis.'

'Is she in your class?'

'Christ, man! What planet are you from? Raven Alexis! She plays in *Lesbian Seductions*. She's a porn star and a hardcore WoW gamer. She's at the highest level.'

'WoW?'

'World of Warcraft. You really don't know anything.'

'Fuck off.'

Tony stuck his hand down his pants with a snicker. 'Did you know that your dick can break?'

'Then you're the only one in the whole world with a bone in your cock,' said Gieles, smoking the joint until his thumb and forefinger burned.

'Seriously. There are these balloons in your cock, and when you get a hard-on they fill up with blood. If you fuck really hard or you fuck at an angle, one of the balloons can pop. Pang! And that's what you hear. Pang!'

'Fucking at an angle?' He realised that this was the friend he had been missing. This was the Tony from before the zits and the souped-up motorbikes.

'You really don't know shit. That's like when a chick lies on her side with one leg raised and you sit between her legs on your knees, and you like hold the one leg that's sticking up in the air ... while her other leg is clamped between your legs ... then your dick is in her ... at an angle ... a kind of ninety degrees Celsius.'

Gieles began shrieking with laughter. 'Celsius! Do you

hear what you're saying? Celsius!'

'Yeaaaah,' hooted Tony, oblivious to everything. 'And if you hear pang! pang! pang! then all three of your balloons are busted. Then you have a serious swinging dick. Ahhh, fuck, this makes my balls hurt ...'

Gieles languidly tucked his hands behind his head. Twigs were tickling his back. A heavy cargo jet took off a few hundred metres away, making the ground tremble. For a moment he was afraid the earth would crack open and he'd be gone for good.

'Ratatatata! We're in the line of fire!' shouted Tony, rolling off the log. His voice sounded very close, as if his mouth were inside Gieles's ear.

'Shit! Shit! They're coming ... The aliens! Take cover! Woo-haaaa! I see a UFO ... Fuck, man, my little sister was watching ET today. That's a film from the year zero. And my mother was bawling her eyes out over that little brown toad! Who died ... "ET phone home" ... Stick your finger out ...'

Tony stuck out his finger and brought it up to Gieles's face. 'Fuck off. I know this one.'

'No, man, I'm not gonna fart ... noho, or burp ... Come on ... ET phone home ... you know that little troll has a flashlight in his finger ... I swear to God, a flashlight!' Tony snorted like a horse. 'You remember that guy, the squatter? That guy next door to us, with the Indian braid ... I once made a bomb with him. A paint bomb. He pulled the insides out of a flashlight ... Or no, it was a light bulb, an ordinary round bulb ... and he put paint in it. He let me seal the top with candle wax.'

'I didn't know that,' said Gieles with surprise.

'No, man, you were really chickenshit. You wouldn't even go near those paint balloons.'

Tony began talking with a weird high little voice.

'We're not gonna smash any windows, are we? Oh, Toooony, we're not gonna smash any windows, are we?'

'I wasn't scared at all!' shouted Gieles.

'And then those golf balls.' Tony lit a new joint. He always bought pre-rolled ones. 'They really went flying.'

'How did you get those balls anyway? Your father doesn't play golf?' Gieles didn't know anyone in the neighbourhood who played golf.

'Oooh, and your dad! When your dad tore up to the runway in his stupid little dinky toy and stared up at your attic window. Fuck, we were shitting bricks.'

'The pilot thought a nest full of eggs had fallen out of the sky,' Gieles roared.

Tony hawked up a big wad of phlegm and took a deep breath.

'You have to know when to attack,' he said then. 'That's the key to a PVP encounter.'

'What are you yapping about?' Gieles wiped the tears from the corners of his eyes.

'I'm talking about World of Warcraft, pinhead. PVP is Player versus Player. But you've also got PVE: Player versus Environment. And RP and RP-PVP or whatever ... Hey, want me to text you that big ass?' Tony yawned.

Gieles peered into the sky and searched for a star, to no avail. There was too much light and too little night. He could no longer hear the rockets his father used to drive the starlings away.

Suddenly he thought of the Somalian girl with her head on the centre spot. He gave her head a hard kick, which appeared to be separate from her torso. It rolled through the sand, and every time her face came up it changed: first he saw his mother, then Gravitation and then Sophia. On and on it went until the head turned into his little goose. He had to go home. She'd be waiting for him at the door. She was so sweet, so tiny. God forbid a fox had gotten her.

'Hey, I'm asking you something.' Tony sat up straight.

'What?'

'If you want that fat ass?'

Was he starting in on Super Waling?

'What ass?'

'From the Fiat, of course!'

Gieles opened his eyes again. 'My mother saw how they stoned this girl. They chucked boulders at her head.'

Tony lit a cigarette. 'Brutal,' he said, releasing a thunderous burp. 'What's she doing there anyway? There's fucking nothing to do in Kenya.'

'She's in Somalia. She's making sacrifices.'

'What?'

Gieles's eyes felt so heavy he could hardly keep them open. He saw himself clinging to his mother and crying. It was the day after his tenth birthday and she was going to Uganda for three weeks. Her first trip with the collapsible stoves. She had explained that you had to make sacrifices in life to accomplish something. Gieles had no idea how he was supposed to say goodbye to her.

'My mother is making sacrifices,' he repeated. 'She has a mission.'

'Big hairy deal,' said Tony. 'My mother has breast cancer. Her whole tit has to come off.'

13

Late the next morning Gieles was awakened by an inspiration. He was going to make sacrifices. Tony's mother might die of cancer, and his own mother might die of Africa, so it was time he sacrificed something, too. He looked around his room. The gosling was drinking water from a dish. He loved that little thing. She was way more than he could sacrifice. Not on your life.

His old toys behind the partition? Lego, puzzles, games, books. Countless stuffed animals from every corner of the world that he hated with intensity. Every flight produced a giraffe or a moose. Gieles even got a stuffed cockroach once. Each cuddly creature was a symbol of her absence.

An audio signal came from the laptop. He looked at the screen. E-mail from Super Waling. 'Subject: Part III of Ide & Sophia. Read only if you feel like it!'

He printed out the story and continued his search for a suitable sacrifice.

The Rizla bird albums! His most precious collection, given to him by his father. He would tear up a couple of pages—no, burn them. Burning was more dramatic. He would call his sacrifice the Bird Burning. Gieles took an album out of the closet: *Exotic Aviary Birds*. Three pages for Liedje's sick tit. Three especially beautiful pages for the best results. After thumbing through the album he decided to destroy the tri-colour tanager, the indigo bunting and the saffron finch.

He ran downstairs with the little goose hidden under his shirt, checked to see if the coast was clear and put her outside. Then he took the matches from the kitchen drawer and ran back upstairs. With pain in his heart he tore the pages out of his album. He flung open the attic window, put the papers in his bedroom sink and set them alight. The thin yellowed pages caught fire immediately, producing black embers that fluttered in the sink. He sacrificed a fourth page: the red-billed leiothrix. And in exchange, Gravitation would have to get back in touch with him.

He wiped the sink clean and threw the embers in the wastebasket. His room was blue with smoke. He felt high, but that may have been the grass. Tony smoked heavy shit, at least that's what he said.

He logged in to see if there were any signs of life from Gravitation and gave himself a good talking to. You can't expect immediate results. Sacrifices don't work that way.

Back in the kitchen, Gieles put a bottle of cola to his lips and watched his uncle come trailing in with a bucket and his crutch. He opened the door for him and took the bucket out of his hand. Uncle Fred dragged himself to the counter. He washed his hands and face. 'There. That's better.' He took a deep breath. 'Smells like smoke in here. Cigarette smoke.'

'I don't smell anything,' said Gieles.

'Do you ever smoke?' Uncle Fred asked, drying his face with a tea towel.

'I saw Tony last night,' said Gieles, who pretended he hadn't heard the question. 'His mother has breast cancer.'

'Liedje Keijzer?' Uncle Fred appeared stunned. 'How terrible.'

He looked down at his hands, which were purple from picking cherries, and then back at Gieles.

'How's she doing?'

Gieles shrugged his shoulders. 'I don't know.' He was silent about the possible amputation and the story Tony told him, that they make pig feed from amputated breasts. It sounded plausible out in the woods, but now Gieles didn't believe a word of it.

'Poor Liedje. Poor children. The youngest one in particular is going to have a hard time understanding this.'

Gieles didn't understand it either: how someone with a cheery name like Liedje—little song—could get cancer.

'I'll call her,' said Uncle Fred, and he began washing his hands again. He scrubbed them roughly with a brush, as if the cancer were clinging to his finger.

Gieles went out to the farmyard and over to the table tennis table. He didn't want to think about gloomy things. The little goose came toddling up to him in high spirits. Her dependence on him melted his heart.

He put the goose on the table tennis table. She hadn't grown much in the weeks she had been living with him. She was the size of a teapot, while her sister had grown as big as a roasting pan. Yet she had surprising strength in her bill and she was smarter than the other geese. Gieles had put a wide plank on sawhorses and shoved it up against the table, and had run a clothesline across the width of it to keep her off her half. Miraculously she understood that she had to stay behind the clothesline. After three training sessions she had already mastered the basic strokes. She was able to shove and block the ball with her bill with amazing precision. Forehand and backhand were the same thing for her. After each stroke she produced an excited quack that sounded like the noise of a paper whistle at a children's party.

Today he was going to teach her to serve. She had to toss the ball up a little higher each time and then swing her neck and smack it with the side of her bill.

Gieles placed the ball on top of her bill and tapped it underneath. Irritated, she snapped at his finger. The ball bounced onto the plank. He tried it again but she snapped at him even more fiercely. Offended, she sat down with her backside towards him. In one second she was asleep.

Gieles lifted the little goose gently and put her down in the shadow of a tree. It was warm and the air was still. Jet fuel vapours stung his nose and eyes.

If he were to let the little goose take part in the rescue training she'd pick up the commands immediately. But she was still too young to fly. Even more importantly: he didn't want to expose her to any danger.

Gieles gazed across the pasture. He saw the elderly couple sitting under an umbrella on the bank of the canal. Their white heads were bent forward, motionless. Gieles avoided them. He was in no mood to look at scrapbooks of plane crashes. Suddenly he saw movement under the umbrella. Johan raised the binoculars to his eyes and looked in Gieles's direction.

Gieles slipped into the house and flopped down on the English rose couch next to his uncle, who was pitting cherries and watching an old Indiana Jones movie. Uncle Fred was as adept at pitting cherries as he was at determining the sex of chicks. It was more or less the same technique. He squeezed the pit out in one smooth motion.

'*Temple of Doom?*' Gieles asked.

'*The Last Crusade.*' Uncle Fred collected all the films Harrison Ford played in.

Together they watched Indiana Jones and his father,

Dr Henry Jones, fly over the forests in a rickety little plane. They were being chased through the air by Nazis. The bullets flew around Indiana Jones and his dad like a storm of hail.

Gieles picked up a handful of cherries and swallowed them, pit and all.

'You know, your father looks more and more like Harrison Ford every day.'

Indy and his dad crashed the plane and emerged without a scratch. The wild chase continued by car. They fled into a tunnel and a Nazi followed them in a plane with broken wings, which exploded. Dr Henry, scared stiff, held on tight to his suitcase and an umbrella.

'I tried to call the Keijzer family,' said Uncle Fred. 'But they weren't there.'

A bomb exploded right next to the car and now they had to continue on foot. They ran down a hill in the direction of the beach. Once they reached the sea they could go no further. The Nazis couldn't wish for an easier target. Indiana and Dr Henry Jones looked up at the fighter plane that was headed straight for them, ready to fire.

'Poor Liedje.' Uncle Fred shook his head sadly.

Reflected in the glasses of the petrified father was the image of the approaching Nazi. All was lost. They were goners! But suddenly Jones Senior pulled his umbrella out of the handle of his suitcase like a sword from its hilt and flapped it open. The seagulls on the beach were so startled by the umbrella that they flew up in a massive cloud.

'A woman from the book club had cancer, too, but now she's completely cured.'

Incredible!

The fighter plane disappeared into the flock of birds.

Seagulls pounded against the window of the cockpit and the Nazi came crashing down.

That was the answer! He would chase the geese off the runway with an umbrella, just like Indiana Jones's dad. But in the right direction. *His* direction. Not in the direction of the pilot.

He jumped up from the couch. He had to revise his *Expert Rescue Operation 3032*.

'Deliver those pots of jam, would you?' asked Uncle Fred, shoving his reading glasses up his nose with a purple finger.

'What do you mean?'

'To Liedje. They're in the kitchen, with a note attached.'

'I really don't feel like it,' said Gieles. 'Somebody will be home later on.'

'I just called. They're not there. Please, Gieles. If I went it would take me forever.'

Indiana Jones looked at his father full of admiration. The old man had saved their lives. With a fucking umbrella.

'Okay,' he said sulkily. 'I'll bring them.'

'We're here when you need us,' it said on the card that went with the jam. 'Take care and be strong. Willem, Gieles, Fred and Ellen.'

Gieles thought it was strange to see her name on the card. His mother wasn't there for Liedje at all.

He'd take the pots of jam over first to avoid running into Liedje. Then he'd do some training with an umbrella. He could throw the vuvuzela away. His geese didn't even hear the noise it made.

No one was at home but the back door was open. Gieles put the jam on the table. The dog was lying in the mint green basket. Lady. Gieles didn't know any animal as lethargic as she was.

Suddenly he heard a loud noise from the living room. Gieles knew right away what it was. It was the glass doors of the display cabinet being pushed closed.

'Now don't start thinking I've lost my marbles,' he heard Tony's mother say. She was making phone calls and polishing furniture, of course: her two favourite activities. 'But you know what's the worst thing about it? At night I always get undressed with the lights on and the curtains open. And then I fantasise that one of the pilots can see me. It's possible. They practically come right through my bedroom window. And honey, that gets me so excited ... But no more of that later on ... No, no. No, I'm not standing in front of the window with one boob. Not this girl. No, ma'am.'

PART III

Ide & Sophia

On the shelves of her market stall Sophia laid out carrots, legumes and potatoes. She swept the sand away with a brush and waited for her first customers. It was eight o'clock in the morning and she was already tired. She was tired all the time now.

A woman with a wicker basket was standing at the herring stall. The woman walked toward her. She smiled and inspected the potatoes for rotten spots. Beneath the broad brim of her hat Sophia saw a carefree, flawless face.

'Very nice potatoes,' she said.

'Thank you.'

'I'll take four kilos.'

She picked up the potatoes one by one and placed them on the scale.

'And two kilos of carrots.'

Sophia admired her red coral necklace. Beautiful things were rare in the life she led. She handed over the change and noticed the contrast: slender fingers with gleaming fingernails. She was ashamed of her own hands, which were full of cracks and calloused lumps. Her nails broke off faster than they grew, the only advantage being that she didn't have to scrape the dirt away.

'What a lovely necklace you're wearing,' Sophia blurted out. She couldn't keep her eyes off it. The woman thanked her for the compliment, revealing a perfect row of teeth, even and white. After the lady left and continued on her way, Sophia ran her tongue over the gap where her two front teeth once had been. She automatically held her fingers over her mouth, as if protecting herself from the punch that had knocked her teeth out. She thought of the battered Belgian with his jaw hanging loose, the drunken polder workers who kicked him so mercilessly and then turned their fists on her and Ide. What she found most loathsome were the bits of skin under her nails from the fellow she had scratched. The skin stank like dead mice. That was seventeen years ago, but the smell had not gone away.

She swallowed back a wave of nausea and straightened her shoulders. The sun was shining. She closed her eyes.

At the end of the day Ide Warrens came to pick her up. His blond hair had grown grey and thin, but he was still an imposing figure at one metre ninety. He winked at Sophia and put the empty boxes in the wagon. The last to go in were the wooden planks. The exertion caused thousands of minuscule wrinkles to appear on his face.

They rode back to the drained lake in silence. The new land. Sophia leaned her head against his upper arm and fell asleep. Ide grasped her with his right arm to keep her from falling forward. In his left hand he held the reins. Every now and then he slapped at a horsefly. Humming, he drove the wagon onto the new land. There were no roads in this wilderness. Reeds, asters and wild endive covered the lake floor, while willow branches made the passage difficult. Ide slowed the horse to a walk. He had tied little planks to the hoofs to keep the horse from sinking into the boggy earth.

The lake had been dry for five years, but Ide was too tired to take any pleasure in it. In all those years he had dug sixty kilometres. Sixty deadly kilometres. He had seen at least that many polder boys die of malaria, typhus, cholera, smallpox or exhaustion. Ide found cholera the most repugnant. One perfectly healthy fellow had fallen down beside him while they were working. He emptied out like the teat of a cow's full udder. Diarrhoea and vomit sprayed out of him. The deterioration of an entire life was compressed into a process lasting fewer than four hours.

The reclamation project had been a fight to the finish. The lake had struggled furiously against its own annihilation and in the end it had given Ide nothing in return. Not the dreamed-of silver coins and chests full of jewels. All the reclamation had left him with was a worn-out body, a dejected heart and a worthless broken clay pipe. He had found the pipe while he was digging.

'Hey, easy now,' Ide said to the horse. 'Easy now.' She had been startled by the ducks that flew up from the bushes. The wagon shook, but Sophia slept through it all.

After the reclamation work was finished they had walked over the ring dike and past the grotesque pumping stations. They were delighted to meet people who had come to admire the new land, but for Ide and Sophia it was a death march. With every step they remembered the men, women and children for whom the dike had become a makeshift grave.

In the distance Ide saw the plot of land belonging to their boss, and his sombre thoughts faded. Their life was finally going somewhere. Not in a straight line—more like twisted willow branches—but things were looking up. They still lived in a shanty, but they didn't have to share it with anyone. Even the boss lived in a shanty because the earth was still too boggy to build on.

'Are we there yet?' Sophia asked with a yawn. She had slept for an hour. She stretched and threw one arm around him.

'You stink,' she said. 'Your shirt stinks.'

'I don't stink.'

'Are we there yet? I'm hungry.'

'Almost.'

She was mystified by Ide's sense of direction. For her the new land was an unfathomable world. The only place that made any sense to her was their boss's land. He was obsessive about keeping his properties free of reeds and willows, but as soon as they turned around the vegetation shot out of the ground like stubble on a man's face.

Slowly they approached the three shanties that stood on a low rise. The boss's was the biggest, with two smaller shanties built up against it in horseshoe fashion.

She saw her vegetable garden, her pride and joy. Carrots, green beans, onions, potatoes, peas, beets and cabbages grew in abundance. She had also planted apple trees and hoped they would bear fruit soon.

The boss was in one of the small shanties, the cowshed. His back was turned to Sophia and he was shovelling shit into the wheelbarrow. He was a small man, no more than a head taller than she. Since the death of his wife and two daughters he had shrunk several centimetres. They had died of smallpox six months earlier. Since then all his joy and desire had vanished. He didn't give a damn about manners. He usually ate standing up at the stove, picking the food out of the pan with a fork. His heart kept him going but he had given up.

'The takings. Your takings,' Sophia said to the short back.

The boss turned around.

She handed him a little cloth sack, which he carelessly put in his pants pocket without counting it. She had kept back some of the money—she always did—but she didn't blush. She felt no guilt. Hadn't for a long time. Nor did she feel guilty about being grateful to have a widower as boss. Women would nag her, pester her with nasty little jobs and rub her nose in the fact of her insignificance. That's just the way women were.

'Tell Ide we're going to start in on the last parcel tomorrow.'

Even his voice seemed to have shrunk. It was a stunted little sound. A peep. It was all she could do to understand him. Sophia nodded and left the shed for her own shanty. Her legs felt heavy. She yawned and crept into the box bed.

'We have to eat,' said Ide. He was sitting in a chair at the window. 'You said you were hungry?'

'There's still soup and bread,' she murmured.

For Ide Warrens, having a window was proof that his life was going well. Now he could be seen. Someone could cast a glance through the window and observe a life being lived. A simple life, to be sure, but the light made it visible. They were no longer hidden away in a dark rat hole like vermin. To his boss he was no more than the farmhand, but he felt like a colonist, a pioneer.

He stared across the endless clay with satisfaction. He would mould that clay with his own hands and create a life worth living. The only indication of human presence now was a plume of smoke in the sky kilometres away. The silence was immense, except for Sophia's snoring. No barking dogs, howling children or jabbering men. One of his landscapes was hanging next to the window, the landscape he had drawn based on his own fantasy. Their farm was the epicentre, and around it Ide had created fields and vast cow pastures that were bordered by fruit trees. The picture was bursting with fertility. Ide could almost smell the ripe fruit. But his landscape was also a model of order and tidiness. Nowhere did he give nature the opportunity to take off on its own. He abhorred the wilderness. Under Ide's pencil all the trees and cows were looking in the same direction.

The morning had a promising beginning. A blanket of blue mist heralded the coming of the sun. Ide shovelled shit, milked the cows and loaded up the wagon. Sophia gathered eggs, fed the chickens and worked in the vegetable garden. At six-thirty they left. Sophia leaned against Ide listlessly and felt heartburn rising in her stomach. She leaned to the side and violently vomited up her breakfast.

'What's the matter with you now?' asked Ide, visibly startled. He slapped her on the back.

'How should I know?' she groaned.

He looked at her, incredulous. His strong Sophia, never sick or weak, always ravenous. It's cholera, he thought, but he didn't dare admit his fear. He looked across the land furtively, as if the source of the sickness lay hidden in the wilderness. For the rest of the journey he kept checking every few minutes for symptoms of cholera. But there was no more contracting of the muscles and intestines. Her body didn't empty out, she didn't turn blue. She kept her eyes closed and slept with her mouth open and saliva on her lower lip.

They passed the remains of a sailing ship. The wreck got smaller by the week. Wood was scarce.

After half an hour they entered the land of civilisation. Here there were roads, brick houses, churches and schools. Ide removed the little planks from under the hoofs of the horse. In the civilised world his horse wouldn't drown in the boggy mud. Sophia didn't wake up until they rode onto the market square. She set out the vegetables with a reluctance that was unusual for her. Ide followed her laborious movements. She was on the brink of collapse, or so it seemed to him. He feverishly went down the list of all the diseases that had anything in common with her behaviour, but drew a blank. All he knew was that death could announce itself with ease and lightning speed.

'Are you going to be all right?' he asked.

'Course,' she said.

He left Sophia at the stall. The boss was waiting for him. Skilfully he manoeuvred the wagon out of the small square. Could it be typhus? Don't stew, he said to himself, and he began counting swallows. There were five. Then he concentrated on the muscular flanks of the mare, with the wet stripes on her coat. She brushed the horseflies away with her dark brown tail. Ide, too, began sweating. The morning sun was already producing heat.

Malaria, or tuberculosis? Don't stew. A pair of shanties were burning on the edge of the former lake. Some of the polder folk refused to leave and the military police set their homes on fire. Or they beat them away. He knew the story of the two brothers who lived with their old mother in a shanty on a farmer's land. The brothers had drained his land and helped build a farm for him, his wife and his seven children. They had planted elms all around the farmyard that one day would serve as a windbreak to reduce wear and tear to the roof. They built stables for the six draft horses and eighty cows. When the work was finished, the farmer no longer needed the brothers. Their shabby shanty spoiled his view. He drummed up a group of men and stormed the place.

Suddenly the old mother appeared in the doorway. Ide had heard that they hardly noticed her. She was the same colour and in the same condition as the wood, grey and mouldering. Terrified, she seized one of the planks, but the men pulled her loose and kicked her outdoors, whooping as they went. The old woman fell. Her head struck a stone and she lost consciousness. When her two sons returned in the afternoon they found their mother dead and the remains of their home a crumbling heap.

'Filthy bastards,' said Ide, and looked the other way, away from the shanties that were burning like torches. But it did no good. Fear had already taken hold of him years before. Fear had sunk its teeth into his head like a tick. Was there really a God? And would that God want to punish him because Ide had created land? Would God get angry because he and all those thousands of other young men had robbed Him of His work? Would He then turn on Sophia and give her some kind of horrible disease? He just didn't know.

'Ide Warrens,' he said in a flood of panic, just to hear his own name.

'Ide Warrens! Ide Warrens!' he roared, at the land and at the sky.

Waiting for him at the farm were the boss with his plough. Sitting next to the boss was a dog he had never seen before.

'You're sweating like a pig,' peeped the boss.

Ide wiped the tears from his cheeks with his sleeve and recovered himself.

'Where did you get that dog, sir?'

The boss shrugged his shoulders. 'He was sitting at the door this morning.'

Ide couldn't get used to the sound of his voice. It was like that of a small child.

They looked at the animal as if they were sizing up a new purchase. His ribs were protruding through his dingy fur. His snout and eyes were all shrivelled up.

'When he's standing he looks pretty decent,' said the boss, and gave him a kick. The dog immediately stood up.

'He sure does,' Ide agreed. 'He's as big as a calf. Are you going to keep him? I mean, a dog like this can come in handy with all that riff-raff scrounging around the polder.'

Again he shrugged his shoulders laconically. 'I don't know. The wretched brute's got to be fed.'

The boss led the way with the horse beside him. In his hand he held a small map showing how the land had been parcelled out. Ide followed, pulling the plough. He looked back and saw that the dog was searching for a place in the shade to lie down.

The little wooden planks under the hoofs of the mare made a clattering sound. Standing beside her long muscular legs the boss looked even punier. They walked over the black parcels. Although the sun had been shining for weeks, the earth was still wet. Swarms of mosquitoes danced above the surface of the ground. Ide wondered whether wheat or rye would ever grow here.

The boss came to a halt at the edge of the ploughed ground and studied the map. A vein on his forehead swelled up and turned purple.

'I think we're somewhere around here,' he said, circling a few squares with his forefinger. 'What does it say?'

Ide leaned over and studied the well-thumbed map, which looked as if it had been dug out of the ground. He digested the text letter by letter. 'S e c t i o n s,' he mumbled slowly. Sophia had taught him to read, but it didn't come easy. 'Sections.' He had no idea what the word meant. What he saw were rectilinear compartments with numbers in each one that he had trouble making out. The boss handed him the map and gazed at the surrounding area.

Ide grew dizzy looking at the hundreds of parcels, all drawn to exactly the same size. The map was a far cry from the chaos that lay before him: stumps with branches and the cursed, never-ending wild endive as far as the eye could see. He stared back at the map and wished his own life were as well-organised as that.

'There's the pumping station,' muttered the boss, rubbing a hand over his grey stubble.

Ide screwed up his eyes and saw little bulge on the horizon. It could have been the mast of a ship or a church tower, but he didn't contradict the boss.

'If that's the pumping station ... then we must be here,' said Ide, pointing haphazardly to a square marked '27.' (Sophia had only taught him to count to sixty. 'We're not getting any older than that anyway,' she had insisted.)

'Do you have section 27?'

'It's possible,' said the boss indifferently. 'Let's get started before the bugs eat us alive.'

Ide chopped away the biggest branches and the boss tried to loosen the reeds with the plough, but to no effect.

'This is pointless,' he said. After five metres the ploughshare jammed. 'We'll have to do everything by hand first.'

Ide felt his impatience more fiercely than ever. Would this never come to an end? If they weren't able to come to grips with the land now, then it would take a hundred years for his own landscapes to become reality.

'It's not the soil,' said the boss, as if he could read Ide's mind. 'It's what you do with it. That determines whether you gain ground or lose it.'

His face showed no emotions, as usual, until his thin lips parted.

'Well, goddamn it,' he cursed. 'The horse is sinking.'

Ide looked over, and indeed the mare was sinking. She whipped her head back and forth wildly, her nostrils distended in hysteria. She tugged at her legs as if she were trying to rear up but her efforts had the opposite effect. The hoofs and ankles had already disappeared. The boss walked up to the horse.

'You'll drown in the mud, too, if you're not careful,' Ide warned.

'I don't care. All I have are two old nags.'

For a couple of seconds Ide didn't knew what to do. Then he ran up behind the boss and grasped him from behind, immobilising him. Ide's iron arms were firmly locked. The boss uttered a desperate cheep as if a little bird were imprisoned in his body. 'Warrens! Let me go, goddamn it ... let me go!'

The animal stopped stamping and whinnying and turned her head toward the voice. Her big eyes softened and she blinked at the men kindly. For a moment all was silent. Nothing moved, not even her tail and the horse-flies. Ide and the boss stared at her, motionless. The horse looked as serene as a saint, even though Ide didn't believe in saints. Suddenly she began to fight against the sucking soil once again. She pulled, lashed, wrestled, snorted and whinnied. Mud was spattered everywhere but she continued to sink, first to the shins and then to the knees, so she looked like a dwarf.

Ide released his boss. He braced himself for a dressing-down, but the boss just turned around, exhilarated. Ide had never seen him like that before. All his movements became mechanical. Fire flashed from his normally lustreless eyes. 'Warrens, lay down branches!' he shouted and ran back to the shanties.

Ide started grabbing indiscriminately at the hacked branches and throwing them at the horse. He tried to ignore her death struggle. It would be at least half an hour before the boss returned. In the meantime Ide turned on the willows as if they were demons. He threw his whole body at the branches, chopping and cursing. 'Is it never enough?' he hissed. 'Don't you ever get enough … ?' And he pulled down a willow trunk with his shoulder. 'A stupid nag … filthy fucking trees.'

His anger was greater than the pain the branches caused as they scratched his arms and face. His saturated body was totally out of control. He screamed and cried and pounded the ground until the boss appeared. The boss, too, was covered with sweat, but as soon as he saw the horse he stopped in his tracks, dismayed. He threw down the planks on the ground beside him, rope dangling from his neck. His horse was almost legless.

'It'll be all right, boss!' Ide wept, wiping away red tears. He threw a new load of branches in her direction. 'I'll get her out! I'm strong! Stronger than the mud!'

The boss looked on in silence as Ide built a bridge of branches and planks, working like a madman. Crawling across the planks on his hands and knees, he tied a rope around the mare's neck. 'It'll be all right,' he said, stroking her between the eyes. She settled down, only shaking her head every now and then to chase the horseflies away. 'Shhhhh,' panted Ide. 'It'll be all right.'

At the market, the woman with the red coral necklace and the gleaming fingernails bought three crates of potatoes. 'The house boy will have to come by this evening to pick them up. The maid is sick. Will that be a problem?'

She smiled so openly that Sophia heard herself say, 'I can bring the potatoes. If you don't live too far away, that is.'

She smiled again. 'That's very kind of you. I live nearby, out past the market.'

Sophia borrowed a wheelbarrow and asked the neighbouring vendor to watch her stall.

The woman led the way and Sophia tried to keep up with her. The fatigue and the heat were merciless. She blew a strand of hair away from her eyes and focused her attention on the woman's dress. The fabric glistened in the sun. Sophia imagined lying under such soft fabric and sleeping for months in a cool, darkened room.

The woman did indeed live nearby. It was no more than five minutes by foot, but Sophia's legs felt paralysed. Her field of vision closed in and she saw the world in fragments. Wheelbarrow, fence, garden path, back door, kitchen floor. Red and black stars.

Later on, she had no idea how long she had been unconscious. She came to in a large chair in a living room. The woman sat crouched beside her. She looked worried. 'Are you all right?'

Sophia stared at the woman's white face. Her skin was so flawless that she wanted to touch it. She looked like a porcelain cup.

'Are you ill?'

Sophia shook her head. She wondered how she had ended up in the chair. The woman didn't look very strong.

'I'll get a glass of water.'

She heard the rustle of her dress as it left the room and looked around her at the heavy furniture. In a recess in the room was a modest library. Sophia stood up carefully and walked towards it. She stroked the spines with her forefinger. She could tell at a glance that the books were in alphabetical order. She pressed her nose against the covers and closed her eyes. This was her reading ritual. First smell the pages, then read. Her father found this a strange habit, and he laughed at it heartily. She tried to conjure up his image but the contours of his face had dissolved. He had become a ghost, just like her mother. Their smell, the sound of their voices: all the memories had faded. It had been a long time since she had felt any guilt about leaving Zeeland. Her father must have carried out a search for her, but she wasn't registered anywhere. And there had been plenty of moments when she wanted to go back to her parents, but nothing ever came of them. One way or another the moment was never right or she thought she was no longer fit to be seen. She felt the holes in her mouth with her tongue.

'Ah, there you are,' said the woman. She handed her a glass.

'What a beautiful bookcase,' whispered Sophia.

'It's walnut. My husband had it brought over specially from England.'

'I mean the books—the case, too, of course—but the books ... beautiful. *Almagro* was one of my favourite books.'

'Can you read?' asked the woman in amazement, and looked at her with different eyes.

'Certainly. But not any more. *Almagro* was one of the last books I read, and that's already ... a long time ago. But I adore reading.'

'I don't read any more either. My son and daughter are still young. They demand so much attention. Your children must all be grown by now.'

It was a friendly remark without a trace of cynicism. Sophia laid odds that the woman wasn't much younger than herself, but she understood. That tender skin and her own rough body. She could easily tear the lady apart with her calloused hands.

'I have no children.' As she said this, she unconsciously placed her hands on her stomach and began to calculate. Sophia handed her the empty glass triumphantly. 'I have no children *yet.*'

The workhorse was irretrievably lost. More than a thousand kilos mired in the mud. Pulling was pointless; Ide would break her vertebrae. As long as he stroked her between the eyes, she forgot the age-old instinct that was urging her to flee and remained reasonably calm, considering the circumstances.

'She's thirsty,' said Ide, and he let her lick the salt from his hand.

The boss looked on for several minutes. Horseflies attacked her colossal back and shoulders without mercy.

'The tail is in the mud,' he said without emotion. 'Lay the branches near her so I can get good and close.'

The boss left Ide alone for a second time. She stopped sinking. She was reduced to a trunk with a neck and a head. Ide was still lying on his stomach, supporting himself on his forearms. The horse pushed her snout against him. She felt safe. There was nothing he wanted more than to stay with her, both of them bobbing on the open land. He remembered drifting out to sea in a little boat as an eight-year-old boy. The sensation that overtook him when he could no longer see the coastline was overwhelming. He wasn't afraid, although he still didn't know how to swim. After a couple of hours a fishing boat happened to spot him and picked him up. His mother was in tears, but his father shouted that Ide hadn't deserved so much of the Lord's help and beat his bottom black and blue.

He scanned the area around him. It was just like being at sea: nothing on the polder to obstruct the view. He could stare into the endless distance without really seeing anything, and it was that very endlessness that made him feel confined and afraid. Would someone please explain something to him? First Sophia sick and now the nag sinking away in the mud.

Ide shook off the panic attack and crept off the plank so he could start in on the job at hand.

'We're going to help you,' he said encouragingly, more to himself than to the horse. With great care he surrounded her with branches, making it look as if she were lying on a raft.

After three quarters of an hour the boss reappeared, this time wearing an apron. His scrawny hands grasped the wheelbarrow on which even more planks were stacked. At the bottom of the wheelbarrow were two jugs of water, a bucket and a box of tools.

'At least she doesn't have to die of thirst,' peeped the boss as he poured water into the zinc bucket. He plunged his own overheated head into the water and held it there for a few seconds, then passed the bucket to Ide.

She drank slowly as if she were sleepy. Maybe she was trying to put off the inevitable. Horses seemed to have an acute awareness that their final hour had come.

'Have you ever finished off a horse?' asked the boss, dripping with water.

Ide shook his head. 'I've slaughtered chickens and rabbits, but never a horse.'

'This won't be slaughtering,' said the boss. 'This is

going to be one big bloody mess. But we can't very well leave her behind. Warrens, lay the planks across those branches,' he ordered, picking up the box of tools.

Ide moved off the plank with the bucket and made room for the boss. With his spare body the man crawled nimbly toward the horse until he was kneeling in front of her, the box of tools between them. He picked up the hammer, and with his fingers he rubbed the triangle between her eyes and ears. The horse licked the hand he was holding the hammer with.

'That old tongue of yours won't be fit to eat any more,' said boss with a kind smile. 'Even my boots taste better than that. Well. So long, Browny. Give 'em all my best. The children will be happy to see you again ...'

Ide stared at the boss. Never before had the man shown any emotion in his presence. He didn't even know his nag had a name. The boss seemed startled himself, and he quickly took a nail out of the box. It was a hefty thing. He placed the point against her forehead. Ide began to whistle nervously and threw a plank on top of the branches.

'Hold off for a minute, Warrens!' peeped the boss when the horse looked over at him with alarm. He waited until she had settled down and her head was still, and placed the point of the nail against her pelt once more as if he were about to hang a picture.

'Okay, Browny. There you go,' he said, and drove the nail straight into the great lobe of her brain. Ide squeezed his eyes shut and heard her groan. He wanted to plunge his fingers deep into his ears as far as they would go, but the boss was calling for a bucket. Ide tossed the bucket over to him and the zinc rim hit his shoulder. 'Goddamn it,' cursed the boss, and he took a knife out of the box. He had trouble staying seated on the planks because the horse's head was twitching in every direction. Mucus ran from her quivering mouth. Her eyes were rolling in their sockets.

Half looking and half not looking, Ide watched the boss lie flat on the plank and push the bucket deep into the mud and against her chest. The dripping mouth hung heavily on the boss's back and left wet spots there. When the bucket was sunken deep enough to give him clear access to her heart, he stabbed the knife forcefully into her chest. Then he jiggled the blade a couple of times until the blood gushed out in waves.

The boss pushed the head aside and dragged himself up. 'It'll never fit in the bucket! Get the jugs! Quick!'

Ide began running back and forth frantically and gave the two jugs to the boss, who held their mouths under the flowing stream of blood. He managed to collect twelve litres at the most. The dozens of litres that remained coloured the mud red. A heavy, sweet odour filled their nostrils.

'What a waste,' said the blood-smeared boss, nodding at the red pool where the horse lay as if she were being marinated. He took a couple of swigs from the jug and pushed it under Ide's nose.

'It's still warm. We'll pour the rest on the fruit trees. It'll make the apples nice and red.'

Ide didn't want to be childish about it so he took a sip. It tasted like rust. In a reflex he turned to the horse. She looked idiotic with her tongue sticking out of her mouth and her glassy eyes almost popping out of their sockets.

The boss looked at her as well. 'Dead as a doornail,' he muttered, picking up the knife. 'I'll cut, you carry.'

They spent the rest of the day dismembering the horse. The boss tried to skin the cadaver as neatly as he could, but it was a terrible mess. Because of the impossible way the horse was lying in the mud he was only able to pull the hide off in strips, making the animal look like a half-devoured zebra. After skinning her, the boss inserted the knife right behind the ears and cut the head off along the cervical vertebrae. It was silent in the polder, except for the sound of tearing tendons. Neither the boss nor Ide said a word. They needed every bit of strength they had. Together they dragged the flayed head to the wheelbarrow, which Ide pushed back to the shanties. As he walked he carefully avoided any glimpse of his cargo.

After he was finished with the head the boss sawed off the neck, and when he had cut away the tail, anus and vulva the horse didn't look anything like a horse any more. It was a monstrous lump of whitish pink fat laid out among the branches, with tufts of hair here and there. Balancing on the planks, the boss cut up the buttocks. Ide helped, or they'd never be finished in time. He went down on his knees and cut the flesh in ragged chunks, while the sickly smell made him feel sensual. He didn't know whether it was from the smell or from chopping the meat.

After carrying away a hundred and fifty kilos of the horse's flanks, they stopped to eat bread in the shade of the shanty. Ide took a bite and looked at the boss, who had turned a reddish brown. He was hideous to behold, but then it occurred to Ide that he probably didn't look much better himself. The stray dog was lying in front of the barn with his nose pushed under the door as if he were trying to crawl underneath it. The smell of flesh and blood made the animal hungry.

Ide could tell by the way the boss was changing position and clearing his throat that it was time to go back to work. They walked past the dog, who promptly began to snarl and curl his upper lip. 'Watch out, you filthy brute,' said the boss, kicking him in the side. 'Or we'll pickle you next.' The dog cringed against the door, whining.

They walked back across the same piece of land. It had cooled down a bit. The sun was sinking in the west and a gentle breeze was blowing up. Insects from all around had smelled the blood and were buzzing feverishly above the shrunken cadaver. Ide and the boss covered their faces with handkerchiefs and pulled their caps down over their ears. Ide wanted to continue working on the hind quarters, but the boss said he was going to start in with the saw.

'If you keep cutting around the backside you'll hit the organs and it'll stink worse than ten dead pigs in a shit hole. And don't touch the gall bladder whatever you do,' said the boss, climbing up on the bare back. He looked absurd, but Ide couldn't even raise a chuckle. His sense of humour had taken quite a beating in recent years. The boss tried to saw the spinal cord loose from the ribs, but he didn't have the strength. After a few minutes he gave up, panting.

'Let me do it,' said Ide.

The boss shook his head. 'We'll never manage to avoid the entrails or any of that other mess. The meat wouldn't be worth eating. Like chewing on shit. No, we'll cut away the heart and breast meat and burn the rest.'

One hour later, while Ide was driving their last old nag to the market to pick up Sophia, he saw thick plumes of smoke rising behind the shanties. The boss had made a big fire and was burning the remains, as if he couldn't bear to leave even one hair of the horse behind on the greedy earth.

14

During the last class, Dutch, Gieles took the class picture of Dolly with Super Waling out of his assignment book. He had made a colour copy of it and had put the original back.

The picture was endlessly intriguing to him because the two hardly looked anything like themselves any more. There was none of that hardness in the face of his neighbour. A life with screaming children, a dead husband and an unsellable house was as yet unknown to her. He looked at the young Super Waling. Every time he saw this handsome, slim version of the man, Gieles was rendered speechless.

'I'll take that,' he heard the Dutch teacher say. Even before Gieles was able to stash it away, the brown hand had grabbed the photo. Mr Muntslag walked back to his desk in his noiseless shoes and sat down.

'Page thirty,' he said, and sent Gieles an encouraging nod. Whenever Mr Muntslag spoke, it sounded just like an exaggerated imitation of a Surinamese.

Gieles opened his book while keeping his eye on the teacher, who was studying the photo. His drew his kinky head closer and closer to the desk. For at least five minutes he sat like that and completely lost track of the time. Only when the room emptied out did Mr Muntslag look up at Gieles, who was standing in front of him. He tapped on the photo with his finger.

'I know him from my first school, where I worked as

janitor,' he said. 'Waling. He was a fine man. Just a boy, actually. Waling was almost as old as his students. The other teachers were jealous of him. Definitely,' he said, straightening his blue shirt. Mr Muntslag had a cheerful face. He gave you the impression that he could burst out laughing at any moment, although it rarely happened.

'Waling was very good with the children, and that made his colleagues jealous. And when Waling got a big inheritance,' he clicked his tongue, 'his colleagues were green with envy. The rumour mill was running at full tilt.'

Mr Muntslag shook his head sympathetically. 'Is one of your parents in the picture?'

'My mother,' Gieles lied. He didn't feel like going into detail.

Mr Muntslag gave him back the copy. 'Go to bed on time for once. You look pale.'

Gieles picked up his backpack and went outside. Some of the boys from his class were playing soccer in the playground. They asked if he wanted to play.

'Next time,' said Gieles, and walked over to the bike rack. He took off, pedalling fast and determined to get answers to his questions.

At the halfway point Tony caught up with him.

'Skitch?' he yelled.

'I'm going the other way,' Gieles yelled back, which was partly true. Tony pulled down the visor of his helmet and sped away.

Super Waling's mobility scooter was parked in his front yard. If he had inherited so much, why was he living in a mini-house? Or did he convert all his money into food?

Gieles hadn't even rung the bell before Super Waling

opened the door. This time he was wearing a copper brown sweatsuit even though it was twenty-two degrees outside. The suit was the same colour as his hair, which gleamed as if he had just gotten out of the barber's chair. Hanging from his shoulder was the linen bag.

'Come on in!' he shouted happily, taking the bag from his shoulder. 'Sit down! What would you like to drink? Actually I was just about to leave for the museum, but that can wait a few minutes. I'm writing a piece about the exhibition on polder boots through the centuries. You're welcome to come along, if you like.'

'I can't,' Gieles said, which was no lie. 'I have a test tomorrow and next week I have to hand in my report.'

'Ah. Exciting. Still have a lot to do?' asked Super Waling on his way to the kitchen.

'It's going pretty well. Your stories about Ide and Sophia have been really helpful.'

Gieles failed to mention that he had lifted whole passages without citing the source.

'I'm curious about how it's gonna end. Sophia isn't gonna die of some disease, is she?'

'Oh, no. Not by a long shot. As soon as I'm finished with Part Four I'll send it to you. Grape soda?'

Gieles shuffled behind him into the living room, lost in thought. How could he ask Super Waling the questions without offending him? They sat down opposite each other and sipped their drinks. Super Waling wiped the sleeve of his sweatshirt across his wet forehead. Gieles couldn't tell whether he was still wearing a bandage on his wrist. He wondered where he bought those sweatsuits. No store would ever stock his size.

Gieles took a deep breath. 'My neighbour Dolly—you know, where I babysit—she used to know you, back when you were a history teacher. Her name is Dolly de Jong.'

He looked at Super Waling's face and expected him to ... well, what *did* he expect? Gieles had no idea, but he certainly didn't expect Super Waling to keep on smiling. He did, though.

'Mmmm. Dolly. Dolly de Jong ... Is that her maiden name or her husband's name?'

Stupid. It was her husband's name, of course.

'She showed me a class picture. You were wearing a leather jacket. Black.'

Super Waling chuckled. 'Oh, yeah. That jacket. Good grief, that thing cost me a month's salary back then. I still have it. Maybe it fits you. Doesn't fit me, that's for sure. It was really soft calfskin.'

He stared wistfully at the mountain motif wallpaper as if he were watching himself wander among the mountains in his gorgeous jacket.

Then he said, 'How great that you're here. I was going to call you with a question. Next week the pumping station association has organised a fair. There will be all kinds of demonstrations of atmospheric machines—steam-driven machines that blow out steam and suck up water,' Super Waling explained, making a pumping motion with his arm. He sounded short of breath. 'We're going to do hydraulic and pneumatic compression, the kids can dress up as dike masters, there will be old Dutch games ... And I would consider it a great honour if you would put on a kind of table tennis demonstration. With your little goose. You don't have to give me an answer right now, of course,' he said hastily. 'Take your time and think about it.'

'No, I think that'd be great,' said Gieles, still brooding over the key questions about the cause of his vast size and his possible fortune.

'Fantastic!' Super Waling slapped his thigh enthusiastically. 'The visitors will really love this! You'll be doing the association a great favour.'

Gieles evaded the gaze of his sincere blue eyes, the last remains of the handsome history teacher he once was. He stared at the fluorescent paintings of the pumping stations and said, 'My teacher knows you, too. From a long time ago. Mr Muntslag.'

'You mean Clark Muntslag? The janitor?' he asked with surprise.

'No, he teaches Dutch.'

'Good old Clark,' said Super Waling. 'So he finally did it. He had his nose in the books day and night. Clark could read and sweep the floor at the same time.' He laughed out loud. 'Give him my warm regards, would you? And your neighbour Dolly, too, of course.'

Gieles began groping for tactful words. 'My neighbour didn't recognise you ... right away ... any more. She had seen you driving by ... when you left my house, and she couldn't believe ... that you ... that you were so ... so ... big ...'

Super Waling looked at him in such a way that Gieles was afraid he was going to fall apart and that even Dolly wouldn't have enough glue on hand to put him back together. His mother would like him. She would certainly like him because she'd be able to save him. It was too bad Super Waling didn't live in Africa.

'I'll tell you all about it,' he said with a calm voice. 'I'll tell you, but not now. Really. I'm not going to give you the run-around and I'm not going to tell you any tall tales. You'll get the truth, from A to Z. But some other time. Is that okay, Gieles? Can you agree to that?'

Gieles agreed. They said goodbye at the orange front door. It took forever for Super Waling to get himself seated in his mobility scooter and drive away. They were each going in a different direction. Gieles could see that people in the other development houses were spying on Super Waling from behind their curtains. Children in the street watched him as he went by. A woman with a stroller went out of her way to avoid him, as if he were leaking chemicals.

What if Super Waling had been on Captain Sully's flight 1549? What if Super Waling had had to stand on one of the wings and wait for the lifeboats? Would the plane have capsized under his weight?

Gieles biked past the main waterway and decided to hold another Bird Burning. A sacrifice of seven pages. In exchange, Super Waling would have to become less fat. But first Gieles had to wait and see whether his sacrifice for Gravitation was going to have the desired result. He still hadn't heard from her.

As he got closer to his house the sound of the planes increased.

Gieles turned into the dead-end street. From the road he could see his father chopping wood. He didn't do this often, only when things were bothering him. During the last year he had chopped more wood than ever.

Gieles wondered whether his father's mood had to do with the flock of starlings. They kept coming back, despite the rockets.

He followed the arc that the axe made through the air. With one firm blow the steel cut through the wood. Maybe his father's mood didn't have anything to do with the plague of starlings. Maybe he had found out that the little goose was sleeping in his room. Or maybe he had left something in the shower after masturbating and his father wanted to talk to him about it. Man to man. But that didn't seem likely. His father never talked about sex. His mother did. One time he had walked into their bedroom after having a nightmare. They didn't realise he was there until he asked them what they were doing. 'We're wiggling,' his mother had explained. The next morning she gave him this big lecture about boys and girls who lie on top of each other, and why they do it. She explained it all with dolls.

Gieles walked into the yard. His father turned around. There were spots under the armpits of his shirt. 'Come over here,' he said.

Shit.

Willem sat down on the chopping block. Volleys could be heard in the distance. A series of volleys. 'They're shooting them,' his father said mournfully. 'The starlings.' He looked up at the sky. Then he fidgeted awkwardly with the handle of the axe and cleared his throat. 'Meike's father called.'

'Meike?'

'Yes, Meike. From Zundert.'

Gieles looked to see if his little goose was walking around. The campground was deserted. The old couple had left with their spaceship. They had to go to the hospital for the stiff leg, the wife had said.

'I don't know any Meike from Zundert. I don't even know where that is.'

'Brabant. West Brabant, I think. It's not a big town ... In any case, she's had a tear tattooed on her face.'

'What's this all about?' he said suspiciously.

'She did it after getting your e-mail about the stoning of a girl in Somalia.'

Gieles felt the blood draining from his face.

Willem traced a line in the gravel with the head of the axe.

'Her parents were shocked by the mail your mother sent.'

Neither of them spoke, and not only because of the Boeing 747 taking off.

'How did they get our number?' asked Gieles.

Willem wasn't very good at difficult conversations.

'They e-mailed Ellen.'

He tried to imagine Gravitation's white face with a tear on it and wondered what colour it was and how big.

'But why a tear?'

'I don't know either. Her father said she's been kind of despondent lately.'

Gieles stood there feeling lost. He saw his little goose splashing around in the blue plastic kiddie pool out in the field. She loved the water. Her sister was standing next to the pool, eating grass. A new series of shots could be heard in the distance.

A nightingale began singing in Willem's pants. 'Wait a minute,' he said, and took the cell phone out of his back pocket.

'A hundred dead starlings? That wasn't what we agreed to! We said fifty!' he barked. 'No, stop immediately. I don't care what management says. They're just a bunch of self-important jerks.'

He hung up cursing and walked over to Gieles. 'Listen, son,' he said. 'I think it's terrible that Ellen sends you e-mails like this. I've told her this before, and I'm going to tell her again. You shouldn't have to think about such things at your age. When I was your age, I had an air rifle and a fishing pole and they kept me entertained all day long. Worries didn't exist.'

'I'm not a little kid any more,' said Gieles, his voice breaking.

'I know. I know.'

That night she called him. Just like that. After supper. Uncle Fred had picked up and handed him the phone. He heard the words 'Hi Gieles' very softly in his ear. She whispered that she thought he had a nice name.

'Better than Captain Sully.' She pronounced the words in a strange way.

He had trouble understanding her because of her accent. She sounded as if she had been to the dentist and her jaw was still full of novocaine. Maybe it was because of the piercing in her tongue.

'And your name is Meike,' he said, and walked outside so his father and Uncle Fred wouldn't be able to hear him.

'Yes.'

'That's not a name I expected.'

She giggled shyly, and he had to strain to understand her response. He felt her blushing against his cheek. The roles were now reversed. On the internet she had been the boss. She said something inaudible.

'What did you say?' He sat down in the mobility scooter with the little goose on his lap. Her yellow down was being replaced by little white feathers. She was having a growth spurt.

'I'm not almost seventeen,' she said.

'Oh.'

'I'm fourteen.'

Gieles began to laugh. 'Me, too. I'm also fourteen. But in two months I'll be fifteen.'

'Yeah, right,' she giggled.

'And my geese aren't called Asterix and Obelix.'

'Oh? What d'you call them then?'

'Tufted and Bufted. And I don't work in a butcher shop.'

Now Meike started laughing uncontrollably. It was a

sweet little peep that switched to a fit of whinnying, until he couldn't understand her any more because of the noise of a passing plane.

'A cargo jet,' explained Gieles a bit later.

'Get outta here!' she shouted, and 'Jaysus!' and he told her in detail what the position of the runway was in relation to their house, how often planes came, and finished his story with a joke.

Again the sweet laugh.

Gieles laughed back, and then there was silence.

The little goose looked at him with one black eye. He thought of her tattoo.

'Did it hurt?' he asked hesitantly. 'The tear?'

'Nah, not really.'

A Boeing filled the next silence.

'Meike?'

'Yes?'

'Sorry about that e-mail. From my mother.'

They talked a while longer, and when Gieles hung up he felt relieved. She had confessed all the white lies, although she had only really lied about her age and the piercings. She only had two piercings—one in her eyebrow and one in her tongue—and not fourteen. And that for him was the greatest relief of all.

When he went to sleep, the little goose nestled up snugly on his pillow against his hair. The fur hat had become too small for her. He felt pleasantly empty. The smouldering battle between his parents, Liedje's cancer, the sprawling Super Waling: all of them kept a safe distance.

15

The ordering 'stay' is going relatively excellent. My geese now stay at the same place, even when I am no longer visual. But they must also stay when danger threatens. For example: I drive in invalid scooter (of my Uncle Fred. Not I am an invalid, but my uncle a little of a paralysed leg). In the road are my geese. I say 'stay' and drive very strong with the invalid scooter towards the geese. This is not yet excellent. They fly away, but they must stay. Do you have a recommendation?

I am going to carry out the ordering 'fly' with silent accessory umbrella. I put the umbrella up and they fly away. I do cry that after a little while the geese no longer carry out the ordering when they encounter the umbrella more often. What do you cry Christian Moullec?

It is going formidable with goose small and ping pong. Service still gives a problem, but the bill manages the forehand and backhand excellent. People often scream: Oh, ping pong is easy. They joke about the paddles and the little ball. They prefer to experience the soccer. Soccer is spectacle. But I tell you: ping pong is difficult for the head. Incorrect thoughts are not allowed! Your person is then suspended in error and loses the good. Your person donates punches on the table, for example, or curses. Or thinking with noise. That is not allowed! Ping pong is a silent sport. Strong exchange of feelings is prohibited. Goose small excels in silent play. Only when she has fatigue does she make noise and fall down dead asleep. I laugh and look at goose small. My mother is returning this summer from Africa. She will have great pride in us.

For Tufted and Bufted the training sessions were more a diversion than anything else. They were given plenty of speculaas to keep them in one place, and they seemed to enjoy Gieles's compliments when they carried out the commands correctly. He was not dissatisfied. They responded reasonably well to the umbrella. They flew away immediately, but in a different direction each time. The wrong direction. The thought of birds in airplane engines, pulverised like kiwis in a blender, alarmed him.

His mother would be landing in eight weeks and two days, Gieles calculated, as Tufted and Bufted ambled along in front of him. They were tired from training. Their webbed feet made a smacking sound on the asphalt.

The little goose was waiting for him in the yard. He didn't want to take her with him to the training sessions because she might get hit by a car. It was just a short distance across the road and cars seldom came that way, but even so.

He picked the little goose up and kissed her bill. It wasn't until he heard his father's voice that Gieles saw him standing in the doorway. He was holding a baking tin. Gieles felt caught, as if he had been seen kissing a girl. The frown his father greeted him with did not go unnoticed.

'Fred asked if you'd take this cherry cake to the Keijzer family before supper,' he said.

'Do I have to?' sighed Gieles.

'Yes, you have to,' said his father, pushing the cake into his hands.

Reluctantly he went.

Tony's mother literally pulled him inside. He hadn't seen Liedje since her diagnosis.

'Gieles, you still know how to find our house!' cried Tony Senior. He was sitting at the kitchen table. 'We haven't seen you in weeks!'

He said this in a buddy-buddy kind of way.

Gieles laughed sheepishly and didn't know what to do with his body, so he leaned against the door of the mint-green refrigerator, which was covered with magnets. Mostly cow and pig magnets. The sound of the TV could be heard from the living room.

'Tony'll be here in a minute,' said Liedje. She put the cake on the counter and turned her attention to a pan on the stove. Then she looked down at his sneakers. Of course, his shoes. Her glance was all it took to get him to take them off and set them on the doormat.

'Tony eats at the snack bar first,' she grumbled, 'and then he comes here and gives me this song and dance that he's not hungry.'

'As long as he leaves it for me.' Tony Senior winked at Gieles. 'Sit down, guy. How you doing? Your father? Fred? Your mother? I'm completely out of touch.'

He shut his magazine (it was a motorcycle magazine) and took a sip of wine.

'Fine,' said Gieles. 'Everybody's fine.'

Gieles had never seen Tony's father anything but happy. A couple of years earlier the local shopkeeper's association had voted him the most customer-friendly shopkeeper in the downtown area. The certificate was hanging in his butcher shop. He had also been given a bronze sculpture of a smiling mouth on a stick. A shrivelled-up cunt, Tony said during the award ceremony. Everyone had heard the comment except for Tony Senior, who was at the microphone thanking every single person he knew.

Gieles thought Tony's father didn't look like a butcher. His idea of a butcher was somebody more of the Super Waling body type, but not so fat. Tony Senior, on the other hand, was thin, and his hair was always so perfectly parted that it looked fake. Like nylon. He'd be great in one of those mail-order magazines for men's clothing that Uncle Fred always used to order his sweaters from.

'Is your mother still in Botswana with those sheets of aluminium foil?'

'No,' Gieles corrected him. 'In Somalia.'

Liedje put a glass of cola down in front of him. There was a piece of wood sticking out of her mouth that she was chewing on laboriously. Gieles wondered whether she had already had the operation. He didn't detect anything strange about her shirt.

'Liquorice root. She stopped smoking,' explained Tony Senior. 'Doctor's orders. Otherwise there's more of a chance that her body will reject the new breast. They've put an expander—a kind of balloon—under the large pectoral muscle.'

Tony Senior took a pen out of a bowl that held a stack of mail and a couple of desiccated tangerines. On the cover of *Motorcycles and Trucks* he drew a curve. He had long, narrow fingers. Gieles wondered whether he had ever slaughtered a horse, like Ide Warrens.

'Then they inject the fluid in the little balloon, here.' On a photo of a yellow cross country helmet he drew an arrow pointing to the side of the curve. 'Until the skin is nicely stretched.'

'Oh, yeah,' murmured Gieles, and he wondered whether the balloon could pop, like the ones Tony said were in your cock.

'He draws it nicer than it is,' said Liedje. She was tying on an apron. 'I'm walking around with all these tubes and a bag under my armpit to drain off the discharge from the wound.'

'That's just temporary, sweetheart. It'll all be fine.'

Liedje put the meat in the pan.

'Sear it gently, two minutes on each side,' Tony Senior instructed, and drew a bulge on the curve. 'The nipple comes later. The doctor tattoos it on. Liedje could have kept her old nipple,' he said with a lowered voice. 'Then they put the nipple in the groin—to keep it alive, so to speak, until they're ready to put it back. On the breast. But Liedje didn't want that.'

'Not on your life. As if you'd walk around with your balls in your groin,' she said bitterly, slamming the lid on the pan.

'Which explains the tattooed nipple,' smiled Tony Senior imperturbably. 'Amazing, huh, what they can do these days?'

'Wow,' said Gieles. He was thinking about Meike's tear. They called each other every day. The volume of her voice increased with every call, and so did his crush on her.

'My own flesh and blood deserts me,' Liedje shouted from under the exhaust fan. She pricked the meat violently with a fork. She was holding the liquorice root in her other hand like a cigarette. The end of the root was frayed like a rope. 'Tony doesn't want to have anything to do with the operation and the cancer. You're different, Gieles. You come here bringing cake. My son comes home with a big mouth.'

'Everyone is different,' said Tony Senior good-naturedly. 'And the most important thing is that you're doing fine again. That's a miracle, isn't it, Gieles? You have cancer and suddenly it's as good as gone.'

The Bird Burning works!

Liedje began to snivel over the frying pan. 'Fucking liquorice root.' She threw the stick of wood into the dog's basket. Lady just kept on sleeping.

'I'm sure Gieles never mouths off to his mother,' she wept, holding one hand under her left armpit with a painful grimace.

'Of course not,' laughed Tony Senior. 'Ellen is never there. How long has your mother been in Botswana again?'

'Somalia. More than seven weeks.' He fervently hoped Liedje would stop crying.

'Tony shaved off his last bit of hair yesterday.' She fixed him with her eyes. 'He looks like one of those skin-heads. I said, "Shouldn't you have discussed it with us first?" And the wise-ass says, "I don't discuss anything with anybody." And then he looks at me with those weird eyes of his.'

Now her grief made way for rage. She slammed the cabinet door so hard that the dog raised her head and their daughter Roxanna disengaged herself from the TV. Roxanna trudged into the kitchen and sat down on her father's lap, even though she was already ten years old.

'Fortunately Rox compensates for her brother's hair shortage,' laughed Tony Senior, pulling on his daughter's long ponytail.

'Are we gonna eat soon?' she asked sullenly. 'I'm hungry.'

'And what about Gieles's hair?' Tony Senior continued. 'It stands straight up! Like a cornfield! There's enough hair in this house to compensate for anything our Tony does to his head.'

Embarrassed, Gieles rubbed his hair flat.

'My meat is ready and that no-good kid still isn't here.' She blew her nose and took a new piece of liquorice root from a drawer. Roxanna trudged back to the living room.

'Did you guys ever get a letter from the airport?'

Tony Senior was rummaging through the mail in the fruit bowl.

'It's enough to make you die laughing,' he said, taking the letter out of the envelope. 'You'll never guess what they've come up with now! They want to buy us all out, tear down the whole kit and caboodle and put up a forest of pyramids!'

Tony Senior threw back his nylon head and made a gurgling sound. His tongue was purple from the wine.

'I don't see what's so funny.'

Liedje was obviously still angry. She bit down hard on the liquorice root, giving herself more wrinkles than ever.

'As long as they don't think I'm ever leaving. Over my dead body. I've been here my whole life. Bred and born here, and I'm gonna die here, too.'

'Born and bred,' Tony Senior corrected her.

Liedje looked at him with incomprehension.

'It's the other way around. First you're born and then you're bred.'

He looked intently at the frying pan. 'The burner, sweetheart. Better turn down the burner or the tournedos will be tough. That would be a shame.'

'You can thank your son, in that case,' she snarled.

Tony Senior took a sip of wine and stuck his finger in the air as if he had had an inspiration. 'I remember what the neighbours said when they left: "We're like extras in a very bad movie." They didn't realise how little time they had to escape when the runway opened.'

'They didn't say that,' Liedje interrupted. 'They said: "We're stuck in the middle of a horror film."'

Tony Senior searched for Gieles's gaze to make sure he

had his attention, then he started reading the letter in a solemn voice.

'Low-frequency sound can be effectively reduced by introducing a sound barrier with canted surfaces, such as pyramids, and combining them with geographic relief in the area behind them, such as hills in the landscape. The canted surfaces of the pyramids serve to block the sound while allowing the wind to pass through, so that no turbulence is created for the airplanes. On the barrier are ... blah blah blah ... pyramids of different heights with different canted surfaces, positioned next to and in front of each other. The pyramids are made of ... blah blah blah ... sound-absorbent materials. The canted surfaces diffuse the sound.'

Tony Senior looked at Gieles with an almost ecstatic expression. 'The canted surfaces *diffuse* the sound!'

Gieles politely joined in the laughter.

'How do these guys think up this stuff!' He raised his hand as if he were trying to calm a wildly screaming audience and continued reading. 'The area *might* also be used for water storage. To preserve the agricultural function, floating greenhouses *can* be developed. Generating sun and wind energy is another suitable ecological innovation.'

Tony Senior now began to talk with a very posh accent. 'Another way to manage energy in an ecologically responsible manner is by storing heat *in* the runway. The heat from the asphalt is stored in a heating element. This can be used for the heating of buildings ... etcetera blah blah.'

'What a load of crap,' said Liedje. 'Every time those cocksuckers from the airport send out a letter, I don't understand a blessed word of it. Anyway, supper's ready. Tony can get lost.'

'That's exactly the idea,' said Tony Senior, handing Gieles a drawing that came with the letter. 'By sending out a message like this, they're saying: we're smart, you're stupid and let's keep it that way. Period.'

Gieles looked at the drawing. It was made by computer. He saw the runway, and in the area around it, where their houses had been, he saw dozens of triangles standing on little hills. That had to be the pyramids. They were red, green, blue and yellow. Exactly the same colours as Lego. He saw row after row of greenhouses as well as strange buildings that were half buried in the earth. It all looked so weird that Gieles could just as easily have been holding the drawing upside down. His old familiar neighbourhood, his house, had been transformed into science fiction. Gieles felt like Ide Warrens when he couldn't make any sense of the map with the sections on it.

'Last week I was at the airport, standing at the check-in desk with three suitcases,' said Tony Senior, his eyes sparkling.

Gieles looked at him with surprise.

'I said to the lady, "This suitcase is going to Milan, this one to Prague and the last one to Berlin."'

Gieles realised he had started in on one of his dumb jokes that no one thought was funny except Tony Senior himself.

'"But sir!" cried the lady. "We can't do that!" "Sure you can," I said. "You did that the last time with my luggage!"'

Liedje sighed very wearily. Then she heard the sound of the souped-up motorbike.

'That'll be our Tony!' cried Tony Senior happily, rubbing his hands together.

After supper he went home. Tony hadn't opened his mouth once during the whole meal, and while the table was being cleared by his mother, he took his bald head upstairs to do some gaming. Gieles said he had homework. More importantly, his mother was going to call— if she could get any kind of signal out there in that sandbox, that is.

The little goose was sitting at the front door. She hopped up and down like a wind-up toy and greeted him with two quacks.

'Hey, shorty,' he whispered, and stuck her under his sweater. He had to give her a name.

Uncle Fred and his father were watching a TV program. He poked his head around the corner, yelled 'I'm back!' and ran upstairs. Waiting patiently for his mother to call, he sat at the computer and continued working on his report. He reread the words of Super Waling: 'After the reclamation work was finished they had walked over the ring dike and past the grotesque pumping stations. They were delighted to meet people who had come to admire the new land, but for Ide and Sophia it was a death march. With every step they remembered the men, women and children for whom the dike had become a makeshift grave.'

Gieles copied the text and pasted it in his own document. He hoped the fourth part of the story about Ide and Sophia would come soon.

He waited for his mother's call and thought about his rescue plan. How would he get the geese to end up next to the runway? Scattering a whole pack of speculaas and running away was out of the question. The cameras would see him. And shooting cookies with a slingshot would never work, either.

He waited and practised a bit with the little goose. She

had already mastered serving with her bill. She was definitely more intelligent than Christian Moullec's lesser white-fronted geese. It was high time he sent that letter. He needed answers to his questions.

He was in the mood for really loud music, which didn't happen very often. Soon his room was reverberating with the sound of guitars. Gieles began to play along (sort of) and to dance, which he never did, certainly not at school parties.

Now the singer was roaring over the sound of the guitars and drums. His voice was loud and raw. It sounded terrific. Gieles's dancing became wilder. He banged his head up and down, playing his make-believe guitar like a master. Nananana naaahaa! The headbanging made him dizzy, which was pleasant. It kept his mind off the bag with Liedje's wound discharge and tattooed nipples and tears.

When his head started spinning he switched to a kind of hop-step-jump. He could see in his computer screen that all his hair was standing on end, just like a porcupine. He didn't give a shit. Anything was better than Tony's shaved cranium. Yeah!

The phone rang. Quick as lightning he turned off the music. Her voice sounded tinny and strange. Gieles could tell that his mother hadn't spoken Dutch in weeks. Despite the coldness of the connection Gieles felt overcome with emotion. He sat on his bed covered in sweat.

She asked how he was doing. She wanted to know everything about his little goose, which he had written to her about at length. Generally his e-mails were short and to the point, but when it came to that little goose he couldn't say enough. Then he asked his mother how it was there. He usually talked about 'there.' He could never remember the names of the villages where she was staying.

'It's okay,' she said. 'It's hot and dry. You'd hate it here. I have yet to see a single bird, let alone a goose.'

Gieles laughed.

'That really got to me, that thing with Meike,' she finally said. 'Were you shocked by her tear?'

'Nah. No biggie. But her parents were. They think she's mutilated herself.'

'You can also see it as a personal expression of grief. Here in Africa tattoos have a more symbolic value. Did you know that prisoners and gang members tradition- ally get tear tattoos when they've killed someone? As a kind of status symbol.'

'Don't tell her parents,' said Gieles.

He pressed the telephone so hard against his ear that it hurt.

'Meike's mother wrote me that you had forwarded that e-mail because you didn't want Meike to go to Africa.'

He said nothing.

'You ought to see what it's like here.' She groped for the right words. 'They have nothing here, sunshine. I realise it's difficult, but ...'

And she was gone. Her voice may have been hanging from a satellite somewhere in the universe, but he could no longer hear her.

The Africans may have nothing, but they have you.

He was going to say that the next time.

He lay down in bed with the phone next to his pillow. He left his computer on. After half an hour a message arrived.

So wonderful to hear you. Something went wrong again, of course, but at least we were connected. What I wanted to say is this: centuries ago, parents tattooed their babies so they could track them down if another tribe stole them. We did that with you, too, on vacation. In big black letters I would write your name and the place where we were camping on both your arms, in case one arm became illegible. Sometimes we wrote down entire route descriptions. 'Follow the path through the woods, after four hundred metres turn left, then upstream along the river.' You didn't mind. You've always been an easy, happy child. Sometimes I wish I was branded, too. 'Ellen, mother of Gieles,' so the people here would see that I'm a mother. Your mother. Let me hear from you, okay?

Love, Ellen

PART IV

Ide & Sophia

Ide had expected Sophia to be completely beside herself when she heard about the gruesome death of the horse, but she wasn't. She didn't want to say another word about it. She refused to go to the place where the slaughter and burning had occurred. She had had more than her share of death and destruction, and now she just wanted to concentrate on the life within her. Ide was standing naked in the yard, trying to scrub off the last traces of blood with water and a brush.

Sophia was sitting on a crate, leaning against the shanty and looking at him with amusement. No one could see them but the dog.

'You have an old cock,' she laughed. 'It's rusty.'

Ide turned his back to her. He was too exhausted to respond.

Reddish brown drops meandered down his white legs. He stared at his feet in the tub. The water was murky.

Sophia stood up. She looked radiant. 'I'm going to fry up some horse cheeks. Delicious tender horse cheeks. Yummy.' She whinnied, made a skip and a jump and trotted inside.

'I thought you were sick,' he shouted after her angrily.

Sophia knew that when she told him about the child later on, the whole episode with the nag would be forgotten.

She was right. One hour later he was smiling so broadly that she was afraid the corners of his mouth would tear. She knew that smile from long, long ago, when she had grabbed his hand for the first time and taken him behind the shed of the doctor's house. Her parents were gone, and Ide was astonished that she let him kiss her. Actually it was the other way around: Sophia had been the first to raise her head to him, waiting eagerly for his mouth with pursed lips.

The next morning when they were out in the yard, when the boss told her there was meat for her to pickle, Sophia blurted out that she was expecting. Ide thought she should wait, that you never knew how the boss would react to the coming of a baby, but she couldn't help it. It was out there before she knew what she was saying. The boss raised his eyebrows, peeped, 'Oh. Well, well,' and gave her the horse's heart, which was considered a real delicacy. From this generous gesture Sophia gathered that she had nothing to worry about with regard to their work.

The months that followed were light and cheerful. Ide was convinced that the greatest trials were behind them. And the daily ordeals that came their way weren't ordeals at all by his way of thinking. Collapsing canal banks, boggy land, grain that wouldn't grow: nothing could spoil his good humour.

Even the boss seemed happy in his own strange way. His voice became less feeble and high and his body grew a couple of centimetres.

When Sophia began lugging crates around, he shouted that she was not to lift anything too heavy. Ide ordered her to eat more and gave her the largest pieces of meat.

Sophia ate, her body expanded and she slowly became the girl she once had been. Her red hair became fuller, furrows disappeared, her skin became soft and her hearty laugh returned. The two men looked on with astonishment at her miraculous rejuvenation. Even her desire for sex came back in all its glory. She fucked Ide with tempestuous abandon, her heavy belly pushing against his. After her orgasm, the child would kick back angrily for half an hour. 'It's going to be a lad, no doubt about it,' Sophia laughed.

Her hunger for reading returned, too. The beautiful lady with the red coral necklace let her borrow books, and Ide brought home magazines and books for her as well. She devoured medical publications on anatomy in particular and the report on the cholera epidemic in Leiden.

There wasn't a doctor to be found in the whole godforsaken region, so Sophia decided to train herself. Her motivation was simple. One in three babies born in the new land never made it, and she didn't want her child to die. She was going to keep all illness at bay and not be as stupid as the peasants who gave their children milk diluted with ditch water that was full of shit and rotting corpses. 'Stupid stupid stupid people,' she would say with an upraised finger.

Her greatest nightmare was the stillborn baby born to Akkie, the Frisian woman from the shanty town whom she thought of constantly now that she herself was pregnant. The woman had been in an alcohol coma and had given birth to a lifeless child. It took three hours for Akkie to come to, and when she did Sophia handed her a dead little boy. After the death of her child Akkie drank even more. Even the town's biggest drunk had disapproved of the amount she belted down. Akkie was washing away the shame. Sophia had lost track of her and wondered whether she was still alive.

No, her boy was not going to die or drown in alcohol. Her boy was going to live to a ripe old age. To make sure that happened, she paid meticulous attention to the hygiene on the farm. She boiled water twice a week and scrubbed the dirt from Ide's body and her own. She inspected him daily for vermin. Not a single spot or fold of skin escaped her probing. Even the boss's thin hair was subjected to her stringent inspections, although she dared not go below his neck. Ide dug a cesspit with the boss's approval and built an outhouse over it, making shitting behind the peat stack a thing of the past. And her hygienic reforms bore fruit. In September there was a fierce outbreak of cholera in the polder, but they were spared.

'Poverty causes disease,' insisted Sophia. She even stopped giving porridge and bread to the children who came begging at her door. She set the hound on all and sundry, and anyone who was foolish enough to ignore him got bitten in the leg.

Sophia was happy. 'The only problem we still have,' she said one autumnal evening, 'is this shanty. I have sworn to myself that my child is not going to grow up in a pig sty.'

'But we have a window and a stove, don't we?' said Ide, shoving a potato into his mouth.

'It's a sty and it will always be a sty. I want a house of brick,' she said in an uncompromising tone, placing her hands on her belly. Sophia's proportions had become immense.

'A house of brick?' he repeated with his mouth full. 'The boss doesn't even have that. Do you know what that would cost?'

'I've saved some money. In my suitcase, on top of the cupboard. Take a look.'

'What do you mean?' asked Ide with surprise. 'Where did you get it from?'

'Just look,' she said, drumming on her belly impatiently. Ide stood up and lifted the suitcase from the cupboard. It was heavier than he had expected. Dust fluttered down on him. He placed the suitcase on the table, opened the lid and expected to see guilders. But all he saw was an old cloth doll and the white clay pipe he had dug up in the reclaimed lake.

'It has a false bottom. You have to take out the cardboard,' said Sophia.

He grabbed a worn corner and pulled the cardboard away. 'Look at this,' he stammered, staring at the guilders and daalders that covered the bottom of the suitcase. 'Look at this. I've never seen so much money all in one place.'

'It's one thousand thirty-three guilders.' Her voice was full of pride.

He ran his fingers through the coins with a blissful look on his face. 'But how were you able to save so much? It's just not possible! Did you steal it?' he asked, half frightened, half in awe.

'Don't be silly. I saved it up from my little food business during the polder project. And sometimes I hold a little back at the market, but it doesn't bother the boss. He's not eating any less because of it.'

She hoisted herself out of the chair with difficulty and went over to Ide, who threw his arm around her and kneaded her upper arm.

'We can't very well build a brick house while the boss is living in a shanty,' he said.

'Then we'll build a farm for him first. After that we'll start on our own house.'

'Yes, but ...' (he couldn't keep his eyes off the money)

'then one thousand thirty-three guilders may not be enough. I'm not well-versed in such things, but a farm could easily cost two thousand guilders.'

'I've thought about that, too.' Sophia hugged her fat belly. Ide was constantly worrying whether the child shouldn't have been born by now. Sophia had grown as big as a draft horse.

'About eight kilometres further down are the remains of an old cemetery. It seems the jewellery in the graves is there for the taking.'

'Who says so?'

'A couple of men in the market. They're always talking about it. And that jewellery may well be our salvation.'

One week later Ide Warrens set off. It was before half past six in the evening. He walked across the wet countryside, meditating on the fact that he had left home as a poor labourer and could be returning in a couple of hours as a rich man. He wondered whether his expectations were realistic. He had no use for critical comments, however. All he wanted to do was fantasise, something he hadn't done in a very long time.

Ide had caught sight of the church tower to the northeast. It was a vague outline, the last relic from the submerged village. The land-hungry lake had gobbled up the inhabitants and their houses centuries ago. Only the church remained. He paid close attention to the path he was following to the village and committed it to memory; he'd have to return in the dark by the light of his oil lamp.

One hour later he was walking through the ruins of the village. There were remains of houses and barns, and even the façade of the pub was still standing. The church was relatively undamaged despite the floods. All that was missing were the windows.

In the twilight Ide could see that the cemetery had already been thoroughly worked over by body snatchers. He shivered, lit his oil lamp and went into the church. Staring into the dim light he saw pulverised pews and crushed stone that he recognised as an altar. Bats fluttered up as he entered.

Ide cursed under his breath. If only it wasn't so dark he'd feel a good deal better. He looked around and set his mind to working out where the entrance to the crypt might be. The weak light cast shadows on the floor that revealed the remains of firewood. The church must have served as a good shelter for tramps, and that thought helped him keep a cool head. After having wandered around for what seemed like an eternity, he found the opening to the crypt. The stone used to seal it off lay beside a square hole with a ladder propped up inside it.

Ide hung back, hesitating. The dark hole was more than he could bear. Its blackness had a hungry look, as if it might swallow him alive, and its maw stank of marsh fumes drained of all oxygen. He couldn't sink any lower than this—robbing from the dead in a crypt. Ide found it difficult to breathe, and he began to cry. Although he tried to restrain himself, his suppressed sobs bounced off the damp walls. 'Ide Warrens,' he said out loud, needing to hear his own voice. 'Make Sophia and the child happy.' He threw a stone into the gaping hole. The toss was immediately followed by the sound of the stone rebounding, so Ide knew that the crypt was not deep.

Slowly he descended the ladder, his heart beating faster and faster. It felt as if he could scarcely get enough air. After eight steps he found himself standing with both legs on the stone floor. 'Come on, Ide Warrens,' he said, egging himself on. 'Make Sophia and the child happy.' He held the oil lamp up with an outstretched arm. Sophia was right: this was where the coffins were. Dozens of coffins. Except she hadn't known that here, too, the body snatchers had preceded him. Ide saw that the oak lids had been pushed aside. Centimetre by centimetre he shuffled past the coffins, doing his best not to look in.

'Nothing to be afraid of,' he said, and he felt his legs swaying back and forth. His fear of a higher power, a God, raised its head once again. Could he go unpunished after having robbed the dead?

'Stay calm.' His voice sounded strange in the airless space. He took a couple of deep breaths, despite the fetid air. This was clearly not his terrain, his territory, which explained the problem he was having with paralysing fear. Suddenly he felt the urge to stake out his claim, like a bear marking tree trunks with his claws to secure *his* part of the forest. With clammy hands, he pulled his penis out of his pants and pissed against the cellar walls until he had pressed out the last drop. This made him feel somewhat relieved; relaxed would have been an overstatement.

'Get to work, Ide Warrens. Make Sophia and the child happy.'

At the back of the crypt there were still a couple of untouched graves. He kicked against one wooden lid with his foot, but it wouldn't budge. Then he began tugging at it with all his might, pushing it aside bit by bit. The lid clattered unexpectedly to the floor. In the weak light he could see a skeleton. Squatting down slowly, he cast his eyes over the bony frame with nervous curiosity. He looked at the skull and pressed his fingers against his own forehead. The skeleton's high cheek bones astonished him. He counted the ribs and then felt under his jacket, how the skin stretched across his own rib cage. He had never seen himself from the inside and now this magical mirror was being held up in front of him. He dangled the oil lamp above the hips and wondered whether this was the skeleton of a man or a woman.

Then he heard a faint rumbling above him; a storm was brewing. Ide inspected the knuckles and the neck and looked next to the skull, but he found no jewellery. He rose quickly and pulled the lid off the next coffin. This skeleton was considerably smaller. One arm was gone and there was no jewellery in this grave, either.

The approaching thunderstorm drove him on. He worked his way through the whole row of coffins, breathing heavily. At the sixth coffin Ide got lucky. He found a gold ring with a small stone on one knuckle and removed it. At the bottom of the coffin was a necklace. Ide tried to pull the necklace over the skull, but the chain was too small. He put the oil lamp on the floor and tried to open the clasp. Tugging on the neck vertebrae made the skull turn to the left. Startled, Ide gave the necklace a jerk, causing it to snap. The shifting of the skeleton exposed a brooch, which he snatched up from between the ribs. He shoved the booty into his jacket pocket and fled through the dark hole.

Sophia waited up all night for Ide. She stood at the shanty's only window and watched the fierce spectacle of thunder and rain. She was not afraid of lightning, and she knew that Ide did not fear nature's violence, either. She took it for granted that Ide wouldn't be stupid enough to stumble around across the open polder, that he'd probably take shelter in the drowned village or with some farmer along the way. And yet. And yet. And yet.

The hours dragged on and the wind died down, while

the storm in her head increased.

By five-thirty the storm had long passed over on its way east. The sun was shining kindly on the new land. Sophia slept in the wicker chair in front of the window and was awakened by rumbling at the door. 'Ide,' she cried, but when she pulled the door open she saw the boss standing there.

'Isn't he awake yet?' the boss asked irritably. Behind him was the dog. The ugly creature followed him everywhere.

'No,' she stammered. 'What time is it?'

'Five-thirty. I've been waiting half an hour. A fine mess.'

'Jesus,' she said. 'Jesus Christ.'

Sophia felt the baby give a kick.

'He left last night.'

'What do you mean, "left"?'

They took the horse and wagon and set off together on the muddy road going northeast. The boss had tied sturdy, broad planks to the horse's hoofs. One more drowned horse would ruin him.

The lurching of the wagon felt like flagellation to Sophia's belly. It seemed as if the amniotic fluid were pouring into her gullet, as if her womb could explode at any moment. She bound her mother's old brocade shawl firmly around her belly. As they rode she scanned the landscape as scrupulously as if she were searching for nits on a scalp.

She groaned.

'The baby's not coming now, is it? That'd be the last straw ...'

The boss's voice sounded squeaky and small for the first time in ages. 'What was he doing out on the polder, anyway? There's absolutely nothing there.'

Sophia didn't know whether she should tell the boss the truth. Suddenly she felt as old as the hills.

It didn't even surprise her when they found Ide further down the road. He was lying on his stomach, stiff as a board and black with mud. When they struggled to lift him and lay him in the wagon, Sophia noticed that his jacket was scorched around the chest.

'Ide Warrens,' she said, smacking his cold face. 'Goddamn it. What's this all about?'

That evening Sophia gave birth to a daughter. The ride with the horse and wagon and the fits of crying had so shaken her body that they set off her contractions. She gave birth in the shanty while the boss stood outside the door, wondering whether he ought to go fetch a midwife from somewhere. But he had no idea where to look.

When Sophia began screaming so loud that even the dog began to howl, the boss stormed inside. He found Sophia squatting over a blanket on the floor. Her upper body was wrapped in a rolled-up nightgown and she was hanging over the seat of the chair. The baby's crown was already visible and made him think of a monstrous haemorrhoid. Once again Sophia screamed like a wounded animal, and just when he was about to shout that she ought to lie down on her back (his wife had borne their three daughters in the box bed), the baby shot out. It landed on the floor with a plop. Sophia clearly knew what she was doing. Laid out neatly on the blanket were a stack of white towels, a pan of water and a pair of scissors on a small plate. She deftly cut the umbilical cord and tied the stub off with a cotton band. After wrapping the baby up tightly in a couple of towels, she dropped down on her hands and knees. When the placenta slid out of her vagina the boss made for the door, retching. He had no idea what had come out of her.

The next morning she asked the boss to bring Ide to her shanty so she could wash him. She was deathly pale but undaunted.

Ide Warrens was still lying on the wagon in the barn. The boss wondered how he was going to move the gigantic Zeelander into Sophia's shanty with the proper dignity. The farmhand was too big for him to lift on his own and the girl was too physically weak to help.

After hesitating for a moment, the boss ran to his own shanty and pulled the straw mattress from his box bed. He dragged the mattress outside and shoved three poles underneath it. Then he pushed Ide off the cart and onto the mattress. Ide fell with a flop, like a sack of flour.

He straightened Ide's stiff limbs, closed his eyes and rolled him to Sophia's shanty. Without exchanging a word they pushed the sides of the stiff mattress together to make it fit through the doorway.

'We'll lay him on the ground,' said Sophia. 'Otherwise the mattress will get wet.'

The boss said it didn't matter, but she insisted. So they dragged the big man over to a blanket on the ground.

Sophia offered him coffee and the boss took a seat, out of breath. They sat at the table, saying nothing. The boss didn't know where to look: at Sophia's dark, sad eyes or the muddy body of his farmhand. A soft sputtering could be heard from the box bed.

'Completely forgot,' said the boss, jumping up. Much relieved, he ran out of the shanty and came back five minutes later with a pouch under his arm.

'Some clothes for the baby,' he said awkwardly. She had taken the baby from the box bed and wrapped her in the shawl. All you could see were a few wisps of fiery red hair.

'He has your hair,' said the boss.

'It's a girl,' Sophia corrected him. 'Her name is Anna Louisa. I named her after Anna Louisa Geertruida Toussaint.'

The boss shrugged his shoulders.

'After the writer,' Sophia explained, realising how idiotic her explanation sounded. The boss couldn't read. 'It was the only name that occurred to me last night.'

'But you said it was going to be a lad,' the boss peeped, crestfallen. He stood up and mumbled that he had something to attend to.

Sophia brought the baby back to the box bed. She boiled some water on the stove and poured it into a pan. Then she knelt down at Ide's feet and pulled off his wet boots. His wet sock, his pants and his underpants. The heavy muddy jacket. The land had absorbed Ide into itself.

She emptied his pockets and found the jewellery: the gold necklace, the ring with the little stone and the brooch. It was a small oval brooch with three little ivory elves on it.

She unbuttoned his flannel shirt and studied the black burns. His left side was scorched in exactly the same way. The lightning had entered Ide through his chest and exited out his side, with the electrical current laying waste to every organ in between. Hesitantly she touched the blackened skin with her fingertips, which gave the impression of being red hot.

Sophia worked on Ide for hours. She scrubbed him so thoroughly that she was willing to bet her last cent that there wasn't a grain of sand left on him or in him. She washed his hair, shaved his face and clipped his nails. She scoured the mud out of his navel, lathered his penis, brushed his toes and dressed him in clean clothes.

As she worked she carried on a pleasant monologue. She told Ide that the brooch would bring in at least enough for a real funeral. The rest of the jewellery and the money she had saved would be enough for a modest house and a piece of the farm. The boss, she said pragmatically, would have to contribute something as well.

'I'll just say that I received an inheritance,' she said, stroking Ide's cheek. He lay there serenely. 'Well, what do you think'? She kissed him on his stiff mouth. 'Hey! Ide Warrens. You never have anything to say!'

She punched his upper arm angrily. The baby began to cry.

She stood up, holding onto the chair and swaying dizzily. Then she carefully lifted the little parcel out of the bed and lay down beside Ide, her head on his shoulder, their child wedged in between them. As the little girl greedily drank, Sophia wept until his clean shirt was soaked with tears.

16

Gieles had gone over his plan step by step and had come to the conclusion that he needed help training the geese. In order to closely duplicate the situation on the runway he invited Super Waling to come over. Tufted and Bufted stayed put whenever Gieles raced at them in the mobility scooter, but he was afraid they would fly away in the face of an approaching plane. The figure of Super Waling on wheels would make an excellent test.

Gieles gave his instructions on the road out in front of the farm.

'It has to look like almost an accident,' Gieles explained. 'You drive straight at the geese at full speed and put on the brakes two or three metres before you reach them.'

Super Waling looked at him doubtfully.

'They have to get used to threats,' he declared. 'I want to register them with a casting bureau, and then they'll have to listen to the director, too. Their leader.'

Super Waling nodded without asking any questions and looked at the two geese, who were wolfing down speculaas a short distance away.

'I'll show you what I mean,' said Gieles. 'If I can use your scooter. My uncle is gone.'

'Of course,' said Super Waling, and hoisted himself out of his vehicle with great difficulty. Uncle Fred and his father had not yet met him, but Gieles didn't care any more. The embarrassment he had felt about his weight was gone. Almost gone.

Gieles rode away from the geese, screamed, 'Stay!' and then hurtled towards them. When he was less than a metre from Tufted and Bufted he put on the brakes. The geese just stood there calmly, without a trace of stress.

'Bravo!' cried Super Waling enthusiastically, clapping his hands. 'What trust! They see you as their leader!'

Gieles blushed and began talking about Christian Moullec, the famous Frenchman in the flying two-seater motorbike and the excellent results he had had with his lesser white-fronted geese.

Super Waling listened and said, 'But I think what you can do with your geese is at least as admirable. I mean, I've never met anyone who could teach a goose to play table tennis.'

Gieles enjoyed his compliments and attention. It was just as Dolly had said: he listened to you as if you were the only person on the earth who mattered. Gieles didn't doubt his sincerity for a single second. Sometimes you just knew what was real and what wasn't.

Gieles began to talk hurriedly. 'Now you do it. But you've got to hurry up. Later they won't be hungry any more.'

'They really won't get frightened when I bear down on them?' he asked again, waving away a wasp. The warm weather was attracting insects.

'That's the whole idea,' said Gieles. 'I'll give the starting signal and the stop sign.'

The geese were restless. Tufted looked at the shoulder of the road with curiosity. Bufted pecked at her plumage.

Gieles counted: 'One ... two ... three ... go!' and Super Waling lumbered forward. Before he had reached the halfway point, the geese got bored and started walking toward the yard.

'I can't go any faster,' he apologised. 'I'm terribly sorry.'

'It doesn't matter,' said Gieles with disappointment. 'They lost interest anyway. We'll do it some other time.'

When they got to the spotters' campground Super Waling gave Gieles a can of grape soda. He himself had water. Gieles had never seen him drink anything else and had never seen him eat a single bite of food.

They sat under an oak tree where there was a set of lawn furniture. Super Waling stayed on his scooter. He was wearing a moss green sweatsuit this time, along with the blue Crocs.

'I know, I know,' said Super Waling, following Gieles's gaze. 'They're terrible. Hopeless.'

'What size are you?'

'Forty-one, sometimes forty-two.'

'That's small,' said Gieles with surprise. 'I'm a forty-four.' He stretched out his legs so his sneakers were clearly visible.

'To be honest, I'm glad that at least my feet are still normal. I can't imagine what they'd look like if they had grown along with everything else.'

Gieles stood up, walked to the barn and came back a minute later with a pair of black sneakers.

'These are my basketball sneakers. Maybe they fit you. They're old and the orange laces aren't cool any more.'

'Oh, no,' laughed Super Waling. 'Orange is a cheerful colour. But you don't have to give me your shoes.'

'I'll take them out.' Gieles started pulling on the laces. 'They're easier to put on that way … and they look much better without laces.'

He put the sneakers down on the footrest of the mobility scooter. Super Waling shook the Crocs off his bare feet. They really were normal feet, a little swollen at the most.

'Well?' asked Super Waling, shoving his feet into the sneakers.

'Perfect.'

An African airplane roared past fifty metres away.

'What a loudmouth,' said Super Waling.

'The airport wants to build pyramids here to block the noise.' Gieles put his legs up on the chair in front of him with its flaking paint. He looked at the black hairs on his lower legs. Why he had no hair on his chin while he was getting plenty of hair in all the other places was beyond him.

'We have to go.'

Down near the canal there were three young men with cameras. They were new camping guests. Uncle Fred had never had such a large group before. They had mounted their cameras on tripods, which looked very professional. Over on the other side of the field the spaceship belonging to the old couple had returned. Gieles hadn't seen Johan or Judith yet. He dreaded the thought of the scrapbooks.

'Would you mind very much if you had to move?' Super Waling asked.

He shrugged his shoulders. 'My father would mind. He was born here. Uncle Fred was born on the farm, too, but nothing ever bothers him. And Dolly would be happy. She hates it here. But Liedje, Tony's mother—you know, that friend of mine who's such a pain in the neck. She'd be hugely pissed off.'

'Mmm. But what do you think?'

There was a long silence. Gieles poked at the slat of the chair opposite him with the toe of his sneaker and loosened it.

'I don't know if it's going to happen or not, of course ... If the pyramids are actually going to be built ... But when I heard about it from Tony's father, it made me think of the horse that drowned in the mud. Maybe he's buried right under the runway, maybe Sophia and Ide lived here. At this very spot. It all really happened, right?'

He gave Super Waling a penetrating look.

'Absolutely. And their shanty could easily have stood somewhere around here. If all the buildings were gone we'd be able to see straight through to the pumping station.'

'Section 27,' Gieles said.

'It's amazing that you remember,' said Super Waling with surprise. Gieles remembered because he had stolen the entire story about the division into sections. Slowly but surely it was becoming more Super Waling's report than his own.

'Our farm will be demolished,' he said. 'That really bothers me. I live here.'

'Landscapes,' said Super Waling, 'remind us that we have a past. Your house tells the story of our ancestors. The soil over there, further on, where the potatoes are being grown, connects us with the first farmers to ever work this land. And that woods—what did you call that woods again?'

'The woods in exile.'

'Right, exile. The trees tell us the story of the people who struggled against the building of the runway. Unfortunately the land tells us less and less,' said Super Waling sadly. 'There's almost nothing left to remind us of Sophia and Ide's time. Everything has to make way for progress. You may think that progress is far away! And then they build a business park or a runway! Or a pyramid! It was even happening when Ide and Sophia were alive. The people were simply chased away by the landowners. Okay, everybody out, torch the place!'

Super Waling began to get excited. The words came streaming out of him.

'And if they still hadn't cleared out, then they beat the poor devils off their land! From the ashes of the farms shall the new edifices rise!' he cried, holding forth over the sound of the engines and despite his own shortness of breath.

'I once read, and I found it quite interesting, that dictatorships destroy culture and landscape. Well, in democracies they're pretty good at it, too.'

Super Waling was inhaling so deeply that his nose created a vacuum. He was clearly having trouble with the heat.

'I think it's terrible that Ide's dead,' said Gieles, in an attempt to distract him. 'He never even had a chance to see the baby. What happens to Sophia now?'

Super Waling fished a handkerchief out of his sweatsuit jacket and dabbed at his face. His hair was plastered against his forehead like wet autumn leaves. 'Don't worry. Sophia manages just fine. The entire female line that issued from my great-great-great-grandmother were a bunch of tough ladies. They all lived to a ripe old age.'

'And they were all filthy rich,' Gieles blurted out cheerfully.

'Whatever gave you that idea?' said Super Waling, as if the word had crushed him. Gieles wanted to say that he was just shooting off his mouth, but instead he said, 'At least that's what I thought. Mr Muntslag said you had gotten a big inheritance.'

His remark did not improve the situation. Super Waling said nothing and looked down at his body, which was still sending out aftershocks like an erupted volcano.

'I made you a promise, remember. I said I was going to explain everything to you. About my enormous size. But I seriously wonder whether you ought to know all this. My personal history is not exactly uplifting.'

They heard a faint quack. There was the little goose coming from the wooden washing shed. They watched her make her way towards them. Then they looked at the three young plane spotters, who had left their post at the canal. They were busy laying out plates on an opened collapsible picnic table. One of them was bent over a small gas stove. He was wearing a ridiculously large pilot's cap.

'Back when I was a history teacher, almost all the girls at school wanted to be stewardesses. And the boys wanted to be pilots.' He said this with forced cheerfulness. It was the first time that Super Waling had ever talked about his job as a teacher.

'My mother used to be a stewardess,' said Gieles, picking up the little goose and putting her on his lap. He caught himself talking and thinking about his mother more and more in the past tense. 'That's how she met my father. They had just taken off and suddenly these flames started coming out of the engine. Enormous flames!'

He was grossly exaggerating on this point. 'The plane had to go back and make an emergency landing. The emergency services were waiting for them, and my father was there on the runway, too. He had to help take care of the passengers and crew. That's how he got my mother in his car.'

Super Waling laughed. His good humour had returned. 'That's great. I can see it all now.'

'My mother did the long-distance flights, intercontinental.' He folded his hands gently around the little goose. She had shut her eyes and was making a purring sound.

'Sometimes she was gone for two weeks at a time. Uncle Fred took care of me then when my father had to work. She always took pens and balloons for the poor children. Or she gave my old clothes to an orphanage. But sometimes she gave away new clothes. One time she gave away my favourite coat.'

Gieles smelled jet fuel and fried eggs. The three spotters were sitting at the small picnic table. Their legs couldn't fit underneath.

'A couple of years ago my mother was fired. She had missed the flight. *Again*. Whenever she helped out in an orphanage she lost track of time. And then she started in on those idiotic solar ovens.'

Gieles felt the tears welling up, but he didn't want to cry. So he said, 'In Africa she wears these rags that they lay across the backs of elephants for tourists to ride on. Really ugly ... she looked much better in that uniform ...'

Gieles started flattening his hair violently, as if he were laying into himself. Then he said, 'When is that fair again?' He wanted to change the subject.

'Oh, right,' said Super Waling, and took his bag out of the basket. 'The registration form.'

He handed the form to Gieles. 'Here's where you put your name and your signature. Then it's all official.'

He rummaged around in his bag. 'Darn. I haven't got a pen. Some journalist I am.'

'I'll go inside and get one.'

When he got to the kitchen Gieles turned on the tap and drank until his head felt cool. Then he went searching for a pen. On the dotted line, after the word 'participants,' he wrote, 'Gieles Bos and ...'

The little goose had to have a name. She couldn't give her first table tennis demonstration anonymously. Without skipping a beat he wrote her name down and then read it aloud: 'Wally.'

17

The day started out hot and looked as if it was going to end up that way, too. Gieles sat in the backyard with the boys. Skiq and Onno were playing in an inflatable wading pool and Jonas was standing mesmerised at the fence, looking at the planes. It was rush hour. 'Wee-wee-wee-wee!' went the little boy. He could even imitate planes in his sleep.

The jet engines were blowing fuel in their direction like a hairdryer. Stupefied by the heat and the smell, Gieles lay under an umbrella, dead to the world. It was the hottest June in years. Gieles's lips felt dry and his eyes were burning. Just as he was about to take off his shirt, Tony appeared in the yard with the lethargic dog. All he had on was a pair of shorts, which hung so low on his hips that his pubic hair showed. His head gleamed in the sun.

Gieles decided to keep his shirt on.

'Fucking hot,' Tony yawned, sitting down in the chair next to him. Lady went for the shade under the table.

Tony unbuckled a pocket knife from his belt. He started cleaning his nails with a blunt blade, carefully scraping red gunk from under them.

'Pork marinade,' Tony said, wiping the blade off on the sole of his flip-flop. He worked in his father's butcher shop on Saturdays.

'It takes pigs five minutes to bleed to death. One stab in the heart and another one in the neck and they're gone.'

Gieles had gone in with Tony a couple of times. In the cold storage locker next to the butcher shop there were slaughtered pigs hanging in a row on meat hooks. Their heads were gone. Tony had jumped on one carcass and swung through the locker, kicking the other pigs as he went.

'Have you ever seen how a horse is slaughtered?' Gieles asked.

'No.' He was cutting the sole of his flip-flop with the knife. 'But I bet it's cool. Shoot the thing right through the head.' He pressed his forefinger between his eyebrows. 'Doof.'

'They used to do it with a nail,' Gieles said, staring at the umbrella over his head. The sun had made the white fabric fade to orange. He wondered how that worked. Why did all the colours fade to white in the sun, but white faded to a colour?

In the meantime Tony had carved the word 'dushi' in the flip-flop. He pushed his foot toward Gieles. 'That means "cunt" in Antillean.'

Dolly didn't like having him around. She thought he was sneaky. Gieles didn't know whether he was or not. He had known Tony so long that he didn't even wonder any more. But lately whenever he was with Tony he felt bad, whereas when he was with Super Waling he felt better.

When he was on the phone with Meike he mainly felt horny.

The little brothers in the wading pool were playing who could stay under water the longest. The toddler at the fence began making a high shrieking sound and holding his arms out wide.

'I'm gonna go check the fridge,' said Tony.

Dolly would absolutely not want him checking her fridge. But ever since the business with the breast cancer Gieles had started feeling sorry for Tony.

Gieles turned his head to the side and spat on the ground. The air he was breathing tasted sticky. He thought about Meike and their daily phone conversations. Her voice was as soft as Wally's new feathers. The softness of her voice didn't seem to match her appearance and the content of her stories, which were raw and angry. Gieles began to wonder why Tony hadn't come back yet, and he shut his eyes.

Suddenly he felt something cool being pressed against his cheek. He opened his eyes and looked straight into the face of Tony, who was swishing some black thing back and forth in front of his nose.

'That dead guy left his dick in the nightstand,' said Tony, holding the thing up and smelling it. 'It's turned completely black.'

Gieles sat up with a start. 'How did you get that?' He looked anxiously at Skiq and Onno, but they hadn't noticed anything. Then he looked at the dildo again, which resembled a big, pointed fungus.

'I just told you, from her nightstand.' Tony dipped the dildo into the glass of cola he was holding and licked the tip.

Gieles felt an intense urge to punch his veal cutlet nose to mush.

'Put it back.'

'Chill, man. I'll put it back. Really.'

Gieles tried to grab the dildo out of his hands, but Tony held it up high in the air. Curious, Skiq and Onno got out of the wading pool. Even the dog woke up. Suddenly the dildo began to vibrate. They all looked at it with astonishment.

'It can go faster or slower,' Tony noted, turning the far end.

'What's that?' asked Skiq.

Tony beat the dildo rhythmically against the palm of his hand. It was surprisingly flexible.

'This is your mother's ...'

'Shut up!'

'Why does he have to shut up, Gieles?'

'Personal ...'

'You shut up!'

'Rubber ducky.'

'Rubber ducky? My mother's?' repeated Onno with amazement.

'It doesn't look like a ducky,' Skiq said. 'It's just a stick.'

'That's right,' agreed Tony. 'A juicy, fat, black stick.'

'Michael Jackson used to be the same colour,' said Skiq in his Spiderman swimming trunks. 'First he was black and then he got this disease and he was white and then he got so white that he died. That was the doctor's fault.'

Tony poked Lady's fur with the dildo. Slowly she stood up.

'Come on, Lady,' cried Tony. 'Go fetch!'

Gieles took a swipe, but Tony threw the dildo into the wading pool. Skiq and Onno ran after it screaming, 'The stick can swim! The stick can swim!' The plucky little thing gyrated through the water.

'Ah-woo-hooo!' howled Tony like a werewolf.

'Give it to me!' shouted Gieles.

'Go fetch, Lady!' screamed Skiq, throwing the dildo into the air. The dog shot out from under the table and ran after it. The vibrating stick had awakened her hunting instinct. She bit into the rubber like a lunatic and ran out through the back gate.

'Lady!' screamed Gieles. 'Come here!'

A little while later Tony came back with the dog. He stood at the back gate, the battered dildo in his hand. Little was left of the black veins. Lady had taken whole bites out of the silicone.

'I'll buy her a new one,' said Tony indifferently. Gieles walked over and blocked the entrance. Although Tony was a head taller, Gieles felt stronger. If he hadn't been holding the toddler in his arms he might have beat Tony to a pulp. Jonas sucked noisily on his plastic squirrel, which was leaking water from the wading pool. Skiq had broken off a branch from a tree and was screaming at Lady to go fetch. But the dog dropped to the ground in a heap.

'Chill,' said Tony. 'Tomorrow I'll go out and buy exactly the same dick. She'll never know the difference.'

When Dolly got back home, Gieles couldn't get away fast enough. He hoped she wasn't going to use the dildo that night. He hoped the boys would keep their mouths shut about the black stick.

He walked along the edge of the fields and heard the cries of the lapwing. Ever since the starlings had been chased off by bullets, the lapwings had come to call. They did not pose an immediate danger, since there weren't more than twenty of them. He could see their white breasts moving across the landscape in the twilight. It was just as if they were calling out their own names.

Back in the barnyard he began looking for his little goose when suddenly he heard screaming coming from the campground.

Jesus, now what?

Gieles looked over at the spaceship, then at the tents of the three young spotters. He couldn't see very clearly, but it looked as if they had been attacked by something. The boys were standing huddled together and making half-hearted karate chops. Above the roar of the planes he could hear angry squawking. Honk! Honk! Honk! Honk!

Gieles ran up to the tents. One of the boys was holding a frying pan and trying to protect himself from an attack that had been launched by Wally's fat sister.

Flapping her wings, and with her outstretched neck, she was lighting into them like something possessed.

'Do something!' screamed the boy with a pale white face. 'That bird's trying to murder us!'

'It's a monster!' cried his friend.

Tufted, Bufted and Wally were looking on from a distance. They seemed bewildered. Even Gieles didn't know how to deal with the aggressive goose.

'Here!' he screamed and walked toward the goose, who was readying herself for a new attack. 'Come here!' Now Gieles was angry. First that fucking dog and now this fucking goose.

She began pecking hard at the hand of the boy with the frying pan. He tried to smack her away but without success. His two spotter friends dove into the tent and pulled down the zipper.

'Catch that thing!' screamed the boy, stumbling over a guy line. He rolled up in a ball, moaning, while the goose worked over his back. Gieles seized the bird right behind her head and dragged her away from the boy. She was much heavier than he had expected. She made flailing movements with her immature wings, but he was able to wrestle her to the ground. He held her neck with one hand and pressed against her with his chest.

Gieles lay on top of the goose for a couple of minutes until she gave up the fight. Then he rose slowly and let her go. She shook her feathers and walked away indignantly.

'She won't hurt you any more,' Gieles told the boy, who was still lying rolled up on the ground.

'Get those other ones out of here, too,' he whimpered.

'They're completely harmless,' Gieles said in a soothing tone. But the boy insisted that all the geese had to be cleared from the field. His friends didn't dare come out of the tent until all four were locked up in the barn.

Gieles looked around and surveyed the damage. The camping stove and the plastic picnic table had fallen over, plates and bottles of beer were lying on the ground among the feathers.

'That one goose was begging,' stammered the boy. He was still holding onto the frying pan. 'And when we gave him some sausage he became aggressive. First he ate all the food off our plates, then he knocked everything over and turned on us.'

'*¡Que ganso!*' whispered the boy next to him.

They were all wearing identical shirts. SPOTTERS INTERNATIONAL was emblazoned across the chest with a climbing airplane below it.

'I'm really sorry. My geese have never attacked anyone before.'

Gieles straightened the camping stove and picked a plate out of the grass. Ants were swarming all over the ketchup.

'I go not to toilet,' peeped one of the boys in English.

'Me neither,' said the other two.

'The barn door is locked,' Gieles attempted, but they begged him to go with them to the washing shed: a small structure with two toilets, a shower and a sink. The door was decorated with stickers from spotters' clubs. Right next to the door handle was a big sticker with a whale on it and SOUTH AUSTRALIAN WHALE SPOTTERS underneath. Gieles thought that was the prettiest sticker of all. The spotters were finished in a flash and came out of the shed like a bunch of skittish horses.

He brought them to their tents and then walked back to the barn. As soon as he got inside the aggressive goose puffed up her breast and began to honk. Gieles honked back, drove her into a corner and picked up Wally.

A little while later he fell into bed, exhausted and fully clothed.

By the next morning the three young spotters had disappeared without a trace. They left without paying their bill. Uncle Fred stood on the site where they had pitched their tents and walked around examining the flattened grass, as if they all might be hiding under the sod.

Gieles tried to explain what had happened without bringing the goose into too much disrepute. 'They challenged her,' he said.

Johan came to join them. He was walking much more briskly since the last time.

'We didn't hear anything last night. We slept like logs.'

He put his hands on his bony hips and looked at the empty site with contempt. 'I didn't trust them from the minute I saw them. I suspect they were foreigners.'

Gieles said he had to go to school and tried to walk away, but Johan grabbed him by the arm. His grip was surprisingly strong. 'Say, Gerard,' he said, 'when are you coming to look at my scrapbooks?'

18

Willem Bos and Gieles were on their way to the public meeting being held to discuss the pyramids. Uncle Fred was not going. He took life as it came, with or without pyramids. His father was silent on the issue, so Gieles kept his mouth shut, too. Discussing problems with someone who had trouble getting the words out was not a pleasant experience. And there were problems. Meike hadn't been to school in weeks. She spent her days in bed. Tony still hadn't bought a new dildo. And two foreign aid workers had been kidnapped in Somalia. His mother had passed the news on to his father by phone. Gieles was lying in bed and he could hear his father's anger. He was screaming, and not just because the connection with Somalia was poor. Gieles counted six 'goddamns' and three 'life-threatenings.' Then he jammed his fingers in his ears.

Gieles was going to sacrifice two extra pages from the third Rizla album that night, and he already knew which ones were going up in flames: the yellow-hooded blackbird and the golden-fronted leafbird.

He looked at his mother's faded passport photo. For years she had been hanging there in a little black frame, stuck to the dashboard with a suction cup. She looked drearier than ever. 'We could put a new photo of Mom in the frame,' Gieles offered. 'This one is so old.'

'Go ahead,' answered his father as he parked the service car on a side street near the town hall.

The doorman said the public meeting in the Fokker Room had already begun. They walked through the corridors, past rooms that were named after Dutch airplane manufacturers: Albert Plesman, Frits Koolhoven, Marinus van Meel. 'Koolhoven,' said Willem, 'was in the NSB.'

Being in the NSB—the Dutch Nazi party in occupied Holland during World War Two—was the worst thing you could be, according to his father. It had to do with treason, Gieles knew, but he didn't know much more about it.

His father opened a door that was marked ANTHONY FOKKER. Hundreds of eyes turned to Gieles and his father and then back to the speaker. They sat down to the side of the podium where there were still a few empty chairs.

Gieles had a good view of the audience. In the first row he saw Liedje and Tony Senior. Liedje was wearing a loose-fitting, gold-coloured shirt with long sleeves. Although there must have been at least seven metres between them, he could still see her heavily applied eye shadow. She didn't look sick, she looked angry. Her pink lips were pressed together so hard that they wrinkled up like a raisin.

Tony Senior was seated next to her, grinning. His legs were crossed and he kept bouncing his left foot up and down. His nylon haircut was impeccable. Sitting at an angle behind Tony's parents was Dolly. He thought about the dildo. It had happened almost a week ago. How often did she use that thing anyway?

He peered at Dolly once again. She was sitting as straight as a ramrod with her chin held high. She held her chin up like this whenever she was warning the boys for the first and last time. It was at moments like that

that Gieles was afraid of her. After the chin came the explosion. She would run after her children, ranting and raging, until her foot or hand made contact with them. He wondered whether Dolly would end up giving the man on the podium a kick in the ass.

Gieles surveyed the townspeople and concluded that all of them, except for Tony Senior and his father, were ready to knock heads together. These people were plagued by airplane noise, and now the airport was coming up with the umpteenth plan to counter the decibels. Most of them were solutions that Gieles couldn't believe any adult would seriously consider. The funniest idea, he thought, was a narrow tent a few kilometres long that was supposed to slurp up the sound like a straw in a glass of soda.

And now they had come along with these hilarious pyramids, but no one could see the fun in them. Gieles wondered what it must be like for this guy with the microphone, addressing a room full of people who wanted nothing more than to eat him alive. But the man seemed totally oblivious. In fact, he was the very picture of good cheer, as if he had been hired to provide the entertainment for a party. He had a little black beard that couldn't have been more than a week old. Gieles reached up and stroked his own baby-soft skin.

The man with the little beard walked back and forth across the podium as if he were taking a stroll and daydreaming out loud.

Behind him was a narrow table at which two more men and a woman were sitting. They weren't paying any attention to Little Beard but were paging through stacks of papers and taking notes. Gieles looked at their clothing. He didn't know anyone around here who dressed like that: with a sports jacket and tie, and trousers with sharp creases. His father wore jeans and a leather jacket. Uncle Fred usually dressed in awful-looking sweaters that never wore out with coloured strips and figures on them.

Little Beard projected an image on a big screen. It was an aerial photograph of the runway. Gieles's house had become a pimple, the woods in exile a birthmark. The runway lay like an alien between the green and grey areas. These were the last agricultural parcels from the time of Ide and Sophia and the sunken horse.

Section 27.

Then Little Beard showed a new picture. The runway was still there, but now it was embedded with brightly coloured pyramids and hills that Gieles recognised from the letter at Tony's parents' house.

Suddenly a buzzing of voices could be heard in the room.

'Over my dead body!' he heard Liedje shriek above the others. 'Over my dead body!'

She had crossed her arms very high so that her shoulders almost touched her ears.

Little Beard seemed not to be hearing any of this. A slight smile even appeared on his face. Maybe he was deaf. He just kept on talking.

'The pyramids absorb the sound. The material and the canted surfaces provide a reduction of at least seven decibels. It's like this,' and he started moving his arms like a traffic cop. 'The noise bounces off the triangular shapes in every direction.'

Little Beard kept on talking about innovative solutions and low-frequency sound, and he looked as if he had worked it out all by himself. Several people in the audience raised their hands. 'You may ask your questions in just a little while,' said Little Beard. 'After the break. Hang onto them.'

He went on with his presentation until a man stood up.

'Do you believe this yourself?' the man said, and his voice echoed through the room.

'You may ask your questions later, sir. *Later.*'

But the man wouldn't let himself be thrown off guard. 'Yes, I know how it all works. Later there'll only be a couple of minutes left for us. So tell me now, do you believe this yourself?'

'What are you referring to?' asked Little Beard, but it sounded more like a reprimand.

The man pointed to the picture. 'I'm referring to that postcard from Egypt. Those pyramids. Those tombs of King Tut.'

The audience chuckled.

'This is an artist's impression,' Little Beard corrected him, articulating through the microphone with great exaggeration. 'What I am showing you here is not a question of belief. This project has been preceded by months of intensive study. *Months.* We present facts, not fables.'

'Yeah, right!' shouted the man. 'That's what you all said *before* the runway came. You said there had been all this scientific study and that we wouldn't have any noise. And what have we got? Noise!'

Little Beard made a face like an overworked teacher.

'I'm asking you once again if you will please ...'

'That constant droning in your body, day and night.' The man grabbed his stomach. 'It's like swallowing a swarm of flies. That's what it feels like. Just so you know, okay?'

'Sir, we base our conclusions on hard facts ...'

'Go fly a kite with your facts. At least that makes a lot less noise.'

'You don't have to be rude …'

'I'm done. I'll shut up now.' The man closed his mouth and locked it with an imaginary key. The audience snickered. The two men and the woman sitting behind Little Beard continued to thumb through their papers stoically.

Little Beard went on with his presentation in an irritated tone. His good spirits had been badly bruised. He rattled on about phase I and phase II. Implementation this, megahertz that. Gieles's mind wandered. His eyes paused on a work of art that ran along the wall of the Anthony Fokker Room. It was a plastic tube that air was being blown through. The tube was at least four metres long and ran up to the ceiling, where an immense kite in the shape of an airplane was bobbing back and forth in the stream of air. Gieles wished the plane would dive down into the audience and take him with it. He would fly to Africa and pick up his mother so she wouldn't be kidnapped. But first he would land at Meike's house and drag her out of bed.

The audience was quiet for a while until Little Beard began talking about the creation of ponds. Sixty hectares of land would be submerged and floating pyramids would be placed in this lake to further reduce the noise.

Then Dolly stood up. She spoke decisively and with restraint, as if she were the queen. 'You see that red pyramid? The third from the left?'

She pointed at the picture with her red-polished forefinger.

Little Beard thrust out his chest, as if he were preparing for a brutal confrontation.

'That's *my* house. I live there with *my* three children. You stand here as cool as you please, talking about your jacuzzi pool, but you haven't checked it out with *me*.'

She put her hands on her hips and raised her chin way up in the air. No one uttered a sound. Dolly looked magnificent, standing there like that. All thoughts of the dildo fled from Gieles's mind.

'I haven't heard you say a word about buying us out. You're acting as if we had disappeared off the face of the earth.'

Now she sounded emotional. Gieles hoped she wouldn't start talking about her dead husband. Liedje had also stood up. She sparkled like an Oscar figurine. Tony Senior kept smiling at Little Beard and his helpers, who had stopped writing and were looking at the women.

'That goes for us, too!' shouted Liedje. 'That yellow pyramid in the curve of the runway, that's our house. I've lived there all my life. I was born in that house ...' She grabbed her left armpit and pressed down. Gieles thought of the tubes and the bag with wound discharge.

She's gonna pinch that bag till it bursts.

'Madam!'

'*You* have wrecked my whole neighbourhood with that damned runway. Almost everybody is gone. And now *you* want to bury the last houses under a bunch of pyramids and ...'

'Please, madam, let me ...'

'I wouldn't leave if you paid me a million! I'm gonna spend the rest of my life there!'

Quite provoked, Little Beard raised his hand. 'Please!'

Even his helpers started making imploring gestures.

'In the near future we will speak to you personally ...'

'There's nothing to discuss!' shouted Liedje, angrily squeezing under her arm.

Dolly said nothing and sat down, satisfied with what she had heard. Gieles knew she wanted to move. Better today than tomorrow.

'Madam, let's talk about this briefly after the meeting. Now sit down, pul-lease.'

Tony Senior pulled gently on her hand while continuing to make friendly nods to the people from the airport.

Little Beard sighed loudly into the microphone. It sounded like a springtime storm. Just when the man seemed to think he had everything under control, a voice was heard from the very back of the room. It was a fluid voice. The voice said, 'The happiest people on earth do not have asphalt-covered roads. The happiest people on earth don't have an airport runway next to their door, either.'

'Pardon me?' said Little Beard, taken completely by surprise. He searched diligently for the voice, but no one in the audience had stood up.

'That's the conclusion of the Happy Planet Index, which is an index that shows how happy we are and in what countries the happiest people live. I can tell you that they don't live here.'

One of the men behind the table took the floor without a microphone and shouted, 'How many times do we have to say that you can ask questions *after* the break! *After* the break!'

'I don't have any questions,' said the voice. 'I just wanted to point this out. To you. Maybe you don't know about the index. Maybe you are not aware of the term Gross National Happiness. I can tell you that very different values are used to measure Gross National Happiness. With all the wonderful research you've done, it would be such a shame to overlook *this* area of research.'

Willem Bos burst out laughing. A couple of people began to clap, and finally the dam burst. The voice was given a resounding applause.

'Go fly a kite with your facts!' shouted a couple of people sitting near Little Beard. Gieles beamed. He tried to imagine Super Waling in his mobility scooter hiding in the back of the room, wrapped in one of his unsightly sweatsuits, armed with a notebook and his dumb linen bag.

Gieles turned to his father. 'I know that man,' he said proudly. Willem Bos bent towards him. 'I know him,' Gieles repeated in his ear. 'That's Waling Cittersen van Boven.'

After the meeting, and as the room emptied, Gieles introduced his father to Super Waling. They shook hands. Willem Bos did not flinch at the sight of all that flesh.

'You have a terrific son. Really terrific,' said Super Waling. 'Gieles saved me when my mobility scooter had broken down once again.'

His remark made Gieles glow for hours like coal in a barbecue.

19

My letter to you is growing formidable. Things go good, things do not go good. The good thing: goose small has a name. Wally. She has been named. Her game with the table ping pong is marching beautifully! The not good thing: goose big is still eating extraterrestrial, but now she is also showing herself aggressive. This is new. She attacks guests of camping. This was for one time, but my father says, for the last time. He says: displaying of aggression cannot happen any more. Goose big cries that she is a predator. She walks prowling across the earth like a tiger. Is my goose dangerous? I cry not. But she is surely defective. By example: yesterday she attacked the lawn. This is now Swiss cheese. And she honks at the man of the mail. I am worried. Do you know how to regulate the situation? Do you have a good ordering?

There was no getting out of it. Johan kept hounding Gieles to look at his plane crash collection. They sat side by side with the scrapbooks at an oval camping table. Wally was under the table taking a nap. It was an impressive stack. He hoped the old man wouldn't be showing him all the books.

His wife served cups of tea and a tray of cookies. She was wearing her hat with the plastic flowers.

'Have you started summer vacation yet?' she asked Gieles, looking at him with her little-girl eyes.

'No, ma'am. Not for five weeks.'

'Ah, summer vacation. I remember it as if it were yesterday. It was endless.'

'Judith,' said her husband, in a tone suggesting that this was serious men's business. 'You're interrupting.'

Johan waited for her to shut the door behind her before he began speaking. Then he cleared his throat and said, 'Let's begin at the beginning.' He pulled out a pair of reading glasses from one of the body warmer pockets. 'On October 13th, 1972, to be precise.'

He took a scrapbook from the stack on which the words '1972 through 1976' had been carefully inscribed by hand. The old man held the book like a precious manuscript and began to intone: 'That was the day an entire rugby team, along with their family and friends, took a nose dive into the Andes mountains. They were flying in a Fokker belonging to the Uruguayan Air Force, and after only a few of days the search for the poor kids was called off.'

Johan laid the scrapbook on the table to show the newspaper clippings.

'All they had left was half a plane. Otherwise there was nothing, and I mean absolutely nothing, at that incredible altitude. Except the ice. Well, who doesn't know the story? The survivors ate the dead. Not dead strangers, either, but their buddies. Family members. Friends. They ate familiar flesh.'

He pointed to a sticker of a film camera. 'I put this symbol on all the crashes that were made into films. Have you seen the film *Alive*, Gerard?'

Gieles didn't know anything about the film or the crash. 'I think so,' he said.

The man cast his eyes upward and then looked over at Gieles. 'I've seen *Alive* maybe a hundred times,' he said, 'and every time I ask myself: would I have done that?'

He grabbed Gieles's wrist and spoke in hushed tones. 'Eat my buddies. Cut strips of flesh off their dead limbs and swallow them frozen.'

Johan gnashed his big false teeth. 'They had no fire on the mountain. They didn't have anything at all, for two months. Only each other. What would you have done, Gerard?'

Gieles tried his best to pry his wrist from Johan's grasp without him noticing. What on earth should he say? The idea of eating someone like Tony filled him with revulsion. He thought of the emergency landing on the Hudson and said in English, 'What would Sully do?'

Johan frowned and released Gieles's wrist.

'Captain Sully, flight 1549,' Gieles said, repeating the question in Dutch. 'What would Sully do?'

'I get it, I get it,' muttered Johan. 'I speak my languages. Captain Sullenberger certainly would have eaten his crew to survive. The man is a survivor. Just like me. I survived the war.'

With these words he concluded his discussion of the crash of the rugby players in the Andes.

Johan turned the pages, all of them packed with clippings, and began talking about the Eastern Airlines Lockheed that crashed among the crocodiles in the Everglades in Florida on 29 December 1972. The man sat bent over his book like an ancient lion trying to protect his kill.

'It was the fault of the pilot. A CFIT. A Controlled Flight Into Terrain. Number of dead: 101. Wounded: 75.'

Gieles shifted restlessly in the lawn chair. This could go on for hours.

'In the years after the crash, the crew members claimed they saw apparitions of their dead colleagues,' Johan snickered.

Gieles sat beside him, staring absently, until he heard children's voices. He sprang to his feet.

'Which was hogwash, of course, but Americans are very sensitive to hocus pocus stories. They're a hysterical bunch. You see that in all those ridiculous flight regulations and security questions. Even so, the crash produced a number of interesting films. I have those films, of course ...'

'I've got to go,' interrupted Gieles. 'I promised one of the neighbourhood kids I'd help him in the woods in exile. That's the woods further down,' he explained.

Dolly's son had begged him to come. Gieles had attended the same primary school, and when he was there his class had done the same thing: go to the woods to clear out dead branches and rubbish.

'But we just got started,' said Johan. He didn't even try to hide his disappointment.

'Sorry.' Gieles stood up.

Johan slammed the scrapbook shut dejectedly.

'We'll go further with this some other time. You got that, Gerard?'

'I got it.'

'Tomorrow?'

'Tomorrow's really bad for me. So's the whole week. I have to finish a report. But after that I think I'm okay.'

Gieles looked under the table. Wally was still asleep. Her neck was draped over her back and she had tucked her head half under her wings. He heard the schoolchildren getting closer. Their voices were as shrill as young starlings.

Gieles left Wally with the disheartened Johan. The other three geese were restless. Tufted and Bufted walked around the yard cackling. Wally's big sister was standing motionless. Only her head was turning around, like a submarine periscope. She surveyed the area with great concentration, her neck stretched out so far that it seemed a metre long.

With his gaze fixed on the goose he walked out to the road. There he saw the teacher leading the way, with a line of pupils behind her in pairs. As soon as they got closer the goose lowered her head to the ground and began moving stealthily in their direction. She hissed. Gieles hissed back.

'Gieles! I'm here!' he heard Skiq shouting.

He and the goose stared each other down until she turned her head and slunk away.

Skiq ran up and threw his arms around him as if he were trying to safeguard his property.

'This is where I say, "Gieles, my how you've grown,"' said the teacher.

It was Miss Barbara. He had had her for fourth, fifth and sixth grade. As the airport grew the school shrank. Miss Barbara looked younger than she did two years before when he left primary school. It seemed like a lifetime ago.

'Let go of Gieles,' she said to Skiq. 'You'll squeeze the daylights out of him.'

Gieles walked in the middle between Skiq and the teacher. Fourteen boys and girls skipped behind them.

Miss Barbara asked how he was doing. Then she wanted to know how his mother was doing. 'I always thought she was so brave. Risking your life to help people. You must be proud of your mother.'

'Yes,' he said, with little conviction. He was proud of her, but he also thought she had changed. When she was home, things didn't happen naturally any more. A peanut butter sandwich could suddenly be a sandwich with too much peanut butter. She didn't say: that's too much, or clean your plate. She never did that. But she could deliver a whole sermon with her eyes and by moving her eyebrows up and down in a way laden with significance.

Suddenly there was commotion at the back of the troop of children. They were shouting, 'Ooooh, how cute' and 'Look! A little goose!'

Wally was looking for Gieles. Once she spotted him she began to honk and stumble over her own webbed feet. The children laughed. The little goose rubbed up against Gieles's legs. He picked her up, and she willingly let herself be petted by a dozen little hands.

The woods were in full bloom. The grass was high and the leaves of the birch trees were succulent. Some of the bushes were bearing red berries. A couple of children ran to the tree that the school had planted to protest the building of the runway. It was a linden tree that was now more than three metres tall.

'The tree is dirty,' one of the children noted.

Gieles saw the black spots on the leaves. It looked just like the layer of soot that formed on their windows and on the airport service car. 'That comes from the planes.' Gieles examined the leaves. 'The jet fuel ends up on the trees and that makes everything black.'

The children listened attentively. Skiq stood proudly beside him, still holding his hand. Wally, too, was resting on his arm with intense satisfaction and looking around curiously.

'Us too?' asked a little girl.

'Yes, us too. That's why you should take a shower every day.' His voice dropped. 'And blow your nose. Or your snot will be black.'

The children all stuck their fingers up their noses.

Miss Barbara was standing near the pond, which was

overgrown with reeds, and she walked back to join them. 'No, guys, that's not jet fuel. It's sooty mould. There are lice in the linden tree and they make this stuff that's a lot like glue.' She ran her fingers over a leaf and showed it to them. 'And that gets black after a while. What Gieles told you is silly.'

Skiq squeezed his hand hard. 'Gieles is really good at ping-pong,' he said, giving his teacher a fierce look. His jaw was trembling with rage. She had made his friend look like a fool. 'And his little goose can play ping-pong, too. They're gonna play ping-pong at the fair and I'm allowed to watch.'

The teacher crouched down beside him. She took his arm and pulled him toward her gently. 'Shall we ask Gieles to tell us about his special goose, Skiq? I don't know very much about geese.'

The boy shrugged his pointed shoulders. 'We were supposed to look for butterflies.'

'The butterflies can wait,' said the teacher. 'Can you find a nice place for us to sit down?'

He pointed to an elm and ran up to it. 'Gieles!' he screamed. 'You have to sit next to me!'

'You're very important to him,' said Miss Barbara. 'He's talked more about you in class than about Michael Jackson.' She followed behind her pupils.

The children sat in a circle and Gieles sat next to Skiq. He put the little goose on Skiq's lap. The children started firing questions at him. Is it a boy or a girl? Can she swim under water? How does she hold the racket? Can she keep score? Does she understand human language? Is there such a thing as fighting geese? Do geese have sharp teeth? Can they bite a child to death?

Skiq hugged the little goose as if he were holding a valuable dish. She liked it for a little while, then she hopped off his lap. She sat in the middle of the circle and began preening herself. She rubbed her bill over the furthest point on her back. Every now and then she looked up at her circle of admirers.

'Geese have a kind of hole right above their tail where this grease comes out,' Gieles told them, encouraged by the interested nod of the teacher.

'Now she's rubbing her bill over that hole and then she'll smear the grease all over her feathers. That makes her waterproof, just like a raincoat.'

'Did you teach her that?' asked a girl.

'No,' said Gieles. 'Animals know those things when they're born. The rest they learn from their parents.'

'Where are her father and mother?' asked another child.

'I don't know. But I teach her a lot.' He said this with pride.

'Look!' cried the teacher, looking up. 'A holly blue.'

A couple of metres above their heads they saw a little blue butterfly with wings that were silver white underneath.

Gieles followed the holly blue with his eyes as it fluttered across the pond, past the bushes and out to the road. And that's where he saw her.

She was standing at least twenty-five metres further on, but he recognised her right away. He stammered something to the teacher and walked toward her. The first thing that struck him was her height. She was much smaller than he had expected, no more than a head taller than Skiq.

'Meike?' Gieles was flabbergasted.

'Hi,' she whispered. 'That man, Uncle Fred, said you were here ...'

She's so white.

It looked as if her skin had never seen the light of day. Her face was flawless, except for the black tear and the piercing in her eyebrow. The piercing was a spider, a minuscule spider with a tiny red stone for a body. Her eyes were much greener than in the photos.

'Yes,' he said, rubbing his hand over his hair, which undoubtedly was standing straight up. 'I was ... uh ... telling them about ... something ...'

Meike plucked at her baggy black shirt. She was wearing army boots and leggings full of holes and runs. There was a cord around her neck with a little bag hanging from it that was decorated with coloured feathers, like the one he used to have with his Indian outfit.

Miss Barbara came up to them. 'How nice,' she said cheerfully. 'We have a visitor.' She put out her hand and introduced herself. Meike reciprocated with her own tiny hand. She had jet black fingernails.

The teacher took her arm as if they had been girlfriends for years and brought her into the circle. 'Skiq told us that Gieles can do tricks with his goose. We're all really curious.'

Meike submissively sat down cross-legged next to the teacher while the children gazed at her from head to foot. They had lost interest in the little goose, who was poking her head into the bushes. With all that black, Meike looked more like a bat that had fallen out of a tree.

'This is Meike,' said Miss Barbara in a voice that was meant to reassure the children. 'Meike, I don't remember whether you ever attended our school.'

Meike sat very still except for her eyes, which shot up and down as if she were searching for something but couldn't remember what it was. Gieles stood outside the circle and didn't know what to do with his arms. They suddenly seemed a metre longer. He put his hands in his pockets, took them out again, rubbed them nervously over his hair and tried to stop the merry-go-round that was spinning inside his head.

'Gieles, when are you gonna do that trick?' shouted Skiq angrily.

But Wally wasn't the least bit interested in playing. She had discovered the pond and was making a path for herself through the reeds to get to the water.

After the children had finished clearing away the dead branches and had gone back to school with the teacher, Gieles took Meike home with him. They walked through the campground. Fortunately Johan and his scrapbooks were nowhere to be seen.

'This is our plane spotters' campground,' he said. 'The Hot Spot.' He pointed to the sign.

'There's almost nobody here,' she said in a whisper.

'The noise drove all the guests away.'

He watched Meike laugh for the first time. Whenever she laughed she wrinkled up her nose. He wanted to go on telling jokes just so she'd wrinkle up her nose like that again.

They walked side by side. He felt an irresistible urge to press his face into her dreadlocks, which looked like the tails of little black lambs. A Fokker 100 took off.

'It's like living next to a highway.' She tried very hard to hide her Brabant accent.

They watched the plane until it dissolved into the air and the next plane went up. Meike sat down on the grass and took a pack of shag tobacco out of the Indian bag. Gieles didn't know she smoked. He had never seen a girl smoke shag. Then she took out the rolling papers. He sat down next to her and groped for words, noticing how practised she was at rolling the cigarette with her tiny hands. He stared at her mouth and cheek and realised how unusual it was for him to see a girl's face up so close.

I'd sacrifice thirty bird pages to kiss her.

'Were you just passing by?' He realised how incredibly stupid his question was. She took a drag and spit out a thread of tobacco from her lip. Then she shook her head, making all the lambs' tails wag. She picked at her leather bracelet, which was decorated with dancing Indians.

'I ran away.' She took a long draw on her cigarette. Meike was sitting cross-legged again. The crotch of her nylon leggings formed a gutter between her legs.

'I've been walking for-fucking-ever.' She unlaced her army boots with great difficulty. 'All the way here from the train station. It must have been ten kilometres.'

When Gieles saw her flaming red blisters he grinned from ear to ear. He wanted to tell her about Sophia and her battered feet in the hollow linden tree, and he said, 'You should put jenever on them. It's good for blisters.'

'I don't like jenever.' She inhaled deeply. 'I only like Malibu.'

Her delivery was tough, but her thick accent made it sound infinitely charming.

Neither of them spoke, and Meike looked with fascination at the airplanes as if she were looking at some kind of performance.

'I didn't know planes were so big.'

Gieles saw that she wasn't making a joke. 'Haven't you ever seen a plane up close?'

'I've never flown in a plane. Our father ... my father is afraid of flying. He'll freak when he sees this.'

Gieles saw the yellow jeep riding into the yard further on. Willem Bos was home earlier than usual.

'My father,' he said, and they watched him shut the car door and walk into the house.

'Your father's tall, too,' she said, greatly impressed.

On impulse he grabbed Meike's hand and pulled her up. 'You better put your shoes on. There's goose shit everywhere around here.'

20

His father and uncle were standing in the kitchen talking when he opened the back door. The little goose tried to worm her way inside, but Gieles pushed her back with his shins.

Gieles knew they were talking about Meike. His father was holding a bottle of beer and leaning against the counter. With that deeply furrowed brow he really did look like Harrison Ford. Uncle Fred was sitting at the table with the newspaper spread out in front of him.

'This is Meike.' She was standing behind him and didn't come any further. His father didn't move either.

'I met her briefly this afternoon,' said Uncle Fred, as if it were the most normal thing in the world for a girl with piercings and a tear tattoo to be standing in their kitchen. To Gieles it seemed like a year before his father disengaged himself from the counter and walked up to her. He held out his hand. 'I'm Willem Bos. Gieles's father.'

Meike lifted her head the way people do when they're looking at a skyscraper. Then she shook his hand. 'Meike Nooteboom,' she said in a voice that was barely audible.

'Nooteboom?' cried Uncle Fred. 'From Cees Nooteboom? The writer?'

Meike raised her eyebrows, making the little spider come to life.

Willem sat down at the table and listened to his brother enumerating the titles of novels in the hope that the girl would recognise them. He drummed on the table with his fingers.

'Fred?' he said and looked at him helplessly. This was a difficult question, something he was not good at.

Uncle Fred took off his reading glasses. 'Meike, I take it you're going to be staying. You brought a suitcase with you.'

Meike gave the impression that she didn't know anything about the suitcase she had dragged along. Her eyes were very big and green. Gicles had never seen a face that kept changing the way hers did. She was like a character in a cartoon.

'And your parents?' he asked casually, walking with difficulty to the counter. 'Do they know where you are?'

'I don't think so.' She whispered and peeked out at the polio leg from under her thickly applied mascara.

'In that case I think it would be a good idea if you called home.' Uncle Fred opened the refrigerator. 'Just tell your parents that we'll call them, too.'

He took a head of lettuce and a cucumber out of the crisper, looking over his shoulder at Gieles. 'Show her the guest room, would you?'

Gieles glanced at his father. He looked worn out. Gieles was hoping for a sign, a wink or something, so he'd know his father wasn't angry. But his father said nothing. He just kept drumming on the table with his fingers.

The guest room was on the ground floor, right near the front door. It was a small room that also served as a repository for junk. Uncle Fred had clearly done his best this afternoon to straighten it up for Meike.

The winter coats, vacuum cleaner and ironing board had been tucked away under the single bed. He had shoved two crates of books under the bed as well. On top of the bed was her suitcase. It was a strange shape. It looked like a baby's coffin.

The window was wide open. She stuck her fingers in her ears and made funny faces, as if the roaring of the engines were rising from her throat.

She had a tongue piercing, didn't she?

Gieles quickly shut the window. She sat down beside the coffin and kicked off her shoes. A blister on the sole of her foot was bleeding.

'You're bleeding!' cried Gieles with a start, and he heard Uncle Fred's crutch in the hall followed by a brief knock on the door.

'Towels,' he said. 'Oh, honey, you need to soak that foot. Gieles, go get a basin of hot water. I'll get the washing soda.'

They were so preoccupied with Meike's feet that Uncle Fred forgot the evening meal. Willem Bos saw his son running around with a basin and his brother taking cleaning products from one of the kitchen cabinets. He had to be at the airport in less than an hour for a rush job. Brooding black-backed seagulls had ensconced themselves in a hangar and had to be driven out.

He walked to the counter and began to clean the lettuce. He cut the cucumber and tomatoes and tossed them in with the lettuce, along with a big splash of salad dressing. On the cutting board were three sausages wrapped in plastic. He looked in the refrigerator to see if there was any more meat. Then he sliced the sausages down the middle and fried them brown on all sides.

Gieles came into the kitchen and was surprised to see his father at the stove. He was making awkward movements, as if he were playing with a doll house.

'I'll set the table,' Gieles said, and raced to the cabinet. They only used a tablecloth for Christmas, but a tablecloth for this meal was essential. And napkins. Meike shuffled through the doorway. Her feet were heavily wrapped in bandages. Only her toes were visible.

'What's this?' said Uncle Fred with surprise. 'Are you cooking, Willem?'

Then he saw the green holly-and-reindeer tablecloth. Smiling, he sat down and invited Meike to take a seat. Gieles suddenly felt embarrassed by the snowman napkins and the tablecloth.

His father gave Meike the biggest helping of sausage. Famished, she attacked her meal with gusto. She swallowed the food almost without chewing it.

'Actually,' she said after a while, 'I'm a vegetarian.'

'Vegetarian?' repeated Uncle Fred.

'Mmm,' she said, wiping her mouth with the snowman napkin. 'For about four and a half years already.'

After supper Willem left for the airport and Uncle Fred told Meike that she had to call home. 'Before you know it we'll have an Amber Alert on our hands,' he said.

Meike looked at him as if he were crazy. After the liberation of a good laugh in response to her vegetarian announcement, they had all become more relaxed.

'God forbid that your poor parents should think you've disappeared.'

'My phone is out of minutes,' she said.

Uncle Fred placed a hand on her shoulder, pushed her into the hallway and handed her the telephone. 'You can make your call here in peace and quiet.'

For the first few minutes they heard nothing, but after a while Meike's voice steadily increased until she was bellowing. They understood little of the Brabant dialect, but just to be sure Uncle Fred closed the kitchen door and turned the radio on. Gieles nervously put the plates and pans on the counter. He had never heard a girl scream like that. Dolly could really blow her top, but that was nothing compared with Meike's tirade. He could hardly imagine so many decibels coming out of such a small body. Gieles couldn't bear the tension.

His uncle folded up the Christmas tablecloth and said calmly, 'Tony called. I'm supposed to tell you that he did the shopping for Dolly.'

'For Dolly?' repeated Gieles, confused. It was as if he had to burrow into his memory just to remember who she was. Since this afternoon his brains had been completely preoccupied by Meike. But slowly the sentence got through to him.

Tony did the shopping.

Now he just had to hope that Tony bought the same dildo and Dolly hadn't missed it.

Gieles heard the door to the guest room slam shut. Hesitantly he combed his fingers through his hair and placed his hand on the door handle.

'Let her cool off a bit,' Uncle Fred said in a fatherly tone.

Half an hour later he knocked on the door a couple of times, with no response, and then pushed it open. Meike was lying on bed. A trail of black mascara was running down her cheek and along her temple into her ear.

'I have tea for you.' He stood in the room with a cup of steaming tea and didn't know what to do.

'I hate them,' she said with little conviction. All the strength had been drained out of her. Slowly she raised herself up. Her tattooed tear was hidden underneath all the black splotches. She looked like a Chinese character.

Gieles put the tea on the little table next to the bed and sat down beside her. They both had their back turned to the lathed wall. Hanging on the opposite wall were framed photographs.

'Is that you with your parents, on that horse?'

Gieles nodded and looked at the little boy sitting on a big brown horse with his father behind him. His mother was next to them on a white horse. The sea was glistening in the background.

'You've got a pretty mother. My mother's a dwarf. She could be in the circus. My father, too, as a matter of fact.'

His mother really did look fantastic in the photo. She was wearing dark sunglasses and her long hair was hanging loosely around her face. Her hair was still black back then. Now it was full of grey streaks.

'That was in South Africa,' said Gieles. 'And that picture of me above it with all those black kids on the ground, that's Malawi.'

'Fuck,' she whispered. 'Malawi.'

'I went to school there for a month,' Gieles bragged. He had gone to the black school because his mother thought it would be good for his development. After the second morning he ran home crying because he was afraid of the teacher, who beat the students with switches.

'They beat the children with switches there.'

Meike looked at him with wide eyes. 'Really? Did they beat you, too?'

Gieles enjoyed the worry in her voice. 'No. They didn't dare.'

Slowly her eyes scanned the wall. Baby Gicles in a batik sling on his mother's back in front of a fruit stall. Toddler Gieles in the jungle crossing a footbridge framed by vines. She laughed at the photo of Gieles and his parents posing in red robes. Standing close together, him in the middle.

'Our suitcases got lost in Kenya. And we had to wear those rags during the whole trip and walk with the Masai. They're nomads.'

Once again Gieles was grossly exaggerating to make an impression on her. After three days with the Masai they were covered with ticks and fled to a luxury hotel with a swimming pool.

'You've really travelled a lot.' She leaned with her chin on her knees. 'We never get any further than Winterberg. That's this German dump where we go every summer. My mother always wants to go in the cable car for the view and my dad stays at the foot of the mountain because he's afraid of heights.'

'The trips we took weren't always fun,' Gieles lied. His memories of them were wonderful. 'A lot of the food was disgusting and I had diarrhoea most of the time.'

Meike had wrapped her arms tightly around her drawn-up legs, as if she were trying to console herself. 'My parents are so boring. They've only been to Amsterdam once in their whole lives. They get up every day in the middle of the night with their Poles. Those Poles—all they ever talk about are women and tits. In Polish, of course, but I'm not stupid. Do you know what *kurva* means?'

'Cunt?' Gieles guessed.

'Whore. And in Romanian it's *pizdâ*. My parents can only get Romanians these days.'

Gieles stole a quick glance at her shirt. Meike didn't just have tits, that was for sure. If she were in his class, she'd be in the big boob category. Meike would also attract a lot of attention. At his school there wasn't a single girl who looked like her.

Suddenly she got up and walked on her wrapped-up feet to one of the photos. 'Where was that? With the little girl on your lap.'

'That was in Suriname,' said Gieles. He preferred not to be reminded of that trip. That was the last time they had travelled as a family. Two months later his mother had lost her job as a stewardess and had become an aid worker.

'We were visiting a children's home where my mother sometimes brought toys.'

She stood with her nose over the photo and blew the dust away. 'What's that triangle on the face of that girl?'

'The mother had pressed an iron onto her cheek.'

This time he wasn't exaggerating.

'On purpose?' She looked at him full of horror. 'Her own mother?'

'Yes.'

'What a bitch.' Meike plopped down next to Gieles on the narrow bed. She couldn't get over the story about the iron and kept repeating the word 'bitch.' It sounded funny the way she pronounced it.

Gieles wondered whether he should tell her such shocking stories. She might go out and get a tattoo under her other eye. After a while Meike changed the subject and began talking about her myxomatosis rabbit, astrology and the actor Jake Gyllenhaal. Then she roared with laughter at Gieles's stories about his geese and the table tennis tournament.

'Why are you alone?' Meike asked suddenly.

'What do you mean?'

'No brother or sister. Just like me.'

'My mother thought one was enough.'

'Because of the overpopulation?' Meike asked sympathetically. He was fully aware that she thought his mother was too cool for words.

'No, for herself. She thought raising me was hard enough.' Gieles tapped his temple. 'Mentally hard.'

Meike frowned but said nothing, as if she had been saddled with an unsolvable math problem.

'I don't understand that,' she said after a while.

Neither do I.

Uncle Fred knocked, but they didn't hear him. 'Gieles!' he shouted, coming into the room. 'Are you going to bed soon? You've got school tomorrow.' He looked at his wrist, even though he never wore a watch.

'Ye-hes,' said Gieles, and he stayed with Meike for another fifteen minutes. Then, giddy with infatuation, he went outside to get Wally.

That night he couldn't sleep. He was fantasising. About them. Meike was wearing a little white dress that fluttered in the wind and her hair was its natural colour, although he had no idea what that colour was. He thought blond suited her best, and he fantasised her with a blond ponytail set high on her head. He erased the piercing and the tattoo. They lay hand in hand on their backs in the woods and listened to the birds. There were geese flying so low over them that they could hear rustling with every wing beat. Airplanes didn't exist. Turning restlessly in his bed, Gieles redesigned the woods according to his own idealised picture. There was a crystal clear lake and a white sandy beach, and the shores were covered with tall reeds so that no one could see them if they went swimming.

The sun shone on their bodies, and later Meike would sit on him the way Sophia had sat on Ide Warrens. But first they went in the water. Meike said she was hot and walked over to the beach. Then she stepped out of her little white dress. Wally pressed herself against his hair. He tried to sketch Meike's body. Her breasts were big and firm. Her nipples were small, but he couldn't decide on the colour. Brown? Reddish brown? Liver-coloured? What colour were nipples, anyway?

And her pubic hair? Blond didn't strike him as particularly beautiful, but a blond ponytail with black pubic hair was an odd combination. No pubic hair at all was juvenile, he thought, although Tony said there was nothing like a bald cunt. But Tony was such a bullshitter.

Meike was naked and he wore swimming trunks. He made himself more tan and muscular than he really was. He didn't want to swim naked, so he fantasised himself in O'Neill surfing trunks.

Gieles dove off the dock into the lake like an athlete while she looked on with admiration. She was standing waist-deep in the water. Strong and bronzed, he swam up to her nondescript pubic hair, grabbed her around the waist and picked her up. At about that point he must have fallen asleep.

At seven o'clock he woke up, dead tired, and dragged himself downstairs with Wally under his arm. He didn't even take the trouble to hide her. The hallway stank of cigarette smoke. Gieles opened the front and back doors for cross ventilation, hoping the smell would go away before the others got out of bed.

He ate a currant bun and walked to Meike's door to hear if she was awake. Then he went outside and gave the geese their waterfowl feed, trying to catch a glimpse of Meike through the window, but the shabby blue curtains were shut tight. Back in the hallway Gieles picked up his backpack and pressed his ear to her door once more. With great reluctance he biked off to school.

21

Judging by what she told him, Meike's first morning on the farm had been chaotic. She was sitting at the back door, wearing the same black shirt and smoking a cigarette. There were dots of black ink on her bare legs. Gieles sat down beside her on the stoop, bathed in sweat. He had biked like a demon to get home as soon as he could. Why did she work herself over with ink like this, he wondered. There was a girl in his class who cut herself and was sometimes home for days because of it, but this was new for him. Maybe scratching with ink was a precursor to scratching with a knife.

He tried to imagine the scene that Meike described. Because the doors had been left open the geese had shat all over the kitchen. The aggressive goose had lashed out at Uncle Fred, and his father gave the goose such a hard kick that the air was thick with feathers. Meike had learned this all from Uncle Fred. She didn't wake up until the goose went for the mailman. She heard screaming, looked out the window and saw the man wrestling with her wings and bill. When Uncle Fred finally turned the garden hose on her head, she stopped. The soaking mailman fled, saddle bags dripping.

Meike chuckled and put her cigarette out in an ashtray. 'And then your uncle went shopping.' She chuckled a little louder. She sounded as if she had screamed herself hoarse. 'But first he gave me an ashtray and said, "Smoking we do outside, young lady, not inside." As if that makes any fucking difference when you're being gassed by airplanes.'

'You didn't say that to him, did you?' Gieles never mouthed off like that.

'Of course not.'

She yawned. 'Jesus, how can you all sleep with that fucking noise? I didn't sleep a wink.'

'You can get used to anything.'

Meike stood up and limped over the gravel. The bandages on her feet were dingy. Her legs looked like they belonged to a Dalmatian. Fearlessly she approached the aggressive goose, who was standing some distance away. She observed the animal like a mother who is concerned about her unruly child. After a couple of minutes she walked back.

'Is blue your favourite colour?' she asked, standing in front of Gieles.

'No. Why?' He looked down at his jeans and shirt.

'You were wearing blue yesterday, too.'

'And your favourite colour is obviously black. Even your legs are black.'

'Oh, that,' she said. 'I colour the holes in my panty hose with a felt tip. It's a kind of nervous tic.' She yawned again and stretched out her arms.

A hundred percent sure she doesn't have a tongue piercing.

Gieles did his best not to get aroused and turned his head away.

'I'm hungry,' she said. 'You want a sandwich, too?'

Before he could respond she was in the kitchen. He heard her opening and closing cabinet doors and probably making a big mess. Chaos suited her. Gieles enjoyed her making him a sandwich.

Tomorrow I'll wear my red shirt.

Wally came scurrying around the corner and lay down

between his feet. He noticed for the first time that at the far ends of her wings, where there were narrow tubes, flight feathers were growing. With flight feathers she'd be able to fly. He stroked her wings.

Meike came back with a stack of sandwiches and two cups of coffee, a pitcher of milk and a bowl of sugar. It was all set out on a tray, astonishingly neat.

She put the tray between them. 'Milk and sugar?'

'Great,' he said. He never drank coffee.

She even stirred for him, and when she handed him the cup he wanted to kiss her. Her face was very close, and only now did he see that she hadn't put any junk on her eyelashes. He wanted to tell her how pretty she was, but Wally's big sister was standing right in front of his nose. Gieles braced himself. He'd throw the mug at her head if he had to. But she didn't do anything. Meike threw her a piece of bread with peanut butter and she raced away with the bit of sandwich dangling from her beak.

'She likes you,' said Gieles.

'Logical. I love animals. They feel it. Animals are smart. I hate my parents, but they don't feel it. No matter how often I tell them, they're just too stupid to get it. They're coming here tonight, by the way.'

'Your parents? Here?' Terrified, he took a big gulp of coffee.

'Yeah,' she said, pulling on her dreads. 'They're coming, but I'd rather die than go back home. My mother thinks your father and Uncle Fred are fags.'

'My father, a fag?' The idea was so absurd that he burst out laughing and choked on his coffee.

'Fred is his brother! His twin brother!' he coughed.

'Yes, I know that. But my mother is such a moron that she thinks that's only an excuse.'

Gieles had trouble keeping his eyes off Meike for the rest of the day. He and Wally gave her a table tennis demonstration. Although the little goose was in top form—her service had reached almost perfect proportions—Gieles kept looking at Meike. She sat in the grass with her legs drawn up under her shirt. She smoked and followed their movements as if in a trance. Even the sound of the planes had no impact on her. After twenty minutes Wally lost interest and flapped awkwardly off the table. The first flutter of her wings escaped Gieles entirely. He only had eyes for Meike.

She asked whether she could come to the demonstration. He said, 'Of course,' and fervently hoped she would still be with him the following week.

Then she wanted to see his room. She followed him up the stairs, while he feverishly tried to remember whether there was anything lying around that might betray his rescue operation. He trusted Meike, but when it came to his plans he aimed for a policy of absolute secrecy.

'Fuck! What a mess.' She stepped warily over the scattered garments and school books as if they were landmines. The sink was full of soot from the Bird Burnings. Next to his bed was the game board, with the runways marked out with masking tape, the blue and yellow geese and the security cameras. He kicked the board under his bed, but Meike took no notice. She was standing at the attic window and tipping it open. Fortunately this morning he had reversed the partition with the schedule on it. Then he walked to his desk to turn off his computer. Super Waling had sent him an e-mail. 'Subject: my mother's double-muscle cows.'

Meike was hanging out the window, just as he and Tony used to do when they were shooting objects on the runway with the slingshot.

'You're really close here!' she screamed, following the flight of a rising plane. She had to stand on her toes to get a good look. Her shirt had crept up a little. He stared at her panties, which were dotted with little pink hearts. Her pale white tummy was slightly bowed, like rising dough. Gieles dove onto the bed so she wouldn't be able to see his hard-on.

Dazed, he picked up a book from the floor and began to page through it while peeking at Meike's bottom. Her buns were so small and firm. He pressed his hips against the mattress as hard as he could, hoping to calm his body down.

Meike waved wildly at the planes, causing her shirt to creep up even further. 'Can they see me?' she shouted as her dreadlocks and breasts bounced up and down.

'I think so.' His vocal cords rattled against each other. He did his very best to concentrate on the text in the book, but the letters tottered and keeled over. Despite his best efforts to avoid it, he came without touching himself.

'Christ,' she sighed. 'It sure is hot in here.'

She was right. The warmth of the whole house had accumulated in the attic. It was as if they were sitting in a sauna.

'Where's the bathroom?'

'Down on the first floor,' Gieles squeaked, burying his face in his hands so she wouldn't see how flushed he was.

She giggled. He broke out in a sweat.

'Your hair. It's so cute. You look just like a little hedgehog.' She laughed and vanished downstairs.

22

Her parents arrived just as Willem Bos was pulling in. They were right behind his service car. It was seven-thirty, and Uncle Fred, Gieles and Meike had just finished eating. Meike had grown quieter as the meal progressed. She had left half her nasi on her plate and had fiddled incessantly with the black band tied around her neck. Not a word had been said about her savage get-up: a black dress with at least a kilo of locks and chains hanging from it. A heavy ring was dangling from her eyebrow.

Gieles began to get nervous when he heard the cars arrive. He was afraid his father would rake him over the coals for that business with the mailman that morning. He had locked the aggressive goose in the barn to be on the safe side.

Uncle Fred click-clacked to the front door with Gieles right behind him. Meike, with all her chains and hostility, stayed seated in the kitchen. What Gieles really wanted was to go to his room, where he could finally read Super Waling's e-mail about the cause of his immense size.

Willem Bos was the first to get out of his car. He was tired and irritable. The brooding black-backed gulls in the hangar had caused him no end of trouble.

Then Meike's parents got out of their Volvo. They were indeed small people, but not the dwarves that Meike had described. They looked far too normal for a circus act, even beside the tall Bos brothers. There were introductions all around, and then it was Gieles's turn. Meike's mother gave him a good strong handshake and looked him straight in the eye.

'Angeliek Nooteboom,' she said with her heavy Brabant accent. She had the same aquarium green eyes as her daughter, but her round-cheeked face was browned by the sun.

Then Meike's father's stepped forward. 'Hey, Gieles. I'm Hannie.' His Adam's apple moved up and down above the neck of his sweater.

Angeliek bent down and reached into the car, pulling out a crate from the back seat. 'Strawberries,' she said hesitantly, using the dialect word.

Gieles noticed she had the muscular arms of a body-builder.

'First-class strawberries. Picked this morning,' Hannie explained. Apparently he had no trouble switching from dialect to Dutch.

'They look absolutely delicious,' said Uncle Fred. Angeliek was about to hand him the crate but noticed, too late, that Uncle Fred couldn't pick anything up on account of his crutch. She quickly pressed the strawberries into Willem's hands. A red streak remained on her white blouse, but she was unaware of it. She was staring with open mouth as an airplane came in for a landing. Meike's father, too, seemed nailed to the ground. The closer the plane came, the more the strawberry farmer shrank into himself. His head sank down between his shoulders and his brown cheeks became ashen and moist. A cold sweat broke out spontaneously from his pores.

'You okay, Hannie?' Uncle Fred asked after the roaring had died down, and he laid a friendly hand on Hannie's arm. Uncle Fred had a way of making people feel as if he had known them for years.

'Hannie, relax,' said Angeliek soothingly to her husband in dialect. 'You're down here, not up there.'

Hannie took a handkerchief out of his pants pocket. Wiping away the sweat, he inhaled deeply and exhaled slowly. 'One, two, three,' he counted.

'Never flown in his life and still he's afraid.'

She lovingly rubbed her husband's back.

'I can't help it,' he said, both hands clutching his head. 'The fear just overtakes me.'

'Happens to the best of 'em,' said Uncle Fred consolingly. 'There are even pilots with a fear of flying. They wake up one morning and just the thought of flying gives 'em the willies. Isn't that right, Willem?'

Willem Bos muttered something under his breath and tried not to look at the strawberry farmer if he could help it. He was still holding the crate. A wasp had settled on it and was feasting on the fruit.

Hannie looked nervously at the next incoming plane.

'Coffee?' asked Uncle Fred. He took Hannie by the arm and coaxed him inside.

Gieles walked straight through to the kitchen in search of Meike. She wasn't there. For a minute the thought flashed through his mind that she had fled, until he saw wisps of smoke wafting past the window. He heard his father approaching. Willem put the crate on the table and fixed his eyes on the strawberries.

'Gieles.' He said it in a way that he reserved for his mother's name alone, as in 'Ellen, it can't go on like this.' Usually she promised to improve—'I'll come home more often'—only to break her promise a couple of months later.

'That mailman this morning. His employer called. As

long as it's not safe here they won't be delivering mail to us. That goose has got to go. He's mad.'

'He is a she.'

'Okay. She has got to go. As soon as possible.'

Without looking at him Willem went over to the counter, to the coffee and tray. Uncle Fred had gotten everything ready.

'And now I want you and Meike to go to the living room.'

Gieles opened the back door. Meike was sitting on the stoop, smoking angrily. Everything about her was dark, except her skin.

'Your parents are here.'

She gave him a black look without really seeing him. 'They can go to hell.'

Gieles shrugged his shoulders and did what his father had asked him to do.

Meike's parents were sitting side by side on the couch, bolt upright. The toes of their shoes barely touched the rug. Uncle Fred and his father were sitting on the other couch. Gieles didn't want to sit next to anyone, so he grabbed a chair. They were talking together about birds. Starlings, crows and jackdaws were a disaster for straw-berry production, Hannie said. He had loosened up a bit but he was still sweating. The cup in his hands was slid-ing all over the place.

'We have a falcon box for two kestrels. They keep the mice and birds away, but it's not nearly enough.'

His wife cast a nervous glance at her husband's coffee cup.

'And recently we got Kees, an inflatable scarecrow. Kees moves and makes shrieking sounds.'

Willem Bos was plainly interested. 'Does it work? Does he keep the birds away?'

'I can't complain but the Romanians don't like it. The sound gets on their nerves. Poles can put up with anything, but Poles are hard to come by these days,' said Hannie.

Angeliek had discovered the stuffed cat with the magpie in the corner of the living room.

Uncle Fred knew exactly what she was looking at.

'What a monster, huh? That's a wild cat my brother caught at the airport. The place is crawling with cats. People go on vacation and dump their pets in the long-term parking lot.'

'I don't believe it!' said Angeliek, stunned. She scrutinised the two brothers closely.

'It's true, I'm afraid,' said Uncle Fred. 'Many people don't realise what they've saddled themselves with when they get a pet. Such a shame.'

'Are you two really brothers?' she asked with scepticism.

'Twin brothers,' Uncle Fred explained. 'You'd never know it, though. We don't look anything alike, except for our height. We're both one metre ninety-nine.'

Angeliek glanced over at her husband with relief, but he ignored her. Hannie went on with his bird problems. 'I used to skewer a crow or jackdaw on a stick and set it out with the strawberries. It did a great job keeping the other crows and jackdaws away, but Meike made such a big fuss about it ...'

Silence fell, and only Uncle Fred knew how to handle it. 'Your daughter,' he said cheerfully. 'I'll go see where she's hanging out.'

He heaved himself up on the crutch and walked out of the room.

They sat there in silence until Angeliek turned to Gieles and asked him what class he was in.

'First year of high school,' he said, a bit more abruptly than he had intended. The problem was that he felt awkward. He wanted to dismiss Meike's parents as stupid simply because she hated them, but the fact of the matter was that they seemed rather nice. There was something endearing about them, just like his geese.

Angeliek didn't dare ask a second question. She lowered her eyes and discovered the red stain on her blouse. Applying a bit of spit to her finger she tried to rub the fruit juice out, and as she did so her eyes strayed to the living room door.

Hannie started in on a new story about his kestrel box. Willem gave him some tips on bird control and offered to show him the service car later on. 'I have a few new distress cries that work pretty well.'

Angeliek was now gazing longingly towards the door.

Gieles felt sorry for her. When she heard Uncle Fred's voice, the muscles in her arms tensed automatically.

'Well, here she is,' said Uncle Fred light-heartedly as the door swung open. He took one step aside and there was Meike, in full regalia and ten centimetres taller than normal. She could have been just about anything: an actress in a cult film, the main feature in a freak show or the prize-winning gothic entry in a dress-up contest. But what she couldn't possibly be was the daughter of the little strawberry farmers from Zundert. They were from two different planets and it was blatantly obvious that they couldn't bear to be in the same orbit.

'Hi, Meike,' said Hannie, and he stood up. He wiped his sweaty palms on his pants and sat back down, since Meike hadn't moved from where she was standing.

Angeliek's round cheeks were as tight as a tarpaulin.

'Okay, Meike, let's all sit down together,' said Uncle Fred. With one hand on her back he pushed Meike towards the couch where Willem was sitting. As she walked past Gieles he noticed her black platform shoes. They looked as if the soles had been mounted onto blocks of wood, that's how tall they were. When she sat down, all the chains and locks hanging from her body jingled.

'Have you any idea how worried we were?' Angeliek blurted out in her heavy southern accent. 'Running away like that. Your dad and I nearly died.'

Angeliek began to cry. Hannie was practically spurting perspiration. Their daughter looked the other way at the wild cat with the magpie in its mouth, her black lips contorted in a spiteful grimace.

'And just look at the way you're dressed. Look at you! You look like Houdini!'

'HOUDINI?' Meike shrieked so loudly that Willem Bos almost had to be peeled off the ceiling. Gieles and his uncle had already made their acquaintance with her sirenic wail.

'WHO THE FUCK IS HOUDINI?'

'Calm down,' Hannie attempted. 'We're guests here …'

'I'M MEIKE, GODDAMN IT! MEIKE! NOT FUCKING HOUDINI!'

'Meike,' said Uncle Fred with unexpected severity. 'Take it down a notch.'

She tried to restrain herself, although she still hurled all her hatred at her mother.

'We'll leave you alone,' said Willem, not knowing what the proper speed was for vacating the room.

Uncle Fred and Gieles went to the kitchen. His father decided to go outside and tinker with his car. For five minutes they heard nothing. Then Meike opened her throat full throttle once again.

Hannie was outside in no time. There were perspiration stains on his sweater the size of soccer balls.

'That screaming just isn't normal,' he said with panic in his voice.

'Oh, come on,' said Willem. 'What's normal? My son sleeps with geese.'

'With that one there? With all three?' Hannie asked. He was pointing to the geese that were walking through the campground.

'No, just the white goose. That little one. He's absolutely crazy about that bird. He carries her around with him day and night. My son is very good with geese,' said Willem proudly. The two men stood watching the geese together until another plane came in and the strawberry farmer's heart was in his mouth.

'Go sit in the car,' Willem suggested. 'Then you can't see them.'

Hannie slammed the car door and planted his hands in his hair. Leaning on his elbows, he swallowed down a series of belches.

'Good Lord, it's hot in here.'

'Should I turn on the air conditioning?'

'Please.'

Hannie sat up and burped. 'I'm sorry. I don't know what's gotten into me. It's probably the tension.'

Willem offered him a handkerchief but Hannie was looking the other way. Deeply anxious, he peered outside as if he were afraid that a plane was about to bore through the window.

'Hannie, would you like a handkerchief?'

'On the farm everybody calls me Arrie, except for my wife. She thinks Hannie is a nice name, but I don't think much of it. I was named after my father, my grandfather and my great-grandfather. All of them are named Hannie, even though it's not even a Brabant name. Fortunately I got a daughter, although recently I've sometimes wished we had had a boy. I don't understand girls at all.'

He stared at the wet circles on his pants. 'For the past six months we've really had our hands full with Meike. All of a sudden she started acting strange, from one day to the next. She has very violent outbursts. Angeliek calls it a short circuit of the brain. And she used to be so athletic. You wouldn't think so now, but she really shone as an athlete.'

'No, sport is not something you'd quickly associate with her,' Willem murmured, and he put on the MP3 player. The warning cries of a black-headed gull shrieked across the farmyard.

'Is that a seagull?' Hannie asked, visibly impressed. He listened attentively while wiping his hands on his pants again.

Willem nodded and switched over to yapping jack-daws. He looked at the strawberry farmer expectantly.

'Jackdaws.' Hannie uttered the word with contempt. 'No better than rats. You can't get rid of them.'

'I'm with you there,' said Willem, noticing some bird poop on the windshield. He had to suppress the urge to get a bucket of water and a sponge. Willem liked a clean car.

'Last week we cleared their nests out from under the overpass. Whole containers full of junk.' Willem kept his eyes glued to the bird poop.

'They even use old condoms to line their nests.'

'Did you know that the rook is the smartest bird in the world?' Hannie said. 'I saw an experiment once with a worm in a glass of water that the rook couldn't reach. The rook threw stones in the glass to raise the level of the water so he could catch the worm.'

'All members of the crow family are smart,' said Willem. 'A jay collects thousands of acorns each year that he hides in order to survive the winter.'

Uncle Fred tapped on the window. 'I wonder if you guys could come inside for a minute.'

Gieles and Meike were sitting next to each other on the couch. There was a pillow between them. Meike's make-up had run so badly that it resembled a war mask of streaks and stripes. She looked like a postcard of the Maori that Gieles's mother had once sent from New Zealand.

Uncle Fred put on his reading glasses and began speaking while leaning on his crutch. The deal was as follows, he said formally: Meike was welcome to spend the next few weeks on the farm as long as she found a part-time job. She had to pay her own way. And if she got a new tattoo, she'd have to go home immediately.

'And no new piercings either,' said Angeliek with red eyes. She was sitting all alone on the other couch with crumpled tissues on her lap. She looked very moist.

'Of course. No new piercings. Are we agreed on that, Meike?'

Uncle Fred raised his eyebrows high. Gieles had never seen him act with such firmness. 'Meike?'

'Sure,' she said with her most blasé voice, and she tottered out of the room in her platform shoes with all the dignity she could muster.

Dear Gieles,

You asked me how I got this way, or to put it in my own words: how I got so monstrously fat. I promised to tell you the whole story. From A to Z.

There's no one else I can blame for my exorbitant weight.

It's my own fault. And I can't reduce my present condition to that one day that my life (and that of my parents) was changed for good. That would mean eliminating the context. So I've decided to begin at the beginning. You already know who my ancestors were for the most part. Regard this as the first half of the alphabet. I still have to find the right words for the second half. Read it only if you have the time and the inclination.

I'm looking forward to Saturday!

My very warmest greetings, Waling

My mother was fonder of her double-muscle cows than of gold necklaces. My father was wild about his land. As soon as the first beet plants came up he would crawl cautiously over the ground to care for them. When beets are big you can slay a giant with them, but when they're young the plants are as vulnerable as babes in arms.

My parents were very simple folk. They had no big ambitions. The only thing of distinction they possessed was my father's family name: Cittersen van Boven. It was a name that didn't suit them, but they didn't complain. They were satisfied with their existence. Everything changed for us (and for many other people) after the accident, but more about that later on.

I was the long-awaited child. When I was squeezed into the light of day by my forty-eight-year-old mother in 1965, they called me a miracle. They had been hoping for a child all their lives and had resigned themselves to the fact that it wasn't going to happen. They had reached the age when most people become grandparents. They looked more at the years that were behind them than those that were ahead. And then I came along. A new promise. Beaming and screaming and as fragile as a young beet plant.

I attached myself to my mother like a suction cup from day one. First literally: she nursed me until I was three. Then by means of her clothing: I held onto the edge of her long skirts and strolled around behind her with my thumb in my mouth. Wherever she was, I was. Day and night. In their bed I pushed my bottom into my dad's face so I could have her all to myself. I lay with my cheek pressed against her head and twisted her red hair in knots as I slept. None of this bothered my parents. Their love for me was inexhaustible. My mother called me her little annex. She was the house, I was cemented on to her and dad was the foundation. Our mainstay. I knew we'd never sink into the clay thanks to my father.

My happiness was further increased by my mother's skill as a storyteller. In addition to me and the double-muscle cows, my mother loved history. Her history. Most people resign their ancestors to the realm of the shades, but not my mother. For years she worked on a family tree that she filled in with pieces of information about her ancestors. I mean the generations of women who issued from Ide and Sophia Warrens.

Three well-thumbed notebooks with diary entries made by her great-great-grandmother constituted the source of the detective work. She knew the texts by heart. She would relate the stories of her ancestors with great passion, as if the reclamation had taken place yesterday instead of in 1852. The characters in her stories were people of flesh and blood, but Sophia was far and away my mother's favourite. Until this very day I don't know why. Maybe because she came to know more about her great-great-grandmother than about any of the others, thanks to those notebooks. Or maybe because she had a boundless admiration for her. After Ide was struck and killed by lightning, Sophia Warrens was left alone.

She kept her promise: Anna Louisa, her only daughter, grew up in a house made of bricks and went to school. They slept upstairs on the farm, the boss slept downstairs. They shared the kitchen, the living room and the bathroom, my mother inferred from the diary entries. But whether the boss and Sophia also shared a bed remained an open question and was for my mother an inexhaustible source of gleeful speculation.

'I think there might have been love there,' my mother sometimes said, musing over her words. 'She wrote that he regularly checked in on the baby during the day to see if she was still breathing. Later he even paid Anna Louisa's school fees. And when Sophia's daughter became one of the first official midwives in the area, he burst his buttons with pride.'

My mother's storytelling was always a casual affair. It happened as she was cooking, hanging up the laundry or doing her exercises for her pelvic floor muscles, which after my birth had become as slack as the elastic in a pair of worn-out underpants.

At other times my mother was a hundred percent certain that the two had never been intimate. 'She keeps talking about "my boss". If she had strong feelings for him, she would have called him by his name. We don't even know what his name was. What do *you* think, *sweetie*? Do you think she remained faithful to Ide Warrens, her great love?'

If we were sitting in the living room with my father and she asked that 'what do you think, *sweetie*?' question yet again, we knew she meant me. I was her *sweetie* and my father had no problem with that. He enjoyed our relationship. He was as warmed by our ritual chatter as if we had been a furnace, until my mother would exclaim with feigned shock that we really had to eat now.

My mother, Louisa, was chaotic in her detective work. She dug around in the city archives, unearthed notarial deeds and worked her way through mortgage registers and the municipal registry. She found yearbooks in the archives that had to do with women's history and read old local newspapers. She spent one morning a week collecting data, usually when I was at school. But as soon as stumbled across a piece of information, she would get so excited that she forgot to write down where she had found it.

In the local weekly newspaper of 1866, for example, she found an article in which Sophia and her daughter Anna Louisa played a role as minor heroes. Delirious with joy, my mother came home and couldn't stop talking about the unique discovery she had made in her family history. Anna Louisa Warrens had been walking on the path near their farm when she came across four little orphans. The children were underfed and unimaginably dirty. Beaming, my mother quoted from memory what she had read: 'The newspaper talked about their being "*so* unclean, *so* vermin-infested, *so* entirely without clothing or shelter." And get this, *sweetie*: Anna Louisa brought the children home with her. Before they were collected by the police, Sophia took them in hand. She hosed them down with water and gave them something to eat. And once the children were clean, they didn't recognise each other! Isn't that incredible, *sweetie*? And wasn't it fantastic, *sweetie*, that it was all in the newspaper?'

When I asked whether she had made a copy of her findings, she slapped her hand against her head with an absent-minded look on her face and shouted theatrically, 'Completely forgot!' Sometimes I doubted the veracity of her anecdotes.

Later, when I undertook my own research of my ancestors in a more organised way and the contact between me and my mother had ended for good, I had to admit that she hadn't fantasised a single word. But now I'm running ahead of myself, Gieles.

It was soon after this discovery that the game of speculation began. She was down on all fours, slowly pushing back her derrière in order to strengthen her pelvic muscles (her daily exercise) when she began musing out loud. 'Sophia must have had her doubts about the wisdom of taking those dirty children into her house. She was terrified of losing her daughter. That was at the time of the umpteenth cholera epidemic, which always claimed an enormous number of lives. Brrrrr. Just thinking about it gives me goose bumps. If you've only got one child it makes you so awfully vulnerable, *sweetie*.'

Slowly my mother raised herself up from her squat until she was back to the starting position. 'On the other hand, Sophia had an especially big heart. She worried about the fate of those poor wretches in the shanties when she herself was just a young girl. And Anna Louisa was already about eight years old by then. I mean, she could put up with a lot.'

And that was true. As I already told you, the whole female line that issued from her great-great-grandmother could put up with a lot. Sophia Warrens died at age ninety in the year 1915. Anna Louisa was buried the day the Germans bombed Rotterdam, eighty-two years old. And Sophia's granddaughter, Johanna, made it to ninety-nine. All their husbands never lived much beyond sixty.

Johanna was my great-grandmother (or have you lost track already, Gieles?). I knew her well. She had a head of thick red hair, just like my mother and grandmother. She always radiated a ruddy glow, even at an advanced age. Besides having the same hair colour, all these women possessed enormous strength and a rebellious sense of humour. Let me tell you an anecdote that says a great deal about their characters.

My grandma became an artist later in life. She took it quite seriously. The last thing she wanted was to be was a bored old woman who produced silly watercolours in her spare time. In her mid-fifties she was admitted to the art academy on the basis of a series of experimental landscape paintings. Her work was pretty shaky as far as technique was concerned, but the admissions committee was charmed by her exotic interpretation of the polder landscape. She had alternated bands of yellow ochre desert sand with strips of black clay. Personally I found her paintings mediocre, but as a child I was terribly proud that my Grandma Aletta was an artist. And what an artist she was! She became totally enraptured by pop-art, a modern art movement that sprang from the spirit of the sixties. I'm sure you've read about it. It all had to do with freedom in every facet of life. My grandma had been to an Andy Warhol exhibition in New York and was fascinated by his work. The irony and light-heartedness with which he made art out of everyday objects really appealed to her. She had no need of mind-altering substances or of walking around with flowers in her hair. For her it was all about the freedom that the movement brought with it, she said. Her late husband (a dull fellow, according to her) had been in his grave for ten years. When they asked her whether she wanted to extend his grave rights, Grandma said, 'Give him a good shake and let him make room for the next one.' For her, his death had been a liberation, and now she found the time to transform her liberated feelings into art.

What Grandma Aletta did wasn't particularly special. She had seen Warhol's images of Marilyn Monroe and had unashamedly copied his method. She set to work in her studio mastering the silkscreen technique. She took pictures of all the cousins, especially of me, and converted them into silkscreens. Then she used fluorescent colours to accent our mouths and cheeks.

I was still a little kid during her Warhol period. I paid regular visits to Grandma Aletta with my mother. After the death of her husband the living room had been converted into a labyrinthine studio. There were canvases and painter's tools lying around everywhere. The antique sideboards and cabinets were scattered higgledy-piggledy through the room and were groaning under the weight of paint cans, spray containers, putty knives and brushes. The passageways all led to the silkscreen press in the middle of the room, where my grandma did her Warhol imitations. My mother railed against the abuse of the antique furniture, which she had hoped at some point to inherit but was now entirely worthless.

It's hardly surprising that I loved visiting my grandma's studio. 'Karel Appel got pretty far by messing around,' she would say, and the two of us would fling a couple of cans of paint at the canvas. This happened on the rare occasions when I was there without my mother. My mother thought throwing paint around was absurd. I think it was her own mother that she found absurd. My grandma was much more modern than my beet-grubbing, double-muscle cow of a mother. You could even see it in the way they dressed. My grandma walked around in shocking pink sweatsuits while my mother wore respectable dresses.

I think my mother was jealous of her, although she never let on. On the contrary, we paid regular visits to Grandma Aletta, and often my great-grandmother Johanna was there. She was as old as the hills and crippled with arthritis, but there was nothing wrong with her mind.

I was a little afraid of her. She usually sat at the table near the window, half hidden behind the sideboard and a stack of silkscreens. She wasn't a chatterbox, my great-grandmother, but whenever she opened her mouth things happened. She could get a rise out of you in no time. She had a sense of humour that got everyone laughing, but she also had an acid tongue that put people's backs up.

She accused my mother of being a duck that had sat on her chick too long.

'You're suffocating that boy,' my great-grandmother insisted. We were sitting at the window and my mother turned her eyes away, chipping at the paint on the table top with a putty knife.

My great-grandmother just kept it up. 'You're right on top of him. You can't even see your own child any more.'

'I can see him all right,' said my mother angrily, hacking into the table even harder.

'It's not normal for him to spend whole days with you. A child ought to play with other children and not be stuck at home with an old bag.'

'Waling is not stuck with me all day,' my mother shouted, hurling the putty knife onto the table. 'And by the way, if anyone around here is an old bag, it's you.'

'Ho, ho, madam,' muttered my great-grandmother as her ruddy glow flared up dangerously. 'If I ever shot off my mouth to my grandma like that I'd have gotten a smack in the face.'

Good Lord, Gieles. I almost crawled under the paint-splotched table I was so scared. That squabbling between my mother and my great-grandmother, while my grand-ma just stood there, mixing paint and chuckling. I almost pissed my pants.

Looking back on it now, I'm thrilled about their fighting. My great-grandmother was talking about *her* grandma: Sophia Warrens. Those moments in the chaotic living room studio were concentrated versions of our entire history. Johanna was the connecting link between the distant past and the present. It was so palpable, so lively.

Of course the two of them didn't spend all their time snapping at each other. When my great-grandmother was in a good mood, she treated my mother to information about Sophia Warrens. She'd tell her about all the outbreaks of cholera in the polder and her sweeping hygienic measures. Or she'd describe the horse's heart that Sophia ate during her pregnancy. 'Thanks to the heart of that old drowned nag,' she would say with upraised finger, 'my grandma's progeny were as strong as oxen.' And then she'd rap the wood with her knuckles.

I listened for two minutes at the most, knowing that I was going to be hearing those anecdotes over and over again. I much preferred working with Grandma Aletta. She took pictures of me and coloured my lips a lurid purple.

'What a splendid child you are!' she would shout during those sessions, hopping around me happily like a little sparrow. 'An exemplary model! A sweetheart! An angel!'

'Knock it off, woman, or it'll go to his head,' came the voice of my great-grandmother from behind all the clutter.

My father never showed his face. All those red-headed women together gave him the heebie-jeebies. To Dad they were a coven of witches. No, all he wanted was to spend time on his land. He loved the silence and order his work brought. Yet my father was the one who came up with the idea of exhibiting my grandma's work in the town hall. By that time Aletta had produced twenty colourful paintings—I was featured in at least half of them—and they were cluttering her overcrowded studio. An exhibition would clear some space, my father suggested. She almost never listened to her son-in-law, but this time she did.

We joined my mother in helping grandma hang the paintings in the great council chamber. Ushers who happened to be passing by would stop and stare at the child's heads with golden eyelids, orange cheeks and fluorescent green hair. I recall one usher standing in front of a canvas and shaking his head, asking grandma why the same picture appeared four times in one painting. He could do that himself, he said.

The day before the exhibition, when the price stickers had to go up under each painting, grandma flew into a panic. She didn't want to make any money on the show. All she wanted at the very most was to cover expenses. 'I'm asking twenty guilders for each painting,' she firmly declared. My mother thought it was a ridiculously low price and she hit the ceiling.

Seething with rage, my mother went back home. She was driving a noisy old Opel, and she shouted over the engine, 'Sophia would never ask such an idiotic amount! She'd go for the top! I mean, just look at how she lives! That mess she lives in, that pink sweatsuit of hers! It's perfectly awful, isn't it, *sweetie?*'

I sat next to her and kept my mouth shut.

'And we can do with a bit more ourselves! You don't get rich on beets and cows! And she's got you in almost every one of her paintings! What I mean, *sweetie*, is that we have a right to our share!'

It was the first time I had ever heard a note of dissatisfaction seep into her voice. She complained about our financial situation, which I knew nothing about. Maybe she had done it more often and had been dissatisfied for years, but I had never noticed. It was in that rusty old car that I first saw my mother sitting grim-faced behind the steering wheel, her big nose almost pressed against the windshield. Every now and then she looked over at me. Her little annex. Her *sweetie*.

My great-grandmother Johanna came to the deserted town hall at the end of the afternoon. She looked at the paintings, cast a glance at the price tags and, without batting an eye, took a pen out of her handbag. It didn't happen very often, but this time my mother and my great-grandmother were in full agreement. She, too, thought the prices were a joke, something only a chump would do. She despised chumps. As she always said, if you act like a chump people will treat you like a chump.

Abruptly, she placed a zero after every figure, so that suddenly each work of art had increased ten times in value.

The exhibition opened the following afternoon. I remember it being insanely busy. My grandma was photographed and interviewed, and dressed in her paint-spattered sweatsuit she looked like a real artist. Her cheeks were flushed with excitement and the stray red hairs stuck out of her bun like a fringe of reeds gone wild. I was proud of my grandma. I walked through the crowd and followed right behind her.

In the midst of all those strangers we formed a family chain. My mother kept a close eye on me and my father traipsed along behind her. He looked both forlorn and funny that day, walking around with his hands in his pockets, which made his pants look short and gawky.

At a certain point, Grandma Aletta was approached by a fashionable man in a black bespoke suit. He questioned her about her work and she told him about the delights of New York, and suddenly my grandma began acting very coquettish. She seemed to be flirting with this man, who had to be at least twenty years younger than she was. When he said he wanted to buy ten of her paintings, she acted very strange. 'Ten?' she stammered with shock. 'Good heavens, that's so many. It's ludicrous.'

After a minute or so she recovered from the shock and began behaving like a teenage girl. My mother, who was curious by nature, came to see what was happening.

'This gentleman is from a bank,' giggled my grandma, 'and he wants to buy *ten* paintings. Isn't that fan-tas-tic?'

'Well, that certainly is fan-tas-tic,' repeated my mother sarcastically. She was still angry about the twenty guilders.

In the meantime a photographer began tugging on the sleeve of my grandma's sweatsuit.

'Oh, I forgot!' she cried with her new little-girl voice, her hands fluttering. 'The picture! I'm going to be in the picture!'

She looked at my mother. 'Honey, the photographer wants me to pose outside. You go with this gentleman,' and she tossed the man a beaming smile, 'and find out which paintings he wants.'

And Grandma Aletta was gone. The bank man and I followed my mother, who strode through the crowd with giant steps. He struck up a conversation with me. 'Later on you'll be featured in all our branches,' he said, or something like that, and ran his hand over my head.

My mother put a little red sticker under the first painting he pointed to—and then she saw it.

'What's this?' she said, completely bowled over. Her mouth literally fell open. The man asked her what was wrong.

'The price ... it's not right ... that zero ...'

Very agitated, she walked past all the works and checked the amounts. Bending over, reading glasses on, reading glasses off. I was standing next to the bank man and I felt a firm little hand grab me by the neck. It was my great-grandmother Johanna, who had kept track of all the goings on, down to the minutest detail.

Finally my mother returned, her face flushed.

'The pri ... prices ... ,' she stuttered.

She looked at my great-grandmother and began hopping up and down, very oddly, as if she were doing one of her silly pelvic floor exercises. My great-grandmother raised her eyebrows ever so slightly, but my mother knew enough.

'Am I to understand that a zero has been omitted from the price tags?' asked the fashionable man.

'Omitted?' echoed my great-grandmother, gasping for breath.

'You're not going to tell me that the paintings aren't *two hundred* but *two thousand* guilders a piece?' he said without flinching.

'Oh, dear,' said my great-grandmother with a slight vibration in her voice. 'I put the stickers up for my daughter. I don't mind telling you that I'm well into my nineties. I'm an old, forgetful lady.' She tapped her temple with her arthritic fingers.

'That's a considerable difference.' The bank man looked at his watch. 'Two hundred or two thousand.'

'Yes, it's ... a very big ... difference,' my mother began, who looked as naive as her double-muscle cows.

The man ignored her babbling and turned to my great-grandmother. 'Let's meet each other halfway. Sixteen for the price of two hundred and four for two thousand. That way we limit the damage for both parties.'

My great-grandmother's red hair blazed like a forest fire. Dropping her voice to a confidential tone, she said to the bank man, 'Don't let my daughter hear this.'

My grandma earned 11,200 guilders that day with her twenty paintings. That was 10,800 guilders more than she had counted on. Grandma was furious. A bunch of money-grubbers, that's what they were! Vultures! My great-grandmother protested that it wasn't about money. She insisted that it was about respect. My mother said that the banks were robbing the common man blind as it was. How was I to know that my parents' beet business was tottering on the brink?

It took weeks before Grandma Aletta got the joke. But once she got it, she laughed so hard that she pissed her pink pants. Grandma never exhibited again though, despite her successful debut and the countless appeals from my mother.

As I said, Gieles, my grandmothers were powerful women with a rebellious sense of humour. They played the lead role in my protected and well-organised life, which ended for good on 4 October 1979, the day my great-grandmother Johanna slipped away in her sleep. We were barely given any time to mourn. One day later an airplane crashed on our beet field. It was just after six and my mother and I were still in bed when we heard a dull clunk. Boofffff. It made the house shake. I ran to the window, and in the early light of dawn I saw a plane lying there like a colossal crane that had flown into something and broken in half. From her bedroom I heard my mother screaming, 'Oh, no, Walter! Walter!'

It was harvest time. My father had gone out to the fields before daybreak. Maybe he was lying under that crane right now. We stormed down the stairs and bumped into Dad, who had come running in.

'Walter! Dear Lord, Walter!' my mother cried, clinging to him.

'That plane. Did you see it?' My father struck me as quite self-controlled.

'I'm going to see what I can do.'

He freed himself from my whimpering mother and walked outside in his work clothes. Without giving it a moment's thought I pulled my coat over my pyjamas and pulled on a pair of boots. I was fourteen years old (just about as old as you are now), and a little excitement was more than welcome. My mother stood at the door, shouting that the whole thing could go up in flames. But that didn't seem likely to me, since it hadn't come down in flames.

We ran across the field, right over the beet plants. The light was still dim, but we could see enough to realise that a calamity had taken place. The wings had broken off, there was a deep tear in the fuselage and the cockpit was pretty much separated from the rest of the plane.

And at this point, Gieles, I'm going to leave the rest until later. As I wrote earlier: I still have to find the right words for the second half. To be continued!

23

Super Waling's story lay like a riddle on his lap. Gieles reread the words he had printed out the night before. 'I can't reduce my present condition to just that one day that my life (and that of my parents) was changed for good.'

Was he talking about the plane crash? Why hadn't he written anything about the inheritance? Or was that coming in the next part, along with an explanation of his fat ass? It frustrated him, not knowing more. He looked yet again at the class photo of Dolly with Super Waling.

It was only a quarter to eight. He could go to Johan and ask him what his scrapbooks had to say about the crash of 5 October 1979. He crept downstairs with Wally under his arm. (She no longer fit under his shirt.) When he got to Meike's guest room he stopped and looked at the closed door longingly—until Wally cackled.

Outside he gave the geese some extra cookies to assuage his guilt. Ever since Meike had shown up on their doorstep with her little coffin of a suitcase he had thought too much about her and too little about the geese. He had completely neglected his training with Tufted and Bufted. The letter to Christian Moullec still hadn't been sent. He'd stopped playing table tennis altogether with Wally. Sleeping was a joke. As he lay in bed he fantasised about the woods in exile. The conditions in his fantasy were always ideal. Sometimes where was a waterfall, with Meike and her glistening breasts standing under it. Then there were fruit trees, where he'd quickly scramble into his O'Neill surfing trunks. He'd push little pieces of peach and pear between her lips and then lick them off. Sometimes he changed the woods and the things they did, depending on his state of mind (which had been pretty horny since her arrival).

But last night it had been impossible to fantasise. Each time he tried, Super Waling came biking in with his grandmothers and the crashed airplane.

He could hear the aggressive goose carrying on in the barn. Gieles threw in a handful of speculaas and she rushed towards him angrily. Then he walked across the field to the spaceship, wondering whether the old couple were still asleep. The lawn chairs were folded up. Between the chair legs a spider had woven a web from which dewdrops were hanging.

Suddenly the aluminium door opened.

'Gerard,' said the old man, who was wrapped in a dark blue bathrobe. There was a sharp part in his wispy hair. 'What brings you here on this beautiful day?'

'I've come for the scrapbooks. But maybe you're still sleeping.'

'Not at all!' shouted Johan, folding out the doorstep as if he were rolling out the red carpet. 'It's never too early for plane crashes. Come on in!'

Gieles inhaled a lungful of musty bedroom air. He hoped the man would leave the door open, but the whole thing was hermetically sealed.

'Have a seat.' He pointed to the small dining nook near the kitchen, where an imitation fireplace was burning. The inside of the trailer looked quite ordinary compared to the high-tech exterior. The cabinets and walls were finished off with beige panels. The brown curtains that screened off the sleeping area looked old and worn.

Johan sat down next to him and turned with difficulty toward the built-in cabinet behind the couch. Gieles heard his upper body creak as he reached for a scrapbook.

The ritual repeated itself. Johan gave a short speech before opening the book. '1982 through 1986' it said on the blue cover.

He had skipped a book. The crashes from before 1982. Gieles didn't dare interrupt him. At this stage he didn't even dare tell him that his name wasn't Gerard.

Johan talked and talked as if he were talking about his grandchildren and not about plane crashes.

Air Florida, flight 90: struck a bridge and ended up in a frozen river.

Air Canada, flight 797: began as a minor fire in the rear toilets and ended in a conflagration.

Air India, flight 182: a bomb on board. 'There have always been terrorists, Gerard.'

Only when he had finished the last page and was about to start in on the next scrapbook did Gieles have the courage to interrupt him. 'You forgot the crashes from 1977 through 1981.'

Johan looked at him peevishly.

'Last time we went up to 1976.'

He turned his creaking body once again toward the built-in cabinet and checked the scrapbooks. 'Doggone it,' he growled. 'Everything's all mixed up. My wife did this.' He redirected his gaze to the closed curtain at the back of the trailer. 'Judith! Have you been messing with my scrapbooks?'

There was no response.

With a great deal of grumbling, Johan opened '1977 through 1981.' He gave a detailed account of the accident on Tenerife: the biggest plane disaster in all of aviation history. White saliva gathered in the corners of his mouth. A sour smell filled the interior of the spaceship.

Gieles's eyes strayed to the curtain, behind which his wife apparently was sleeping, and to the clock over the fake fireplace. Eight-thirty. In two hours he had to be at the pumping station. Today he and Wally would be giving their table tennis demonstration.

Johan seemed to sense that he wanted to leave. Suddenly the man slammed his hand on the table. '... and this Airbus from the Soviet Union,' he said with a loud voice, 'ended up right here, further down the polder, on October 5th, 1979. Thirty dead.'

Gieles was one hundred percent present and he dove head-first into the scrapbook. In the blurry black-and-white photo he could see a tractor hooked up to a trailer on which passengers were sitting. In the background was the plane, broken in half.

'Farmer Cittersen van Boven provided care for the victims' were the words below the photo. Gieles's heart began to pound.

Johan launched into a technical recitation of the circumstances surrounding the crash while Gieles tried to decipher the yellowed clippings.

IT WAS GOD'S WILL THAT WE WERE ABLE TO HELP he read in big display type. Johan turned the page mid-oration ('the black box was irreparably damaged') to a dim photo of a man and a boy looking dazed and staring into the camera lens. The man was wearing a cap and was resting his hand protectively on the boy's shoulder.

'Farmer Cittersen van Boven and his son Waling hastened to assist the survivors of the wrecked Airbus,' read the caption.

'Most likely it was malfunctioning ailerons that

caused the thing to come crashing down,' Johan went on, but Gieles was no longer listening. His new fat friend was a hero! Maybe not of the same order as Captain Sully, but he was easily a match for Moullec. Or his own mother.

'How many passengers did they save?' Gieles asked eagerly. The sour smell no longer bothered him, nor did the globs of saliva in the corners of Johan's mouth.

'Forty.'

'*Forty?*' cried Gieles ecstatically. His pride was beyond description. Once he had recovered from his astonishment, he asked Johan what had happened to the farmer and his son.

'I don't collect that kind of information,' he answered tersely. 'I'm more interested in the type of airplane and the facts of the crash. That kind of thing. The people involved don't concern me. Dead or alive, doesn't matter. As I said, Gerard, the audio recording in the black box was irreparably damaged. Did you know, by the way, that the black box is never black but orange?'

The curtain at the back of the spaceship opened. Johan's wife was sitting up in bed in her nightgown. 'Good morning,' she mumbled. Her mouth was sunken. 'How nice to see you here.'

'You're interrupting.' Johan was irritated. 'Please go back to sleep.'

'I really have to go,' said Gieles. It seemed like the perfect moment to take his leave.

Everyone at the farm was awake. Even Meike had put on her clothes. She was sitting on the edge of the guest bed in a tight vinyl dress, digging through her coffin suitcase. Her breasts and midriff were so compressed that the sight of it alone made him gasp for air. She took out a black piece of cloth and tied it around her neck.

'There's also a hood on the cape,' she said, pulling it over her head. The velvet hood was so wide that two heads could easily have fit into it. The hood was lined in pink.

'Isn't that too warm?' Gieles asked. He thought the cape was just as ugly as the robes his mother wore.

'Black clothes help keep you cool.' She spread out her arms and moved them slowly up and down. Then she gave Gieles a penetrating look, something she was very good at. Every time she looked at him like that he had to turn away after a few seconds because her eyes were too much for him.

'People who live in the desert also wear black,' she said, sliding her blister-covered feet into the platform shoes.

Meike was going to meet Super Waling today. He knew she would like him. Meike loved anything different, which is why she thought the aggressive goose was so funny. Gieles hadn't told her that the goose would soon be going to the butcher. But he did want to brag about Super Waling, about what an awesome hero he was. Gieles could hardly believe it himself. Back then, Super Waling was as old as he was now. If Gieles had rescued forty people from a busted up airplane his life would look very different. His mother would never go away again. It was a known fact that everybody liked to be near their hero. You could see that with Captain Sully and with the great table tennis player Jan-Ove Waldner. They were always surrounded by fans. If Gieles had rescued forty passengers, he would have kissed Meike ages ago. That was also a fact.

His father was outside tooting the horn. They had to hurry up. He had his car window down and didn't bat an eye when he saw Meike stumble out of the house in her cape. His father had the same neutral facial expression as when he shook Super Waling's hand after the rowdy pyramid presentation in the town hall. He hadn't said a word about Super Waling, not even on the way back home.

Gieles and Meike were sitting in the back with Wally. Uncle Fred was sitting next to his brother and providing an animated running commentary on the passing scenery. It was a beautiful day. The air was clear, but Gieles's head was cloudy. There was too much going on.

The grounds around the pumping station had been catapulted back in time at least a hundred and fifty years. A settlement of shanties had been built that were supposed to show what life was like for the poor polder workers. Ramshackle little huts made of wooden panels with branches and reeds painted on them were leaning against each other. Gieles was sure that Super Waling had been responsible for the basic design of the fair. He could almost see Ide and Sophia Warrens walking around among the hundreds of visitors.

He shuffled past the stands with Meike, holding Wally under his arm. His father and Uncle Fred had stayed behind at the pumping station to get a cup of coffee.

Meike could barely walk on her heels. There was no rhythm in her stride. With every tottering step she took her velvet cape touched his body. It was as if they were walking hand in hand. No one looked at her. The men and women behind the stands were all decked out in historical costumes, and everyone probably thought she was one of them. Not that he was ashamed of Meike. He thought she was the prettiest girl around. But the stuff she put on and smeared on her face was hideous, to his mind.

Meike had lowered her hood and was trying to catch a glimpse of the polder workers' tools and utensils that were on display. There were people crowded together in front of every stand, except the stand for jenever tasting. Apparently it was still too early for that.

The little orchestra that called itself Not Afraid of Wet Feet consisted of three elderly gentlemen playing folk music. They were drowned out by the screaming children at the old Dutch games stand. Suddenly Skiq and Onno popped up in front of them. They were walking on wooden blocks with strings attached, which made them as tall as Meike.

Skiq had his Michael Jackson hat on. 'This is Meike,' Gieles told the boys, who stared at her with undisguised curiosity. 'I know that,' said Skiq. 'She was in the woods.' He bumped up against his little brother, who in turn lost his balance and slammed into Meike. Onno dragged her down as he fell, like a row of dominoes. She lay stretched out in the straw with the little boy on top of her, her cape fallen open. Shocked, Onno crept off the vinyl dress and ran away.

'You okay?' Gieles asked. Meike sat down, brushed the straw from her cape and shook her dreadlocks. Skiq sat on his haunches and studied her platform shoes. 'Whoa,' he said, greatly impressed. 'You have wooden blocks *in* your shoes.'

Gieles tried to pull her up with Wally under his arm. Finally she got to her feet, still tottering.

'I'm gonna ask Mom if I can have shoes like that,' said Skiq, and he stood up on the wooden blocks.

Gieles saw Dolly sitting further down on a long bench. The toddler was lying with his head in her lap. She was wearing a pair of large sunglasses, her mouth tight and impatient. He wondered whether this was the right moment to introduce Meike. Dolly had this it's-all-too-much-for-me look on her face, which meant it was better to stay out of her way. He wanted to keep walking, but Skiq was calling them over.

'That's Dolly,' Gieles told Meike, who was still busy brushing off the straw. 'You know, the hairdresser.'

Uncle Fred had called Dolly and asked whether Meike could work for a few weeks at the beauty parlour. She could wash hair and sweep the floor, Uncle Fred suggested. It wasn't easy finding a summer job. Meike had applied at a bakery, a florist and a nut shop, and all of them had sent her away without an interview. 'They must not want anybody from Brabant,' Meike had said angrily at supper, plunging her knife into the meat as if the animal hadn't been killed yet.

Dolly had said she wanted to meet Meike first. It looked as if the time had come. Dolly and Meike: he could hardly imagine a worse combination. They'd annihilate each other. Meike would start shrieking with her siren voice and Dolly would treat her to a kick in the ass.

On top of his worries about the Meike/Dolly combination was the dildo. Tony had done his 'shopping,' but Gieles hadn't seen him since then.

'You coming?' shouted Skiq impatiently. He was now walking backwards on the wooden blocks. Gieles looked at Meike's dreadlocks. Dolly hated dreadlocks.

She probably also hated black eye shadow and piercings.

'There's still some straw in your hair.'

She shook her head. 'Gone?'

'There's still something in it … no, there.' With one hand he helped her pull the bits of straw out of her tangles. Wally was on his other arm and she was starting to get heavy. He knew Dolly was looking at them.

'Come on!' Skiq was standing right next to his mother.

Gieles and Meike cleared a path through the crowd of children.

'Hi, Gieles,' Dolly said, smiling at him sweetly. 'You ready for the contest?'

No, she still hasn't missed the dildo. Otherwise she'd act very differently towards me. Maybe she never uses the thing. The dildo didn't look worn out. On the other hand, what does a worn-out dildo look like?

Gieles laughed shyly. 'Oh, it's just an ordinary demonstration.'

'Call it ordinary if you want. A goose who plays table tennis. I haven't seen too many things in my life that were so unordinary.'

Then Dolly turned to Meike, as if these last words applied to her as well. Gieles could read nothing from her face, however. Dolly's eyes were still hidden behind the big sunglasses, camouflaging any impression that Meike might be making on her.

'This is Meike,' he muttered. Meike's pale face contrasted so sharply with her cape that she looked like a ghost.

'I thought so,' said Dolly.

Skiq hobbled on his wooden blocks and pointed to Meike's towering soles. 'Look, Mom! She has blocks *in* her shoes.' He admired the shoes avidly. 'Can you moonwalk in them?' he asked Meike in all seriousness.

'Moonwalk?' she repeated with surprise. She said this with a thick Brabant accent, which indicated to Gieles how terribly nervous she was.

Dolly told Skiq to shut up. Then she turned to Meike.

'The draining of the lake,' she began, taking off her sunglasses, 'was in around 1850. But looking at you right now, I'd say we were somewhere in the Middle Ages.'

Meike looked at her in utter confusion.

'That cape,' Dolly explained, without ridicule or cynicism. 'People in the Middle Ages wore capes like that. The rich ones, that is. Because if you were poor you'd have to work, which you couldn't do in such a long garment.'

Dolly sat straight up and laid a hand on Jonas's sleeping head.

Gieles followed her example. He laid a hand on Wally and began to stroke her breast nervously.

'So, Meike, you want to work at a beauty parlour, is that right? That's what I understood from Gieles's uncle. But you can't wear a cape or wood-block shoes there. No way. In my shop we have a certain dress code. Is that a problem for you? A dress code?'

She took a breath. 'Because if it's a problem, we don't have to bother coming to an agreement. That would be a waste of our time. And time, Meike, is something that I absolutely don't have. So it's up to you.'

Dolly said this without blinking her eyes, even though she was looking straight into the sun. Gieles didn't dare look at Meike. He was afraid she'd start wailing like a siren. He began rubbing his hair frantically to dispel the silence that had fallen.

But Meike didn't scream or wail. She didn't start cursing and roaring like a longshoreman. She simply answered, as cool as you please, 'No, a dress code is no problem for me.'

'Well. I'm glad about that,' said Dolly, and laughed with unexpected warmth.

Gieles breathed a sigh of relief.

'Can we have a pancake?' asked the boys, jumping up and down in front of their mother.

'All right,' said Dolly. 'Everybody gets a pancake.'

She stood up and put the sleeping Jonas in the stroller and then laboriously pushed it through the straw. Gieles and Meike walked behind her. The boys ran ahead, but came right back. 'Mom!' Skiq tried to whisper. 'There's that fat bean-bag man!'

Gieles saw Super Waling in the mobility scooter. But why was his father crouched down over the left rear wheel? And why was Super Waling wearing a jute sack with a rope tied around it?

Jesus, he looks like a water barrel. Why is nothing ever normal?

Dolly greeted Willem and Fred with a friendly hello but ignored Super Waling completely. She just stood with her back to him.

'How nice that you've brought Meike along,' said Super Waling, as if nothing was wrong. He turned a bit to the side so he could see her better. 'You are Meike, aren't you?'

Out of nowhere Skiq threw himself in front of her and pulled her cape aside, revealing pale white legs covered with ink spots and impossibly high shoes.

'She's wearing wood blocks!' he screamed. 'They're hidden in her shoes!'

All eyes were on Meike, who looked anguished.

Dolly yanked her son up roughly by his antenna-like arm. 'Behave yourself!' she hissed and gave him a good shaking.

'Mom, weren't we were gonna have pancakes?' Onno whined.

'That's a good idea,' Uncle Fred put in, and pointed to the patio of the pancake shack. 'I see an empty table there in the corner.'

Willem Bos stood up and wiped his hands off on a handkerchief. 'The problem is the differential. It has to be replaced. The gears,' he explained. 'That's why it squeaks so much when you're driving it.'

'Well, thanks for the advice,' said Super Waling gratefully, and he started up the scooter.

'I've got something to do. I have to see whether they set up the table tennis table properly.'

'Waling, you're not going to abandon us already, are you?' shouted Uncle Fred heartily. 'We've just met. Come on, have a pancake. We've got heaps of time before the demonstration starts.'

Dolly and the boys were already seated. She was leaning her elbows on the table and massaging her temples.

'When I see your gorgeous cape, I'm ashamed to be wearing this monk's habit,' said Super Waling as they zigzagged through the crowd. 'Historically speaking I'm totally out of sync. The polder boys didn't wear habits. But I couldn't fit into the work pants. That's why I put this on.'

Meike was tottering next to him. 'Apparently what I'm wearing doesn't fucking fit in here, either, but I'm used to it.'

Super Waling stayed far away from Dolly, much to Gieles's relief. He parked at the other end of the table, next to Meike. Her silence from the morning had vanished into thin air. She wolfed down a polder pancake with bacon and syrup, and in between bites she told Waling that since the past week she had given up being a vegetarian. Perhaps she was going to do what Nicolas Cage, 'you-know-that-actor-guy,' was doing. 'He only eats animals that have sex with each other in awesome ways,' she said with her mouth full. 'Like horses and fish. But Nicolas Cage doesn't eat pork because their sex is gross.'

Gieles looked at Dolly, but she was feeding the toddler

and talking to his uncle and father at the same time.

'I've never seen that with pigs,' said Meike. 'I've never seen geese having sex, either. But I swear I'd never eat a goose.'

She stroked the little goose on Gieles's lap. Super Waling listened with amusement. Every now and then he took a sip of water. He had declined the pancake.

For Gieles, the contrast with the photos was so enormous he could hardly take it in. First there was Waling the little boy with his father at the site of the plane crash. Then there was Waling the handsome teacher in the calfskin jacket. And finally the Waling of today: the lump of lard that wouldn't even fit into seven calfskin jackets. Gieles hoped he could have a few minutes alone with him. He had to know the truth about the plane crash.

When Dolly's children finished eating, things threatened to go dangerously wrong. Gieles could hardly breathe from the tension. Onno told his mother that all Meike was wearing under her blanket was a plastic bag. Everyone ignored him, but the little boy kept it up and blared, 'There's a garbage bag under that blanket! I've seen it myself!'

He jumped off his chair and stared at Meike defiantly.

'Shut up,' said Dolly with a low voice. She hurled her fork onto the table with noisy finality as if she were throwing her towel in the ring.

'I'll go settle up,' said Willem, not knowing how soon he could gracefully get away. Meike and Uncle Fred left to find the toilets. The little brothers went over to the bales of straw and promptly started kicking them.

'Now I remember!' cried Super Waling. 'You're Dolly de Boer! You were in my class, and as I recall you wanted to be a doctor.'

His eyes twinkled, but Dolly avoided all eye contact and began rubbing Jonas's face briskly with a bib.

'Most of the girls wanted to be stewardesses or hairdressers, but not you ...'

Super Waling became uncomfortable. Even now that he was speaking directly to her she ignored him.

'Golly, I just didn't recognise you,' he continued, feeling his way. 'I believe you used to have blond hair ... Gieles told me all about you, that you were in my class ... Did that ever happen ... becoming a doctor?'

'No,' she snapped. She put on her big sunglasses. Her poker face. Only then did she look at him. 'I ended up just like all those other girls. I never got any further than hairdresser. The doctor idea didn't work out.'

She raised her head and then slowly lowered it. Her dark lenses made their way down the length of the brown monk's habit, and Gieles was grateful that her eyes were hidden.

'I did have blond hair in high school. That's why you didn't recognise me. But you know ... ,' she said, and then she paused. She crossed her arms and jabbed at her upper arm with her sharp nails. 'I still don't recognise *you*. With all the will in the world, I cannot recognise my wonderful history teacher in that ... *that* body.'

She clamped her hands onto the handle of the stroller. 'See you later, Gieles. I'll go find a place to sit. Do your best and put a comb through your hair. It's all over the place.' And with that Dolly was gone.

Fucking fucking fucking bitch!

Gieles stared at the rest of the food on his plate. All the tension had drained his appetite and now he felt sick.

'Well, that didn't go very well,' said Super Waling.

Gieles squeezed his eyes shut. 'I hope she doesn't show up. What a lousy rotten thing to say.'

'It's all right, Gieles. She's allowed to be disappointed.'
He slapped his arm.

'If she knew about you ... she wouldn't act like, like that.' He was fighting back tears.

'If she knew what?'

'About you! That you rescued all those people from the plane! You and your father!'

Super Waling shook his head despondently. 'No, you're wrong.'

'You're heroes!' cried Gieles with emotion. 'I'm sure Dolly doesn't know anything about it!'

'I was absolutely no lifesaver,' interrupted Super Waling. A woman in a long skirt and an apron stacked up the plates. As she worked she greeted Super Waling warmly.

He waited until she was gone. 'Listen, Gieles. I was anything but a hero.'

'But it was in the newspaper! You were in the newspaper!'

Super Waling sighed. 'That whole plane crash, it was completely different than what everyone thought.'

Gieles looked at him with bewilderment.

'It's not an easy story to tell ... Dolly knows nothing at all about the crash. I never mentioned it later on.'

'Dolly is a fucking bitch.'

'No, she's not,' said Super Waling soothingly. 'I understand her reaction. I know that people look at me with disgust and shame.'

'I don't. I'm not ashamed ... I was a little in the beginning, but not any more.'

'Thank you, Gieles.'

'I named Wally after you. Waling, Wally.'

'I saw it on the registration form ... You have no idea how deeply that touched me. Right in the heart.'

'I don't want you to explode ...' He could no longer

327

hold back the tears, and he hid his face.

'Oh, Gieles. It's all right. Nobody can see you anyway. I'll sit like a bunker between you and the rest of the cafe. And hey, I'm really not going to explode. You probably can't tell by looking at me, but I'm trying to lose weight. Really. And you know, in the last few weeks I've actually started to take a little pleasure in life.'

24

Gieles lay in bed. Wasted. Wound-up. Miserable. Horny. Over-stimulated. His head was reeling from the day's impressions. His body was a hormonal frappuccino. Gieles tried to concentrate on his breathing, but by the time he got to the fourth deep breath a new thought would blast its way into his head. He wondered whether all that worrying might cause his brain to crash. It made him think of the wiring of their stereo installation that one day had simply burnt out.

He tried to find a relaxing position, although the little goose was pressing against his skull to scratch herself. He did his best to reconstruct the afternoon.

Meike is sitting next to me in the car and she says our table tennis demonstration was absolutely incredible and she pets Wally, who's lying on my lap. Her hand touches my hand and I'm absolutely sure she's doing it on purpose, because she doesn't have to touch my hand. Dad's driving. We're listening to an old song. Uncle Fred says it's The Beatles. I don't miss anything or anybody, not even Mom. It's just as if we were one family. We stop at a traffic light and there's a woman there who looks into our car. I try to look at us through her eyes and I chuckle out loud. We must look like a pretty bizarre family. Dad turns onto our street and slows down. He leans against the door and stares out at the runway and the sky, the runway and the sky. Then Uncle Fred shouts, 'What's that over there?' We see a white pillow lying on the shoulder of the road. It's torn apart. There are feathers everywhere, and then I know that it's no pillow. 'Goddamn it,' Dad curses, and he pulls over and parks the car. We get out and Meike starts to cry. She cries the way she screams. She falls on her knees and buries her face in her cape. The goose looks very strange. Flight feathers have been torn out of her wings and her neck is twisted like a rope. I know right away that she wasn't hit by a car or attacked by a fox. Dad picks the goose up by her twisted neck and Meike cries even louder.

'You asleep yet?'

Gieles wasn't aware that she was standing next to his bed. He sat straight up and automatically reached for his hair, trying to act as if having a girl in an undershirt standing next to his bed was perfectly normal.

'No, I'm still awake.' His voice cracked horribly.

'Can I lie next to you?'

'Sure,' said Gieles, much louder than he intended, and he edged over with his back to the wall so that Meike had almost the entire bed to herself.

'Downstairs I sleep under a duvet, but up here it's sweltering.'

She lay on her stomach and stroked Wally's neck. Wally was sleeping with her head tucked into her feathers.

'All I can think about is the goose,' said Meike. 'When I see that mailman I swear I'm gonna murder him.'

Gieles looked at her profile in the darkness. She had a perfect face with a creepy spider pinned to her eyebrow and a weird tattoo. He wondered whether her appearance was the reason why she didn't go to school any more. Maybe she had been bullied.

'Why don't you want to go to school any more?' Now that she was lying to close to him he wasn't afraid to ask. He was wide awake.

She didn't answer for a couple of minutes.

'I was suspended, and after that I didn't want to go back. It's a shitty school.'

'Why were you suspended?'

Don't ruin it! She didn't come here to talk, obviously!

She rested her chin on her forearm.

'You don't have to tell me if you don't feel like it. We can listen to music or something.'

He should have sacrificed more Rizla birds. Whole albums full. There was so much going on that he hadn't had time for any Bird Burnings.

'I pissed in my gym teacher's car.'

'Your gym teacher's? On purpose?'

She nodded.

'No way!' He accidentally hit his head against the wall. 'Why would you do that?'

'He came in when I was taking a shower. I had to stay after, to clean up the gym. And when I was in the shower he walked in on me, the filthy pig. One week later two girls and I walked in on *him* in the shower. He's a big guy, but he had a teeny little dick this big.'

She held up her pinkie. 'From that day on we started calling him Mouse Dick. Mousie Dick.' She fiddled with her piercing. 'We really busted his chops. On Sports Day there were all these events that I'm good in.'

'You?'

'I'm really good in running.'

Gieles laughed. 'But you have to have long legs, don't you? ... and you have to be athletic?'

She gave him a jab, but she didn't break into her customary fit of giggles. She was serious. 'It's not a matter of height, it's a matter of stamina. But that's not what I'm talking about. On Sports Day they handed out prizes. There was a stage set up next to the track where Mousie Dick was announcing the winners. I was first, and as he put a medal around my neck I could see from his face that he was gonna jerk me around. After a minute he said,' and she put on a weird, distorted voice, "'Oh, no, I got the names wrong. The first prize doesn't go to Meike Nooteboom from 2b but Meike Bla-dee-bla from 2e." That asshole came up with some bullshit excuse about too many Meikes at school and he took the medal away from me.'

She spoke faster and faster, as if she wanted to get through her story as soon as possible. 'Mousie Dick drives around in this macho sports car with an open roof. He had left the thing parked behind the clubhouse. I was with the same girls from the shower incident. First we spat all over the windshield of Mousie Dick's car. One of the two girls took off her underpants—we were wearing those long gothic dresses—and hung it on his rear-view mirror. I stuffed my underpants in the muffler and squatted down behind the steering wheel. When I was finished pissing, Mousie Dick came up. The other girls were able to get away, but he caught me. I was in bare feet and there were these little pebbles all over the ground. He dragged me back to his car and he kept screaming, 'What did you do to my Lexus? If you did anything to my Lexus ... !' He didn't know yet that I had pissed in his car, but he did see the windshield.'

Meike shivered for a second, although she couldn't possibly have been cold.

'He rubbed my face all over the windshield like a sponge. Until some other teachers came up. Then he stopped.'

She laid her head down. Her face was hidden under the dreadlocks. Gieles remembered biking to school once with Tony. They spat up into the air, and the trick was to ride under the spit as fast as possible. Tony's spit ended up in Gieles's eye. The whole day he could feel it. As if the enzymes were consuming his eyeball.

'And you were suspended?' he asked. She didn't say any more. From her silence he gathered that that's what had happened.

'But why didn't that Mousie Dick get kicked out of school? I mean, he walked in on you in the shower.'

She turned her head to him and said loudly, 'They didn't believe me. They kept talking this shit that I was a sore loser and that's why I made things up. I went to the principal with my parents and the guy was such a hypocrite. He was like, 'Why would I walk in on your daughter in the shower, of all people? Give me one good reason.' And they all looked at me as if I was the sister of Charles Fucking Manson, and then they looked at each other and laughed themselves silly.'

Now she was speaking very loudly. 'My mother just started flirting with Mousie Dick! She couldn't keep her eyes off him, the dwarf! She wanted ...'

'Shhh,' interrupted Gieles. He was afraid she'd start screaming.

She snorted angrily.

'Super Waling once rescued forty people from an airplane,' he said to distract her. 'The plane crashed on their property and thirty people were killed, and all the newspapers wrote about him and his father. Super Waling was only fourteen at the time.'

'Wow,' she whispered. 'He's really awesome.'

'Yeah. Super Waling is super awesome.'

Gieles wanted to stroke her cheek and whisper in her ear that she was the prettiest girl in the whole wide world. But he didn't dare. Tomorrow he'd sacrifice a record number of birds. She yawned and he felt her warm breath on his skin. Her breath smelled delicious and sweet. He wouldn't mind at all if she spat all over his face.

She was so close that Gieles could hear her eyelids fluttering. He held his eyes wide open, but despite all his attempts to stay awake, sleep got the better of him.

25

I am once and for all making an end to my letter. There are
many developments and I am becoming timeless. I bring
first of all the bad news. Goose big was murdered. We suspect by a person. Her neck was screwed and the wings
torn were lying further away. In the back side of my head I
know who the author of the murder is. My father is going
to investigate the bottom. He suspects the man of the
mail. As you know, we live next to the flight path. The
cameras are hanging everywhere. My father is going to
study the tapes. Meike wants to attack the author of the
murder. I do not want her to do this. She must behave herself. Otherwise she must go to her parents back. Her parents keep strawberries. Meike hates strawberries and
Meike hates the teacher of physical education. Her teacher
of physical education, entitled the Laughing Dick, peeked
secretly naked in the shower. She now has temporary asy-
lum with us. I have very strong feelings on Meike. I hope
for mutual traffic.

And now I bring the nice news! Goose small, entitled
Wally, show the stole with the table ping pong. We were at
a spectacle and played excellent. The whole world clapped
for goose small. She was in great form. Her game was
silent and strong. I have great pride. Tufted and Bufted
also listen better. They saw me as a brother to obtain tricks
on. But today I am more like an adopted father. They rest
on 1 place, even when I am no longer visual.

Yet I crack my head whether my geese will stay on 1 place

if 1 great threat approaches. Will they still listen to me, or will they forget all the orderings and start flying every which way without their heads? You know the answer with certainty. Your geese lesser white-fronted always listen. Even with the balloon trip. I read that the humanity with you can rise in a balloon driven by your pulling varieties. Formidable! I read that you say: it is the wind that decides my destination.

I hope really much that the wind blows to my direction and brings you and your pulling varieties. I hope we can be friends! I thank you for your hearing and your accumulated answer.

Gieles Bos (fellow goose explorer)

Three days after the murder of the goose Gieles went to the beauty parlour with his father by car. Meike had completed her first workday. During the ride, Willem Bos kept looking at him strangely. Ever since Meike had moved into the house he had starting acting like a father who would bend over backwards for his daughter. During a meal the previous week he had spent way more time in conversation than he usually did, talking about brooding terns. He must have been at it for at least fifteen minutes. He said he was able to think like a bird, which made it possible for him to come up with a good solution to almost every bird problem. His father said that the terns were brooding on the flat roof of one of the airport caterers and were creating quite a nuisance. He had put himself in the tern's shoes, so to speak, had flown over the buildings near the airport and had settled on the roof, which was strewn with pebbles. He hopped around (and when he said 'hopped' his father had actually made a hopping movement), laid his eggs and discovered that the eggs were the same colour and size as the pebbles. Then Willem knew—Meike was hanging breathlessly on his every word—why the terns had chosen the camouflaged roof. So the pebbles were removed, the roof was sprayed orange and the terns moved on, never to be seen again. When his father was finished, Gieles and Uncle Fred stared at him with their mouths hanging open.

They rode past a fence. Sitting on the fence was a bright green bird with a red beak. 'A rose-ringed parakeet,' said Willem, slowing down to get a better look. 'You see them here more and more often.'

Gieles didn't respond. He closed his eyes and sank down in the seat. He was totally worn out and he nodded off, until he heard his father say, 'Tony killed the goose.'

Gieles sat up so fast that he practically hit the dashboard.

'I knew it!' His face was bright red. 'What a bastard! I knew it!'

'Calm down, Gieles,' said Willem, lurching over the roadway. 'I looked back over the images. I couldn't see everything, but Tony himself was attacked. It was self-defence.'

Gieles hit the car door. 'What do you mean, self-defence? What can a goose do to somebody like Tony?'

Willem watched his son explode with a surge of testosterone.

'I don't know either. I couldn't see everything in the images. I saw Tony running across the road with the goose on his back. I think she had the skin of his neck in her bill and was giving it a twist. That hurts.'

'HURTS?' roared Gieles, who was bouncing through the car. 'THAT BIRD DOESN'T WEIGH ANYTHING! IT'S STILL JUST A CHICK!'

'I'm sitting right next to you. You don't have to scream,' said Willem.

'It was still just a chick!'

'It was a *very* big and aggressive chick. And now stop the screaming or you'll end up walking to the beauty parlour.' He cleared his throat. 'Tony had probably left our yard and she went after him.'

'How is that possible?' said Gieles angrily. 'I had put her in the barn. Tony is a filthy sadist. He always has been. Even when we were little. When you had that CO_2 gas tank in the barn, he put a rabbit in it just for fun.'

'I didn't know that,' said Willem, shocked. He glanced up from the corner of his eye. About twenty jackdaws were flying west. They were relatively small birds, but in a group they could snap off a plane's engine blades. He picked up the walkie-talkie and reported the jackdaws to his colleagues.

'That rabbit,' his father asked a bit later. 'Did you gas that rabbit?'

'Tony, you mean,' said Gieles, correcting him angrily. 'He put him in the tank. Not me.'

Willem rubbed his furrowed brow. 'But I *always* disconnected the gas tank. For safety's sake. How did you guys get that thing running?'

'Jesus, Dad, Tony can get anything to run. He can even soup up a lawnmower to go eight kilometres an hour. He fixed Mom's old curling iron, right?'

Willem was visibly upset.

'The cylinder was empty,' said Gieles. 'There was no more CO_2 in it. I let the rabbit go.'

They drove down the main road in silence for several minutes, until Gieles started in on the goose. 'But why did he pull out her wings? And the neck isn't normal, either. She must already have been dead and he twisted her neck anyway.'

'I couldn't see that from the images.' He knew his son had a point. Tony Junior had maliciously brutalised the goose.

'He tried to beat her away. I saw Tony take a club out of a bag. A short, black club. That's what it looked like, anyway.'

Gieles stared at his father in amazement.

'Did you guys have a fight? Why would Tony bring a club along if he was going to stop in and see you?'

'No idea,' answered Gieles abruptly.

Willem parked the service car in front of Dolly's Hair Corner. The beauty parlour was at the end of a faded shopping arcade, next to The Meat Hall. There was a permanent smell of bleach in and around The Meat Hall. Dolly was at war with The Meat Hall because it made her shop reek of bleach. She had called in the food inspection authorities several times. The man in the upstairs apartment was fighting with Dolly, too. He had a Rottweiler who carried on all day long on the balcony. The barking was driving her crazy.

When Gieles got out of the car, his father said, 'I think it's better if we don't say anything to Meike.'

Gieles nodded. She was fully capable of giving Tony the same treatment that he had given the strangled goose. He slammed the door shut. The Rottweiler started up immediately, his blunt head pressed against the balcony bars.

He opened the door that said CLOSED. Dolly closed her shop fifteen minutes earlier than the other shops so she wouldn't be late picking up the boys from daycare. She was tallying up the cash and writing down the results in a ledger, mumbling the numbers aloud as she went. These were not large amounts. She had a small business with only four chairs, and since the expansion of the shopping centre the competition had become cutthroat. Dolly had to make do with the older clientele who hated loud music and austere interiors. That's why she never changed anything in her shop. The walls had been the same terra cotta colour for years, and all the furniture was wicker. There were flowers everywhere: plastic flowers in the window and plastic flowers worked into garlands—Dolly called them festoons—that hung from the modular ceiling.

Gieles sat down on a little wicker bench. He wondered where Meike was. Had she been fired on her first day of work, and was she wandering through the shopping centre? Or had she run away after some biting remark from Dolly?

Suddenly he felt an enormous aversion. Her harsh words, her snarling and screaming, her comments about everything and everybody, the tirade against Super Waling. Gieles could tell Dolly about the noble deed Super Waling had performed in the beet field, but he was too angry at her.

'Meike is doing some shopping for me,' said Dolly as she shut the drawer of the cash register.

She walked up to one of the mirrors and took a lipstick out of a make-up display. As she coloured her lips red, she looked at Gieles in the mirror. The skirt came to just above the knee. Her turquoise vest, the sandals with straps around the ankles. It left Gieles cold.

She pouted her lips and put the lipstick back in the display.

'Meike didn't disappoint me,' she said, pulling the elastic out of her hair. 'She knows what work is.' She brushed her hair slowly while observing Gieles in the mirror. He had picked up a magazine and was paging through it indifferently. She can go jump in a lake. The only reason he was sitting there was because she had given Meike a summer job. Without a job she'd have to go back to Zundert.

'Do you ever go into my bedroom?' Dolly blurted out.

Gieles looked up from his magazine and met her eyes in the beauty parlour mirror. He stretched himself to his full length and pushed his shoulders back. Gieles felt like a man.

'What do you mean?' he bluffed.

'Oh, you know,' she mumbled, and she broke eye contact.

He felt so angry and strong that he didn't care that Dolly was fishing for her dildo, which had been missing for at least two weeks.

Meike came into the shop with two bags full of groceries. Only when she handed Dolly the change, accompanied by a torrent of words, did she see Gieles sitting on the wicker bench. They smiled shyly at each other, and Gieles was impressed by her new outfit: a pair of black jeans and a white shirt that had DOLLY'S HAIR CORNER printed on it. Except for the piercing, the tear and the dreadlocks, Meike looked like an ordinary girl. Gieles stood up. 'We have to go. My father is waiting.'

Meike spontaneously gave her boss three big cheek kisses, shouted out 'how-do!'—the Brabant way of saying goodbye—and skipped after Gieles. She sat in the back of the car and babbled ecstatically about their working arrangement. Dolly cut and dried. She was allowed to wash and sweep. Tomorrow Dolly would teach her how to set hair. Gieles and his father remained silent. The murdered goose sat like an obstacle between them.

It wasn't until Willem Bos had parked the car in the

yard and stuck one foot out the door that he coughed nervously and said to no one in particular, 'From now on everybody sleeps in his own bed.'

26

Sunshine,

I really enjoyed the newspaper article about your table tennis demonstration. Fred scanned it and fortunately I was able to check my messages at a medical aid station near Galkayo. That paragraph that says you're a talented young man with a sixth sense for the training of geese made me especially proud. Obviously it was apparent to everyone, because Juan (a Spanish doctor from Doctors Without Borders) asked me why I was sitting there grinning from ear to ear. I showed him your picture.

I'm doing fine, by the way! There have been some foreign aid workers who were kidnapped by criminals, but they were naive Americans who were travelling through the country in a luxury camper as if they were on a school trip. That level of stupidity is not something I see very often here. But just as a precaution I'm staying with the Spanish doctors at the medical aid station.

On the same day you were giving the table tennis demonstration, I was giving a cooking demonstration that unfortunately went awry. Ahmed, a six-year-old boy, got into a fight with his older brother about which of them could assist me. The brother (age eleven) then stabbed Ahmed in his leg and shoulder with a carving knife. Little boys attacking each other with knives is quite normal here. Everything in this country is extreme. The dryness. The heat. The hunger. The war between the clans and family members. Somalia is a country adrift. The people are adrift. The children are adrift.

After Ahmed was treated at the medical aid station (fortunately the knife wounds weren't serious), Juan (the Spanish doctor) and I brought him home. He lives with his mother and brother under a rusty car hood. The walls are made of flattened soft drink cans and plastic bags. That's their house, but the weird thing was that it didn't get to me. I felt no emotion. I thought: there, the boy's back home. I also don't feel guilty that a stabbing took place because of my cooking demonstration. Which is idiotic when I think about it now.

Tonight I'm going with Juan to a wedding. A sixty-year-old man is marrying an eighteen-year-old girl. Distasteful age differences like this are also quite normal here. The great thing is that the meals for the guests are all being prepared on my stoves. Tell Meike I said hello!

Love, Ellen

(Your father is terrified that Meike's going to get pregnant. I told him to stop carrying on about it. If you need condoms, they're in the chest of drawers in our bedroom between all the guarantees and the insurance papers.)

Time was running out. In less than four weeks her plane would be landing. He had dreamt about his mother. It was her birthday and Gieles was allowed to wake her up with breakfast in bed. She was asleep. Her face was soft and motionless, and when she woke up she ran her hand over his cheek. She ate her toast and sipped her tea. Gieles waited until the cup was empty before giving his mother her present. He watched with expectation as she tore off the wrapping paper and a crystal vase appeared. For a moment she looked at the gleaming vase as if it were something totally foreign to her. Then she threw the vase against the window. The glass in the window remained intact, but the vase ended up on the carpet in a million tiny pieces. 'You know I hate beautiful things!' his mother shrieked. She opened the window, jumped out and disappeared into the void.

Gieles turned the partition around and studied the schedule.

'July: train for all commands—stay/go up/come down.'

The month of July had come and Gieles still hadn't practised all the commands at the same time. He also didn't know how to get the geese out to the runway. He reached into a plastic container behind the partition and took out a little Playmobil man. It was a cowboy. He put the cowboy down on the game board, right behind one of the pins: the security cameras. That made him invisible to the lens. The airport couldn't see him. He then put the cowboy in front of the pin. His act of heroism would have to be filmed by the airport. So they'd be able to repeat his rescue operation endlessly on TV.

He would make the following statement: 'I was standing there waiting for my mother. I wanted to welcome her home in a special way, and suddenly I saw those geese sitting on the runway. I knew right away what I had to do.'

It made Gieles happy.

I was sure I could do it.

Whistling, he went downstairs two steps at a time. Before heading for the domestic noises in the kitchen, he slipped into his parents' bedroom. He opened the drawer where the papers were stored, but there were no condoms among them. He searched the drawer with the socks and underpants, but no condoms there either. Maybe his mother had taken the condoms with her to Somalia.

He closed the drawers and headed for the chattering voices.

Meike was standing at the stove. She was stirring a pan with a wooden spoon while Uncle Fred sprinkled sugar from a measuring cup. She had on a long shirt with skulls on it that went down to her knees. Over that she was wearing an apron. It was her first free day and she couldn't stop talking about her work at the beauty parlour. It was totally awesome, she said.

Gieles noticed how her bottom moved rhythmically as she stirred. The black ink spots on her lower legs had faded to grey smudges. He had a strong desire to pull up her shirt. He fixed his gaze on the flowers on the table to keep from getting a hard-on. There hadn't been any flowers in the house since his mother left, but now Meike had picked an armful of wildflowers. She was going all out to do her best. A few days back her parents had been up for a second visit. Meike had barely said a word to them, but she hadn't shrieked at them like a seagull either or called them every name in the book. Count to thirty when you feel the urge coming on, Uncle Fred advised. It helped. She didn't scream any more. She worked at the beauty parlour, she ate what was put on her plate and she smoked her cigarettes outside. She hardly ever spoke with a Brabant accent, and no one had even asked her to give it up.

Willem came into the kitchen, poured himself a cup of coffee and smiled with emotion when Meike called out that she had made her own cherry jam. 'With my name on the pots!'

Gieles knew for certain that if there had been a daughter in the house his father would have been more communicative. But his mother didn't want another child. A job in the air and a second child on the ground was an impossible combination. Foreign travel pulled at her like a strong river current. There was no turning back.

'Don't put too much pectin in it,' warned Uncle Fred, 'or the jam will be so stiff you'll be able to knock off heads with it.'

She poured the warm mixture into the glass pots on the counter, chatting away at the same time.

Gieles stared out the window because he didn't want to look at his father. His father assumed they were already doing it. Gieles was flattered, but the expectation also put pressure on him. They hadn't even kissed yet. He had fallen asleep next to her that night, and when he woke the next morning she was lying there beside him in a deep slumber. Her face was lightly covered in sweat. He had crept out of bed by carefully climbing over her, fully aroused.

'Now the jam has to cool,' said Uncle Fred, running the pan under the tap.

Meike took off her apron and went outside to smoke. After she had flicked the butt into the water, Gieles took her along for his training session. He told her the same white lie he had told Super Waling. He was training the geese so he could register them with an animal casting bureau.

They walked together toward the shed. Wearing her new Hello Kitty slippers (a gift from Dolly), she strolled behind the geese.

Gieles had left Wally at the campground with a bath full of water and some fresh feed. For the time being she wouldn't miss him.

'You know what Dolly said to me?' They were walking down the grassy path. 'She said you had to be highly motivated to look the way I do.'

'I don't understand what she means.' He was still mad at Dolly.

'Oh, I do. She means it's much easier to look like you. Just get a pair of jeans.'

He looked offended. 'So why do you make it so difficult for yourself?'

'I don't know,' she said musingly, and rolled another cigarette.

They walked behind Tufted and Bufted in silence. Once they got to the shed, he continued to the pasture where the cows were grazing. The last time, just before her arrival, he had practised outside with the geese.

'What do they have to be able to do for the casting bureau?' asked Meike.

'Different stuff,' answered Gieles, pushing the wooden fence open. 'Say the geese are cast for a film. Then they have to be well-trained. You know *Indian Jones and the Last Crusade*?'

She shrugged her shoulders.

'The part with the airplane and the birds?'

'Never heard of it. You know what? Dolly told me I look like that actress Lara Flynn-whatchamacallit.'

'Never heard of her,' said Gieles, and he looked at his watch. He had to be at Dolly's in an hour to babysit.

The geese walked into the pasture and began to nibble at the grass. They paid no attention to the nearby cows.

Meike began climbing up the fence with a cigarette in her mouth.

'My father and Uncle Fred can never know that the geese can fly.' He pronounced the words with utter seriousness and tried not to stare between her legs.

'So *can* they fly?'

'If they find out, the geese will have to go,' he said ominously.

'That would be terrible.' Horrified, she pulled the skull shirt a bit further over her luminous thighs.

Gieles led the geese as nonchalantly as he could to the edge of the pasture, where he scattered some speculaas. He repeated the 'stay' command a few times and then walked away. Swaggering, he balanced the umbrella across his shoulders and hung his arms over it.

I'm cool.

When he got to the end of the pasture he stopped and turned around. Now he was right near the cows. Jokingly he faked a lunge at them, which made them recoil. He kept stealing glances in her direction. Meike giggled flirtatiously.

Gieles was standing next to a compact cow pat, and that gave him a brilliant inspiration. He would mix the speculaas with gelatine in order to form balls, spherical speculaas balls that he would shoot over the canal with the slingshot. Onto the runway.

'What happens now?' shouted Meike.

He flapped opened his umbrella, and at that very moment the geese stopped eating, sprinted forward and shot into the air. They flew higher than usual. Their wings seemed broader. For a moment Gieles thought the geese were considering flying past him, to freedom. But Tufted and Bufted came down in a smooth line and landed at his feet in the tall grass, cackling loudly. He could hear Meike whooping from the fence, which convinced him more than ever that the exercise had been very successful.

He was late because of the training session, but Dolly wasn't angry. In fact she was in an especially good mood. She was sitting leisurely at her laptop as if she had all the time in the world. Jonas was sitting next to her on the floor, sucking on his squirrel. All that drool had turned the animal's head white. Meike picked the toddler up and tickled his neck. Then she plopped down comfortably next to Dolly as if she'd been coming here for years.

'What's that?' Meike asked, peering rather rudely over her shoulder at the screen.

'A sleep log,' Dolly explained. 'I'm keeping a night book for a research bureau. They're studying to what extent airplane noise disturbs sleep.' She read the question out loud: "How many times were you awakened last night by the sound of airplanes?" Hmm, that was ... let me think,' she stared at the ceiling, which was full of leakage spots. 'Five times.'

Dolly pressed the 5 key. 'Twice because Jonas was crying, but no doubt he was awakened by a plane, so I'll keep it at five.'

She read the following question: "'How long does it take for you to fall back asleep?" Pfff ... the first time I went to the bathroom, the second time I read for a while ... The third time I had to give Jonas his puffer because he was starting to wheeze again ... I think it was easily twenty minutes on average before I fell back asleep.'

Without a dildo. Or has she bought a new one?

She filled in 'thirty.' 'You always have to exaggerate. You guys should take part in the study, too,' said Dolly, looking at Gieles over the screen.

'It never wakes me up,' he said.

'Yeah, that's what you think. I know for sure that you're a light sleeper. It's very bad for your concentration.'

His school performance hadn't been what you would call terrific lately, but that had nothing to do with the planes. He just wasn't studying hard enough since Meike's arrival. He got a five for economics. But for his report on the pumping stations he had scored a nine (or Super Waling did).

The soccer ball banged against the back window. Dolly didn't even look up.

'And you get high blood pressure from all that racket,' she said, typing further. 'And everything that goes with it. The father of my children never lived to tell the tale, at any rate.'

Jones pulled on a dreadlock and gave a fluty sort of laugh. Dolly looked up for a moment and asked Gieles to get his puffer.

Do it yourself, why don't you?

Obediently he went upstairs to the medicine cabinet in the bathroom. Out in the hallway he put his hand on her bedroom door handle. He could check her nightstand. He held his breath and pushed the handle down, but Dolly had locked the door. Apparently she didn't trust him any more. Well, he always did think she was a bitch, and this proved it.

Gieles got the puffer and threw it carelessly on the table, next to the laptop. She kept going without even looking up.

'What's the name of that actress you said I look like? Lara ...'

'Boyle,' said Dolly. 'Lara Flynn Boyle. Wait, I'll google her.'

'Are you gonna play soccer?' screamed Skiq from the garden. His face was purple.

'God, how awful!' shouted Dolly with a start. She clapped her hand over her mouth.

Meike's face clouded over.

'"Celebs who won't need a Halloween mask,"' Dolly read aloud. 'What did she do to her face? It's all crooked and bulgy.'

'I don't look like her at all,' said Meike angrily.

Gieles went to stand behind them and saw a woman with huge, swollen lips twisted in a grimace that made her look like she was in a freezer.

'Good God,' said Dolly indignantly at the screen. 'She was a knock-out when she played in *Twin Peaks*. Wait a minute.' Dolly scrolled quickly down and clicked on old images of Lara Flynn Boyle. The actress became younger and younger.

'Got it! There she is as Donna, Dale Cooper's honey. This is all before your time. So, just like I said! Meike all over.'

Meike's face slowly brightened. On the screen a young girl appeared with light eyes, pale white skin and short black curls. She was wearing lingerie and sitting on a red bed, and everything about her was charming without looking slutty. She really did look like Meike. Except Meike had green eyes.

Before they could say anything about the photo, Dolly slammed the screen shut and stood up resolutely. 'And now I've got to high tail it out of here.'

'Gieles!'

The soccer ball slammed against the window so hard that the glass shook in its frame.

Once again, Dolly didn't blink. She slipped into her high heels and said decisively, 'They can kick the windows in for all I care. Finally they're going to buy me out, and not just for peanuts either. Has the airport been to see you guys?'

'Not that I know of,' said Gieles. He had forgotten the whole eviction story with the arrival of Meike.

'In less than a year our houses will all be turned into pyramids. We can finally escape from this hell hole.'

Dolly picked up the suitcase of vitamin pills. 'Well, have a good time and don't forget the boys' puffers.' She caught one last glimpse of herself in the mirror. Gieles looked at her slim, tanned legs as she rushed out of the house. He much preferred white legs.

Meike sat down on the couch with the toddler, who leaned against her breasts as if she were an air mattress.

'WHY AREN'T YOU COMING?'

Skiq stood in front of him with his fists on his hips. His soccer pants had been pulled up so high that his underpants peeked out from the bottom.

'Yeah, what are you doing standing there twiddling your thumbs?' Meike teased, and she pushed her nose into Jonas's hair.

'Do you like him?' Skiq gave Gieles a wise-guy look.

'Who?'

'Him, of course!' He pointed to Meike.

'Him is a her. And for the zillionth time, don't scream like that!'

'Do you like her?'

Now Onno came into the living room. He had pulled his shirt off up to his forehead. The tight neck was pushing his eyebrows down to his eyes. He looked ridiculous.

'Gieles likes Meike!' shouted Skiq. He made a circle with his thumb and forefinger and stuck his other forefinger into it.

'Cut it out, Skiq! You don't even know what that means!'

'Do, too.'

Meike laughed in amusement and made braids in Jonas's fuzzy hair.

'Well, what does it mean then?' she asked.

'The pee-pee kisses the wee-wee!' Skiq and Onno bellowed. They fell into each other's arms and rolled around on the floor. Gieles stood there watching them sheepishly. As usual, the horseplay turned into fighting. Most of the time Gieles had the patience of a saint, but now he wanted to kick the boys apart.

Meike suddenly stood up and walked over to the window with Jonas in her arms. She pushed the perishing ficus aside.

Tony was standing in the middle of the road. He had put his helmet on the gas tank. He was wearing a sleeveless shirt to show off his biceps.

The boys released each other from their stranglehold and ran to the window. 'That's Tony! Gieles's friend.'

'*Was*. He was my friend.'

'What a creep.' The toddler had wrapped his chubby arm around her neck. He pressed his finger against her inky tear.

Gieles saw Tony waving a plastic bag over his head.

The dildo!

The boys were pounding on the windows. 'Tooo-neee! Tony! Come on, let's go out and see him. I want to show Tony my new MJ hat!'

It was too much for him. The brothers' screaming, Tony with the dildo. It felt as if the back of his head was short-circuiting, as if something inside had snapped. Pofff!

'WE'RE NOT GOING OUT TO SEE TONY!' He cursed and ranted his lungs out until the three brothers started crying and Meike had to address him like a school teacher.

'That's enough of that,' she said firmly. 'I'm sure they know now that Tony is a fucking idiot. Look, he's already riding away on his fucking motorbike.'

27

They had agreed to meet the next day at the beauty par-lour. Super Waling had offered to take Meike on a tour of the pumping station. Gieles biked to the edge of the shopping centre with his school books in his backpack. Super Waling was waiting for him. He was sitting in a car, leaning his elbow out the open window. Gieles had never seen him in a car before. He looked good in it.

Meike came walking up just as Gieles arrived. Traips-ing along beside her was a Rottweiler with a muzzle on his snout. With his massive chest and muscular thighs the leashed dog looked even bigger than Meike.

'Now that's what I call an impressive dog,' said Super Waling, when she came to a halt in front of him.

'He lives over Dolly's shop.' Meike placidly petted his black-brown fur. Her dreadlocks were pulled back in a ponytail, revealing her round face in all its glory. The dog sniffed Gieles's pants and stared at him intently over the edge of his muzzle, which looked like a ventilation grill. Gieles took two steps to the side. Then the dog raised his head toward Super Waling's forearm. With a wrinkle suddenly appearing in the skin above his eyes, Super Waling quickly pulled his arm back into the car. 'Sorry, but I'm a coward,' he said.

'That's not true,' said Gieles with unexpected ferocity. It irritated him that Super Waling kept presenting him-self as some kind of goofball.

'You rescued forty people.'

Gieles looked at Meike. 'He really did rescue forty people. It was in the newspaper.'

All that screaming at the boys the night before had made him hoarse.

Super Waling shook his hand and his head. 'That was a long time ago. And you shouldn't always believe what you read in the papers. Real acts of heroism are usually performed in silence.'

The Rottweiler began to bark savagely at the balcony above Dolly's shop. Standing at the railing was a bent little man.

'That's Dino's master,' said Meike.

He waved his walking stick, gesturing her to come up.

'I asked if I could take the dog out.' She stroked his head and said in a hushed voice, 'The old loon had a cap over his mouth. The cap has a tube hooked up to a kind of scuba diving tank.'

Dino's master began smacking the railing of the balcony with his stick.

'I'll go and take him back,' she said, and she took her time walking over to the apartment entrance. When they passed The Meat Hall, Dino began pulling on the leash. Meike gave it a tug and Dino obeyed immediately.

SPECIAL OFFER: TWO KILOS GROUND BEEF FOR TWO EUROS, Gieles read on the advertising sign.

'Well, she's no shrinking violet,' said Super Waling with admiration after they had turned the corner.

Gieles could see a shadow moving behind the windows of the beauty parlour. That had to be Dolly. He knew that Dolly was waiting until they left. She didn't want to bump into Super Waling, of course. It was obvious that she detested him.

He studied the offer from The Meat Hall once again. Two kilos of ground beef for two euros.

Suddenly Gieles knew how he would take revenge on Tony for tearing his goose apart. It would be a brilliant punishment. Then he turned to Super Waling. 'What's the big secret behind that plane crash? You guys did rescue those people, didn't you?'

'Things are often not what they seem,' answered Super Waling. 'Listen, I finally finished my plane crash story.'

He said this like a schoolboy who was handing in his homework too late. 'I'll mail it to you tonight.'

'Okay,' Gieles responded, and he looked up at the Rottweiler, who was barking insanely from the balcony. Meike came sauntering back. She took one last drag on her cigarette and crushed the butt under her flip-flop. Then she showed them a piece of candy wrapped in faded cellophane. 'Look what he gave me. For taking Dino out. He thought I was still in grade school.'

She got in the front seat. There was no room next to Gieles. Super Waling's seat had been pushed back as far as it would go.

'Is this a handicapped car?' Meike asked as she looked around with curiosity.

'You might say that. The rental company said it was a car for senior citizens. Because it's higher off the ground and easier to get into. And this one has extra wide seats.'

They rode through the centre of town towards the N201.

'What's it like living in Zundert?' Super Waling asked, his eyes glued to the road. He was driving at a snail's pace and holding up traffic. It was obvious he wasn't used to driving.

'Shitty,' she said. 'It's a shit hole. This month there's a flower pageant and all those retarded farmers crawl out of the woodwork to get sloshed.'

'Vincent van Gogh was born in Zundert, wasn't he?'

asked Super Waling as he put on the brakes.

'Green,' said Gieles. 'The light's green.'

Super Waling forgot to shift to first, thereby killing the engine. There was honking behind him. He started pulling wildly on the gear shift. GRRRRRRR. The car bounded forward a metre.

'Red! It's red again!' shouted Gieles.

Meike was having a laughing fit. She asked Super Waling if he had his driver's license. He looked in the rearview mirror and raised his arm in the air apologetically at the driver behind him, who was tapping his forehead with his finger.

'Waling, go! It's green!'

'Okay, okay, okay,' puffed Super Waling, and he stepped on the gas again while shifting, but not far enough. GRRRRRRR. Beeeeeep! Beeeeeeep!

Weak with laughter, Meike hung out the window and extended her middle finger to the cars behind her.

Super Waling tore off with a jolt and accidentally ran the next red light, leaving the angry drivers in the dust.

'I think the radar nabbed me,' he said, looking around in panic.

'This is so funny,' shrieked Meike in hysterics. 'Do you really have a driver's license?'

Gieles wanted to lie down in the back seat so no one could see him.

'We're almost there, guys. We're almost there,' said Super Waling encouragingly, mostly to himself. His enormous hands had the steering wheel in a stranglehold. The N201 was bursting with traffic lights, but he got better at accelerating. By the fifth traffic light Super Waling was confident enough to look around at the residential area on the left side of the road.

'You used to be able to see the dunes from here, that's how grand the view was.'

'Where we are it's all old crap. Here everything is new,' said Meike, closing the window. She smelled her hands. 'Dino stinks. It's from that man. His whole house stinks like cigars.'

'All the buildings you see there are the product of graft and corruption,' Super Waling said, nodding at an industrial area. He didn't dare let go of the steering wheel. 'It was built by a bunch of crooks. In Italy they call practices like that the work of the mafia. Here graft and corruption are perfectly normal. What do you think of those houses over there?'

'Pffff,' Meike sighed, looking outside with disinterest. 'I don't know. Not much, I guess. Everything looks the same to me. I got lost here a couple of times when I had to go shopping for Dolly.'

'Exactly!' shouted Super Waling. 'You put that so well. The stuff they throw together here evokes almost no emotion. People get hopelessly lost. They wander around because the soul has been cut out of their environment. There's no love in it. Bah.'

'Uncle Fred says you can't stop things from happening. Everything changes,' said Gieles, yawning from the back seat.

He was at least forty hours behind in his sleep cycle. His sex fantasies with Meike in the woods in exile were wearing him out. Last night he had found her on a rocky plateau where she was sunning herself naked. She was afraid of getting sunburnt, she whispered, and Gieles began rubbing her body with coconut milk. His hands slid down her vertebrae and buttocks and then pushed her legs apart.

'Uncle Fred is a Buddhist,' Super Waling concluded. 'Nothing stays the same. He's absolutely right. But that doesn't mean that all changes are well-considered. Some of them are totally, how can I put it … stupid, short-sighted. And sometimes the changes need adjusting. You have to let your voice be heard. You don't have to agree with everything.'

'What are you droning on about?' said Meike. 'You sound just like the priest from our church.' She had put her feet up on the dashboard. One of her black-polished toes was sporting a little ring.

'Do you go to church?' asked Gieles with surprise, leaning between the two front seats. He was awake again.

'Are you kidding?' cried Meike. 'I don't. My parents do. Sometimes. All the old folks do by us.'

'I used to go. With my parents,' said Super Waling. He was keeping up with the traffic and was more relaxed. 'But the last time I sat in a church pew was at my father's funeral.'

'The last time I went, my father told a joke,' said Meike. 'There was this choir of nuns, and my father asked me why nuns didn't wear bras.' Meike turned to face them. 'Well?'

'It's a riddle?' asked Super Waling. 'Oh, fun. Uhhh, let's see.'

He drove at a snail's pace into the empty parking lot of the pumping station.

'Their tits are too big?' Gieles said, and he felt his cheeks blaze. He had never used the word 'tits' in the presence of a girl before, and now it just slipped out. Tits. *Tits.* What a fantastic word. He wanted to scream it out the window.

'God supports everything,' said Meike.

'What do you mean?' Gieles asked.

'Why don't nuns wear bras? God supports everything.'

Super Waling laughed his infectious laugh. 'God supports everything! Ha! That's a good one from your father.'

'Yeah,' said Meike quietly. 'It is pretty good.'

He parked the rental car as close as he could to the entrance. Gieles got out and began to wonder how Super Waling was planning on getting inside. He never went anywhere without his mobility scooter, and here he was without it.

'I have crutches with me,' said Super Waling as if he had read his mind, and he began pushing himself out of the car. 'They're in the trunk. Way in the back.'

'Can you get out?' Meike asked. She was holding her pack of shag and watching Super Waling exert the most enormous effort, as if she were watching TV. A kind of strongest-man-in-the-world show.

'What goes in ... must ... come out ... ,' he puffed, and pressed himself through the open car door.

Gieles gave him his crutches. Super Waling hung over the car door, gasping for breath. He looked better. He was still a blob of fat, of course, and he was wearing a weird shirt that had a hippie with braids on it, and there were lakes of moisture under his armpits. But he had grown a little beard, which made his neck look less spongy. His auburn locks fell onto his shoulders and looked pretty decent. And he was wearing the basketball sneakers, without the laces. Gieles wondered whether Super Waling had any friends. He doubted it. You would really have to overcome your objections to appear with him in public. Or not give a shit about anything, like Meike.

'Great shirt,' she said. 'Cool text.'

WILLIE NELSON, it said on his chest. BORN FOR TROUBLE.

'I'm afraid this has become my motto,' Super Waling

muttered in his fight with the crutches.

'Last one there is a rotten egg,' said Meike, pretending to get ready for a sprint. 'Just joking. We'll help you.'

Meike grabbed his gigantic upper arm. Gieles hesitated.

'Come on, give me a hand,' she ordered.

It was the first time that Gieles had ever touched Super Waling. He felt his warm, soft flesh.

'Your arm is as fat as my ass,' Meike giggled.

'Goodness. I hope not,' said Super Waling, taking the first ponderous step. 'That means you have a very fat ... behind.'

Gieles laughed with them and concentrated on the short distance between the car and the pumping station.

Stumbling between them on his crutches, Super Waling entered the building.

'Hello, Mrs Geerts,' he squeezed out of his lungs with his last bit of strength.

The lady at the ticket counter looked up from her work. A smile appeared on her face that immediately switched to an expression of alarm. Gieles remembered the woman with the protruding gecko eyes from their last visit to the station.

'Waling! Are you on foot?' She said it with total disbelief and rushed to his side. 'Where's your mobility scooter?'

'At the car rental,' he panted, leaning heavily on his crutches. Gieles and Meike stood resting against him like bookends.

'Wait a minute! We have a wheelchair!' She dashed off to the storeroom and came back with the chair. It was black and it looked quite new.

'You'll never fit in that,' said Meike. She had let go of his arms.

'Oh, yes he will,' said Mrs Geerts resolutely. 'Anyone can fit in a wheelchair, so Waling can, too.'

The slender woman stood behind him and pushed the seat against his legs. 'Now just lower yourself slowly. Very slowly, that's right.'

'You think the rims can take it?' Super Waling asked uncertainly while trying to force his black sweatpants, filled with his massive bottom, between the arm rests. 'I don't think this is going to work.'

'I don't think so either,' said Meike stoically. 'You're too fat for the wheelchair. Is there a bathroom here?'

'In the back, near the cloakroom,' answered Mrs Geerts. She followed Meike disapprovingly with her reptilian eyes.

Super Waling had heaved himself up and was standing there on wobbly legs.

'The arm rests come off!' Mrs Geerts stood bent over the chair and pulled on a couple of levers. 'Look! What an invention.' With a beatific smile she released the arm rests and put them on the floor. 'Try it again. Very good, take it easy ... yes, a bit more to the left, no, the other side to the left ... yes, yes, very good.'

His flesh spilled out over both sides of the seat, but he was sitting. Mrs Geerts was satisfied and looked at Super Waling as if she had just tucked her baby in.

'There,' she said. 'And what can I do for you all. A glass of water? Apple juice? Gieles—you *are* Gieles, aren't you?' She grabbed hold of him and took him to the bulletin board, which was filled with clippings. 'You're a big celebrity here. We talked about your performance for days.'

Gieles had the same newspaper photo of himself and Wally hanging in his room.

Gieles Bos and his little goose steal the show at table tennis.

Below the headline he was shown sitting on the table tennis table. He was smiling and his hair was relatively smooth, luckily. Standing next to him was Wally, who refused to look into the lens. The photo was a little out of focus because she kept turning her bill away.

Mrs Geerts was standing right next to him. She was even smaller than Meike. The top of her head was as flat as an end table.

'I so enjoyed your demonstration. I kept thinking: how does that young fellow do it? I had a cat once, but I was never even able to teach him to use the litter box. And you, Gieles, you can teach a goose to play ping pong!'

Gieles was glad when Meike returned. She stood behind the wheelchair and began to push. With the sudden movement Super Waling almost fell off.

'You have to provide a counterbalance,' said Mrs Geerts. 'With your crutches. That's right, as if you were propping yourself up. Just walk along with the chair. Very good!'

After having had something to drink they went into the museum. Super Waling took the elevator next to the stairs. On the first floor Meike took off her hairdresser's shirt and tied it around her waist, which had an overwhelming effect on Gieles. He turned away from her little pink top and began staring into the closest display case he could find. There were inanimate objects in it that proved to be an excellent remedy for his erection: a battered jug, eroded coins, a rusty rifle. 'Found at the bottom of the lake after the reclamation of 1852,' it said on a small card.

He turned his head towards Meike as inconspicuously as he could. She was standing with Super Waling near a collection of pumps. There was a round band-aid on her shoulder blade that he hadn't noticed before. The band-aid was right above the edge of her top. He focused once more on the display case, where his eye fell on a brown notebook. 'Diary of Sophia Warrens (1825-1915).'

Gieles felt a strange kind of excitement that was entirely new to him. It had nothing to do with his hard-on, but it was as if he had been a witness to something great for the first time in his life. It was like Uncle Fred: each year on September 11th he'd start talking about what he had been doing when the two planes flew into the Twin Towers. ('I was shopping for a new electric kettle and I saw a plane fly into a skyscraper on this huge bank of TV screens.') Gieles had been too young then to understand all the commotion, and now he was right in the middle of it. As if he had seen Captain Sully land flight 1549 on the Hudson River with his own eyes.

He saw the footprints of Super Waling's ancestors. The fluorescent pumping station paintings by his Grandma Aletta next to the collection of pumps. It was an ode to Waling's history. But there wasn't a trace of his parents or the plane crash.

Meike, too, noticed the paintings. She thought they were cool. Super Waling said there were very few people who thought his grandma's pumping station art was *cool*. Hideous, more likely. Gieles heard how his voice wrapped itself gently around the paintings and around Meike. He told the story about his Grandma Aletta. He did it in a very compelling way, as if Meike had actually been there when Grandma Aletta spread the fluorescent green paint on the canvas.

Gieles began searching for more points of contact and found a large print of a scrawny woman with two braids. She had reins around her shoulders that were meant for pulling a boat. Her gaze was so empty that she could easily have had no eyes at all.

'Is that that Akkie?' asked Gieles. 'From Friesland?'

Super Waling looked at him gratefully from his wheelchair. He didn't know any adults who were able to look like that. With such sympathy.

'She could have been Akkie. I bet all the polder women looked like her.'

'Akkie?' snorted Meike. 'What a stupid name. Who's Akkie?'

'Well,' said Super Waling. 'Akkie was an unfortunate woman.'

'I believe it, with a name like that.' She stood in front of the grainy photo and frowned. 'She doesn't look happy either.'

'This woman had little reason to be happy,' said Super Waling, using his crutches to make a quarter turn with the wheelchair. 'First she had to shovel more than sixty kilometres of mud while her children were dropping down dead. Then she had to do the work of a horse *in* the canal—which she herself had dug, for crying out loud. Every day she was rigged out in a strap that was connected to that barge, with her husband at the helm screaming at her to pull harder.'

'What a prick,' Meike concluded, rubbing the round band-aid on her shoulder blade.

'You're telling me. And it seems like long ago, but that woman in the strap could have been your great-grandmother. The life we live today with all its comforts was something even the nobility back then couldn't have dreamed of, let alone a workhorse like her. That's why this woman doesn't look happy.'

'Nah,' sniffed Meike. 'I don't know any happy people either.' She said this with an ice cold voice. Gieles and

Super Waling were silent because they didn't know what to say.

Gieles thought about the people he knew. Dolly and Liedje were unhappy. So was his mother. She looked for happiness in the unhappiness of others, which made her unhappy, too, and she was dragging his father into her trap. When Gieles got right down to it, who really *was* happy?

He pressed his nose and forehead against the display case. The glass was pleasantly cool. Super Waling came rolling up to him, paddling with his crutches.

'I have the keys,' he said. 'Open it up.'

Gieles opened the display case and carefully removed the diary. It felt like a dried flower. The notebook's paper was so brittle that he didn't dare open it. He put it back and ran his finger over the cover. Just touching it was enough. He looked at Meike.

I am happy.

After the pumping station they drove past a bowling alley and Meike shouted ecstatically that she *had* to go bowling because she hadn't done it in a hundred years, so they went bowling. Mrs Geerts had let them take the wheelchair, and Super Waling threw three strikes and eight spares from his chair, to his great delight. The music blasted over the lanes and Meike danced a slithery dance on lane three until the personnel told her to get off. Super Waling asked whether the music couldn't be turned down a notch, they could hardly hear themselves think, but the girl at the bowling shoe counter said the boss wouldn't allow it because it wasn't fun without loud music.

I am happy.

Meike handed them the bowling balls, and every time she did her pectoral muscles strained out over her top, which drove him nuts. She grabbed Super Waling's fat fists and led him in a rolling rock, a rocking roll, a rock-and-roll until he almost tumbled out of his wheelchair, and then she grabbed Gieles around the waist, weak with giggles.

I am happy.

Dear Gieles,

A promise is a promise. Here is the rest of the alphabet. My story. The story of my father and mother. I wish I could have given you a different version, a heroic epic in which I play the lead and vanquish all injustice. Undaunted. Fearless. But sadly I am not the hero that the newspapers claimed I was back then. Not even a little. I am also fully aware that I am making you party to our family secret. I'm not asking you to keep it to yourself. On the contrary. Secrets are bad for your system. One look at me says enough.

My warmest greetings, and thanks for the wonderful day with you and Meike.

Until next week!

Waling

I remember it being eerily silent when the plane came down on our property on that 5th of October, 1979. It was like watching a silent movie. It was so bizarre. There was this immense monster right in front of my nose, a gigantic beast that weighed at least a hundred and seventy thousand kilos, and I expected it to produce impressive sounds. But it didn't even roar or shriek. It didn't even breathe.

My father began to scour the plane in search of an entrance. I looked through one of the little windows and saw a dead body for the first time in my life. I knew immediately that the man was no longer alive because his head was twisted ninety degrees and not even a contortionist can imitate that. A little further on I saw a passenger in convulsions. Feeling no emotion, I continued walking past the windows where horrible scenes were being played out. I'll spare you the details, but it was true that the dead were scattered all over our property.

Suddenly I heard sounds. It was as if my ears had been full of water and suddenly popped open. My father had discovered a hole in the fuselage at the other end of the plane and was helping the first survivors to get out. I heard people moaning, I heard distant sirens approaching. And I heard this: 'Help me, please, help me ...' The voice was begging for help, quietly but insistently, and it came from the direction of the torn-off cockpit.

I walked toward the voice and tried to comprehend what I was seeing. Pieces of loose insulation, a chair, crushed metal, a leopard-print ladies' shoe, a jumble of wires. In all that mess there were undamaged perfume bottles. It said FATALE on them in black letters, and it flashed through my mind that it was as if I had landed in some kind of absurd commercial.

'Please, help me ... help me ... my leg ...'

In the disembowelled intestines of the plane I searched with my eyes for the voice. I knew for certain that the supplication was coming from the cockpit, but I had no idea how to get inside. I wasn't able to think clearly and the penetrating smell of jet fuel didn't make it any easier. I walked past the crumpled nose of the plane, which had bored its way deep into my father's land. The windows were black with mud. I wiped the earth away

with my coat and looked straight into a pair of bespecta-
cled eyes.

The pilot was wearing round eyeglasses and a yellow
polo shirt.

The pilot was a boy my age.

I looked at him with astonishment. His mouth and
eyes were wide open, as if he were riding in a roller
coaster and had been captured on film just as he was
about to loop-de-loop. Except for one shattered eyeglass
his face was unharmed. My astonishment turned to
curiosity. If the pilot was a child, then who was the
co-pilot for heaven's sake?

A baby?

Once again I wiped the mud away, but the window
remained dirty.

'Help! Help me ... my leg ...'

The voice could hardly be the co-pilot's. His head was
smashed against the glass like a fly.

'Good God Almighty,' I heard behind me. It was my
father. I didn't turn around. My eyes were fused on the
boy. I wasn't aware that my father was trying to get into
the cockpit in order to help the moaning voice. I hadn't
noticed that our beet field was inundated with firemen,
police and ambulance workers. Their vehicles were parked
in the farmyard and along the side of the road because
the muddy earth was too soft for their tyres.

In all that chaotic mass of spotless uniforms and
bloody clothing I suddenly heard my mother. She was
calling to me, but I couldn't say a thing. I was crouched
down in front of the cockpit and my brains had entered
another dimension. Later on she told me I was in shock.
What I had seen was more than my immature adolescent
brain could take on. I fled from reality and hid in the
wonderful stories my mother had told me about our
ancestors.

I was Ide Warrens and the plane was the workhorse that sank in the mud of the drained lake. I spread out my arms and laid them comfortingly on the windows, with my cheek pressed against the glass. I murmured incoherently that everything was going to be all right. Finally my mother had to step in and pull me away from the cockpit.

I was in a stupor for the rest of the day. My father hooked his tractor up to a trailer and drove it back and forth over his beet plants to carry away the dead and wounded. Our farm was cordoned off with crush barriers and tape to keep out the camera teams and rubberneckers. A tent was set up in our farmyard where the lifeless bodies were laid, and our living room was transformed into a beehive where first-aid workers and men in suits and ties zoomed past each other. The survivors who were not visibly wounded were put up in the barn.

My mother ran around like a chicken with her head cut off, serving coffee and pitchers of fresh milk from her double-muscle cows.

The most terrible thing about that day, she told me a couple of months later, was that I kept calling her 'Sophia.' My mother thought I had lost my mind because of the plane crash, and she tried to shield me from the suffering. I wasn't allowed to go with my father on the tractor. I wasn't allowed inside the tent with the dead. Again and again she found me in the barn where the survivors were being held and she made me leave. One woman sat on a little stool that had once been in my bedroom. She was black with mud and she shook uncontrollably. Her shoes were gone and her skirt was torn. I still have a crystal-clear memory of that image.

According to my mother, who kept pulling me out of

the barn, I was exceptionally cool, considering what I had gone through. I rattled on about the building of new shanties and shouted that she didn't have to worry about hers. Things like that. The poor woman didn't know what I was talking about. Most of the passengers were from the former Soviet Union.

By the end of the morning all thirty bodies had been removed and forty survivors had been rescued from the wreckage. Some of them had been trapped in the plane and were in very bad shape. As I walked across the yard I heard someone say that the co-pilot was in a critical condition, a piece of information that didn't really sink in. I was wandering around in another era, searching for wood to build a new shanty. I can't even remember posing with my father for the photographer.

And there was Grandma Aletta. She had managed to clear a path through the crowd and had quarrelled with two police officers at the crush barrier who refused to let her in. Grandma was around eighty at the time, but with her inner strength she still blasted her way through every obstacle. The guy who could hold her back hadn't even been born yet.

Grandma Aletta saw the stupefied look in my eyes, grabbed hold of me and made a run for it. We saw that image of the two of us on the evening news. You see me in my pyjamas and with a muddy coat thrown over my shoulders, and with Grandma Aletta on my arm in a fashionable silver sweatsuit. Even though she was already a head shorter than I was and covered in wrinkles, it was abundantly clear to the viewers that she was leading me and not the other way around.

We walked through the crowd of rubberneckers, who moved to make way for us. And as we listened to one journalist say, 'The rescue operations at the site of the crash were quickly set in motion,' you can see my grandma saying something to me. She was whispering, 'Stop that nonsense this instant, Waling,' because I had been mumbling that the crash was a punishment from God.

By nightfall I had returned to reality.

Two days later I went home. The plane was still on our property and the red and white police tape danced merrily in the wind. The morgue tent was gone. My father and mother looked twenty years older. Dad's back had become stooped and there was pain deeply embedded in his eyes. My mother staggered around as if there were a ball in her vagina that was throwing her off balance. They were dead tired, but they were too polite to shut the door on the intrusive outside world. Everyone was laying claim to these model citizens. The mayor, the acting mayor, the director of the airport, the director of the responsible airline. And then all the media that descended on them with exactly the same force as the plane that had crashed on our property earlier that week. My parents were suddenly being praised to the skies.

They were unpretentious people, the kind who sat in the back of the church because that was good enough for them. And by this I'm thinking especially of my father. He was happy to live a modest live. He usually pronounced his last name in a kind of mumble because he thought Cittersen van Boven was too presumptuous. But my mother wanted more. She longed for a place at the front of the line, although I didn't realise it at the time.

Walter and Louisa Cittersen van Boven suddenly found themselves heroes, nationally and internationally. My poor old man, who barely spoke a word of English, stood there stuttering on TV in foreign living rooms. 'I hear boom and I see plane. I drive tractor and I help.' And then you see him pointing to his tractor and shyly pulling on his cap, while he says once more, 'No problem, I help.' No problem.

They were an endearing, respectable Dutch couple, and entire populations embraced them with open arms. Even my mother's double-muscle cows made the news. She had fed their milk to the victims in the barn, and journalists saw this as an apparently amusing addition to their stories.

A Catholic weekly interviewed my parents about their faith. If you can believe the article, they were the two most pious creatures around and had acted out of pure religious devotion. Sheer nonsense. My mom and dad went to church once a month at the most, but the reporter twisted all their words. She quoted my dad as saying, 'It was God's will that we could help,' while he had just told her that if he hadn't helped, his neighbour would have stepped in ('because he has a tractor, too.')

Then they came for Grandma Aletta with their cameras, but she slammed the door right in their face.

And so it went, for days and weeks on end. Our life revolved around the crashed plane. When we stood in the yard and watched the pieces of wreckage being hoisted up and dragged away, we had to live through it all over again on the evening news.

Eight days after the crash I woke up in the middle of the night. There were bits of information that had been deleted from my memory, and suddenly I found I could recall them. I spliced all the bits back together and my memory returned.

The pilot was a boy with glasses. On his yellow polo shirt there was a little crocodile. The co-pilot's head was smashed to jelly on the windshield and he was as dead as a doornail.

But the media reported that after the amputation of his leg the co-pilot was out of danger. I went to my parents' bedroom, woke them up and crawled in between them. When I began talking about the boy, the light went on and they both sat bolt upright in bed.

First my mother said that there was no boy. 'You're mistaken, Waling.'

My father stood up and started pacing through the room, listening to me say that I *had* seen a boy at the control stick.

'There was no boy, *sweetie*,' repeated my mother, and at that point Dad stepped in.

'No, Louisa. We're not going to lie. Waling has to know what happened. He has a right to know.'

My father sat down next to me and told me about the cause of the accident without a trace of emotion. What it all boiled down to was that the plane was flying on automatic pilot, and the pilot, and in defiance of every known law of aviation, let his son take his place at the control stick. He had adjusted the course a couple of degrees for effect, so his twelve-year-old son would think he was really flying the plane. It was the very first time the boy had flown with him on an international flight and the pilot wanted to make an impression on his son. The boy inadvertently applied force to the control stick, which partly disconnected the automatic pilot. The plane switched over to manual, but no one noticed it until the aircraft began descending dangerously. After a brief struggle with gravity the pilot succeeded in pulling the plane up a bit to prevent its encounter with the earth from resulting in an inferno.

My father shuddered a moment and then began shuffling across the linoleum again in his bare feet. My mother was still in bed, and she grabbed my hand. She began to cry. Tears rolled over the swollen bags under her eyes.

'We're not allowed to speak of this to anyone, *sweetie*. No one. You understand?'

No. I didn't understand at all.

'We promised the people from the airline,' she said through her tears. 'It would be disastrous for the pilot's family ... Do you understand that? For the wife of the dead pilot ... it would be terrible to learn about this. A loving father, and then it all goes so horribly wrong ... Just a few seconds at the control stick ... Just think, they still have two little daughters ... Their father, their big role model, from one day to the next ... because of such a stupid mistake ... we're not allowed to talk about it to anyone ...'

She kept crying and squeezing my hand, and I swear with that same hand over my heart that her tears were sincere. She was sincerely sorry for the pilot's relatives. What's done can't be undone, she kept saying. The truth can't bring the dead back to life.

But the intentions of the airline, I discovered years later, were far from sincere. Their official story was that in all probability the crash had been caused by defective ailerons. Thanks to the quick thinking of the experienced pilot and co-pilot the lives of forty people had been saved. The black box was found, but the tape it contained of the last cockpit conversations had broken into pieces and was unusable.

After the crash nothing was the same. All the media attention dried up, thank God, but in our circles we were still heroes. I was looked on differently at school. Older boys turned out to know my name, and they greeted me with a slap on the shoulder as if I were their best pal. I was invited to everything, and—what I liked most of all—girls began to find me unexpectedly interesting. Not that they treated me like a jerk before the crash. I was a nice boy to look at. And I don't want to brag, but I was fairly well-built. Girls just weren't interested in me, so I wasn't interested in them.

Three weeks after the plane ruined our beet crop I had my first real kiss. It was with Alice, the prettiest girl in the class, and from that day on she was my girlfriend. My passionate infatuation kept me from noticing that at home the next disaster was creeping up on us.

While we were involved in voyages of discovery in her bed, my parents were meeting with the people from the airport. Day after day, men would come by with various proposals, arguments and contracts. They wanted my father's native soil for their own, and they were prepared to pay for it. The airport already had plans to expand, and now that at least a thousand litres of jet fuel had seeped into our land and left it seriously polluted, they decided to get right down to business. My mother hesitated, my father refused outright.

But the airport people were very professional and they drove my parents into a corner. They were already getting on, weren't they? Their grandson was still too young to take over the farm. Oh, is he your son? Our apologies. Well, he's still got years of school ahead of him. And Louisa (you don't mind if we call you Louisa?), let's face it: how attractive is farm life for young people these days? Not very, right? And then that land. Walter, be realistic. Even if you were to dig down deep and level it off, sowing is simply out of the question for now. It'll be at least two years, Louisa and Walter, before the land even begins to recover. Nobody wants polluted beets. These plane crashes can have very long-lasting effects. They knew from experience.

My father gave in. With his beloved soil still under his fingernails he signed the contracts—and thereby brought about his own downfall. We were allowed to stay on the farm and to keep the double-muscle cows, but in fact my father had nothing to do. For the first two months he put on his work clothes every morning and kept himself busy in the barn and the stable. There were plenty of neglected chores that had to be done. Sometimes he lumbered over to the fence and stood there staring at the excavating machines that were wrecking his land.

I saw him standing like that at the fence many times, but I biked away. I only had eyes for Alice and her bedroom.

Grandma Aletta was well aware that my father was going downhill. You had to be blind not to see it. He stayed in bed longer and longer and wandered around aimlessly. Sometimes I asked him what he was looking for—because that's what it looked like to me. It looked as if he had lost something.

'You've got to get help for your husband,' Grandma said to my mother. Her tone was severe. 'He's wasting away. Just look at him. Before you know it there won't be anything left of him.'

My mother brushed her warnings aside. She had already come up with the solution: moving. Then he wouldn't be tormented by having to look at his land every day.

As I said, my mother and I were blind. Five months after the disaster we found him one morning dead in his chair. His farmer's heart had given up.

My mother sold the farmhouse to the airport, too,

and we moved to a spanking-new detached villa six kilometres down the road. It was a flashy place to live with a flat roof, white plastic panels, and maintenance-free window and door frames. My mother thought it was gorgeous but it meant nothing to me. I cut myself off from everything having to do with my parents. My dad dead? Not much you can do about that. That Mom cashed in on her loss? So what? I had taken my grief, along with the secret of the boy and his pilot father, and hidden them so far away that I didn't even have to work at suppressing them any more.

I had a fantastic life thanks to the plane crash, and I hung onto it grimly. I was accepted at school. I didn't ask myself why I was accepted. I didn't go in for self-reflection. I was egocentric. For me just being accepted was enough. Nor did I wonder where all that money was coming from. My mother bought an expensive car and two fur coats, and for the first time in her life she experienced the pleasure of travel. She flew alone to the cities of Europe and came home with jewellery. Her new passion was flamboyant gold necklaces and rings. She never said another word about double-muscle cows or her beloved ancestors. Sophia and Ide Warrens were dead and gone. She had sold the double-muscle cows.

But that, too, left me completely cold. I was no longer a mama's boy. I had cut the apron strings for good. I was a tough customer, with money in my back pocket and a dazzling girlfriend. The fact that my mother did so much shopping abroad was all to my benefit. At home I was sitting pretty with my new friends and my new gaming computer. No one had anything like it, so we all crowded around the little screen and played Digger, Firepower and Pacman all night long.

I almost never went to see Grandma Aletta any more.

She had become a tiresome old lady, with all her critical questions. 'Waling, where are you?' she used to ask, giving me a penetrating look and knocking on my head with her knuckles, as if I were an egg. I thought her maze-like studio was a filthy mess. Her glittering sweatsuits and eccentric personality irritated me. I covered up the great love I felt for her with a mountain of shame and rage. I was angry at her because she was constantly talking about my dad. I didn't want to talk about him because if I did I would miss him, and that would put an end to my Fantastic Life.

Fortunately there were others who took care of this for me. The status of hero has a limited best-before date, unless you die before your time. After a year and a half the plane crash had become history. Now all people saw were the gaudy maintenance-free villa and the expensive car my mother chugged around in. It was a beige Mercedes convertible with a dark blue roof. Fellow villagers began to make fun of the tacky jewellery she hung all over her tanned body. She became a source of amusement, of nasty gossip. Her new riches failed to conceal her lack of class and taste. My mother was still a farmer's wife, a flat-footed arriviste, despite her exclusive last name and lifestyle.

I didn't notice it at first, until my girlfriend's parents started asking questions. The airport had been exceptionally generous to us. With all due respect, said Alice's father, his voice dripping with contempt, that little bit of land couldn't have been worth all *that* much. Alice's mother knowingly remarked that no bought-out farmer she knew was able to afford a city excursion every month. Dispossession wasn't exactly the same as winning the jackpot, said her parents, rubbing my nose in the obvious. And my mother had clearly won the jackpot.

My relationship with Alice ended, and it was all my fault. Their suspicious questions convinced me that I didn't belong any more. That wasn't actually the case, now that I think about it, but I acted like an outcast and that's exactly what I became. I crawled into my shell and spent all my time alone behind my not-so-new gaming computer. My grief and my secret burrowed into me like water rats. My last year of high school was the loneliest year of my youth. I went into hiding inside myself and only came up for air when I left home for teacher's college in Amsterdam.

My mother had bought a modest apartment for me. She thought renting was throwing money away, and I didn't protest. I never protested when she slipped me a bit of cash. Since the plane crash I had become a spoiled little boy, but once I got to that apartment the fog in my head lifted, thank God. I cried for my father and let myself be comforted by Grandma Aletta, with whom I had re-established contact. We had four fine years together. Usually I went to her, and I'd drive Grandma and her painting stuff all around the polder. She had put pop art and abstract expressionism behind her. Grandma had returned to her polder art days. Her specialty was oil paintings of pumping stations. We sat side by side on our folding chairs in the grass of the ring dike. She painted, I read. She used mainly fluorescent colours. My grandma was a thrifty soul, and the paint from her Warhol period had to be used up first.

The Cruquius was her favourite. Sometimes she pointed out the neo-Gothic elements, such as the pointed arches, or she told me how the pumps worked and explained the principle of the steam cylinder. My mother had stopped telling stories and my grandma had taken over through her painting.

'When I'm dead, you get all the pumping stations.' She said this every time we drove back home. And she kept her word. She left me twenty-four paintings.

The contact with my mother became superficial and sporadic. On the evenings before I went to see her I often came down with a migraine that didn't go away until I left. The visits were completely predictable: first I was given a tour. New purchases had to be admired, such as the stone Greek gods in her garden and the tall decorative fencing with LCB engraved in gigantic letters. Louisa Cittersen van Boven.

'My initials,' she said needlessly. As she stood there at the fence, isolated from the gossiping outside world, I felt a flash of sympathy for her. She must have been deeply unhappy, the way she had done herself up. Her red-gray hair had disappeared. My mother had become a blond in her old age with a doughy powdered face and wrapped in white tennis shorts (although she'd never hit a ball in her life).

Very occasionally I interrupted her endless babble with a question. Usually I did this after dinner, when I knew the visit was almost over. Then I would start talking about being bought out by the airport. About the secret of the boy, the reckless pilot father and the one-legged co-pilot. Didn't the relatives have a right to the truth?

My mother would invariably burst into tears. She'd stamp around in her boat shoes (she didn't even have a boat) all over her marble-coloured, heated tile floor, fuming with blame and rage. Had I started in on this again? Her own flesh and blood? (She had stopped calling me 'sweetie' long ago.) Hadn't she suffered and sacrificed enough? Didn't I think for one second about her or the pilot's family? What gave me the idea that the pilot was a murderer? I used to sit behind the steering wheel of the tractor when I was ten! What if I had ridden someone over with that tractor! Would that have made Dad a murderer? And that's essentially the way it was with that pilot! Walter and the pilot weren't murderers but loving fathers, and I was to let the matter rest once and for all. At moments like that she looked so menacing that I kept my mouth shut. We were never able to work it out. The plane crash remained an issue between us, as if the pieces of wreckage were still lying there.

After teachers' college I went back to my native district. The house I bought was far enough away from that of my nouveau riche mother. I taught history at a high school. I was doing well. I met a nice woman, Pieternel, and soon she moved in with me. Pieternel and I had a lot in common. We loved history, books and walking. We spent all our vacations in our hiking boots climbing through the Swiss Alps. Pieternel was also a good ally in the grudge I bore against my mother. She regarded my mother as an insult to humanity (and she said this with a laugh, as if my mother were the joke of the century).

The only thing Pieternel didn't like were my grandma's pumping station paintings, which were hanging all over my house. She thought the colours were horrendous, and since I had always been a fairly docile type I took down all twenty-four of them to please her.

As I said, I was doing well. But as I got older, the airplane secret deteriorated into a leaking vat of chemical waste. In my dreams I was visited more and more frequently by the boy with the shattered glasses and his pulverised father.

One Saturday morning, after the pilots had been

pursuing me for the umpteenth time and my head was bursting with migraine, I decided to go to my mother to get some answers. I was not going to let myself be silenced by her hysterical fits of crying. I was going to persevere. The crash was almost ten years behind us and the daughters of the dead pilot were adult women. They could handle the truth by now.

I found my mother working out on her new home trainer in front of the sliding French doors. The doctor had said she'd stop being bothered by stiffness if she exercised more. 'He thought I'd been playing tennis all those years,' panted my mother with astonishment. She was still wearing those white tennis shorts at the age of seventy-four.

'I'm not surprised that the doctor thinks you play tennis,' I responded. 'He probably also thinks you have a boat because you always wear boat shoes and boat shirts.'

I was in a rare vicious mood.

'I don't wear boat shirts,' she said. Then I asked if she'd overlooked that whopper of a gold anchor on the blue-and-white striped shirt she was wearing. I looked at the shirt and saw a heavy gold chain necklace on her shrivelled décolleté. The sight of that tasteless necklace and her brown skin gave me the strength to start asking questions. I couldn't stop. I opened up and let her have it.

How much money did you and Dad get for the land? Why couldn't the truth come out? Was the airline afraid of getting a bad name? Was it afraid of insurance claims? Were you and Dad given hush money? Was the co-pilot paid off?

She slogged away on the home trainer, furiously pedalling in her boat shoes while she screamed at me to leave the past alone. How dare I think such things about herself and Dad? She could just hear Walter turning over in his grave because of my slanderous talk, even at a distance of ten kilometres.

For a moment I thought she was going to have a heart attack, and that thought made my body relax and the migraine dissipate. She gasped for breath and turned as white as a sheet, which was almost impossible after all those hours on the tanning bed. She threw back her head and pushed against her chest with both hands. Then she started to sputter, *errrrr errrrr*. The whole display lasted at least two minutes. Finally she pulled herself together, sat straight up on the home trainer, and began to pedal again.

'I'm going to the press,' I said. 'I'm going to tell them what really happened on October 5th, 1979. I'm going to tell them that a child was flying the plane.'

My mother stopped biking and looked at me. With contempt. As if I were a poisonous jellyfish in the surf. She said, 'The declaration made by the airline is the only existing declaration. I'll say you're talking nonsense. That you're making it all up. Everyone will think you're crazy—your students, your colleagues, even Pieternel will think you've lost it.'

'I'll find witnesses,' I said, clutching at straws. I wish it were different, but I've never been a hero. That hateful look in my mother's eyes paralysed me. 'I'll find the co-pilot … ,' I bluffed, but my mother crushed me completely. 'Ha!' she burst out. 'Ha! The co-pilot! Waling, that's brilliant!'

She dabbed her brown forehead off with a white monogrammed towel. LCB. Louise Cittersen van Boven. Jesus, it was all so ridiculous. I was a big *Dynasty* fan back then. That was a TV series from long before your time, Gieles, but I watched every episode. It was about a loony family of stinking rich oil magnates, but obviously it was about my mother, too. She was that soap opera personified. It only hit me then that she had even adopted the impeccable hair-do of the main character, Krystle.

'And I'm sure that co-pilot is just sitting around waiting for your so-called truth,' my mother screamed at me, and that was the moment that I did it. I left the soap. I turned my back for good on her villa with its Greek statues and fussy little fountain and I've never seen or spoken to her since.

No, I didn't go to the press. No, I didn't look for witnesses or the co-pilot. Cowardly? You bet. But I was afraid. I clung to what I had. Just like before, I held onto a pair of apron strings and lurched blindly behind a woman. My wife. I didn't want to lose Pieternel. In the meantime the secret was eating at me. Or rather, I tried to eat the secret away. It happened very gradually. Every year I gained five kilos, and during the summer vacation I walked three of them off. I wasn't yet overweight. When we got married I was on the hefty side. Pieternel herself was plump. We found out that she was infertile, and we sat together on the couch with cookies, doughnuts and Toblerones. We each had our own sad reasons to anesthetise ourselves with sugar.

Fifteen years after seeing my mother for the last time on her home trainer, I heard that she had died. The lawyer called me to his office. I didn't want to go. I didn't want to have anything to do with that insane woman. But Pieternel insisted. It was just when we were working on losing weight. Pieternel was one metre seventy and weighed ninety kilos, about twenty kilos too much. And I had hit a hundred and ten on the scale. We had to quit hiking because the fat got in the way.

We sat in the lawyer's office, and he told us that as the

only heir I was getting her property and the villa. That's what I was afraid of. After deducting the mortgage her property was estimated at one million euros. And then came the worst part. She had socked away the rest of her assets in a Swiss bank account. This was around 1.2 million euros, the lawyer said nonchalantly.

Speechless, Pieternel and I thumbed through the will and the bank statements from Crédit Suisse. It was there, on the lawyer's Biedermeier chairs, that our marriage came apart.

What I had always known finally hit me like a ton of bricks. My father and mother had let themselves be bribed. They had accepted hush money, and now—a quarter of a century after the plane had crashed in our beet field—it had landed on my plate.

I didn't want those 2.2 million. But Pieternel did. I told her my nauseating secret and she listened. Patiently, full of understanding. She thought it was awful that I had had to live with such a heavy burden for such a long time. With her chubby arm around my chubby shoulder, she explained lovingly why it would be better for *me* if I accepted the money. I had a right to compensation. I had suffered. I was a victim, too. And I didn't earn all that much as a teacher. All things considered, my salary was a mere pittance, she declared. Her opinion of my salary was news to me.

I stuck to my guns. I did not want my mother's inheritance.

Pieternel withdrew her consoling arm and sat down across from me. She explained with great passion why it would be better for *us* if I accepted the money. Two-point-two million euros! We could go to America and buy a baby. Happiness was finally within our grasp. It wasn't just for wealthy homosexuals. She had a right to a baby, too, she wept. We were almost too old to adopt. She was so unhappy. I had no idea how unhappy she was. Did I want to make her unhappy? Was that what I wanted?

I surprised myself. I held my ground. Pieternel was dumbfounded. She stood up and began screaming. She aimed her forefinger at me as if it were a gun. I *must* accept the money. Who was I to talk anyway? I had always known about the bribery. What did that say about my credibility? F--king this, f--king that.

Once again, the plane crash came between me and a woman. For weeks we had fights that became so heated that I had to move to the guest room, which once had been intended as a nursery. But this time I refused to capitulate. I did not want the money, and that was that.

'Then I'm going to divorce you,' Pieternel said finally. 'Because I *do* want the money. We were married in community of property, so I have a right to half.'

And so we divorced. She got 1.1 million euros and stamped out of my life. The lawyer advised me to donate the other half to a worthy cause, which I did. My parents' hush money was used to restore my grandma's favourite pumping station.

And while the Cruquius was being restored, I ruined my body and my life by eating. More than ever. I felt so sorry for myself that in less than a year I had gained sixty kilos. My students supported me through thick and thin (apologies for the bad pun). I can't do much, but must admit I was a pretty good teacher. The kids really liked me and I liked them. Long after my colleagues had dumped me because I was so fat and because I called in sick so often with migraine attacks, the students kept coming to see me. But even the most persistent ones finally gave up—the ones who kept coming to my door while I hid myself away with a plate of junk food.

For a long time I tried to eat myself to death. It seemed like the best way to be rescued from the migraines and from a loathsome body that was no longer mine. I made a deal with myself that if I crossed the two-hundred-fifty kilo border and still wasn't dead, I'd start living my life again. And that's what I've done, more or less. I'm almost forty-seven years old and—wonder of wonders—my fat heart is still able to pump the blood through my silted-up arteries to keep me alive, day after day.

So that's what I'm looking at now. Once again, Gieles: I'm not asking you to keep the information about that cursed plane crash to yourself. You're free to tell it to anyone you wish.

28

'You scared me to death,' said Liedje, who was smoking under the stove exhaust fan. Gieles was startled, too. He had sneaked into the kitchen thinking that no one was home. Liedje hastily put out the cigarette under the tap and threw the butt into the garbage.

'Tony isn't here. Again. But sit down. I haven't seen you in such a long time.'

Gieles wanted to do an immediate about-face, but Liedje had already opened the door of the mint green refrigerator and taken out a soft drink. He put his sneakers on the doormat and sat down. His backpack, filled with two kilos of ground beef and Super Waling's life story, was on the floor at his feet. Two kilos of ground revenge. He hoped the dog wouldn't smell it. But Lady was lying unconscious in her basket as usual.

'Did you know that Tony had been left back again?' said Liedje with a weak voice. Normally she was shrouded in a golden glow, but now she seemed sallow and lustreless. She looked like one of those emaciated polder children from Super Waling's stories.

'Later on he'll be as old as his teachers. He's in a class full of little kids.' She handed him the drink. 'You passed, of course.'

Gieles nodded uncomfortably. 'Skin of my teeth,' he said, to make her feel better. He emptied the glass at breakneck speed.

'I wish he hung around with you more. A nice game of

ping-pong or football. But what does m'lord do with his time?' She was asking Gieles, but she answered the question herself. 'Smoke dope. I'm a thousand percent sure he's smoking with his no-good little friends right now. He's always talking about Flippertong. Flippertong! That boy must have morons for parents. Tony's smoking his brains away with that Flippertong. Do you smoke?'

She asked him as if she hoped he did.

'Pretty often,' he lied.

She didn't even hear him. 'No, of course you don't smoke. You're *making* something of your life ... Tony was gonna call you about your goose ping-pong. He read about it in the paper. He calls you the goose whisperer. What a laugh. The goose whisperer. Tony thought maybe you could play ping-pong at the shopkeeper's association party. With your goose.'

'Oh,' said Gieles.

Now he really wanted to leave.

'You'd get paid for it, of course. I just wish that lousy kid would do something useful with his life. Smoking dope and gaming. That's all he does. And eating French fries.'

She stared out the window and put a hand on her neck as if she were trying to strangle herself.

'I've got to go ...'

'And now he wants to join the army. He wants to be a soldier in a fighting unit. Can you picture it? Tony? A soldier? He can't put a dent in a pack of butter. Our little Tony. Give me a goddamn break.'

Gieles actually could imagine Tony as a wild, rapid -fire Rambo. The problem was that his mother saw him so differently. Rabbit killed by slingshot, school windows smashed, firework through the mail slot. Little Tony couldn't possibly have done that, Liedje used to shout.

And if he did do it, well, those others must have put little Tony up to it. Gieles could tell her about the assaulted goose, but she'd never believe him.

'You don't even need a diploma to join the army. That's what Tony said. Heh heh. That stands to reason,' Liedje sneered. She scratched her head. Her hair was thin. He could see her scalp right through it.

'I told him, 'Since when do you need a diploma to let yourself get shot in the head?' And you don't even have to be eighteen. No, you can't vote unless you're an adult, but children can let themselves be blown to bits.'

She took another look outside. Three women biked past, and a man with a carrier bicycle. The carrier was full of garden tools. One of the women had a Palestinian scarf wrapped around her head like a turban. Normally Liedje would have jumped to her feet and shot off a barrage of criticism that would have shattered glass. But now all she said was, 'There's those filthy hippies again. Bunch of goofballs. Going to clean up that little woods. And what's the point? That's where they're putting the pyramids.'

She stood up and fished a pack of cigarettes out of a vase. She inhaled down to her toes. Gieles couldn't find an opportunity to leave. She just kept on talking. 'Two arrogant assholes from the airport came to see us. They didn't even have the decency to wipe off their muddy feet. All I can say is this: if they flatten my house, they'll have to do it with me in it. I'm not gonna let myself be chased out of my own house. Go to hell.'

Gieles could just see it: a bulldozer flattening her house while Liedje was still in the kitchen smoking. He saw the old woman anxiously clutching onto her shanty while the men pulled her out and tore the shanty down.

Gieles wanted to tell her Super Waling's story, but he

had a feeling that Liedje wasn't interested in hearing it. He stood up.

'Tony isn't here.'

'I left something in his room. A while back.'

'That dildo? Is that yours?' She didn't even sound shocked. She could just as easily have said, 'Those shoes? Are they yours?'

'No, a ... uhh ... a book.' He was redder than red.

'Tony and books,' she said passively. 'That's like smoking under water. Hopeless.'

He had grabbed his backpack, but she put out her cigarette and started in on the next subject.

'I saw you with a girl. She looked like a white black kid. With that Ruud Gullit hair. When he was still playing soccer.'

'Meike, you mean.'

'Is she Dolly's niece? She works with her in the shop, doesn't she?'

'Something like that, yes.'

'She doesn't live with her, does she? Dolly can hardly take care of her own kids. Those boys are doomed.' She thought a moment. 'Those boys will come to a bad end. How's your mother doing?'

Here we go again.

'Fine. Great.'

'Where's she hanging out now?'

'She's in a hospital with some Spanish doctors.'

She's always talking about that Spanish doctor. Juan this, Juan that ...

'I have to go to the hospital this afternoon. I have to go to the hospital every day. For radiation,' sighed Liedje. 'Well, you know how to get to Tony's room.'

She gave him such a lonely look, as if she were the only survivor left on earth. He got goose bumps on his arms.

Tony slept at the front of the house, near the road. Unlike Gieles's room, Tony's was extremely neat. His bed looked as if no one ever slept in it. Next to the wardrobe were six pairs of sneakers, perfectly aligned. School books were arranged on the shelf above the desk from large to small. Above his bed was a poster of a brunette dressed in a tiger bra with fishnet stockings and buttocks as round as cantaloupes. She was posing with her back to Gieles and looking at him provocatively over her bare shoulder. RAVEN ALEXIS it said under her stiletto heels. DIGITAL PLAYGROUND.

That was the porn actress and gamer that Tony loved to talk about. Gieles thought she was so-so. That was all that Tony had on his beaten-up walls. Sometimes Tony put his fist through the hardboard out of frustration. Or he used the wall as a dartboard for his pocket knife and Tony Senior would come and repair the holes with filler.

Gieles had to hurry. He took the plastic bag of ground beef out of his backpack. Hanging in a corner of the room was a red punching bag. There was a zipper running along the top, which he opened a few centimetres. He pushed a glob of ground meat in with the stuffing and closed the zipper. He also spread some ground meat behind porn star Raven Alexis. It stuck surprisingly well. He chuckled to think of the maggots that would soon start crawling behind her long legs.

He stuffed a raw meatball in one sock and shoved it under the other socks in the wardrobe. Another clump went into the slit on the back of the piggy bank that bore words KEIJZER BUTCHER SHOP. He placed two chunks on the wardrobe and under the mattress. One small ball went into his down pillow. Gieles remembered the time he and Tony had thrown roasted meatballs out the attic room window. Tony had swiped the balls from the butcher shop. They were so tough that they bounced across the runway. He thought of the speculaas and gelatine balls he was going to throw for his *Expert Rescue Operation 3032*. Gieles gloated over his brilliant solution, until he heard music.

Elvis Presley. Liedje played this number all the time. Elvis would fall into a laughing fit and Liedje would laugh along with abandon. But this time he didn't hear any laughter.

Quickly Gieles smeared the last of the raw meat on the disc drive of Tony's computer as if it were a sandwich. Mission one successfully accomplished.

Downstairs Gieles called out 'bye!' right through 'Are you lonesome' and fled from the house. It was two in the afternoon. Dolly was working, the boys weren't there. He pushed Super Waling's life story through her rusty mail slot. Hush money or not, in his eyes Super Waling was still a hero.

Mission two accomplished.

Satisfied, he biked back home.

He took a biology book and sat down under the cherry tree, out of sight of the plane spotters' campground. Wally was beating her wings cautiously next to the wading pool, but Gieles didn't see her. He had closed his eyes. He smelled the sun, the jet fuel vapours and his own sweat. He thought about Meike's lips and the cantaloupe buttocks of Raven Alexis. They were standing under the waterfall in their forest: their tropical jungle with purple and orange birds and moss as soft as silk. Meike laid down on the moss invitingly and spread her wet arms and legs for him.

29

Super Waling was turning forty-six. He had said he wanted to celebrate his birthday among a very small circle of friends.

Gieles flattened his hair with a lick of gel, put on a clean shirt and walked to the barn. He saw his father standing at the fox-tail workbench, bent over a wooden box.

'Hey, Dad,' said Gieles. Startled, Willem turned around. He was holding a screwdriver, and it almost looked as if he had poked the point of it in his eyes, which looked very irritated.

'The box isn't finished,' he said with a nasal voice.

Gieles had asked his father to make a box for his bike so he could carry Wally around.

'No big deal.'

His father blew his nose.

'You sick or something?' Gieles asked with concern. He was almost sure his father had been crying.

'No, no. Nothing's wrong.' He straightened his long back and tossed the screwdriver in the tool chest. Earlier in the week Gieles had heard his father screaming into the phone again. This time it was about the Spanish doctors.

He grabbed his bike and lingered at the door.

'Have fun tonight,' his father said, trying to look cheery. 'I tightened the screws on your rack. It was loose. Very dangerous if you're carrying somebody around.'

That somebody was Meike, and they both knew it. Up until now his father had never worried about his loose rack.

'Thanks a lot!' he said, and left. Biking down the road, Gieles felt guilty about leaving his father behind in the barn.

'Fucking mess,' he said to the open air.

After fifteen minutes he turned into Super Waling's street. His front door was ajar and Super Waling was in the kitchen. There was rice stuck to his hair. His purple sweatsuit was covered with stains.

'The sushi bombed,' he announced, glancing over the detritus. There was rice everywhere, and crumpled sheets of seaweed. The handmade sushi rolls looked like dead magpies. Waling's basketball sneakers crunched on the kitchen floor, which was covered with a thick layer of uncooked grains as if a wedding had just been performed there.

'Did you ever make sushi before?'

Super Waling was holding up a garbage bag. 'No. But I thought: why don't I make a nice healthy, delicious meal for you. I thought young people only ate sushi.' He threw the black rolls into the garbage bag one by one.

Super Waling surveyed the area. There was rice sticking to his three-day-old beard as well.

I wonder if the maggots have started crawling out of the raw meat yet?

'Good heavens. Meike will be here any minute. She'll think I live in a state of squalor.'

He looked meditatively at the kitchen wall with its folders and torn-out ads for home deliveries. 'What do you feel like? Shawarma, Chinese, pizza, spare ribs, French fries, roti? I'm afraid it's not going to be a very well-balanced meal.'

'Spare ribs,' said Gieles, with the floor crackling beneath him. He wanted to talk about the plane crash but this wasn't the right time. Super Waling looked seriously stressed. 'Shall I vacuum?'

'No, Gieles. You don't have to clean up my mess. Go have a seat. I'll be ready in a minute.'

The living room was impeccable. It smelled of cleanser. A vase of fresh peonies had been placed in the window. Several remote controls and telephones were lined up on the glass coffee table. He sat in the massage chair and resisted the urge to turn it on. There were books stacked on the small table next to the chair. *Sit-Down Exercises. Get Up and Lose Weight. Eat Yourself Beautiful, Trim and Happy. Tame Your Food Monster.* Next to the stack was one weighty tome: *The Complete Works of Chuang Tzu,* a book that probably didn't have anything to do with losing weight. But Super Waling had clearly started out on a new path, and that was good news. Very good news. He picked up the book and began leafing through it. The sound of the vacuum could be heard from the kitchen.

One chapter was about Perfect Happiness. The writer with the unpronounceable name was writing about the Marquis of Lu who offered hospitality to a sea bird. Gieles read that the Marquis gave him the best pieces of meat, but within three days the sea bird was dead. 'If you want to nourish a bird with what nourishes a bird, then you should let it roost in the deep forest, play among the banks and islands, float on the rivers and lakes, eat mudfish and minnows, follow the rest of the flock in flight and rest, and live any way it chooses.'

Gieles turned the page. 'Fish live in water and thrive, but if men tried to live in water they would die. Creatures differ ...'

A toilet was flushed. The doorbell rang. Gieles tossed

the book on the small table and dashed to the front door.

Meike was standing on the doorstep in her hairdressers' clothes, with Dolly in her wake. 'Hi,' said Meike, and walked right in.

'Is Waling there?' asked Dolly. She had not been invited to Super Waling's birthday.

'He's in the bathroom.' Gieles had no intention of letting her in, but suddenly Super Waling was standing behind him. He was wearing clean orange sweatpants and a long-sleeved shirt with JOHNNY CASH IS A FRIEND OF MINE written on it. The rice in his hair was gone.

'Dolly,' he said happily. 'What a surprise. Come in.'

'I'd rather stay outside.' She clutched her shoulder bag tightly.

Gieles wriggled past Super Waling's belly and went to the living room, where Meike was walking around inquisitively. He kept the door and his ears wide open.

Dolly's voice echoed through the front hallway. He heard her say, 'I read it. About you, your grandmas, the plane crash of 1979. The way they bribed your parents. The death of your father. Your heartless ex-wife. Your unfulfilled desire to have children. I read it all. Word for word. And it's nothing to sneeze at, what you've gone through. But that's no reason to eat yourself to death. Jesus, Waling, how long have you been holed up here shamelessly gorging yourself? Five, six years?'

Silence. 'I tell you, Waling, I'm not going to stand idly by while my favourite teacher assumes the proportions of a hippopotamus. I'm not offering you an apron string, like your mother and your ex did. But I am offering you this.'

Gieles and Meike stood stock-still at the door, but they couldn't see what Dolly was giving him.

'The window,' whispered Meike. Between the flowers

on the window sill they watched Dolly take all kinds of stuff out of her handbag.

'What's she giving him?' she whispered.

'Pills,' said Gieles knowingly. 'She's giving him health pills.'

'What was she talking about just now?'

'I'll tell you later. It's a long story.'

They watched Dolly's lips move, but they couldn't understand what she was saying. Then she stopped talking and listened. First impassively, her red lips forming an uncompromising line. Slowly she relaxed her mouth muscles, and after a short time a tiny smile even appeared. She cast her eyes skyward as if the answer were somewhere up in the clouds, and then she stepped into the house.

'Just a few minutes then,' they heard her say. 'I have to pick up the kids.'

Still clinging to her purse, she walked in.

'I'll get the drinks,' shouted Super Waling, with his hands full of pill bottles.

Dolly walked around as if she were in a museum. She shuffled past the bookcase and studied the Alpine wallpaper.

'Is this one of those chairs that move?' Meike asked, plopping herself down.

She pushed the remote control and her body began to vibrate.

Dolly was still exploring. She looked in a display cabinet containing Country and Western knickknacks. A lighter featuring a photo of Merle Haggard, a Tammy Wynette button, a cigarette tin with THE MAN IN BLACK written on it, a bandana signed by Willie Nelson.

'Hey!' shouted Meike. 'Those are the paintings by Waling's grandma.'

Dolly looked up from the cabinet at one of the fluorescent paintings. 'I know that picture,' she said.

'Isn't it cool?'

'No, I think it's hideous. During history class Waling once took us to the pumping station, and even then I thought those paintings were awful.'

'Well, I'm finally here,' Super Waling panted. He was carrying a tray on which cans of grape soda and tumblers were precariously balanced. Gieles took the tray from his hands, and he lowered his backside awkwardly onto the couch.

'All right,' he said. 'You're all here. Welcome to my cabinet of curiosities.'

Dolly stood next to the massage chair and took a book from the pile. 'I see you still have the same passions,' she said, leafing through *Tame Your Food Monster*. 'Pumping stations, mountains, country music. But I bet you don't do any more hiking.'

'Sadly not,' Super Waling said apologetically. 'Who wants a grape soda?'

'I remember a school camp on one of the Wadden Islands. Was it Texel?'

'Terschelling. We always went to Terschelling.'

'Christ. All we did was hike. One month later I still had aching muscles.'

She sat on the couch across from Super Waling and Gieles. 'You were always scared to death you'd lose one of the students. You spent all your time counting heads.'

'Sometimes I still have nightmares about it.'

She slapped her leg and laughed. 'Remember that time we went for a field trip to see the flowers in the Keukenhof? It was after closing time and there were these two old ladies standing at the fence. The touring bus had forgotten them. It had left for Maastricht *hours* before.'

'Yeah,' said Super Waling. 'I can still see them standing there with their canes and their long raincoats.'

'And you felt *so* sorry for them. The people at the Keukenhof told us: "This happens every day. We always have a couple of them left over. We'll put them up in a hotel and they'll be picked up tomorrow."'

She laughed until she cried. Gieles couldn't remember ever having seen her like that. All the muscles around her mouth were tightened and at the same time she looked totally relaxed.

'Then you took the old ladies in our bus,' she said, wiping a tear from her cheek. 'And from the school you drove them by car to Maastricht.'

'What a ride that was,' Super Waling recalled. 'The one lady cried the whole way and the other one was incontinent. By the time we got to Utrecht she had peed all over the back seat.'

'Yuck,' said Meike, moving her legs up and down with the adjustable support. 'Did you kick her out of the car?'

'Oh, that poor old thing. She was totally out of it. She thought I was her father. She kept calling me papa.' He shook his head.

'I remember,' Dolly continued with a quiet voice, 'that I thought it was incredibly sweet of you. To drive the whole damn way to Maastricht.'

'Oh, it was a minor inconvenience.'

'No, Waling,' she said. 'That was no minor inconvenience. I thought it was a magnificent thing to do. And this,' she tossed the book *Tame Your Food Monster* onto the coffee table, 'is not going to save you. In your case, food monster is an understatement.

'What a thing to say!' cried Meike from the massage chair. 'That's really rotten! You have to be highly motivated to look the way Waling does.'

'Wise ass,' said Dolly, taking a folder out of her purse.

Meike looked at Super Waling with motherly affection. 'Don't let her get to you. She's in a super grouchy mood. The pyramid project has been dropped, and now she can't move away.'

'How dreadful for you,' said Super Waling, but he sounded relieved.

Gieles was sitting next to Super Waling on the couch and he jumped to his feet. 'Why has it been dropped?'

'The pyramids are too expensive,' she said with restrained rage. 'All those airport people are bastards. But I don't want to talk about that. I was talking about you, Waling.'

Testily she resumed her story, while Gieles and Super Waling exchanged a conspiratorial look.

'In your case, a tummy tuck is the most effective way to lose weight. This clinic does outstanding work. A customer of mine lost seventy kilos that way.'

Super Waling took the brochure from her and folded it open.

'Wow,' he said.

'The operation is covered by insurance.'

'"On to a new life,"' he read aloud solemnly. 'But I have to have a BMI over forty.'

'Don't worry about that,' said Dolly. 'I think you've broken all the records.'

'What's a BMI?' asked Meike as she crawled out of the massage chair.

'Body Mass Index,' Dolly explained. 'The ratio of your height to your weight.'

'And now enough about me,' said Super Waling, folding the brochure back up. 'Let's have a toast.'

'I really have to go.' She looked at her watch and stood up. 'The boys.'

At the living room door she turned and stared at Super Waling intently. 'The old Waling. The history teacher who all the girls were secretly in love with. The Waling who could make a boring day at school worthwhile with his stories. That's who I want to see again. Okay?'

Super Waling's face was redder than the peonies on the window sill. 'Okay,' he stammered.

Dolly went out into the hallway but came right back. 'One more thing. Those rompers you wear all the time. They're hopeless. Orange sweatpants? What were you thinking? Next time I see you, we're going on the internet to order clothes. There's a million American websites for tubbies like you.'

And she was gone.

'Ooh-la-la,' sang Meike, flopping down next to him. 'Were all the girls really hot for you?'

'I don't know. My antenna isn't very sensitive.'

Outside Dolly was starting up her old car. Super Waling wanted to stand up and wave her goodbye, but by the time he got to his feet she was gone.

He's falling in love with her! His flab will be gone and his abs will be tight again and Dolly will fall in love with him and then he'll finally have kids and her own kids will stop screaming. That's what has to happen. I'll burn a million Rizla birds to make it happen.

'Your present!' cried Meike. She skipped in her bare feet to the dining room table, on which she had placed a bag from the liquor store.

'Dog biscuits.' She shook the cardboard package. 'For Dino. He barks much less now that I'm walking him. Did you know that his master has a son with a tattoo shop? ... And this is for us.'

She held up a bottle of Malibu. Super Waling raised his eyebrows dubiously. Meike continued unpacking her bag.

She handed the birthday boy three presents.

'Who could have imagined,' said Super Waling with emotion, 'that I would live to be forty-six?'

'Jesus, Waling,' said Meike. 'You're old, but you're not that old. Now my grandma—she's old.'

'That's true.' He seemed to be smiling through his tears, but Gieles wasn't sure. Maybe he was still sweating from all that vacuuming.

'Shampoo! What a good idea!'

'And conditioner. For after you wash your hair. Really good quality. They're from Dolly's shop.'

'How wonderful. How sweet. How nice.' He held up the hair products as if they were high-priced bottles of wine.

'And I downloaded this especially for you,' she said, tearing the paper from the CD box.

'*Fever Ray*,' Super Waling read aloud. Meike had written on it in pink pen: 'When I grow up I want to be a forester, run through the moss on high heels.'

'That's what the singer sings. She's Swedish, and she's the best thing you've ever heard. She transforms from one day to the next. Want to hear it?'

'Of course we want to hear it. Right, Gieles?'

'Sure.' He had settled into the massage chair and had begun to vibrate. Chuang Tzu was still beside him on the little table. The story of the sea bird was worrying him. If you want to nourish a bird with what nourishes a bird, then you should let it roost in the deep forest, play among the banks and islands, follow the rest of the flock in flight. Wally was locked up in his room right now. Was that bad? But if she was free, she'd start looking for him and then she'd panic. The little goose couldn't live without him. He picked up the book and read on the back cover that Chuang Tzu had lived in China four centuries before Christ. Gieles decided that the old Chinese geezer was just shooting off his mouth. What did they know back then, anyway?

Meike put on the music and turned up the volume. Sinister noises engulfed the room. A bleak, dark wind arose. The voice of the singer sounded wispy, hypnotising. Meike closed her eyes and began to move. She writhed and twisted and swung her head around. She danced as if she had been released from the face of the earth.

Gieles stuck his fingers in his ears theatrically and Super Waling listened to the lyrics with interest.

When the number was over, Meike opened her eyes. 'And now we'll have some Malibu.' The Swedish band launched into the next number with a whine.

'Alcohol ... do we have to do that?'

'Of course. Do you have any chocolate milk? It's really delicious mixed with chocolate milk.'

Super Waling shook his head.

'Then we'll drink it straight.' She filled three tumblers.

'It tastes like coconut,' Super Waling said, sucking on his tongue.

Gieles turned up the massage chair to level three.

'We really should eat something with this, you guys, or it'll hit us too hard. Spare ribs? Meike, you want spare ribs, too? If you don't, check out the delivery services, on the kitchen wall.'

She walked away, singing and rolling a cigarette.

Gieles looked up. 'Waling, do you mind that I passed your story on to Dolly? I wanted her to know what happened. With your mother and that pilot boy ...'

'No problem, Gieles. I'm glad you gave it to her. As I said, secrets can make you sick.'

'Pizza! I'm totally psyched for pizza. One of those

folded-over ones!' She came back and sat down next to Super Waling with her legs drawn up.

He called the pizza delivery service. 'One calzone and one pizza with only vegetables,' he said in a loud voice, to make himself heard above the Swedish singer. 'Pizza Bianca? With bacon? No, no, I only want vegetables. Veggie Pizza? What's that?'

'Vegetarian,' said Meike, inhaling.

'Zucchini and peppers, yes. Artichokes are ultra fantastic ...'

Then he called the spare ribs line.

'"If I had a voice, I would sing,"' sang Meike to the music.

'With a baked potato and herb butter. Excellent. Lava? Guys, you want lava cake? Two servings ... Cittersen van ... exactly, van Boven. I'm in the database.'

'You know all those phone number by heart?' asked Meike.

'I'm afraid so.' He rubbed his forehead with the back of his hand.

Meike screwed up her eyes and leaned her chin on her knees. 'Do you have kids?'

Super Waling took a long swig of his Malibu. 'My ex-wife and I couldn't have children. But we really wanted to.'

'Why did you get divorced?'

Super Waling stared at his stomach. 'How should I explain this ... We grew apart, more or less.'

'Grew apart?' She gave him a bewildered look. 'Did you get too fat? Or was she just as fat as you?'

Super Waling put his glass down. 'Oh, no. Pieternel was plump, but she certainly wasn't as fat as I am now. I haven't always been like this. This is from the last few years.'

'I know. Dolly showed me pictures of you.' She chugged down red-brown beverage. 'She had ten of you, at least.'

Super Waling beamed and opened the folder Dolly had just given him. The page was filled with before and after tummy tuck shots. He saw an apron of flab hanging over a man's underpants. The apron was as big as kid's swimming tube. The after shot showed a trim man's stomach. Super Waling would have been intensely satisfied with the swimming tube.

'But why did you get divorced?' Meike persisted.

'I think ... well, I think we no longer felt at home with each other. We were going in opposite directions. Does that make sense?'

'Mmm.' She poured herself another full glass. 'No.'

'Take it easy with that stuff. It's powerful.'

Gieles turned the chair off. The Malibu and the vibrating made his body feel like a cocktail. He turned his head toward the couch. Meike looked like a minuscule doll next to Super Waling. Like one of the Chinese good luck dolls his mother had on her key ring. She must have had at least thirty.

'What direction did she go?'

'Pieternel left for America. She's been living in Santa Barbara in California for the last five years. She has a husband and two small children.'

'Naah! And she couldn't have children!'

'Turns out the problem was with me.'

'Be glad you can't have any kids,' snorted Meike. 'My mother says I'm gonna give her a heart attack. She only thought I was fun when I was a baby.'

'I would have liked having a daughter like you.'

'Get out of here. With piercings and tattoos? Yeah, sure.'

'With piercings and tattoos. To tell the truth, I'd like to have a tattoo myself.'

'YOU!' She pounded on the arm rest, laughing uproariously. 'That would be too cool, Waling!' She crept across the couch towards him, grabbed his upper arm and pushed up the sleeve of his JOHNNY CASH IS A FRIEND OF MINE shirt. 'You could fit a whole pumping station here! Or two! Two pumping stations!' She drew the outline of the station with her black finger nail.

The front doorbell rang. 'I'll get it,' said Gieles, nauseated from the hunger and the Malibu.

It was the spare ribs delivery boy. Not long afterwards the pizza delivery boy arrived. While Meike threw out ideas for tattoos for Super Waling (Celtic crosses! A skull! A tribal tattoo on your back! Or Thumper, that Disney rabbit, on your ankle!) Gieles unpacked the food.

The calzone had been torn open, which left the box soaking wet. The Veggie Pizza turned out to be a Bianca anyway and the spare ribs were tepid. Gieles sat on the couch opposite them and began to gnaw. His mouth was red from the marinade. Meike, still smoking, tore off small bits of pizza and popped them in her mouth. Super Waling ate very neatly with a knife and fork, as if he was sitting in a three-star restaurant. He had transferred the pizza to a large plate. It was the first time Gieles had ever seen him eat.

'You know,' said Meike, blowing smoke up to the low subdivision ceiling. 'You have to get a tattoo that suits you. You can't just pick any old thing. I know a kid who's a guinea pig for beginning tattooers. He's covered with them. On his forearm he got a mermaid and the face is a total catastrophe.' She grimaced. 'Mermaid with a stroke, he calls her.'

Super Waling wiped his beard with a paper napkin. 'A tattoo would be wasted on my body. I have to lose some kilos first. Lots of kilos.'

She raised a pedantic finger. 'You're only as fat as you feel.'

'My body doesn't have anything to do with the way I feel any more.'

'But what kind of tattoo would you get if you were to lose all those kilos?'

'Something with mud,' said Super Waling, and took a bite of his Bianca. 'It all begins with mud, doesn't it?'

'Deep,' said Meike.

'That doesn't make any sense,' Gieles said, smacking his lips. 'Mud on your arm would look like shit.'

'That's true. Let's see ... Yes, I know! I'd get a tattoo of Sophia Warrens. My great-great-great-grandmother.'

'But do you know what she looked like?' asked Meike.

'Sure. I don't have a photo or portrait of her, but in my mind I know exactly what she looked like.'

Meike shook her head. 'You didn't know her, right? Great-great whatever? When was that?'

'Sophia lived from 1825 to ...'

'1915,' said Gieles, sinking his teeth into the soggy baked potato.

'You really remember everything.'

'Then you never knew her,' said Meike. 'So your tattoo won't mean anything.'

'I know her thanks to history.'

Gieles nodded in agreement. He knew what she looked like, too. Even naked.

Meike stubbed out her cigarette in the gnawed off spare ribs. 'I'd get a pumping station. On your back. A great big one. In exactly the same colours as your grandma's painting.'

'That's an even better idea,' said Super Waling, deeply moved. 'What station would you get?'

'The gold one with the purple things sticking out,' she

said resolutely. 'I think it's super fantastic.'

'You mean the balance arms for pumping up the water. Okay, you can have it.'

'What do you mean?'

'The painting. Take it with you. It's yours.'

'Get out of here.'

'Go on, go get it,' he said encouragingly when she stood up.

Meike carefully lifted the canvas from the wall. She stood there for a few minutes as if she were imprisoned in time. Gieles looked in her direction, but he didn't want her to think he was staring straight at her. So he let his eyes circle her instead: the ceiling, the Swiss Alps, the tile floor, the wooden table. Only now did he notice the faded traces of paint on the legs and along the edges. The table was unmistakably an heirloom from his grandma. And the threadbare chairs probably were, too.

Meike put the painting on the table and wiped her face clean with her shirt. 'Fucking mascara,' she said and walked up to Super Waling, planting a kiss on his three-day-old beard. 'Let's play musical chairs. It's time we had a real birthday party.' She tried to pull him up by the hand, but she couldn't get his body to budge.

Meike sat on the back of his bike. She had shoved her hands under his shirt, around his stomach. Her small fingers felt cool and glowing hot at the same time. She moved her face slowly across his back, as if she were drying herself off. And all the while she babbled nonstop. About shampoos and music. About her pumping station painting that Super Waling would soon be dropping off. He biked slowly into their dead-end street to prolong the sensation she aroused in him. If he were to stop at their woods, he'd take Meike by the hand. He felt confident.

I'm sure I can do it.

This afternoon before he left he had sacrificed a whole bunch of pages from part 4 of *How to Identify Birds*.

About two hundred metres further down, standing in the middle of the road with his hands in his pockets, was Tony. Gieles hadn't seen him in the approaching evening light and he was startled. He couldn't make out his face, but his manner told him enough. The excited jubilation in his stomach turned to a mixture of fear and fury. They had never fought before. It was too late to turn back. Gieles didn't want Tony to think he was afraid, and Tony would easily catch up with them.

He wondered if it would hurt. Gieles thought of the battered bedroom walls and the time at the town fair when Tony gave some kid a head-butt with his helmet on because he beat him at the Mega Booster.

Gieles biked up to him in slow motion, while Meike played piano on his stomach and hummed. The gleaming head came closer and closer. He was wearing combat pants and a sleeveless shirt. His small eyes were hidden beneath his eyebrows. It was abundantly clear that the raw ground meat behind porn star Raven Alexis and in the other places in his room had come to life.

When he got to within four metres he put on his brakes. His house was nearby. If he should start screaming, his father and Uncle Fred might be able to hear him. But he wasn't going to scream. Meike got off, her arm still around his waist.

'Who's that?' she asked drowsily.

He saw that her arm made Tony even nastier. Tony had never seen him with a girl before, and now here was a girl virtually glued to him.

'That's Tony Keijzer. He lives down the road,' he said, and he knew that 'he lives down the road' was oil on the fire. For the first time in their lifelong friendship, Gieles was indicating that it was over as far as he was concerned.

From now on, Tony would be someone-who-lived-down-the-road.

'Oh, yeah, him,' said Meike.

Tony walked up to them threateningly and stood with his knee pressed against Gieles's front wheel.

'You stuck that meat in my room.' Tony pushed the wheel rhythmically with his leg.

Meike looked at his leg and then at Tony's rigid face, which towered above her.

'I don't care one way or another,' he went on, and made a hawking sound in the back of his throat. He spat next to Gieles's sneaker. 'But my mother wasn't real pleased by the explosion of maggots.'

'Explosion of maggots?' repeated Meike. She was hanging onto Gieles as if she were leaning against a bar. Two glasses of straight Malibu had made her tipsy.

'Shut your face, dwarf.' Tony clamped the front wheel between his legs and stuck out his acne-dotted chin.

'Dwarf?' laughed Meike. 'Did you hear that, Gieles? The creep can talk.'

Tony stared at Meike in a way that frightened Gieles.

'Hey, Bos,' he said. 'Can't you do better than a butt-ugly whore with a speech defect?' Tony gripped the handle bars firmly.

Meike was instantly sober. She took a deep breath and screamed, 'YOU'RE THE ONE TO TALK, CHEMO HEAD!'

Surprised at the gigantic volume of her voice, Tony just looked at her. Then he said, 'What did you say?'

He let the handle bar go and walked over to Meike, planting himself firmly in front of her. His nostrils were open so wide that they looked terrifying.

'Try to repeat that one more time, and just remember that I don't discriminate. I knock butt-ugly whores around, too.'

Cancer was a sensitive topic for Tony.

Meike looked at him defiantly and put her hands on her hips. 'I said, 'You're the one to talk, chemo ...'

'I'VE SEEN EVERYTHING!' Gieles interrupted with a roar, hoping Tony would keep his hands off Meike. 'I saw that you trashed my goose! My father has video images of you ...'

'That fucking bird attacked me! He bit me with his filthy ...'

Now Tony was standing so close to Gieles that saliva flew into his face.

'You son of a bitch. You tore her apart!'

'Yeah! Homo whisperer!' screamed Tony, and pushed him hard with both hands. 'And the next time I'll rip up those other fucking birds of yours!'

Gieles threw his bike down. He wasn't afraid, even though Tony had always surpassed him in physical strength. His advantage was his rage, which was far greater than Tony's. It churned through him like white-water rapids, and the only means of release for Gieles was through his fists. Meike stood next to him screaming. Brabant dialect shot out of her throat like poisoned arrows, but he didn't hear it. The only things he could see were Tony's veal cutlet nose and flabbergasted expression when he slammed his fist into the middle of Tony's face. Tony had no time to hit back.

Meike dove onto him and sank her teeth into his forearm. Tony groaned and pulled on her dreadlocks, while Gieles jumped on his back, clamping one arm around his neck. For a moment Gieles thought he heard geese taking wing. Thousands of geese, in search of green places to eat and mate. He saw red and white stripes dancing before his eyes. They were the same as the ribbon his father used to keep the geese off the grasslands near the airport. As he tried to grip Tony's head with his fingernails he found himself admiring the intelligence of geese. After a year the geese had figured out that the flapping ribbon was not a threat but an indication of where the tastiest grass was.

What he heard was not thousands of geese flying overhead. It was Mcike ripping Tony's combat pants to shreds. It was his father, who was charging toward them.

30

Meike had pure white spikes no more than a centimetre long. If Gieles hadn't known her, he would have sworn she was a model. Her skull was perfectly round and flawless, except for a couple of minor wounds. Tony had pulled the dreadlocks out of the left side of her head as if he had been pulling up weeds. Sophia had been subjected to the same treatment, Gieles remembered, when she stood up for the Belgian with the hanging jaw. Her hair had been torn away too, scalp and all. Gieles was going to let Meike read the stories of Ide and Sophia.

'Well?' asked Meike. She was sitting nervously in the hairdresser's chair with her back to the mirror. Gieles put Wally on the floor, which was littered with black sheep's tails, and she ploughed through them with her bill.

'Nice,' he said.

'Nice?' Dolly crossed her arms. 'There's an incredible babe sitting in front of you and all you can say is "nice"? Are you out of your mind?'

'Beautiful,' he stammered. There was something else about Meike. Her face was empty, as if some heavy obstacle had been cleared away.

'Dolly made me up, too,' she said with a look full of expectation.

'I unmade you up,' Dolly corrected. 'I took off more than I put on.'

Now Gieles saw it. Her tear had been made invisible. Meike had stopped crying.

'Beautiful,' he heard himself say again, and he sat down awkwardly on the wicker bench.

Dolly took off her hairdresser's belt with all its paraphernalia and shut the cash register. 'I have some shopping to do, then I'll swing by and take you guys home. Meike, will you do the floor?'

'I feel a thousand kilos lighter,' she said, shaking her head. She walked barefoot through her own remains and swept them up into a pile. Without her dreads Meike was even smaller. Wally walked behind her. The little tails formed a mountain. She looked at it meditatively.

'You're Virgo, right?' They stared at each other. 'Your astrological sign is Virgo, isn't it?'

'I think so,' said Gieles. He breathed a sigh of relief.

'I'm Leo.' She stirred the dreadlocks with her toes. 'I read that a female Leo and a male Virgo are a bad combination. Leos are open and Virgos are closed.'

'Where did you read that?'

'In some gossip rag.'

'Those things are full of lies.'

Meike picked up a dreadlock. She held it above her lip for a few seconds, then stuffed it in the pocket of her jeans. Silently she swept up the hair with a dustpan and brush, then ran a dust cloth over the counter. Gieles wanted to tell her how beautiful her face was, but the words stuck in his throat. Since the bloody confrontation with Tony three days earlier there had been a strange silence between them. They both knew what would have happened that evening if they hadn't run into Tony. Maybe they wouldn't have done everything. The whole idea of fucking, which Tony talked about all the time, was not a matter of urgency for him. Not yet. But he had wanted to taste Meike with his mouth. Her mouth, her neck. He had wanted to touch her breasts. He had wanted to find out for himself why breasts were so exciting. But now her mouth and the rest of her body seemed miles and miles away. Meike no longer played piano on his bare stomach and no longer rubbed her head against his back.

That evening, Uncle Fred had taken care of her plucked head while his father had dragged Tony off to his parents. The next day Meike had shut herself up in the guest room until Uncle Fred announced to the closed door that she had to come out and eat supper. Or he would call her parents.

Dolly appeared with the shopping. 'We really have to go now,' she said in her familiar impatient tone. Ever since the cancellation of the pyramid project her good mood had vanished.

Meike sat in the front. She kept fingering the white spikes. Gieles sat in back with Wally and kept his eye trained on the back of her head.

'The boys won't recognise you,' said Dolly. 'You look like Demi Moore after she got her head shaved in that film G.I. Jane. She had a nice little head, too, just like yours.'

'Never heard of it,' said Meike, and reached up to touch her head again.

'With most people you see the edge of the skull, and there are ugly bumps and indentations. Or they have scars.'

Gieles wondered how quickly the spikes would grow. Would she have long hair again by the end of the summer? Would she go back to Zundert with dreadlocks and black lips? Would Meike look as if she had never been gone? Would he have tasted her before that happened?

Will we keep seeing each other?

He pushed Wally off his lap. Suddenly she felt terribly

hot. The little goose took two steps toward the car window and stretched out her neck, peering outside with great curiosity. They were riding along the straight canal where ducks and coots were bobbing around. Wally shook her plumage and tapped her bill against the window.

Dolly dropped them off in front of the farmhouse. Meike ran inside to show off her new look. Gieles checked the mailbox. Nothing from Christian Moullec.

They were in the kitchen. Meike spun around and basked in the compliments. Willem leaned against the counter, a bottle of beer in his hand. Gieles could see from his face that something was wrong. This was just how he looked that day in the barn, when he was working on the box. Tony? Had Tony trashed his other geese? Wally had been with him all the time; nothing could have happened to her. Maybe Tony was in the living room, waiting to apologise.

'That white looks great on you,' Uncle Fred kept repeating.

Willem fixed his eyes on Gieles and said, 'Ellen is coming home this Saturday.'

'Home?' Gieles looked at him with bewilderment.

'Yes, here. With us. The medical aid station where she was staying has been attacked. She was shot in the upper arm, but not seriously. She was lucky. The two Spanish doctors are dead.'

Gieles dropped into a nearby chair. Saturday? Jesus, it was Tuesday afternoon! Only three more days. Three! He hadn't even had an answer from Christian Moullec!

'You mean this coming Saturday?'

His father nodded.

'But that's three weeks early!'

'Aren't you glad you'll be seeing her?' He had expected happiness or concern about the bullet she took in the arm. But not this. He looked at his brother.

'Ellen is really looking forward to meeting Meike,' Uncle Fred attempted cheerily.

'That's not the point! That wasn't the deal! She was supposed to come back on August 7th!'

He stood up so abruptly that the chair fell over and he stomped upstairs.

Now it was his turn to shut himself up. He kicked the game board across the room. He kicked one of the slanted walls until he made a dent in it. He kicked the partition with the schedule written on it. Then Gieles laid down on his bed and ignored Uncle Fred's calls for supper. After a couple of attempts they left him alone.

He dozed off and was awakened by Meike's excited voice. She was downstairs, and he couldn't understand what she was saying. She was too far away. He heard high-pitched sounds alternating with lower-pitched buzzing. It was as if they were speaking another language, a primitive language. He found it pleasant, not being able to understand. Gieles stood up slowly and walked to the landing.

Through the skylight he could see Super Waling's mobility scooter. Gieles waited until they were in the living room and then crept noiselessly down the stairs.

'You really must come with me to one of my book clubs,' he heard Uncle Fred say. Gieles tried to imagine what was going on. Uncle Fred babbling affably. Next to him his silent father. Super Waling on the other couch, sweating from the short distance he had had to walk. Meike was probably sitting next to him, jabbing his blubbery arms. She seemed obsessed by his fat. Whenever she got the chance, she kneaded his arms like a baker's wife.

Gieles crept on without knowing why, but creeping seemed logical to him. His father was in the kitchen so he couldn't creep away. Willem had spotted him.

'There's food here for you,' he said, putting cups on a tray. Gieles had never seen his father carrying around coffee on a tray as much as he had in the past several weeks. Which meant they'd never had so many visitors before.

'I'd rather have a sandwich.'

Willem let his strong arms hang limp at his sides. He was standing at a bit of an angle, as if he were falling in slow motion.

'Waling's here. He came to bring Meike a painting.'

'I know.' Gieles had never been abrupt with his father, but even his abruptness suddenly seemed completely logical now.

Gieles took the butter and cold cuts from the refrigerator. It was as if the roles had been reversed. It felt good. Then he poured himself a glass of cola. Cola at meals was unthinkable, but his father kept his mouth shut. Gieles ate as if he were alone. He sat down at the table and read the newspaper.

Looking out of the corner of his eye he watched his father's hands rise upward, followed by a rasping sound.

'I thought you'd be glad she was coming home early. The circumstances aren't ideal, but at least she survived. That Spanish doctor Juan and his colleague were killed.'

'When is she landing and what's the flight number?' Gieles asked tersely, without looking up from the paper.

'About two-thirty in the afternoon. I'll have to look up the flight number.'

He felt his father watching him work his way through the sandwiches and cola.

'Want to join us? Waling's here.'

'Can't. I have to study.'

Upstairs Gieles sat down on his bed and stared at the partition. He ran through the plan in his head. Going up and coming down with the umbrella was no problem. But Gieles was still uncertain about the 'stay' command. Would the geese stay put with a plane thundering toward them? Another thing he hadn't done yet was to train the geese for the first step of *Expert Rescue Operation 3032*: to fly over the canal on command. He had to buy gelatine and speculaas. Very important.

It was a short day, but he just might succeed—if he played mental hardball. No emotions that would throw him off balance. He had to focus, to prepare himself as he had done a couple of years before for the table tennis contests. He had to stay away from everyone. And by everyone, he meant Meike.

Don't think about Meike!

After pondering this for an hour or so, he heard the front door close. Super Waling. He had to call Super Waling with the instructions. Gieles stretched out on his bed and looked at the faded lion and birds on his ceiling. Leo was Meike's sign. A Leo and a Virgo didn't mix, according to astrology.

Gieles felt himself nod off, but no sooner had he slid into sleep than the door opened a crack. Only then did he notice that he had forgotten Wally. He couldn't tell who it was who put her over the threshold. They looked like big hands, but he couldn't be sure. The hands that had just held his little goose moved him. He gave himself a good talking-to. No emotions!

31

As soon as Gieles got out of school, he did his math homework and then called Super Waling. The phone rang seven times and then switched over to voicemail. Gieles called again. He imagined Super Waling groping around in his linen bag in search of his cell phone. Voicemail. Or he was waddling from the couch to the hall, where his bag was hanging on the coat rack. On the third attempt he managed to reach him. In the background Gieles could hear passing cars.

'Are you going somewhere?' He heard honking.

'Yes, I had another problem with my scooter. Something with the rear wheel. But it's great that you called. We missed each other last night.'

'I want to ask you something,' said Gieles, and he remembered that he hadn't yet thought about *how* he was going to ask the question.

'Okay, shoot.'

Gieles rubbed his hair, and in the midst of the chaos in his room he noticed a lipstick lying on the floor. It had probably fallen out of Meike's jeans pocket when they were lying on the floor together. They had pretended they were dead, and Wally had walked around them in desperation. After a while she peeped so fiercely that they stopped. It was funny and pitiful at the same time.

'Gieles, are you still there?'

'This coming Saturday at two-twenty I want you to be at the fence. The big fence near the runway.'

'That fence right near Dolly's house?'

'Right. At two-twenty. Not a minute later.'

Gieles heard the sound of a bus or truck.

'Did you get that?'

'Absolutely. This coming Saturday, two-twenty. Does this have to do with your mother coming home?'

'And bring your camera,' said Gieles, forging ahead.

'My camera. Good.'

'And your notebook.'

'Yes, sir. I'll be there.'

Gieles felt awkward. He had never given orders to anyone before, except his geese.

'I can't tell you any more. It's still a secret.'

'Watch out for those secrets.'

'Till Saturday,' said Gieles, and cut his voice off.

Outside, hidden behind the barn, Gieles shook the cookie tin. He didn't want Wally to come with him for the training session, but she followed him anyway. If he brought her back, then Johan would see him. He was polishing his spaceship, and undoubtedly he'd start moaning about his scrapbooks.

He tapped the geese with the tip of the umbrella and took his regular route to the pasture near the shed. He became more and more determined with every step he took. The rescue operation had to succeed.

That afternoon he had Tufted and Bufted fly up and down while Wally sat next to him. She ate grass and did a little napping. Gieles opened his umbrella and the geese took flight. He admired their brown bellies and orange webbed feet, which were stretched out so beautifully. Their necks bobbed elegantly on the waves of air. He kept repeating his commands until Tufted and Bufted were exhausted. Their wing beats became burdensome, their bodies heavier and heavier. He understood that they had had enough. The geese sat down in the tall grass, panting. Gieles stroked their tufts with satisfaction.

He spoke very little during supper. Instead he concentrated on chewing his meat and ignoring Meike. She was chattering with Uncle Fred about Dolly's beauty parlour and her children. Meike was crazy about them. Gieles was jealous of the physical attention they got from her. The toddler pressed up against her breasts like a bumper sticker, and she let the little brothers smear the remains of their food onto her vinyl dress. It was a demonstration. Meike was showing them how handy plastic clothes were. Skiq and Onno took turns squirting gobs of mayonnaise from a tube onto her plastic thigh. Meanwhile his hard-on was pointing at her thighs from inside his pants.

'I can't babysit tomorrow,' said Gieles without looking at her. 'I have to study for exam week. Would you go?'

'Sure,' she said coolly. She didn't look at him either.

Uncle Fred was unaware of the icy atmosphere between his nephew and Meike.

After clearing the table, Gieles vanished upstairs. In his sink, which was full of black smudges from the Rizla Bird Burnings, he threw speculaas, water and gelatine. The result was brown mush. He kneaded it and diluted it with water, and rolled a whole lot of small, firm balls. They were just as big as the fish dough balls he had had at his ninth birthday party for shooting stuffed animals out of a tree with a blowpipe. The fish dough had been his father's idea. Tony came up with the idea of rolling nails into the dough. That worked fine until Gieles got a nail in his forehead. The point had bored into his skin.

He kept on rolling with the dexterity of a butcher.

Tony hadn't been over to see him yet. And if Gieles

ever did find him standing on the front step, he'd slam the door in his face. But first he'd slam a nail into his fat head. Right between the eyes.

32

The day before his mother came home, Gieles cut school.

He hadn't been happy with the geese's landing skills, and he had to test their obedience. Gieles waited until he heard his father and Meike leave in the airport service car. Meike could easily bike to the beauty parlour, but every morning his father offered to drive her there. As if she were a silly goose chick who couldn't take care of herself.

Up in his room, Gieles counted the speculaas balls. Twenty-nine. Wally was sitting on his bed. She had ceremoniously installed herself there, with her butt on Super Waling's story. Last night he had read the airport story for the fifth time. Or was it the sixth? It intrigued him enormously. When Super Waling's mother almost had a heart attack on the home trainer he had fallen asleep.

The little goose watched him arrange the speculaas balls on the floor. She had a strange fascination for anything round. Gieles left a couple of balls behind for her to munch on and put the rest back in the plastic bag. He thought once again of Chuang Tzu's sea bird. The Chinese marquis gave the imprisoned sea bird the best pieces of meat, but within three days it was dead.

How harmful was speculaas for geese?

He erased the thought by hitting himself hard in the head a couple of times.

Going down the attic stairs, he saw Uncle Fred in his

parents' bedroom. He was removing the pillow cases and fluffing the pillows. Countless minuscule particles of dust whirled through the room in the clear sunlight.

'Aren't you going to school?' his uncle asked as he put on a new pillow case.

'No, not until this afternoon.'

Uncle Fred had no idea what his class schedule looked like. 'I'll be back in an hour or so,' said Gieles.

There was no time for breakfast. He ate a banana and a muffin on the way. Tufted and Bufted walked ahead of him. Waddling, gabbling. Forever cheerful. His mother used to be cheerful all the time. Maybe you became less happy as you got older. Or when you had children. All Dolly and Liedje had were worries. Meike's parents stayed awake day and night, fretting about her. She kept Gieles awake, too, but for very different reasons. If her parents knew what he was fantasising about they'd never sleep a wink.

Gieles whipped his umbrella against the tall roadside grass and the yellow flowers. They were the same as the flowers on the kitchen table. Meike had picked them for Ellen. Uncle Fred said they were primroses. He struck his umbrella against the streetlight that the security camera was mounted on. Beneath the camera was the number 185 written in black.

There were no cameras posted along the main road. He walked down the bike path (there was no sidewalk). The geese had entered unknown territory and were becoming restless. They looked up fearfully as if some dangerous thing were hanging over their heads. Gieles gave each goose a speculaas ball. Food helped calm the nerves.

He sat down on the shoulder so they could get accustomed to the traffic, but the road seemed deserted. Gradually the geese relaxed and began pecking at the grass. He concentrated on the sounds around them. It was a typical quiet countryside—between airplane take-offs.

He heard the nibbling of his geese and the buzzing of a bee. He heard the leaves rustling in the poplars and the quacking of ducks. He enjoyed the calming effect of these sounds, until the geese looked up again and began to utter their cries. They explored the sky with their piercing gaze. They weren't afraid. They were curious.

From behind the row of trees he saw a small group of geese appear in the sky like a dark cloud. These were bean geese; he recognised them from their black-gray wings. Bean geese were a rarity here. They sounded different, too. Their cackle was more like the gravelly cough of an old man. When they flew overhead he could hear their flapping wings creak like rusty hinges. They coughed their birdcall from the air, and his geese responded with loud, high-pitched honks.

They all turned their attention to the bean geese. Gieles counted nine. He watched them disappear behind the empty shed. They had probably landed in the pasture where the cows were and would continue their journey later on.

Gieles saw a car coming far down the road. He stood up and tried to gauge the distance. If he were to put the geese in the road right now, he'd have time to get to the bicycle path unseen. He lured them to the middle of the road with the speculaas, placing the balls on the white stripe that divided the road in two. Then he trotted away and hid himself behind the poplars, the umbrella poised.

It seemed like a year before the car finally arrived. It was a dilapidated old white sedan that was going fifty at the most, while the traffic signs were marked for eighty.

Uncle Fred always used to drive too slow on the highway. After fourteen tickets he quit driving for good.

The geese gobbled down the balls without even looking up. Gieles saw their complacence as a good thing. Promising.

When the car was about ten metres from the birds, Gieles flapped the umbrella open and expected the geese to fly away, as they had done during practice. But they didn't move. The car honked. It sounded as hoarse as the bean geese. Still no response. At the very last moment the driver tried to avoid the geese by turning sharply to the right. With a bang the nose of the car ended up crashing into a tree.

Gieles was two trees further down the road. From his hiding place he tried to see into the car. He saw a man with a beard behind the steering wheel. The man wasn't moving.

He's dead.

His heart was in his mouth. This was his own horrible, terrible fault, screamed a voice inside him—and just then the man got out of the car. Gieles now saw that the driver didn't have a beard at all, but that his mouth and chin were smeared with blood. Using the sleeve of his white overalls he was trying to staunch the flow of his bloody nose. Terrified, Gieles walked toward him.

'You all right?' he asked quietly. He appeared to have lost his voice. The geese were standing behind him as if they were taking cover.

The man said nothing. He stood there pressing his sleeve against his nose. It was a terrible sight, Gieles thought, and he turned away. He looked at the car. The front was dented. DACIA it said on the battered hood. Gieles didn't recognise the make.

The man held his arm in front of his face and looked at

the stain. The bleeding had stopped. Then he walked around the car, inspecting it like a car salesman. Gieles had no idea whether the man was angry or not. Feeling uncertain, he followed the man's shuffle. The geese walked behind him. The man didn't look as if he came from around there. He had thick, black, frizzy hair and pale skin. His face and posture were as angular and ungainly as the jalopy leaning against the tree. The man kicked one of the tyres and opened one of the car doors. Several cans of paint fell out. A strong smell wafted from the car.

'Can I help you?' Gieles asked, but the man didn't say a word in response.

He began to pick up the cans that were lying on the ground and put them back in the crates on the back seat. He pulled a grubby rag from one of the crates, splashed some turpentine on it and cleaned his face. He did this with the same rough movements that his father used to scrub seagull shit from the windshield. The man glanced quickly at the blood and then threw the rag back into one of the crates.

The man's car was full of dents. The rear bumper was held on in several places with masking tape. The country initials on the license plate were RO.

RO? Rowanda?

His mother had been in Rowanda once. Big drama. Ellen had been doing cooking in some village and suddenly an American relief organisation descended on them, another bunch of solar cooking missionaries. It turned into an all-out competitive battle. The Americans cooked on reflectors that cost two hundred dollars apiece. Within fifteen minutes they could bring several litres of water to a boil, while her rickety units took at least two hours but didn't cost chicken shit, and the local people could make them themselves. And in an environmentally responsible way! His mother was beside herself. The villagers wanted the expensive reflectors. They—and the Americans—laughed in her face. Ellen had called home in tears and told them the whole story. His father had tried to calm her down. He said that poverty and compassion don't go well together, not to mention the fact that they didn't give a damn about the environment. That made Ellen cry even harder.

But that wasn't the way you spelled Rowanda. It was Ruwanda or Rwanda.

Romania!

Tufted and Bufted pecked at the plastic bag, which still had a few speculaas balls inside. He wanted to keep them calm, afraid the man was going to get angry at the geese for causing the accident. Gieles gave them each a ball while the man shut the car door once again. He looked at the geese and then at Gieles, and suddenly he seemed just as pathetic as Liedje since the breast cancer business. Before he really knew what he was doing, he offered the Romanian a speculaas ball. The man took the ball in his blood-spattered hand. He chewed on it with some difficulty. Gieles didn't want to be left out so he took the last one. The speculaas with gelatine tasted as dry as dust, but there was something pleasant about the two of them chewing together. As if they were out on an excursion and were having a roadside picnic.

The Romanian gave Gieles a slight nod, got into his car and started the engine. He backed up his jolting, jerking wreck, stuck up his hand and drove out onto the road. One taillight became detached and dangled by a wire. Gieles waved. Tufted and Bufted honked a bit. Like watching the passing bean geese, they gazed at the Dacia until it had passed out of sight.

33

It was 11:07 a.m. Gieles had all the time in the world. He tried to concentrate on the teletext because he didn't want to think about anything else. The Romanian and his bloody nose, for instance. He also didn't want to give any thought to the fact that the geese had completely ignored his command. Last night, still wide awake at around four-thirty, Gieles came to the conclusion that the geese simply couldn't see the umbrella. He had been too hidden behind the trees. Of course. That was the only explanation, and if there were any others he didn't want to think about them. His brain felt stretched to the limit. Even the tapping of Uncle Fred's crutch today had been too much for him.

So Gieles concentrated on the teletext. The expected arrival time of flight 9321 was still 2:28 p.m. His mother had to practically travel around the world to get back home. There was no airline that flew directly to or from Somalia any more.

Tap tap tap. The sound reverberated neurotically through his skull. Uncle Fred came into the living room. He was wearing a bright orange batiked shirt with short sleeves, one of Ellen's souvenirs. Uncle Fred had washed the shirt several times in boiling hot water but the colour refused to fade.

'You sure you don't want to go with us?'

'I'm sure,' Gieles growled.

Uncle Fred's voice was dripping with concern, which

wasn't at all like him. Usually he never got worked up about anything. Gieles's new blunt attitude had caused his father and uncle to pay a whole lot more attention to him over the past few days. But not Meike. She acted as if he was nothing but air. And if she happened to cast him a glance by accident, it was icy cold.

'I have a surprise for Mom,' Gieles said more indulgently. 'It's something I have to get ready for at home.'

Picking up Ellen had become a fixed routine over the years. Gieles and Uncle Fred would wait for her at the frosted sliding glass doors that yielded up the passengers one by one. Usually she came through the doors alone, but sometimes she would still be conversing with a fellow passenger. He hated that. The fact that her eyes didn't start searching for him right away. He wanted to be the first one she saw.

Willem Bos always made a point of waiting for her at her plane's gate. He couldn't see her through the little airplane windows, but that wasn't the point. He stood there like a final beacon, piloting Ellen safely back to the polder. As soon as the jet bridge was attached and began filling with passengers, Willem would drive back home to wait for them.

It was a ritual that they were now breaking with. This time everything was different. This time he wouldn't be waiting at the sliding glass doors. This time his mother had a hole in her upper left arm. The bullet had been removed.

Suddenly Meike was standing near the couch. She was wearing a short black dress that he had never seen before. She looked soaking wet, as if she had been sitting in the bathtub, dress and all. Meike conferred on him her most glacial stare. She had set aside her bat image. The little witch had disappeared. The tear was camouflaged. Meike looked dazzling. She picked up her Indian shag-bag and spun around, giving him a glimpse of her bare back, where the dress was laced up. The round band-aid was still on her shoulder blade. Gieles wanted to tear the laces out of the wet dress. He wanted to hit her and kiss her at the same time.

Later she would discover the hero in him. Not that he had the appearance of a hero, but Captain Chesley Sullenberger wasn't exactly a sex bomb either with his bristly grey moustache. Sully looked more like a good-hearted doorman on the verge of retirement. But the world adored him. Sully had made the ultimate gliding flight.

Gieles cast one final glance at the teletext and went to his room. He opened his desk drawer and took out a pair of scissors and a roll of white tape. He had thought of everything. On his desk was a copy of the letter to Christian Moullec. He had reread the letter over and over, hoping for an answer. According to Uncle Fred, the answer lay hidden in the question, but he hadn't been able to find it.

Granted, Sully would *never, ever* lure geese onto a runway. If Gieles's act of heroism were made into a movie, that part of the rescue operation would naturally have to be kept secret. But Sully didn't know anything about geese and Gieles was a geese trainer. In fact, he was a pupil of Moullec. Gieles knew what he was doing. And what was wrong with putting two geese near a runway in order to give happiness a helping hand? People had been doing that for centuries. Sophia had gotten Ide to rob graves for the sake of their happiness. Things hadn't turned out too well in their case and Gieles didn't want to dwell on that right now. But what was wrong with giving his happiness—and that of his father and mother—a little nudge? His parents' relationship was pretty shaky anyway.

Nothing wrong with it at all.

Gieles gave the tape a good rub. There was almost no room for the last letter, the 'e.' And the 'o' had ended up as a weird-looking square. But seen all together, from a distance, the words were clearly legible. Satisfied, Gieles shut the umbrella, opened it, and shut it again. His alibi was watertight.

12:00 noon.

He checked the arrival time on the internet once more. Flight 9321 was on schedule. His mother was probably suspended somewhere over Eastern Europe, her arm in bandages. No bones had been hit, which was a miracle considering how skinny her arms were. Whenever she went away she always lost so much weight that she came back looking emaciated.

Gieles picked up the speculaas balls and put them in his backpack. He had rolled thirty new ones in the sink the night before. It had clogged the drain. The balls gleamed like otter fur. They had turned out incredibly well.

Gieles's movie would have to start with, 'Based on a true story.' That sentence always had a big effect on the audience. It made the experience more intense. 9321 would be a catchy title for a movie, but there was already *Flight 93* about that 9/11 business. Maybe something like *Gieles and his Magnificent Geese.*

He had to call Super Waling. Check, double check. Captain Sully did that all the time. Checking was essential. Super Waling was an important link who had to be checked. Were there any really fat actors who could play him? No one immediately came to mind. He called. After getting voicemail four times he finally reached Super Waling.

'I just got out of the shower,' he apologised.

'Will you be there on time?'

'Of course I'll be there on time. A little before two-thirty, next to the big fence.'

'No!' shouted Gieles in exasperation. 'Not a little before two-thirty. Two-*twenty*. It's *very* important. Make it two-fifteen. To be on the safe side.'

'Gieles, I'll be there. Don't worry.'

'With your camera and your notebook. And a pen.'

'Packed and ready to go ... Gieles?'

'Yes?'

'I want to apologise to you.'

'What for?'

'For my story, the plane crash. I shouldn't have given it to you. I mean, I didn't realise until later that I shouldn't have bothered you with it. With such ponderous things ...'

'No big deal.'

'Yes, it is. It is a big deal ... I think in the past few years I've lost my sense of proportion, literally and figuratively.'

His voice faltered. 'It's no excuse, but I just needed to say it—for myself, as a way of explaining why I saddled a young man, a very special young man, with all my troubles. I'm not a teacher of anything.'

Gieles felt his brain starting to swell painfully.

12:20.

No emotions!

'I've got to go.'

'Yes, of course. I won't hold you up any longer. I'll be there at two-fifteen. Sharp.'

Gieles checked the arrival times once again, then he checked his e-mail. Nothing from Moullec. So what? Christian Moullec could go to hell. He read through his list one more time.

Balls
Slingshot
Rizla albums
Matches
Umbrella

He had more than an hour to get through. He picked up a physics book.

'Chapter 2. Sound and sources of sound.'

He tried to understand what he was reading, but the words wouldn't penetrate. Calculating sound. Whenever there was a thunderstorm he used to crawl in bed with his parents and they'd calculate how far away the storm was. After the flash of lightning they'd start counting together until the thunder came. How did that work again? ... 3 seconds times 340. Or was it 320?

Adults were never afraid of thunderstorms, except for Dolly. She was terrified that the lightning would strike a plane and the plane would land on her family.

'Section 2.1. Measuring sound.'

Gieles underlined the words with a pencil. Again his thoughts wandered. The airport didn't want to measure sound. The airport calculated sound with programs that were too complicated even for computers. If the sound was to be measured from now on instead of calculated, everyone would see that the airport was producing much more noise than it had led people to believe. The airport was built on lies, according to Uncle Fred, but he shrugged it off. It made Dolly furious, but Uncle Fred accepted reality. He was a river, after all. He rolled with the flow. Dolly was a chain of volcanic mountains. Meike was a Leo. He was a Virgo. And—best of all—almost a hero.

Gieles drew a female bosom in the margin of the book.

He made the breasts extremely large and thought of Meike.

Concentrate!

Check arrival times. Check geese.

He left his room. The house smelled of perfume. It had to be Meike's, although she didn't wear perfume. It must be part of her new look. Her parents were coming to visit next week. Angeliek would fall on the ground, moaning with happiness. Hannie's sweat glands would gush with joy. Would she suddenly like her parents? He hoped not, with all his heart.

His father was outside waiting, leaning against the service car and staring at the shed. Gieles had made up his mind to ignore his father, but Willem spoke to him.

'Did you hear that?' his father asked.

Gieles stood still and listened. Yes, he heard it. A dry cough.

'Those are bean geese,' said his father with surprise. 'I haven't heard them around here in years.' Willem turned his practised ear toward the shed and enjoyed this secret pleasure. 'Must be ten of them, I'd say.'

He knew his father thought it was a shame that later they'd have to drive these geese away.

'My guess is nine,' said Gieles, and he saw Tufted and Bufted further on drinking from the wading pool. Willem laughed and looked at him with that meditative look he'd reserved lately for Gieles alone.

Gieles turned away. The sky was clear blue. The polder was bathed in sunlight. The conditions were ideal. No clouds, hardly any wind.

Just act normal.

'Maybe we can go to the Cheese Market with Mom,' said Gieles, realising how incredibly dumb that sounded. They used to go to the Cheese Market together whenever his mother came back from a long flight. She always had a craving for French cheese. But that was back in her stewardess days, before the flights to disaster areas.

'If she feels reasonably up to it. Then sure, we can do that.'

His father's answer sounded just as stupid. Luckily Meike and Uncle Fred came outside. She walked right past him.

'Can I sit in the front?' she asked without waiting for an answer.

Gieles held the door open for Uncle Fred and helped him with his crutch.

Willem stretched his arm along the back of Meike's seat and backed out of the yard. It was just as if he had put his arm around her. Gieles watched until they turned onto the road.

His heart started beating double time. He ran back to his room and picked up all the Rizla volumes. He was going to make a big sacrifice. His biggest yet. The stack of blue-fronted redstarts, red-billed firefinches and red-cheeked cordon-bleus wouldn't fit in the sink. He took the birds outside, behind the house. Gieles pulled the pages out of the albums and tossed the colourful wads of paper into a cast iron bucket.

Although he didn't want to, he thought about his grandpa. Grandpa had been dead for at least five years, but suddenly Gieles had the feeling that he was looking over his shoulder. A sense of guilt gnawed on one of the strained lobes of his brain. Goddamn it, this was more than he could handle. He would have to reassure his grandpa and send him away. Speaking out loud, Gieles said, 'Dear Grandpa, your birds are going to make your son and his wife ... my mother, that is ... Ellen ... happy again ... Just like you, these birds will ...' He heaved a sigh. So? What will these birds do?

1:50 p.m.

'You were cremated, too,' he said hurriedly, 'and now your birds will come and ... fly ... up to you.'

Gieles threw a couple of matches into the bucket. Flames licked at the birds. In just a couple of seconds, years of collecting went up in smoke. But he paid no attention to that. His grandpa disappeared.

His next serious concern was Wally. Where was Wally? *Damn!*

He had to get the little goose up to his room. He went out to the campground, walking nervously. Near the washing shed he almost bumped right into Johan. This was the last person on earth he wanted to meet (except for Tony). Under his arm Johan was carrying a roll of toilet paper.

He raised his white eyebrows. 'Expecting rain?'

Gieles shook his head with irritation. These dumb questions about his umbrella.

'Because I believe it's going to be a beautiful day,' Johan said.

'Have you seen Wally? My little white goose.' He was extremely agitated.

'Wally,' repeated Johan. 'Sure. She's sleeping in my chair.'

'In your chair?'

'Lawn chair.'

Goddamn it!

'I'll come get her right away.'

'Your little goose is waiting for you,' he said plaintively. 'Just like me. I've been waiting for you for weeks, so we can finally pick up where we left off. 1981. The emergency landing of the Douglas DC-9-31 on a highway. Seventy dead. That's as far as we got in my scrapbooks. And it was a spectacular emergency landing, let me tell you ...'

'I don't have time for plane crashes!' thundered Gieles.

Johan was taken aback.

'I have some very important things to do!' shouted Gieles, enunciating each word with exaggeration as if he were addressing a deaf man.

'You know, Gerard,' said Johan. 'I'll take care of your goose. You go do your things.' He patted Gieles on the shoulder and sauntered back to his spaceship.

Gieles ran to the wading pool and roughly prodded Tufted and Bufted with his umbrella to get them moving. He ignored their complaints; there was no time to lose. It was just like a game of table tennis: the outcome was mostly a matter of preparation and psychology. Winning had little to do with chance.

2:08 p.m.

He was three whole minutes behind schedule. With all this tension he was going to have a stroke right on the spot.

Calm down!

The best place for driving the geese to the other side of the canal was behind the house. No one could see them there, except for the landing planes. The slingshot and speculaas balls were lying ready next to the bucket of cremated Rizla birds. Gieles let Tufted and Bufted smell the balls, as if they were police dogs being put on the scent. As they picked at the balls he pulled his hand away and grabbed the slingshot. He waited for a plane to land and taxi past.

Gieles shot. He shot one ball after another over the canal in a straight line. The balls fell right next to the water. The geese began bobbing up and down hesitantly.

Go on, goddamn it! Fly!

They were supposed to fly over the canal, after the cookies. This is what they had practised behind the shed. Going after the ball was the easiest part of the whole rescue operation. And here he was shooting the balls and the fucking birds were refusing to go after them. Okay, this was a different canal, but all the canals in the polder were the same.

Gieles began hyperventilating. He shot the second volley of balls, which landed about eight metres from the canal. That was better—closer to the runway. The geese flapped their wings wildly, but their webbed feet remained stuck to the ground as if they had been glued there.

2:17 p.m.

Gieles's head was exploding from the tension. His heartbeat was pounding behind his eyeballs and pressing them against their sockets. He wanted to cry, to scream. His central nervous system was going wild. He felt a tremendous urge to kick the birds over the canal. He shut his eyes and counted. A landing plane went past, its engines whistling.

He picked up the slingshot for the third and last volley of speculaas balls.

His shots were perfect. The balls fell right next to the runway. Tufted and Bufted kept flapping without rising one centimetre off the ground.

'FLY!' he screamed, anxiously scanning the sky. The headlights of the next plane were still far away, pin pricks.

'GO!' He clapped the umbrella as if he were shaking off raindrops.

'GET OUT OF HERE!' shrieked Gieles, totally beside himself, and he gave the geese a wallop with the umbrella.

And so they did. 'Gak-gak-gak-gak!' they cried angrily, flapping into the air.

'Thank You,' whispered Gieles reverently, although he had no idea who he was thanking. The geese flew over the narrow canal, but it felt as if they had crossed the Atlantic Ocean. Gieles ran to his bike and tore out of the farmyard.

2:22 p.m.

He was still behind schedule, but not too far behind. He estimated his chance of success at ninety percent. Captain Sully had to manage with only one percent.

Gieles knew exactly how long it would take—3 minutes and 20 seconds—to cross over the road to the fence. It was faster along the canal, but there he would be too easily seen by the pilots. There were still a couple of last-minute uncertainties. One more plane had yet to land before his mother's flight. The pilot might notice the geese and raise the alarm. But by the time the bird controllers arrived he would have carried out his act of heroism.

Gieles expected to see Super Waling in his mobility scooter at the end of the road, but he was nowhere in sight. And the weird thing about it all was that Gieles didn't flip out. He felt himself growing calm. When Sully made his emergency landing there hadn't been any press in attendance either, yet his silent gliding flight became world news thanks to a security camera mounted on a nearby building.

2:25 p.m.

Gieles tossed his bike against the tall fence. Less than fifty metres further on the geese were eating the speculaas balls, right next to the runway. Just as he wanted. He followed their movements with fascination. Gieles felt an enormous love for them well up inside him. It was different than the feeling he had for Meike. That was infuriating, arousing, paralysing. But his love for the geese gave him the power of a meteorite.

Two identical points of light were approaching in the distance. Flight 9321.

Noiselessly and unsuspectingly, his mother was gliding in from space. Gieles squeezed the umbrella with damp hands. The lights grew larger. They were two floating herring gulls in a lightly rolling sea. He had run these images through his head a thousand times already, and now it was really happening. His concentration was clear and imperturbable. He had a command of the whole playing field, while his attention was focused on the ball and his opponent: the geese and the plane.

It was so quiet that he could feel the blood coursing through his body. Then Gieles heard quiet coughing. Super Waling. The coughing got louder. Gieles turned around. It wasn't him.

What he saw were bean geese. Nine bean geese flew over the treetops of the woods in exile and the spotters' campground and came down near his own geese.

Gieles's breath got stuck somewhere around his oesophagus. He felt ultralight, but it wasn't the pleasant lightness that he experienced in the company of Super Waling. It felt like he was going to faint. He couldn't get any oxygen. Maybe he was dying. He was almost certain he was dying. He was frozen. He couldn't even move his fingers any more.

The wings and nose of flight 9321 became visible. His mother was flying straight into the geese.

Eleven geese!

That was nine too many. Even Captain Sully didn't have to deal with a flock that big. 'I smelled a burned bird smell,' the pilot had explained to the platinum blond reporter. No plane stood a chance against eleven geese.

The bean geese were eating. On the runway! But he hadn't shot any balls *onto* the runway, had he?

2:27 p.m.

The plane, a Boeing, was coming down low over the head of the runway. The coloured strips on the tail were clearly visible.

'Gieles ... I'm so sorry,' he heard someone say breathlessly. Gieles turned with a jerk. Super Waling's hands were black with grease, and he was pressing them with great force against his belly as if he was afraid his organs were oozing out. There was a black-and-blue spot on his forehead.

'The damn cart broke down again ...' Then he looked up with big, terrified eyes.

'My God, geese! Gieles! A whole flock of geese! On the runway!'

Gieles felt an air bubble float upward inside his head. 'Pop,' it went. He wanted to tell Super Waling about the pop. His fat friend had also had a popping experience when he saw the dead and wounded in the shattered airplane on his father's beet field. Super Waling's ears had popped open and he was able to hear again. But Gieles sensed that this was not the right moment. He turned around and began to run.

The roar of the engines came rolling forward, preceding the plane itself. The tyres hung above the asphalt, while the bean geese and Tufted and Bufted fought over the speculaas balls. Gieles ran along the canal and flapped the umbrella open with exaggerated gestures, as if he were opening a bottle champagne.

And just as he opened the umbrella, Tufted and Bufted raised their tufted heads. They spread their wings like trained commandos, broke into a run and shot forward. The bean geese followed them immediately. It was an unbearable sight. Geese, eleven geese, and hot on their heels a monstrous bird with a deadly sucking beak. The air around the wings was vibrating and their cries of distress were drowned out by the noise of the plane.

Now they were flying at the same height. The wheels hit the ground with a thunderous thud. The landing gears seemed to be collapsing. The engines howled. Black smoke flew up from the overheated tyres.

Never had Gieles seen a plane brake so insanely. A smell of scorched rubber filled his nostrils as the plane shot past. Johan had shown him pictures in his scrapbook of what happened when a pilot braked too hard. The 'hot brakes' caused the plane to catch fire and transformed it into a liquid mass.

Gieles was terrified that his mother would die in a sea of flames.

She wasn't killed. The geese weren't either. They flew toward him, but Tufted and Bufted did not make their customary awkward belly landing. They skimmed over the canal with the bean geese, and then in the blink of an eye they disappeared from his field of vision.

'Gieles.' Super Waling came tottering up to him with foam on his mouth. His green sweatsuit was completely soaked.

Gieles paid no attention to him. He stared into the sky from under the umbrella.

'"Welcome home,"' Super Waling read aloud, looking at the white letters on the black umbrella fabric. 'What a fantastic welcome ... for your mother ...'

He pulled out his camera and took a picture.

From the sky there came a chirping sound. Super Waling followed Gieles's gaze. It was Wally. The little goose was working her way skyward, as if she were swimming against the current. She flapped her wings disjointedly. Gieles screamed her name. The next plane was off in the distance, preparing to land.

She flew higher and higher, her breast and neck angled upward. She played with her outstretched wings and cut through the air, feeling for the first time the wind around her. Bravely she was discovering all the new things she could do.

'WALLY! WALLY!'

Exultant, the little goose turned a somersault. But there was something wrong. She kept turning somersaults. The image of the electronic golden eagle crashing to the ground flashed through Gieles's head.

'WALLY!'

Down she tumbled and came to a stop between the canal and the runway, her wings limp and formless.

34

I'll kill him.

That was the first thing that occurred to Gieles when he saw his father. He was standing on the other side of the runway, holding a hunting rifle. But as the emergency services approached, Gieles was overcome by panic. He left Super Waling behind in a state of anguish and fled. The only place he could think of to go to was the shed.

Leaning his back against the corrugated metal plates, he kept his gaze fixed on the sky. In every passing bird he recognised his own geese and sprang to his feet. But as soon as the bird came closer he would drop back against the corrugated plates. He combed the grass with his eyes, hoping his little goose was looking for him. Maybe she had only been grazed. Maybe it was just a slight injury to the wing. His father was not an expert shot. The sirens in the distance died away, much to his relief. He knew they had only come out as a precaution. But even so.

Gieles closed his eyes. Snatches of film began to play behind his eyelids. Black smoke, bean geese, Wally in a nose dive, black smoke.

He fell asleep in the shadow of the shed. When he finally woke up and went back home it was getting on to seven.

Almost all of them were there. His parents. Meike. Uncle Fred. Super Waling. Dolly. They were sitting in the living room as if they were mourning. When Gieles appeared in the doorway, everyone stood up at once. They looked at him as they had never looked at him before. It was a mixture of happiness, tenderness and remorse.

His mother was the first to break the silence. 'Sunshine,' she sighed, and flew to him with one arm around his neck, her wounded arm dangling in a sling between them. His face disappeared in her salt-and-pepper hair. She smelled like a long flight: microwave meals, sweat, flat wine, fresh-up tissues.

Her shaking body told him that his mother was crying. He returned her hug, but it was forced. She felt angular. He used to take pleasure in her hugs. Only now did it occur to him that he had grown. They had become the same size.

Through the curtain of her hair he could see his father standing at the window sill, his hands in his pockets and his head bowed. His neck looked dried out, as if he wasn't getting enough water.

His father had shot Wally out of the sky. Gieles was willing to bet his right hand that Wally was the first goose he had ever killed.

Meike was sitting on the couch and leaning against Super Waling with her legs drawn up. Her cheeks were smeared with mascara. She had exchanged her wet lace-up dress for a pair of jeans and an African tunic.

Super Waling was still covered with grease from his broken down mobility scooter. The bruise on his head had turned a dark colour. Dolly and Uncle Fred were sitting rigidly with their backs to him.

'Did you see me chase away the geese?' Gieles asked, although he really didn't care any more.

His mother raised her head from his neck. Her face

was tanned and wrinkled. Now she had as many wrinkles around her eyes as Tony's mother did around her mouth.

'No. I couldn't see that very well,' she said evasively. 'I saw you pass by in a flash ... with your umbrella ...'

'I taped WELCOME HOME on it. Did you see that?'

She shook her head sadly and wiped the tears from her cheeks. 'No, I couldn't see that either. The landing was a little rough. We had to brace ourselves.'

She stroked his cheeks and then his chin. 'You need to shave.'

Then she said, 'I'm sorry.'

She buried her face in his neck again and kept repeating it.

'Did anybody see me chase the geese away?' Gieles asked, his voice cracking.

No one said anything.

'Not one person saw how I saved my mother? Waling? You were standing right behind me? You saw everything.'

Gieles didn't even look at Super Waling. He just stared at his father.

'Son, you know how disastrous this could have been.' Willem didn't sound angry. He sounded anything but angry. 'Luring geese to the runway. I didn't even know they could fly ...'

Gieles freed himself from his mother's one-armed hug. 'I didn't. Suddenly there they were. I saved people's lives. I saved Mom.' His voice had become fluid.

'I found speculaas,' his father said with great reluctance. 'Balls of speculaas ... And a letter to Christian Moullec. We found the letter. On your desk, next to the game board ...'

After his rescue operation they had put the puzzle

pieces together. They had rummaged through his room like detectives, searching for clues about their exhausted son. Then they had all talked about him. Here, in the living room. And Meike was there. He was the biggest idiot she'd ever met in her life. Meike must have laughed herself silly.

And he said he was training the geese for a casting bureau. Welcome home! On an umbrella! What a jerk! Ha-ha-ha.

But no one laughed. His mother took his hand.

'I didn't know you were so worried. About me. I never realised.' She began crying again.

'This could have been disastrous,' his father repeated. He was chewing so doggedly on his lip that it looked like he was eating up his mouth.

Gieles saw his mother's bare feet, where the journey had left its traces. Her toenails looked like crushed shells on the beach. Her tanned feet were full of white scratches. Then he looked around the room and said calmly, 'I knew exactly what I was doing. But you don't know what I'm doing, not one of you. You don't even know what *you're* doing. And that's … *that's* disastrous.'

35

Meike took him with her. He didn't put up a struggle. He felt no resistance. Everything that evening had pretty much been said after his mother had bluntly asked, 'But what do you want, Gieles?'

Everyone had looked at him, while what he was thinking about was Wally. His little goose had been sacrificed, a sacrifice that far surpassed all the volumes of Rizla albums he had. Tufted and Bufted had disappeared. In one fell swoop he was gooseless. In exchange for his geese he had made his mother promise she would never again go on a disaster flight or get involved with the solar ovens. He showed her how to solemnly swear by spitting between two fingers onto the tile floor. She followed his example and swore. It felt incredibly liberating to say what he wanted to say. So Gieles kept on going. After his mother it was Super Waling's turn. Gieles made him promise not to eat himself to death and to go in for a tummy tuck. After some hesitation, Super Waling gave him his word of honour and spat right on the floor.

He told Dolly she had to be nicer. Dolly looked so furious that the whole living room fell silent, but finally she agreed. She spit between her fingers like a Boy Scout. Then she began to cry. Gieles didn't know she could cry like that. She cried with plaintive howls as if she were singing opera.

Gieles had wanted to make Meike promise she would never go away again, but he didn't dare. He wanted to tell his parents that they had to get married, but he didn't do that either. He had a hunch that things were going to get better between them. At least the dead Spanish doctor was no longer a threat.

It was the worst day of his life, and at the same time it was the best. A kind of Christmas in the summer. Uncle Fred put on some music and bottles were uncorked. Tony Senior and Liedje dropped in to toast Ellen's homecoming. They were totally oblivious to the near-accident with the geese.

For the first time since the coming of the runway all of them were sitting in one place together. Only Tony didn't show his face. The neighbourhood had been practically dismantled, but they still formed a community of sorts. His father had put his arm around Ellen and was gently rubbing her bandage with his hand. Tony Senior teased Super Waling that the spot on his head made him look like Gorbachev. Next he started telling a joke about a drunken Russian, a drummer and a terrorist that only Super Waling laughed at.

Then Super Waling told the story behind the painting of the pumping station that Meike had put on the mantelpiece. While everyone was talking to everyone else, Meike took Gieles by the hand and led him away.

'We're going downtown,' she said.

'Okay,' Gieles answered, and got his bike. For the first time he didn't have any horny or insecure thoughts. What he felt most of all was—well, what? It was bigger than happiness. It was the feeling he used to have after a day at the beach. Sitting sleepily on the back of his mother's bike, ice cream spots on his shorts, sand in his face. His father biking next to them. Under his father's bungee cords the beach bag with a fishing net sticking out. Ice cream spots and a bed full of sand: that's how he felt.

They didn't say a word, yet the silence was not uncomfortable. Meike hugged his waist and, just like the last time, she nestled her head against his back.

With a clear voice she directed him to a side street in the shopping centre. 'Here it is,' she said. 'Number 38.'

The building looked deserted, but Meike knocked confidently on the window as if she knew she was expected. The dark curtain parted a few centimetres. All Gieles could see was a hand clutching the curtain fabric. Soon the door opened.

They were standing in a poorly lit beauty parlour. The man who had opened the door said, 'Well, look who's here. I almost didn't recognise you.'

He was wearing glasses with thick black frames, as if he had been watching a 3D movie. He was still young, but the glasses and his lush head of hair made him look older.

'Short and blond looks good on you,' said the man.

He must work with Dolly. He's a fag. Of course he's a fag: he's a hairdresser and he's wearing overalls with nothing under them. There's probably a pair of scissors in that front pocket.

'And that's the boyfriend you called about.' The man gave him a firm handshake and introduced himself as Lazy Lex.

A fag name.

'Gieles,' said Lazy Lex, with mock suspicion, 'I have my doubts about your age.'

'He's really sixteen,' Meike quickly responded.

'But then again,' said Lazy Lex, turning on a lamp next to one of the chairs, 'I have to be careful about refusing anything to a girl who managed to tame my dad's no-good dog.'

Gieles looked at the walls and realised he wasn't in a

beauty parlour but a tattoo shop. It didn't frighten him, though. He took in the images of freshly tattooed limbs with a dreamy indolence. The skin around the anchors, swallows, dice and broken hearts was bright red.

'I'm old-school,' said Lazy Lex, following Gieles's gaze. 'So if you want a tribal on your butt, you've come to the wrong guy.'

Lazy Lex leafed through a folder full of drawings.

'What else don't you do?' Meike asked. She was standing next to the tattoo artist and looking over his shoulder.

'An animal's backside around the navel, so it looks like you're staring into his asshole,' he said. 'That I refuse to do. I also don't do tattoos on animals.'

Meike burst out laughing. 'Get out of here. Who would put a tattoo on an animal?'

Lazy Lex pointed to a picture. Meike nodded in agreement as if they had been married for a hundred years and no longer needed words to understand each other.

'The Chinese do,' continued Lazy Lex. 'On goldfish. They laser a good-luck symbol on their bellies before they sell them.'

He opened a drawer in a wooden grocer's cabinet and took out a sheet of carbon paper and some pens.

Gieles strolled through the shop and looked at a case full of art books.

'Does your boyfriend want it in the same place as yours?' asked Lazy Lex, placing the carbon paper on the picture.

I'm getting a tear.

'Yes,' said Meike. 'In exactly the same place.'

He traced the drawing with a steady hand. Satisfied, he then studied the result through his 3D frames.

'Have a seat, Gieles. Take off your shirt and hold your arms like this.'

It's gonna be a tattoo on my back. Maybe a pumping sta-tion. A little one, because it didn't take him long to draw it. Or a fairly large tear.

Obediently, Gieles took off his shirt and rested his forearms on the back of the chair as Lazy Lex had demonstrated, completely relaxed. It was a desk chair with a back that tipped horizontally.

'Put it there,' said Meike resolutely, touching his left shoulder blade. 'Gieles still doesn't know what he's get-ting.'

So that round bandaid on her back was meant to hide her new tattoo.

'You don't know what you're getting?' asked Lazy Lex as he pulled on a pair of black latex gloves.

'No,' answered Gieles.

'Yet you're so relaxed. I can tell by your skin. Stressed skin is tight, and tattooing it is a waste of time. If you're getting an anchor suddenly it goes all crooked. But you're relaxed. That makes you,' a razor slid over his shoulder blade, 'the coolest dude I've tattooed in a long time. Either that or you're stoned. You're not stoned, are you?'

Gieles felt cold liquid and shook his head. He smelled antiseptic.

Maybe a skull.

'Good,' said Lazy Lex. 'I thought so. I can tell right away. I worked as an art teacher for a little while, and when the kids were screwing around with drugs I was the first to see it.'

Meike picked up a stool and sat down right in front of him. Her batik tunic looked like a bad watercolour of a rainbow. Too much water, not enough paint. His moth-er's souvenirs were usually awful.

Her pretty face shone above the blurred colours. The carbon paper was pressed onto his skin. Lazy Lex told him to wait a few minutes. In the meantime he removed the needles from their plastic wrappings and assembled the machine with the precision of a marksman. Gieles was surprised that the tattoo artist himself had no pictures on his body. None that were visible at any rate.

Lazy Lex turned on the radio and tuned it to a classic station.

'Like I said.' His hands danced through the air like a conductor's. 'I'm old school. How is my old man, by the way? Is he still smoking on the sly?'

Meike giggled. 'I think he is. The last time I came to pick up Dino for a walk I noticed smoke coming from behind the curtains.'

She laughed at his father with his oxygen canisters, but Lazy Lex pinned her with a serious gaze.

'You know, I can get rid of that tattoo on your cheek if you want. With a laser. That powder you put on it makes you look like you're walking around with a liver spot.'

Without waiting for an answer, he turned around and switched the machine on. The sound of a dentist's drill joined in with that of violins and Lazy Lex's humming.

Gieles felt the needle in his skin and the latex hand supporting his back.

A heart with our initials.

'Does it hurt?' Meike asked with concern, stroking his forearm.

Gieles shook his head.

'Sit still, buddy.'

'Shall I show you what you're getting?'

He nodded.

Meike turned around and pulled up the new tunic. He admired her bare back.

So beautiful. And she's wearing a black bra.

'See it?' she asked, and she pulled the fabric up further

so that her head disappeared in the watery rainbow. 'No? See it now?'

'Sit still!'

'Yes,' he said huskily. 'I see it.'

On her shoulder blade was Wally. His perfect and innocent little goose, the size of a ketchup bottle top. With black outlined wings she was gliding toward Meike's neck, motionless, her plucky little bill pointing forward. Gieles stretched out his hand and touched her.

'You'll end up with a dragon if you don't sit still,' warned Lazy Lex.

Meike let her tunic drop and bent her head toward Gieles.

Her mouth slowly moved closer and landed on his lips.

They kissed each other without moving.

I was sure I could do it. I was sure I could do it.

On the Design

As book design forms an integral part of the reading experience, we would like to acknowledge the work of those who went into creating the form in which the story is housed.

Tessa van der Waals (Netherlands) is responsible for the cover design, cover typography and art direction of all World Editions books. She works in the internationally renowned tradition of Dutch Design. Her bright and powerful visual aesthetic maintains a harmony between image and typography and captures the unique atmosphere of each book. She works closely with internationally celebrated photographers, artists and letter designers. Her work has frequently been awarded prizes for Best Dutch Book Design.

Mischa Keijser is a Dutch artist and photographer who regularly exhibits and publishes his work. His relationship to Dutch nature and landscape is a major theme, and he often includes elements of his personal life in his images. The red overalls on the cover belong to his 14-year-old son. This picture was taken on a regular windy day in the open fields of North Holland, on special request of the publisher. The photographer's assistant had to throw the overalls up in the air approximately fifty times before obtaining the desired effect.

The cover has been edited by lithographer Bert van der Horst of BFC Graphics (Netherlands).

Suzan Beijer (Netherlands) is responsible for the typography and careful interior book design of all World Editions titles.

The text on the inside covers and the press quotes are set in Circular, designed by Laurenz Brunner (Switzerland) and published by Swiss type foundry Lineto.

All World Editions books are set in the typeface Dolly, specifically designed for book typography. Dolly creates a warm page image perfect for an enjoyable reading experience. This typeface is designed by Underware, a European collective formed by Bas Jacobs (Netherlands), Akiem Helmling (Germany), and Sami Kortemäki (Finland). Underware are also the creators of the World Editions logo, which meets the design requirement that 'a strong shape can always be drawn with a toe in the sand.'